Literary Theory:
Some Traces in the Wake

Alexander C. H. Tung

Taipei : Showwe Co.

First published 2007 by
Showwe Co.
F1, 25, Lane 583, Rei-guang Road,
Taipei, Taiwan

ISBN 978-986-6732-25-6

Preface

As a ship moves, it always leaves behind a track or trail in the water. The track or trail is particularly called the wake. But the wake of a boat is no better than a footprint or a wheel rut. The wake may seem to be always there so long as the boat keeps moving. Yet, no trace in the wake at any single moment is ever actually the same trace made of the same body of water with its original quantity and quality, and thus each trace is, theoretically and practically, as transient as a bubble or a ripple. It is only that similar traces will always come to take the place of the vanishing traces, and this succession or continuation of traces replacing traces can make us feel that the wake is still there and the ship is still moving. Now, literary theory is like a moving ship in this way: it also constantly leaves behind a succession of traces replacing traces, which are seemingly the same wake but actually the composite of ever-varying critical opinions.

To be sure, the wake of a boat may vary at times in regard to its size, shape, color, motion, manner, or any other aspect, as the boat carries a heavier or lighter load, moves faster or slower, veers south or north, sails over deep or shallow waters, meets strong currents, violent storms, or normal conditions, fares at a bright noon or at a dark night, etc. Yet, in the light of constancy rather than variation, the wake of the moving ship may seem roughly the same all the time: a torrential composite of water with flying drops or foam recording not only its temporary but also its permanent existence. That is why one can say there has never been anything new in literary theory since Plato, just as one can say there is nothing new under the sun.

On Keats's tomb in Rome, it is said, are carved, according to his request, the words: "Here lies one whose name was writ in water." If Keats's name had really been "writ in water," no trace of the "writ" could still be seen today. Yet, his name, together with our associations with that name, is still there, like the wake of a boat, calling our attention and gaining momentum from those of us who go one step further to add weight and energy to the "name-ship" by tracing its wake, getting on board, and refueling it with new ideas about it.

Hopefully with this comparative understanding, I have collected herein, under my name, 15 papers on literary theory which I have written since I came to Chung Hsing University and started my academic career there. For me, these 15 papers are like so many traces in the wake of literary theory imagined as a ship. And for me my name is also "writ in water," leaving among other things only those traces to join the wake. This is a fact to be deplored, and a fact to achieve self-gratification as well. For, while the traces do not guarantee my eternal name, they have at least joined the wake for a time and helped it sustain its enduring appearance.

Ours is a postmodern world. This world is ringing occasionally with deconstructionist voices, with Derrida's coarse voice denouncing "the metaphysics of presence" and pronouncing the phenomenon of *differance*, of grams supplementing one another, or of traces representing and erasing traces. Now, my 15 papers in the wake of literary theory are indeed not just 15 pieces of a written message left in the sixteen traces of writing, much like those imprinted on the wax of a children's writing pad. They are, besides, so many signs that have completed their history of *differance,* of supplanting (that is, adding something to and taking the place of) other signs (call them grams or traces if you like) in due time.

I came to Chung Hsing University in 1965. The year 1965 is a significant year not only politically (especially about the Civil Rights Movement) but also in the field of literary theory. By publishing their *Critical Theory Since 1965*, which is a sequel to *Critical Theory Since Plato*,

Hazard Adams and Leroy Searle say that they have attempted to "bring the history of literary theory reasonably up to date." What leads to this attempt of theirs is the fact that since the 1960's, the critical or theoretical views of literature have rapidly been expanded in so many widely different directions that multifarious voices are indeed as constantly heard in the literary circle as in the arena of political struggle. In a sense, my various interests in or concerns with divergent topics of literary theory, as demonstrated in the 15 papers, can be seen as an echo to or witness of the plurality or heterogeneity that the postmodern or poststructuralist world has ushered us into, with quicker and quicker paces since 1965.

Most of these 15 papers of mine were published in the *Journal* of the College of Liberal Arts, National Chung Hsing University, the name of the *Journal* being *Journal of Arts and History* (*JAH*) at first and *Journal of the College of Liberal Arts* (*JLA*) later and *Chung Hsing Journal of Humanities* (*JH*) presently. The *Journal* has not been ranked very highly in the world. Nevertheless, it should not lower the real value of any paper published therein. For me, each of my papers represents some original thinking of mine. The place of its appearance may affect its readership and popularity, but the truth, if any, it contains cannot be devalued.

Still, I fear that my critical opinions may reach very few people if they keep being embedded in a journal like ours. Paradoxically, while I know it is unavailing to keep bubbles or ripples from disappearing, and futile to hold some traces in the wake, I still wish that more critics might be cognizant of my profitless efforts. That is why the 15 papers are reprinted here in book form, and I have taken the trouble to write this vain preface for the collection.

Contents

On "Modernism" as a Literary Term

We cannot be certain when the term "Modernism" first came into being. The *O.E.D.* fails to give us this information and so do such excellent reference books as *Encyclopedia Britanica* and *Encyclopedia Americana*. However, in the *Encyclopedia of the Social Sciences* edited by R. A. Seligman and Alvin Johnson, it is said that in the eighteenth century Rousseau had, in a letter to M. D., January 15, 1769, used the term to describe the humanitarianism, rationalism and tolerance of the *philosophes*, in contrast with the traditional privilege, authoritarianism and coercion prevailing in society as a whole. And in his *Ulysses, The Waste Land, and Modernism*, Stanley Sultan tells us that in the same century the term was used pejoratively by Swift in a letter to Pope (23 July 1737) to designate the doctrines and practices of one side in the "Ancients and Moderns" dispute (4). These early uses of the term, to be sure, are conceptually far from identical with our uses today. What, then, does the term denote in our times?

This is a very difficult question. Before we can answer it, it may behoove us to decide first whether or not the neologism has become a well-established term in our glossaries. Sultan, in the above-mentioned book of his (1977), states that he checked six glossaries of literary terms published during the last dozen years but found none of them listed "Modernism" (4). I have also checked quite a number of dictionaries or handbooks of literary terms. I seem to be luckier, for I find the term entered in at least two books: namely, Joseph T. Shipley's *Dictionary of World Literary Terms* (1970), and J. A. Cuddon's *A Dictionary of Literary Terms* (1977). With this fact, however,

I still deem it beyond dispute that up to now the word "Modernism" has not yet established itself as a solid literary term (like Romanticism, Realism or Symbolism) not to be rejected or neglected by compilers of nomenclatural books.

But, in view of this, we cannot conclude that the term has not been in frequent use in the literary circle. In fact, there is positive evidence that the term has enjoyed increasing currency nowadays. In the 1920s, the term was used by such critics as John Crowe Ransom, Robert Graves and Laura Riding in speaking of the art of that "present age" of theirs. The latter two even published a book entitled *A Survey of Modernist Poetry* in 1927. In 1935 we had Janko Lavrin's *Aspects of Modernism*, which is a study of various European twentieth-century writers. In his Prefatory Note, Lavrin proclaims that the term had become hackneyed by his time. From that time onwards, we witness the publication of, at least, the following works bearing direct usage of the term and large-scale discussion of things related to it: Louis Kampf's *On Modernism* (1967), Irving Howe's *Literary Modernism* (1967), and Peter Faulkner's *Modernism* (1977). Meanwhile, we find that Frank Kermode, in the sixties, was prompted to discriminate between "paleo-modernism" and "neo-modernism"; the Autumn1971 issue of *New Literary History* was devoted to "Modernism and Postmodernism"; and in 1982 Ihab Hassan tried to define the concept of post-modernism as against that of modernism in his *The Dismemberment of Orpheus*: *Toward a Postmodern Literature*. All these apparently suggest that a historical movement or period of literature under the heading of Modernism has already been clearly delineated.

Yet, this is not the real case. Despite the increasing number of books and essays concerned with Modernism and Modernist literature, many of us still hesitate to adopt Modernism as a name with an equal force and status to, say, Romanticism or Realism if we want to designate a movement or a period of modern literature. An obvious example of this is seen in the volumes of world masterpieces edited by Maynard Mack et al. In the earlier version of the volumes (1956, entitled *The Continental Edition of World Masterpieces*), we find such rubrics as "Masterpieces of neoclassicism," "Masterpieces of Romanticism," "Masterpieces of Realism and Naturalism," and "Masterpieces of Symbolism and the Modern School" for the sequence of chapters dealing with European literature from early seventeenth century to the present time. The last rubric "Masterpieces of Symbolism and the Modern School" evidently suggests that the editors of the volumes believed in the existence of a "Modern School" of writers, and this in turn suggests the possible existence of a "Modern," if not "Modernist," period or movement in modern literature. However, in the later version of the volumes (1980, entitled *The Norton Anthology of World Masterpieces*), the rubric "Masterpieces of Symbolism and the Modern School" is significantly altered to "Masterpieces of the Modern World." And in the introduction to this chapter, we are asked two provoking questions: "But what is 'Modernism'? Is there such a thing?" The change of the chapter heading, along with the two provoking questions, gives us a broad hint: Have the editors become doubtful of the existence of a "Modern" or "Modernist" school or movement in modern literature?

All depends upon the definition of the term "Modernism." As we know, the term is not reserved for the special use of literary men only. In fact, it can refer to anything (a practice, an attitude, a usage, an expression, a way of thinking, a way of living, etc.) characteristic of or peculiar to modern times. It can refer, for instance, to a radical view or practice of sex in our age. So, it is suggested in Seligman and Johnson's *Encyclopedia* that almost everything except perhaps pure sciences—from economics, sex and politics to religion and art—has its own aspect of modernism in history. But, of course, the epithets "modernist" and "modernistic" have been attached preeminently to religion and art (565) . In the realm of religion, in effect, the term "Modernism" has already taken on a more or less fixed meaning, and in many encyclopedias the religious meaning is the only meaning given for the term.

As a religious term, it is usually explained either as a movement in the late 19th century and early 20th century in Roman Catholic Church for a reinterpretation of traditional doctrines in the light of new philosophical, historical and psychological theories, or as a similar movement in Protestant Christianity at about the same time to reconcile Christian faith with present human experience and unify traditional theological concepts with modern scientific knowledge.

As a term of art, "Modernism" has seldom occurred in encyclopedias. But where it does, it is explained as something related not only to modern literature but to almost all other branches of modern art: painting, sculpture, music, theatre, etc.[1] As our concern here is not with non-literary arts, we can bypass the modernistic in painting, music, etc., and go straight to the modernistic in modern literature. But before we get started, a big problem arises. What is modern literature?

As "modern" is only a relative term, we find we cannot be sure what modern literature exactly is. To Buckner B. Trawick, anything from the Renaissance period downwards is modern, for his two-volume *World Literature* simply divides the world's literature into three main periods: the ancient, the medieval, and the modern. For Dorothy Van Ghent and Joseph S. Brown, the modern world began in the later eighteenth century or, more specifically, with Rousseau or *Confessions* or the Romanticism he raised. In contrast, Richard Ellmann and Robert O'Clair's *Norton Anthology of Modern Poetry* begins with Walt Whitman (1819-1892), while Mack and others, as we have seen in their anthology of world masterpieces, seem to think that the modern age begins with Baudelaire (1821-1867). But Gerald DeWitt Sanders et al., list Hardy (1840-1928) as the first chief modern English poet, pushing the meaning of "modern" even nearer towards our present world.

Of course, what is modern is not necessarily modernist. And, conversely, modernity can be found in rather old things. Therefore, insofar as we are concerned only with the modernist, it may not be a serious matter if we cannot define what modern literature exactly is. However, it *will* be a serious mater if we cannot even for our purpose tell exactly when and where modernist literature occurs.

It is well-known that Virginia Woolf once inadvertently suggested that Modernism had its advent "in or about December 1910."[2] The date was indeed set up too arbitrarily. Nevertheless, Peter Faulkner does consider the first era of literary Modernism to be from 1910 to 1930 in his *Modernism*, although he traces its source of development to the "realism" of the Victorian novel, to the Pre-Raphaelitism of Rossetti and Swinburne, to the aestheticism of Walter Pater, to the new drama of Ibsen and Shaw, to Hardy, James, Yeats, etc. And there are people who claim T. S. Eliot's "Tradition and the Individual Talent" and Virginia Woolf's "Modern Fiction" (both published in 1919) to be two manifesto-like documents (much like Wordsworth's "Preface" to *Lyrical Ballads*) for modernist poetry and fiction, and claim Joyce's *Ulysses* and Eliot's *The Waste Land* (both published in 1922) to be two typical works of the Modernist triumph.[3] Naturally, these claims can be justified in some sense. But there are other equally justifiable considerations. For instance, as far as drama is concerned, Modernism can be dated back to Ibsen (1828-1906).[4] And if we are willing to consider the term in an international magnitude and in view of all creative arts, then "since the latter end of the 19th century" may prove to be a more proper dating.[5]

Another thing adds to the difficulty and complexity of setting off a period for literary modernism. That is, our contemporaries have begun to sense the existence of different phases in the Modernist period if such a period does exist. For example, in Frank Kermode's view, the art of Virginia Woolf, Eliot, Joyce, Proust, Stravinsky, Picasso, etc., is to be distinguished from the art of Duchamp, Beckett, Cage, Tinguely, Rauschenberg, Burroughs, etc. (i.e., from the Dadaists and Surrealists onwards). And Kermode calls the two phrases "paleo- modernism" and "neo- modernism."[6] Similarly, Ihab Hassan sees great differences between the art of Valery, Proust, Gide, Kilke, Mann,

Musil, Faulkner, the middle period of Joyce, Yeats, Lawrence, Pound and Eliot, etc., and the art of the later Joyce and Pound, Duchamp, Artaud, Roussel, Bataille, Broch, Queneau, Kafka, etc. And he uses the two terms: Modernism and Post-modernism.[7] But neither Kermode nor Hassan tells us clearly when the older modernism ended and the newer began. J. A. Cuddon's *Dictionary* says that "paleo- modernism" concluded "perhaps, c. 1914-20, while neo-modernism refers to movements...since that time" (399). Yet, like any other date for any literary period, this must not be taken seriously.

Now, perhaps we have begun to have an idea, though a vague one, of the time or age when literary Modernism, older or newer, prevails. But is literary Modernism a universal phenomenon? From the information we can gather, it seems fairly safe to say that Modernism has at least as much international impact as any previous literary trend or movement. We cannot agree to A. Alvarez's opinion that "Modernism... has been predominantly an American concern."[8] For, as we know, many people such as Virginia Woolf, Joyce, Proust, Ibsen, Strindberg, and Kafka (i.e., many of those mentioned in the last paragraph) are not American in any sense; even Eliot and Pound are dubious cases if we want to consider their expatriation. In my opinion, America has been only a great world for experimenters from Europe. Literary Modernism perhaps came to America just as Beat Music or Rock 'n Roll. Whatever is begun in Europe is soon taken up in America.[9] In the case of literary Modernism, we find that it even spreads to Latin America and Asia. And I have the impression that while Europe and the United States began to feel the term "Modernism" unsatisfactory, the other parts of the world had established it as a sonorous (and seemingly meaningful) word in their vocabulary. To prove this, we need only to go to *Encyclopedia Britanica* and see that there "Modernism" is only a religious entry whereas "modernismo" is already a set-up literary term for a movement with its school of writers in Brazil and other parts of Spanish America as well as in Spain.[10]

And if we examine our own literature (here in the Republic of China), we find that in February 1956 Tsi Hsien (紀絃) and some other poets founded their Modernist School of poetry in our country and they even proclaimed distinctly their credos of Modernism and had their own periodical.[11]

As time passes and the term undergoes various interpretations (or misinterpretations), applications and modifications in various nations among various groups of people, "Modernism" has naturally assumed quite different meanings or emphases to the extent that it may have lost its definable character. For a more conservative one like Peter Faulkner, the "sense of the almost overwhelming abundance of the experience to be made into art" coupled by the "spatial form" Joseph Frank finds in *The Waste Land*, *The Cantos*, *Ulysses*, Proust, and Djuna Barnes's *Nightwood*; or, more specifically, the use of myth, the stream of consciousness technique, the notion of "objective correlative," the objection to the "dissociation of sensibility," the paradoxical quality in literature—all those which show the artist's apparent self-consciousness of his art and tool are central to the concept of "Modernism." But for a more liberal one like those who see two phases in Modernism, the term can cover almost everything that is *avant-garde* at some recent time. The Modernist School in our country, for instance, took the term to cover the Symbolism from Baudelaire downwards, Cubism, Dadaism, Surrealism, Imagism, the art-for-art theory and practice, etc.[12] And in Cuddon's *Dictionary*, the term is said to be associated with the following: Anti-novel, Anti-play, Beat Poets, Dadaism, Decadence, Existentialism, Expressionism, free verse, Happening, Imagists, New Humanism, *Nouveau Roman*, *Nouvelle Vague*, stream of consciousness, Theatre of the Absurd, Theatre of Cruelty, Ultraism, Vorticism. Indeed, if we still want to be more inclusive, to the list we can add Pataphysics, Futurism, Supremotism, Constructivism, Merzism and the cult of De Stiji—those listed in Hassan's book—and theatre of panic, theatre of silence, theatre-in-the-round, etc., etc. But, of course, this is too much to many. The Modernists of Spanish

America as well as any other Modernist at any particular place and time simply cannot allow such a great anarchy of ideas in their minds.

Perhaps for us it is more pertinent and effective to point out the keynote, if any, of the term "Modernism" than to try to define it. If the keynote of Romanticism is experimentation and rebelliousness,[13] what then is the keynote of Modernism? It is said that

> *Modernism may be described as that attitude of mind which tends to subordinate the traditional to the novel and to adjust the established and customary to the exigencies of the recent and innovating. The practical effect of this attitude may be either conservative or evolutionary. It is conservative where the subordination of the old to the new saves the old from destruction through desuetude or attrition. It is revolutionary where the subordination takes the form of a nullification of the old via desuetude and attrition. The conservative species of modernism occurs among religions; the revolutionary species occurs in the arts.* (Seligman & Johnson 564)

If this statement is true (I think it surely is), then isn't the keynote of Modernism in literature practically similar to that of Romanticism? "Revolutionary" is synonymous here with "rebellious," and "experimentation" is the practice of trying to "subordinate the traditional to the novel and adjust the established and customary to the exigencies of the recent and innovating." It is no wonder, therefore, that Peter Faulkner should remark that "Modernism has come to seem a broadly homogeneous movement, *with roots in Romanticism* and a flowering in the first third of this century" (74, my italics).

Of course, very few of our Modernists would admit that they are Romantics in the sense the word is usually understood. And, indeed, their revolutionary theories and practices are in many respects different from those of the early Romantics. For one thing, what the early 19th-century Romantics valued was "diversity, fluidity, a loose open form to which there is no sharply defined end" (Danziger & Johnson 119). But the "great experimental novels of early modernism—Kafka, Proust, Joyce, Musil, for instance—are all characterized by a kind of formal desperation," (hence they "made a cult of occult forms") while the neo-modernists from the Dadaists downwards all tend to deny the value and even the existence of forms (Kermode 662-74). In other words, although the Romantics revolted against the neo-classicists' extreme emphasis on formal order (together with the notions of proportion, balance, symmetry and decorum), they still kept order in their art. It was only that their way was subjective and thus tended to probe into the subconscious, the dreamy and the visionary. But we should grant that the paleo-modernists' stressing the mythical, the archetypal and the psychoanalytical is akin to the Romantic way in spirit. What makes them radically different is this: the former seeks consciously a new order (e.g., the stream of consciousness) in their formal desperation, while the latter simply let, as it were, their imagination decide the order of their art. But the case of the neo-modernists is totally different. They seem to depend for their "art" on chance, on "aleation," ignoring intentionally any artistic order, formal or psychological.[14]

For another thing, we know the typical Romantic hero, no matter whether he is Byronic or Faustian, is often a lonely figure immersed in a sort of melancholy solitude and in a feeling of isolation characteristic of a sensitive and sentimental genius (e.g., Chateaubriand's Renè, Pushkin's Eugene Onegin, Rousseau in his *Confessions* and Wordsworth in his *Prelude*). Later in the realists' literature we also find lonely figures (e.g., Tolstoy's Ivan Ilyitsch and Flaubert's Frèdèric Moreau), and still later the Modernist heroes, to be sure, also feel solitariness (e.g., those of Kafka, Musil and Joyce). However, as Georg Lukács has pointed out, the solitariness of the Modernists is felt not just as a condition attendant on a Romantic or Realist individual, which becomes only "a specific social fate," but as "a universal *condition humaine*" (476), in which man "is reduced to a sequence of unrelated experiential fragments... inexplicable to others as to himself" (480), thus describable only by way of "Joyce's stream of consciousness, or of Musil's 'active passivity,' his 'existence without quality,' or of Gide's '*action gratuite*,' where abstract potentiality achieves pseudo-realization" (479).

In this last connection, we are led to the third thing that distinguishes Modernism from other types of writing. We acknowledge that all literary movements have their own critical theories for their practical bases. Thus we have "Neo-classical criticism," "Romantic criticism," "Naturalist criticism," etc. However, it seems to me that the previous movements never relied so much on their theories as does Modernism on its own. We can read Pope, Wordsworth and Zola without much difficulty if we have not read their "Essay on Criticism," "Preface" to *Lyrical Ballads*, and "Preface" to *Thérése Raquin*. But it would be exceptionally difficult for us to appreciate Virginia Wolf, Brecht, and Ionesco if we do not know the theories and techniques of the "stream of consciousness," the "epic theatre," and the "theatre of the absurd." C. S. Lewis says that "modern poetry is not only a greater novelty than any other 'new poetry' but new in a new way, almost in a new dimension" (Lewis 448-9). Indeed, the difficulty, if any, with Alexandrian poetry, Skaldic poetry, with Donne or Wordsworth can be easily solved after some scholastic effort on the part of the reader. Yet, the difficulty with Eliot's *Cooking Egg* or Joyce's *Finnegans Wake* may forever be there puzzling all readers without knowing their methods of writing. The Modernists have really overindulged in theory and technique; they seem to pursue theory and technique as an end, rather than a means, of art.

Perhaps the complexity of modern life does require a complex literature to express it. After nihilism and existentialism, we cannot but let anarchy, void and uncertainty reign over the world in order to display the absurd in us. And this intellectually painful consciousness of absurdity in life (let us call it skeptical absurdism) may be the central philosophy of Modernism, contrasting sharply with the rational optimism of the Neo-classicists and the emotional mysticism of the Romantics. When Dryden and Moliére wrote, they believed there was truth in the present, in the "good sense" of society; when Wordsworth, Thoreau and Hugo wrote, they imagined there was truth deep in our soul or somewhere we could reach by transcending this physical world; when Sartre, Camus, the Dadaists and the Surrealists write, they are convinced that there is no truth except that life is meaninglessly absurd. With the Modernists we do have "no exits"; we are living really in a "theatre of the absurd" where we are "but walking shadows ... full of sound and fury, signifying nothing."

Everything comes from something; even a literary movement professing *nada* as its aesthetic object is no exception. Neo-classical literature might be accounted for chiefly as the outcome of the rationalist philosophy which came to dominate the later 17th and early 18th century Europe after the Renaissance humanism. Romantic literature, with its inclination towards individual liberty and rustic commonalty, is manifestly a corollary of democratic thought. Now, we have the ingenious remark: "Never regarded as modernist in itself, science has been the occasion of modernism in everything else" (Seligman & Johnson 565). Today, we never doubt that Realism or Naturalism tries to be in complete accord with the spirit of modern science, because it publicly asks its writer to be "as objective as a chemist" and to present us with a "slice of life" like a botanist.[15] But we are not quite aware that Modernism is even more unmistakably under the sway of modern sciences. The stream of consciousness technique, for instance, can be directly associated with Freudian psychology. The mythical approach to literature can be linked to the modern development of anthropology. And it is the availability of modern acoustic and optical equipment that helps advance such things as the theatre of cruelty, which depends largely on spectacle, lighting effects and the exploitation of the full range of the "theatrical." To cite quite a different case as example, most of us know that both impressionism and expressionism are originally terms of modern painters, but few of us know that their theories and practices were a reaction precipitated by the impact of science, especially Helmholtz and Young's theorizing about color vision and the invention of photography (see Seligman & Johnson 566).

So, science indeed plays a very important role in the shaping of literary Modernism. But this is not the whole story. In actuality, philosophy and democracy are equally important, too. Even a surface examination will show that all branches of philosophy, not just humanism or rationalism, seem to have co-operated with all branches of cultural or human sciences especially aesthetics, linguistics, ethics and theology, to give rise to many of the cults associable under the term "Modernism": Existentialism, Dadaism, Surrealism, Ultraism, Nouveau Roman,[16] and what not. And it is the spirit of democracy that allows the co-existence of so many opposing or merely different theories and ways of writing in our times. In our free world, we seem to have become "democratic" enough to tolerate all kinds of experimenters who are on the verge of making an ungovernable anarchy out of Modernism.

So far I have made a general discussion of Modernism in literature by tracing the origin of the term; judging its present status in our terminology in consideration of its circulation in nomenclatural works, literary periodicals, and other relevant books; pointing out its usage in realms other than that of literature; clarifying the various notions of modern literature; distinguishing the Modernist periods, types, and locales; showing the difficulty of defining the term; dealing with the keynote and chief characteristics of Modernism in contrast with other previous literary movements; and fixing it against the background of our modern world to view its relationship with philosophy, democracy and science.   This, of course, may be too general a discussion to serve many specific purposes, and many of my points are of necessity oversimplified—e.g., what makes Modernism is more than just the combination of philosophy, democracy and science; history (the two World Wars) is another obvious conducive factor in the development of nihilism, Dadaism, etc.   Nevertheless, this is enough to serve my present purpose: to discuss the utility, or rather the futility, of the term "Modernism" in our literary circle.

I have been, and will forever be, against using the term.   And I have my reasons.   First, as is said above, the word "Modernism" has been established as a special religious term with a meaning quite different from that of literary Modernism.   We can prevent unnecessary confusion by choosing not to use the term.   Second, even though we have tried to clarify the difference between "modern" and "modernist," there are still people who would mistake "Modernism" for any modern literature, while we know on one hand modern literature can refer to literature very far back in time and on the other hand not all modern literature is modernist (it can be old in content and method). Third, the term "Modernism" is itself too vague a term; it is so inclusive as to be too evasive to be useful.   As we have seen, it contains two broadly different phases (paleo-modernism and neo-modernism); it includes, as we have enumerated, too many trends and movements which have occurred in the "modern age"; it is, as we have also said, adopted in many parts of the world, but with different emphases and even different interpretations.   Under such circumstances, when we mention the term, I doubt if we can successfully convey what we mean by the term even though we have the help of the context.   It is very likely that our meaning will be considerably distorted somehow in the hearer's or reader's mind.   Fourth, although the term denotes some aforesaid keynote ideas and characteristics, it is not yet clear whether it is really a movement with a fixed period and a fixed set of writers or a mere historical process, a mere human attitude.   In a sense, all writers that refuse to cling to the traditional and try to do something new can be called modernists. And modernization of literature occurs at any time, any place. Fifth, notwithstanding that what the term denotes was actually born out of a certain background and then continued to exist up to now, the name is an unhappy choice. For time never stops; what is modern or modernist will surely become "out of fashion" or merely "time-honored" in the course of Chronos. We witness "New Criticism" is no longer new today. There is no sense, similarly, in inventing a term which will soon prove ironic in time. In fact, we have already the terms "neo-modernism" and "Post-modernism." What then will come next for the even newer or more modern trend? "New neo-modernism" or "After Post-modernism"? Sixth and last, to sound worldly wise, since after more than eighty years the term is still not well-established, we must think there is reason for it and had better avoid using it. I do not know for certain why the three-volume *Encyclopedia of World Literature in the 20th Century* fails to list the term therein, together with such terms as Dadaism or Surrealism. But I guess the editor must have purposely rejected the term rather than carelessly neglected it.

In his *Essentials of Contemporary Literature*, Donald W. Heiney says:

> *The year 1900 is more than an arbitrary chronological milestone in literary history: it marks the onset of a new era in literature as it does in the field of social activity. On first examination the striking characteristic of twentieth century literature is its extreme diversity. There is no one single school, no one tendency, which can be said to typify the age. Never before in literary history have there been so many cenacles, so many schools, circles, and movements existing simultaneously. This diversity is social development: the twentieth century, having no one dominant social philosophy, cannot hope for unanimity in literature. (ix)*

If, to single out a dominating movement, our contemporary literature proves to be our despair, let us not aggravate our situation by using the despairing term "Modernism," unless for some otherwise unpreventable expediency,

Notes

1. In Seligman and Johnson's *Encyclopedia,* it is asserted that "Architecture cannot be said to be modernist because there has never been any creed for the building art to seek or to repel reconciliation with science. Functionalism and internationalism in architecture are modern but not modernistic." I think these statements should be accepted with some reservation, as in architecture a revolutionary idea is not wholly preventable.
2. In fact, Virginia Woolf stated that at that time "human character changed." (See her "Mr. Bennett and Mrs. Brown" in *The Captain's Death Bed and Other Essays*, 1950). That was the time of the exhibition of Post-Impressionists like Cézanne at the Grafton Galleries in England. That was also the time when Freud's major works began to be felt as an impact on life. See Peter Faulkner's *Modernism*, pp. 34-5.
3. On this point see, for instance, Peter Faulkner's and Stanley Sultan's works.
4. For example, Joseph Wood Kruth does this dating in his *"Modernism"* in his *Modern Drama.*
5. On this point see Cuddon's *Dictionary*, p.399.
6. See his "The Discrimination of Modernism" and "Objects, Jokes and Art" in *Continuities* (1968).
7. See his "Postface 1982" in *The Dismemberment of Orpheus*. This article was recently translated into Chinese and published in *Chung-wai Literary Monthly*, vol. 12, No. 8 (Jan. 1984).
8. The statement is seen in his *The Shaping Spirit* (1958), and quoted in Peter Faulkner, p. 70.
9. Kruth argues that it is not the case in speaking of modernist drama. See Chapter 6 of his "Modernism" in *Modern Drama.*
10. Cf. also the entry "Modernism" in William Rose Benet's *The Reader's Encyclopedia*, 2nd ed. (New York: Harper & Row, 1965).
11. See Han-liang Chang & Hsiao, pp. 383-92.
12. *Ibid.*, p. 387.
13. This is a truism stated in Danziger & Johnson, p. 119.

14. This is the central theme of Kermode's "Objects, Jokes, and Art."
15. These are two slogans made by Chekhov and Zola.
16. In his *The New Novel*, Vivian Mercier considers *le nouveau roman* as the result of a literary rather than a philosophical movement, but he admits that many critics see the New Novel as an embodiment of phenomenology. In fact, in its tendency towards *inventing* rather than recording reality, *le nouveau roman* also betrays its scientific spirit.

Works Consulted

Chang, Han-liang & Hsiao, eds. *Hsien Tai Shih Tao Tu (A Guide to Modern Poetry)*, vol. 2. Taipei: Ku Hsiang Publishing Co., 1982.

Cuddon, J. A., ed. *A Dictionary of Literary Terms.* Harmondsworth, England: Penguin, 1979.

Danziger, M. K. & W. S. Johnson. *An Introduction to Literary Criticism.* New York: D.C. Heath & Co., 1961.

Ellmann, Richard & Robert O'Clair. *Norton Anthology of Modern Poetry.* New York: Norton, 1988.

Faulkner, Peter, ed. *Modernism.* London: Methuen & Co., 1977.

Fleischman, Wolfgang Bernard. *Encyclopedia of World Literature in the 20th Century.* New York: Frederick Ungar Co., 1977.

Ghent, Dorothy van & Joseph S. Brown. *Continental Literature.* 2 vols. Philadelphia: Lippincott, 1968.

Graves, Robert & Laura Riding. *A Survey of Modernist Poetry.* New York: Haskell House, 1969.

Hassan, Ihab. "Postface 1982: Toward a Concept of Post-modernism." *The Dismemberment of Orpheus*, 2nd ed. Madison: U of Wisconsin P, 1982.

Heiney, Donald W. *Essentials of Contemporary Literature.* Great Neck, NY: Barron's Educational Series, Inc., 1954.

Howe, Irving. *Literary Modernism.* Greenwich, Conn.: Fawcett, 1967.

Kampf, Louis. *On Modernism.* Cambridge, MS: MIT Press, 1967.

Kermode, Frank. "Objects, Jokes, and Art," rpt in Lodge, 662-74.

Kruth, Joseph Wood. *"Modernism." Modern Drama.* New York: Russill & Russell Inc., 1962.

Lavrin, Janko. *Aspects of Modernism.* Freeport, NY: Books for Libraries Press, 1968.

Lewis, C. S. "De Descriptione Temporum," rpt. in Lodge, pp. 448-9.

Lodge, David, ed. *20ᵗʰ Century Literary Criticism.* London & New York: Longman, 1972.

Lukàcs, Georg. "The Ideology of Modernism," rpt. in Lodge, pp. 474-87.

Sanders, Gerald De Witt, et al., eds. *Chief Modern Poets of Britain and America.* 2 vols. New York: MacMillan Co., 1970.

Seligman R. A. & Alvin Johnson, eds. *Encyclopedia of the Social Sciences*, IX. New York: MacMillan Co., 1957.

Shipley, Joseph T., ed. *Dictionary of World Literary Terms.* London: George Allen & Unwin Ltd., 1970.

Sultan, Stanley. *Ulysses, The Waste Land, and Modernism.* Port Wastington, NY & London: Kennikat Press, 1977.

Trawick, B. Buckner. *World Literature.* New York: Barnes & Noble, 1955.

*This paper first appeared in 1984 in *JAH*, pp. 1-6.

The Value of Genre Classification

"When we name something, then, we are classifying. The individual object or event we are naming, of course, has no name and belongs to no class until we put it in one" (Hayakawa 210). If these conclusions reached by a semanticist are right (and I think they *are*) and can be applied to my present topic, then I may hold that when we give names to genres of literature we are classifying literature, and that the genre names we have had so far never existed before we felt it necessary to classify literature by inventing such names. There was a time, I presume, when mankind had the idea of writing only, without bothering to divide it into literature, history, philosophy, religion, etc. And there was also a time when the idea of literature was enough for mankind to distinguish it from other sorts of writing. However, as literature "developed" further and further, its size and variety began to increase to such an extent that in many cases people no longer found it convenient to have merely the general and vague idea of literature. For the sake of ordinary communication, not to say scholarly studies, people at some time in the past found it somehow unavoidable to divide literature into classes and give them suitable names. Thus, we Chinese began to have such names as *Shih* (poetry), *Wen* (prose), *Fu* (verse prose), etc., in our country.

"What we call things and where we draw the line between one class of things and another depend upon the interests we have and the purpose of the classification" (Hayakawa 209). As in other processes of classification, genres of literature (i.e., literary kinds or classes) are arbitrarily made. They are made "arbitrarily," of course, not in the sense that the name-giver never, in the process of classifying and naming, makes any consideration as to what or which name will better serve his interest or purpose, but in the sense that the adopted name usually has no necessary intrinsic connection with the represented external or internal object.[1] There might be reason, to be sure, for the Greeks to call a play like *Oedipus Rex* or *Medea* "tragoidia" (goat song), but there was no reason why the same people should not call the same thing another name. Indeed, "That which we call a rose/By any other word would smell as sweet."[2] The choice of a name for any literary genre is like the choice of a name for a newborn child: it is the result of a "willful" if not random decision made on the part of the namer (and the namer is the classifier). It may be "meaningful" (may denote and connote a good deal) for the name giver. Yet, it is "meaningless" for those who cannot associate the name with anything other than the name. So, for a person who has not read any epic and has no idea of what an epic is, the genre name *epic* is just a series of phonological sounds or a putting together of four alphabetical letters.

With this understanding, then, we can begin to discuss the value of genre classification in literature. Since classification or naming is always an arbitrary process, we cannot accept any classifying or naming system as absolutely "true" and dismiss all others as "false." When the Renaissance critics based their division of dramatic genres on the rank of characters presented on the stage (tragedy dealing with high-ranking people; comedy with the middle class; farce with the lowest class), they thought it was a "true" system,[3] and it might well be so in their own right. However, it might not prove really "true" if Shakespeare's plays were to be taken into account. Think of *A Midsummer Night's Dream*, for instance. It has in it all the three ranks of characters. Is it then a tragedy, a comedy, or a farce?

Even a system of genre classification is "true" in a high degree at a certain time, it may not seem so "true" when time shifts. It is generally admitted that drama, epic, and lyric were considered the three basic literary types of the ancient West; they are replaced, however, by drama, poetry, and fiction in the modern times.[4]   This replacement implies, of course, that the old way of classification is no longer thought to be valid while the new way is regarded as more feasible.   So genres, indeed, never remain fixed.   "With the addition of new works, our categories shift" (Wellek & Warren 216).

Genre classification varies not only with times but also with places.   In the West, in view of the language used a piece of literature has been assigned to either poetry or prose until relatively very modern times.   In our country, the dichotomy was at a very early time replaced by a trichotomy: *Shih*, *Wen* and *Fu*.   That is why we can say "Every 'culture' has its genres" (Wellek & Warren 225).

Since no system of genre classification is to be regarded as absolutely true for all times and places, the value of genre classification does not obviously lie in the truth a system claims to possess.   Aristotle's system (lyric, epic, drama), Hobbes' system (heroic, scommatic, pastoral), E. S. Dallas' system (play, tale, song), and Northrop Frye's system (epos, prose, drama, lyric) are all true and all false.   For they all base their classifications on certain criteria (manner of imitation, represented worlds, grammatical ideas, and rhetorical rhythm), which are mechanically and "willfully" chosen for their own interests or purposes, regardless of all other considerations.[5]

But, as we know, the idea of genre (with at least one implied system at one time) has been useful to many critics since ancient times.   The neo-classical theorists, for instance, were especially interested in such topics as "purity of kind, hierarchy of kinds, duration of kinds, addition of new kinds" (Wellek & Warren 220).   These topics, besides giving these critics pleasure of exercising authority through argument and debate, have all influenced more or less writers' as well as readers' attitudes towards works through the critics' authoritative statements concerning the idea of genre and the act of genre classification.

For instance, for those who advocate the purity of genres, works of mixed genres like a tragicomedy are held to be against a rule of "decorum";

they are hence not to be appreciated and not to be written. However, for those who do not believe in this decorum of a "pure breed" in literature, "hybrid" works of mixed genres are to be encouraged.[6] As to the idea of generic hierarchy, it influences even more widely and deeply those writers and readers who are conscious of their literary tradition. Under the influence of a hierarchical idea, an ambitious writer naturally will not be content with writing a lesser kind of literature (e.g., the sonnet, the pastoral, the masque, the ballad, etc., in the classical West). He will aim to establish his name on one of the highest or greatest kinds (e.g., the epic or the tragedy).[7] And as writers and critics agree on a hierarchical order of this nature, readers, especially those "common" readers who have no taste of their own and cannot judge independently, will naturally form a similarly "snobbish" idea of genres and base their criticism largely on generic considerations (just as people judge a person in terms of blood and social ranks). So, no matter on what basis a critic constructs his hierarchy of genres,[8] that hierarchy is sure to have a far-reaching effect on readers and writers alike.

In an aristocratic feudal society, or in a classical world in which people believe in order, authority and "the Great Chain of Being," the purity or the hierarchy of genres may win applause as an obvious and trustworthy notion. However, in a time of democracy when equality dominates over the idea of nobility, the two generic topics naturally lose their significance for most writers, readers as well as critics. In a fashionable term, the idea of generic purity or hierarchy is an aspect of the "logocentric" tendency of the whole past Western culture; it is an established value most vulnerable to the process of "deconstruction" in our times. So, any system of genre classification connected with the idea of purity and hierarchy may not have a permanent value.

If to consider genres in terms of purity or hierarchy is to be aristocratic and thus prove of no great value in modern times, it is not so to examine the duration of genres and to notice the addition of new genres to the literary world.　We might say that to talk of purity and hierarchy is to maintain a static order, to neglect the process of change, to act against history, while to talk of the new birth of a genre and to attend to a genre's duration are to admit the "evolution" of literary species in the long history of human culture.　In our country, the idea of "generic evolution" is most prevalent.　We Chinese have become accustomed to accepting as true that our literature "developed" different types with various durations in different periods: the *Fu* in Han Dynasty, the Poetry in T'ang Dynasty, the *Tz'u* in Sung Dynasty, the *Hsi-chü* in Yüan Dynasty, and the Fiction in Ming and Ch'ing Dynasties.　In the West, pastoral, elegy, sonnet, epigram, ode, satire, drama (including tragedy, comedy and farce), epic, etc., were accepted genres up to the time of Boileau. After the eighteenth century, novels of various types gradually made their appearances.　Today the basic genres have ramified into so many sub-genres and sub-sub-genres that critics, especially most recent French and German writers, begin to speak of some sub-genres (the sonnet, the rondeau, the ballade, etc.) as "fixed forms" and differentiate them from genres (see Wellek & Warren 221).

　　The purity of kind, hierarchy of kinds, duration of kinds, and addition of new kinds, as well as the number or detail of kinds and the way of distinguishing kinds (prescriptive or descriptive; based on form or content, etc.), are all problems of literary critics or historians.　Any system of genre classification can be of great value to these literary specialists so long as it can provide them with necessary data for probing the problems they are interested in.　And the conclusions these specialists have drawn may really have a great influence on those writers or readers who trust them.　However, for a writer or reader who is not aware of, or simply does not care a fig of, these specialists' words, the generic problems and conclusions may be worth nothing.　Nevertheless, the very knowing of the fact that literature has various kinds will influence a writer or a reader to a certain degree.

Naturally, a writer completely unaware of any genre classification may start his writing without any connection with the idea of genre. But one doubts if there is any writer of this sort except the world's first writer (or writers if you like). Did Homer write *Iliad* without knowing he was writing something like an epic? The answer could be in the affirmative only if Homer were really the first Western writer. If there were already many examples (which were lost to us) before him, the answer should be "No." If we really have "born writers," writers who can write literature without having to read and "learn" from other writers' works, then these "geniuses" certainly will not have any notion of genre and will not be affected by any genre classification. However, who are the "born writers"? Even the Romantics who claim to learn mostly from nature are in fact eager "grazers" of literature.[9] Now, in reading others' works, a man is forming among other things the idea of these works' shapes, is recognizing literary kinds although he may not bother to know what these kinds are called. Then, the next time when he himself begins to write, he cannot but write either in conformity or in "deformity" with his learning.

In fact, today's writers often determine to make themselves poets or playwrights or novelists or essayists or what not before they make themselves known. And this choice of career is a choice based on the notion of genres. Then, when a poet starts writing a poem, he may be fully conscious of what sub-genre of poetry he is writing: lyric or ode or elegy or ballad or epithalamion or sonnet or what not--just as a novelist may choose to write a Gothic novel or a picaresque novel or a *Bildungsroman* or a *roman à clef* or any other type. But, of course, a writer may also choose to write none of the established genres; he may intentionally break with tradition by writing something "very different" from any known genre of literature.[10]

If a writer chooses to work within certain genres, they may find the accepted traits or conventions that go with the genres either becoming an obstacle or fetter of his writing or becoming a stimulating test of his skill and craftsmanship in making new the old stuff. (Let us not forget Wordsworth's pleasure in being bound within "the Sonnet's scanty plot of ground."[11]) Conversely, if a writer can really break with all traditional genres and write something clear of any established generic traits or conventions, then he is entirely free, of course, to do whatever he likes and he may claim "original" by striking out entirely on his own. Yet, this liberty, like political liberty or any other sort of liberty, may also breed danger. An entirely free man may not know where to begin his wander, may roam aimlessly without getting anywhere, and may end his vagabondage in a state of anarchy. So, the notion of genre is important to a writer. And a clear idea of the existing literary genres can help the writer to know where to conform and where to "deform."

The notion of genre is equally important to a common reader. If a reader can know to what genre a work he is reading belongs, then he will usually be able to judge it better, just as we normally can judge a person more accurately if we know to what race or nationality or social class he belongs. In effect, a reader often has his favorite genre. A lover of chivalric romance may find pleasure in anything pertaining to that genre. To see a form or content familiar to one can be a pleasant experience.[12] Yet, of course, there are cases in which people are repulsed by something too familiar to them. A reader may also dislike a work replete with stale conventions or stereotyped traits of a genre which he knows only too well (see how Dr. Johnson disliked Milton's "Lycidas").

In Danziger and Johnson's *Introduction to Literary Criticism*, it is convincingly pointed out that in general a work, by being written in a particular genre, "may gain yet another dimension , an additional complexity, and … its very meaning may, as a result, be in some way amplified or perhaps even qualified" (85-89). The same critics also point out that a work in which "no recognizable genre has been chosen is also significant," and that to fail to recognize what genre a work is written in can be very dangerous --e.g., one might miss the very meaning of a work, might be baffled by any kind of parody, might be left in doubt about the structure of a work or some of its details, etc. (89-90). In his *The Act of Reading*, Wolfgang Iser says, also convincingly, that "Art exists only for and through other people," that "The combined efforts of author and reader bring into being the concrete and imaginary object which is the work of the mind" (108). Now we may say that one of the combined efforts of author and reader is the knowledge of genre classification.

So far I have discussed the value of genre classification in relation to critics, writers and common readers. I cannot say which of the three groups can benefit most from the notion of genre and the details of a genre classification. But I can add that if a culture has more genres of literature, that culture may be said to have more developed literature. For, as I have stated at the outset, the act of genre classification and the process of giving names to genres occur only after works of such genres have appeared. Variety is an index to development. We may classify genres arbitrarily,[13] but we normally cannot classify works with new generic names unless new types of literature have really been developed. So genre classification has the additional value of serving as an index to a nation's development in literature.

Notes

1. This idea is similar to the structuralists' assertion that the signifier and the signified (or the sign and the object) cannot be said to have any "real" relationship.
2. This is said by Juliet in Shakespeare's *Romeo and Juliet*, Act II, scene 2.
3. See, on this point, Hall's *A Short History of Literary Criticism*, pp.38-39.
4. See, on this point, Danziger & Johnson, , p.67 & p.76.
5. For details of these systems, see Wellek & Warren, pp. 217-8; Hall, p.57; and Frye's fourth essay in his *Anatomy of Criticism*.
6. In his "An Essay of Dramatic Poesy," for instance, Dryden makes Neander defend tragicomedy by claiming that it is a more pleasant way of writing for the stage, and comic relief can make the tragic even more tragic.

7. Notice, for instance, that many major English writers (Spenser, Milton, Wordsworth, etc) have attempted to do so by imitating or emulating Homer and Virgil whose names are celebrated for their epics.
8. Aristotle, Hobbes, Dryden and Blair, for instance, construct their hierarchies in consideration of the rank of the character, the style, the seriousness of tone, and the length or size of the work.
9. Wordsworth, for instance, read voraciously in William Taylor's library; and Coleridge was admittedly one of the most learned men of letters.
10. In theory a new work is never identical with any old one, though they may belong to the same genre.   Conversely, a new work is never wholly different from any old one, though they may belong to different genres.   Here the Russian Formalists' idea of "defamiliarization" is useful.   A writer's intention to write a "totally new" genre is only a strategy of trying to "defamiliarize" his work so as to "foreground" it on the old stage.   "Totally new" is impossible in practice.
11. See his "Nuns fret not at their convent's room."
12. This is why so many of our people like to watch a Peiking Opera staged in strict accordance with the established conventions.
13. For example, genres of poetry have been classified in terms of subjective and objective (the lyric is held to be the most subjective, the epic the most objective, and drama somewhere in between).   See M. H. Abrams, *The Mirror and the Lamp*, p.241.

Works Consulted

Abrams, M. H.   *The Mirror and the Lamp*.   New York: Norton, 1958.

Danziger M. K. & W. S. Johnson.   *An Introduction to Literary Criticism*.   New York: D. C. Heath, 1961.

Frye, Northrop.   *Anatomy of Criticism*.   Princeton: Princeton UP, 1957.

Hall, Vernon, Jr.   *A Short History of Literary Criticism*.   New York: New York UP, 1963.

Hayakawa, S. I.   *Language in Thought and Action.* New York: Harcourt Brace, 1952.

Iser, Wolfgang.   *The Act of Reading*.   Baltimore: Johns Hopkins UP, 1978.

Wellek, Rene & Austin Warren.   *Theory of Literature*.   New York: Harcourt Brace, 1949.

*This paper first appeared in 1986 in *JAH*, pp. 195-202.

On the Originality of Literary Works

This essay aims to discuss three questions. First, what is meant by originality in reference to literary works? Second, where and how is literary originality known to exist? And third, to what extent is originality a valid criterion for the evaluation of literary works?

In trying to discuss the first question, we have to admit at the outset that the word *originality* is capable of quite widely different interpretations in reference to literary works. If we take the word to mean, as the O.E.D. puts it, "the fact or attribute of being primary or first hand," or "the quality of being independent of and different from anything that has appeared before," then we may, paradoxically, doubt on one hand that any existing world-famous work has any originality at all, and claim on the other hand that no existing work today is without originality. For on one hand even such earliest known writers as Homer, Pindar, and Anacreon are only "accidental originals," not real originals; it is only that the works they imitated are lost.[1] If we stick to the principle of being "primary or first hand," the really original writers could very probably be those ancient barbarians who somehow happened to have worked out some prototypes of literary pieces. However, if on the other hand we are willing to be loose about the principle of being "independent of and different from anything that has appeared before," we should admit that except in the case of a pure plagiarism, no two works are identical just as "no two faces, no two minds, are just alike" (Young 288), and therefore each work is original to a certain degree.

To clarify the meaning of originality, we often get inextricably involved in the theory of imitation. As a Romantic preaching the value of original genius, Edward Young has told us that "Imitations are of two kinds; one of nature, one of authors: The first we call originals, and confine the term 'Imitation' to the second" (279). This is plainly a refutation to Pope's neo-classical thought: "Those rules of old discovered, not devised,/ Are nature still, but nature methodized" (ll. 88-89). Indeed, it may seem a peremptory act to a mimetic theorist that one should call the imitation of nature original while calling the imitation of man imitative. But this is the common case we still witness today in the literary circle, though we have not forgot that Plato has suggested that literary works are merely copies of copies.

The idea of originality begets another serious problem when we refer it to something from which some other thing or things are derived, rather than to something which is imitated by others. In his "The Origin of the Work of Art," Martin Heidegger repeatedly asserts that the artist is the origin of the work, that the work is the origin of the artist, and that art is the origin of both artist and work, if by origin is meant "that from and by which something is what it is and as it is" (77 ff.). These assertions of Heidegger's are all true in their own tight, although we seldom give them any thought when we consider the originality of literary works.

There are then many people for whom originality simply means "newness" or "novelty" or "freshness" which the reader feels in a work. This impressionistic interpretation of the word has, of course, its dangers. For one thing, an inexperienced reader or a beginner of reading, for example a first grader, may very probably find an idea or an expression or a technique very original (as it seems to him fresh and new) which in actuality is but commonplace, trite, and disgustingly repetitive. And the other extreme case is, a terribly well-read connoisseur of literature (if there really is such a man) may find very little novelty in a recognized world masterpiece; he may assert with Emerson that "every new writer is only the crater of an old volcano," or simply agrees that there is nothing new under the sun.

Still for some people the word *originality* may suggest "authenticity" or "genuineness," as when we are concerned with the originality of Macpherson's Ossianic poems. In this sense, originality becomes the establishment of true authorship or the prevention from literary forgery or hoax. It is, therefore, the concern of a few textual scholars or editors, not that of the common reader, whose sense of novelty or freshness in a work may not be affected by the fact that the work is a mere fabrication, as the above-mentioned pseudo-Gaetic poems indicate.

In connecting *originality* to the idea of "dissimilarity" or "novelty," we need to pay attention to a special type of work: namely, parody. As a parody recognizably copies the manner of a known writer or work, it may seem too similar to the "original" to be called "original." But does it then lack novelty, unprecedentedness, or "originality"? The answer is No. The fact is very paradoxical: a parody is often highly interesting and genuinely original just because it follows so closely the original in so many places. Its originality seems to concur with the fact that it imitates so perfectly!

Parody may be an exception or merely a small portion when we discuss literature in the light of originality. But how about such works as said to be "influenced" by other works? It is said that Jacopo Sannazaro's *Arcadia* (1504) was indebted chiefly to Boccaccio's *Filocolo* and *Ninfale d'Ameto* for style, diction, and subject matter while it borrowed also from Theocritus, Bion, Moschus, Catullus, Virgil, Ovid, Apuleius, and Petrarch (see Trawick 24). It is also said that the same work of Sannazaro's had as its direct descendants Guarini's *Faithful Shepherd* (*Pastor Fido*), Montemayor's *Diana*, Sidney's *Arcadia*, and D'Urfé's *Astrèe* while it also influenced Tasso, du Bellay, Spenser, Marlowe, Shakespeare, Phineas Fletcher, Milton, and Keats (see Trawick 25). If these statements are true, can we then call those (Boccaccio, etc.) original who have influenced others and regard those who have been influenced (Guarini, etc.) as lacking originality?

The problem of "influence" is very complicated as one work can be influenced by another in countless ways. After reading Shakespeare, for instance, a writer may start writing something very obviously Shakespearean--e.g., with a *King Lear* plot, or a Hamlet character, or a setting of *Midsummer Night's Dream*, or anything reminiscent of Shakespeare's peculiar dramaturgical device, or just a line allusive to Shakespeare. The same writer, however, may also start writing something non-Shakespearean or even anti-Shakespearean. After reading *Macbeth*, for example, he may write an *Oliver Twist* or a *To the Lighthouse*, showing very little, if any, influence from the great playwright. Or it may chance that having read the lines beginning with "tomorrow and tomorrow and tomorrow," the writer suddenly strikes out an idea of writing something temporal and after a long persistent effort finishes a *Remembrance of Things Past*—an influence certainly from Shakespeare but hardly Shakespearean at all.

It follows, therefore, that to say a work is influenced by such and such authors or works is not necessarily equal to saying that it is not original. Those are indeed never original who, as Arthur Schopenhauer says of them, "in order to think at all … need the more direct and powerful stimulus of having other people's thoughts before them"; who always adopt others' thoughts as their immediate themes (3). And those of course are also in want of originality who merely adopt others' techniques or devices idly without using their own brains for "creating" their own works, just as the strong adherents to a certain school or movement of literature often do. Yet, if one receives someone else's influence within the extent of being "inspired" only, of being able to strike out on one's own with a mere hint from someone else, one surely may not fall short of originality through that "influence."

So far in trying to define the meaning of literary originality, I have discussed some concomitant difficulties in the job. From this discussion, however, we can conclude temporarily that in reference to literary works originality does not mean real unprecedentedness, nor total uniqueness, nor sheer lack of imitation, nor complete absence of origin, nor absolute newness, novelty and freshness, nor authenticity or genuineness in authorship, nor entire freedom from any influence or affecting source. It means rather the quality that the reader feels existing in a work which *seems* to him unprecedentedly or uniquely different from anything he has already known to exist in all other works.

In giving this definition, I have implicitly touched on the second question of this essay: Where and how is literary originality known to exist? My definition clearly holds that originality as a literary quality certainly exists (or *consists* if you like) in a literary work. But this objective existence is changed into a subjective existence through the reader's feeling. That is to say: in order to be known, any literary originality has to be removed from the dead body of the work to the living consciousness of the reader. At this point, one may argue thus: But isn't it possible, too, that the author (especially the really creative genius) rather than the reader may subjectively foresee the quality of originality in his work to be written, that is, originality can be a pre-existence in the writer's consciousness to be moved from there into the dead body of the work (i.e., the manuscript or the print). To this argument, I concede that the subjective existence of literary originality can be found indeed in both the writer's consciousness and the reader's. But as a criterion for judging works, it is only the subjective existence in the reader's consciousness that counts. In a plainer word, an author may claim (and that truly without any falsehood) that his work is original in such and such a way because he has intended it to be so and he has known no former examples quite like that before. Nevertheless, the writer's consciousness is never wholly equal to the reader's consciousness; what is *in*tended often runs short of or in excess of what is *ex*tended, to use the two words in a philosophical sense. The originality which looms big in the writer's own mind may fail to be seen in the reader's eye. And as evaluation of literary works is normally a job of the reader (especially the special reader called "critic") rather than the author himself, originality as a judging criterion can naturally be understood as referring only to the subjective existence of that literary quality in the reader's consciousness.

The discrepancy between the writer's and the reader's consciousness of literary originality can be best demonstrated in the well-known case of Edgar Allan Poe's suspecting Nathaniel Hawthorne of plagiarism. In his Review of Hawthorne's *Twice-Told Tales*, Poe once charged Hawthorne with writing in "Howe's Masquerade" a passage which "resembles a plagiarism [from his 'William Wilson'] –but in which *may be* a very flattering coincidence of thought," not knowing that Hawthorne's "Howe's Masquerade" had been first published in the *Democratic Review* more than a year before his own "William Wilson" appeared.[2] Poe's unfortunate misconception arose, as we know today, quite innocently from his double role as both writer and reader of something claimable of literary originality. As a writer he presumed confidently he was creating something novel and fresh without knowing "a very flattering coincidence of thought" did occur. As a reader he was disgusted with something which was really unoriginal to him at that time but which was truly original to Hawthorne some time earlier.

This fact leads us to think of the third question: To what extent is originality a valid criterion for the evaluation of literary works. Since originality as an inherent property of literary works is to be appreciated in the reader's subjective consciousness, it is subject to the reader's sensibility to and knowledge of literary works. To give an extreme example, the comparison of a woman to a rose is too stereotyped to claim any originality for most readers today. Yet, to a person who hears the metaphor for the first time, the comparison is as fresh (hence original) as when it was first made in the ancient times. So, theoretically, literary originality is never a stable objective existence. It has a relative quality which changes its value as time and space change with the individual reader. Consequently, a work claimed to be highly original at a particular time in the past might become stale in a future reader's mind just because similar works have since been repeatedly produced and crammed into the reader's mind.[3] For example, Shakespeare was said to be original for his "tragical harmony," the harmony of blank verse.[4] But after so much blank verse has poured into English drama and other types of literature today, can the present-day reader of Shakespeare feel any trace of originality merely in the great dramatist's use of the blank verse form?

Facing this question, one may protest thus: "But it is unfair to efface a former writer's marks of originality by later writers' imitation." True, if we all have a sound historical sense. However, is it obligatory that a reader should have such a sense? Is it necessary or possible that one reads works according to chronological order and has a clear sense about what goes first and what comes next? If the answer is in the negative, what can we do to restrain the individual's whimsical use of originality as judging criterion for literary works? We allow that there is no absolute originality, that literary originality is a relative matter, and that the degree of originality varies with various readers of various times and places. But, after all, evaluation of literary works is a social behavior. In order to become a valid judging criterion for literary works, originality must be understood as something pertaining not to an individual's consciousness only, but to the consensus of a social class (in reality, the so-called literary circle). Otherwise, literary evaluation on the basis of originality is liable to become a matter of purely personal taste.

If originality is limited to the quality communally felt in a work by a literary circle, we still have to admit that what seems original to a particular circle may not prove the same to another circle. It is often asserted, for instance, that we Chinese have no tragedy nor epic of the Greek sort. If this is true, isn't it also true that a Chinese imitation of Greek tragedy or epic is likely to be found original among the Chinese people while felt to be obviously derivative in the West? Facing a case like this, shall we then widen the judging literary circle to an international one? The answer may be Yes, but then we know it is very hard to find a modern work which is original in any way to people of all times and all places. Accordingly, originality becomes an unworkable criterion for literary evaluation if the judging circle grows too big, just as it does when the judging circle is reduced to a single individual. Therefore, to judge works on the basis of originality, the ideal judging circle should be a moderate size only. And this incidentally betrays the fact that originality as a subjective literary existence cannot be a permanent nor a universal quality.

As a judging criterion, originality has another danger. One may easily take what is merely novel for originality. And the easiest way to beget originality in that sense is to frantically break away from all established forms or conventions of literature, leading thus to an overvaluing of the merely odd or eccentric as it does in the case of the Dadaists.[5] That originality is not just the prevention of the hackneyed or trite, of the remarkably derivative or the flatly uninspired, has been a stressed point of critics, East and West alike. For instance, Liu Hsieh in our country recognizes the fresh and extraordinary as one of the eight styles of literature, but he observes at the same time: "The literary stutter results from a love of the odd. In chasing after the new and strange, the writer naturally embrangles his throat and lips" (222 & 258). And in his Introduction to *Criticism: the Major Texts*, Walter Jackson Bate says: "… one can be 'original' in any number of ways. For example, to react counter to the truth in every respect is, after all, a form of 'originality." (3). Thus, we find it indispensable to hold the pursuit of originality within the bounds of other essential literary principles, e.g., the principle of pleasure or that of unity.

In talking about artistic creativity, Vincent Tomas affirms that creativity must be denied where mechanical borrowings are detected, where self-repetition is found, where novelty and freshness are impertinent or bad, and where unity and clarity of artistic objects are lost.[6]   I think these conditions of denying artistic creativity are also conditions of denying literary originality (here creativity is the synonym of originality).   To sum up Tomas's and any other similar affirmations known to us, we might say that no act of artistic creativity should surpass the ultimate aim of art (the means should forever serve the end); therefore, to be original in any way is to be original in an artistic way, that is, to achieve the final aim of art (be it to delight or to instruct or both).   And therefore, in using originality as a judging criterion for literary evaluation, we shall see that what is original in a work is really in keeping with the work as an artistic object, and not just the pursuit of originality for originality's sake.

Aesthetic excellence is seldom the result of going to extremes. Originality in the sense of novelty is for that reason expected to keep a due "aesthetic distance" from tradition.   In his "The Sense of the Past," Lionel Trilling rightly asserts that "the work of any poet exists by reason of its connection with past work, both in continuation and in divergence, and what we call his originality is simply his special relation to tradition" (29). Modern studies of reader response also come to the conclusion that "the right kind or degree of novelty brings pleasant surprise, too little novelty gives boredom, but overmuch novelty is bound to result in frustration and indignation, or even complete wreckage of the reading process."[7]   Indeed, originality should also observe Coleridge's principle of beauty, namely "unity in multeiry,"[8] in order to become a valid judging criterion.

So far, I have discussed my proposed three questions, and have, to be sure, left much unsaid.   For instance, originality can lie either in a work's content or its expression.   And any discussion of this division will lead to further difficult problems.   But as such a discussion need not concern us here, I will be content with quoting a few words from a critic, which can best conclude my points presented herein:

Originality ... does not necessarily consist in being different from everyone else; it does mean thinking independently of others and making every opinion so much one's own that it does not matter whether one is the first to hold it or not ... The fundamental, the important things are as old as man himself. There are endless permutations and combinations of these prime factors in the problem of life; there are endless new ways in which an old idea may be presented. Herein lies the originality of the artist; if the conception comes with new force and meaning from his pen it is to all intents and purposes original. (Nithie 62-63)

Notes

1. This is a point made in Edward Young's "Conjectures upon Original Composition." See Paul R. Lieden and Robert Withington, eds., *The Art of Literary Criticism*, p.281.
2. See Note 5 in Sculley Bradley, et al., eds., *The American Tradition in Literature*, p.886.
3. This is a phenomenon to help explicate T. S. Eliot's truism in his "Tradition and the Individual Talent": "... the past should be altered by the present as much as the present is directed by the past."
4. Samuel Johnson doubts this claim of Dennis's in his "Preface to Shakespeare."
5. This is a point made in Danziger & Johnson's *An Introduction to Literary Criticism*, p.174.
6. I derive these points of Tomas's from the Liu Shih-Tsao's Chinese translation in Liu Shou-yi, ed. *Critical Essays on Western Literature*, pp. 99-116. Tomas's original is published in *Philosophical Review* (1958, January), Vol. IV, No. 2.
7. See Chi Ch'iu-lang, "Liu Hsieh's View on Novelty and Russian Formalists' Concept of Defamiliarization," p. 508. Chi's statement is based on the study of Liu Hsieh, Wolfgang Iser, and some Russian Formalists in regard to their conception of novelty which has much to do with our present topic.
8. For this point, see Coleridge's *Biographia Literaria*, II, and also his *On the Principles of Genial Criticism*, Essay III.

Works Consulted

Adams, Hazard, ed. *Critical Theory since Plato*. New York: Harcourt Brace Jovanovich, 1971.

Bate, Walter Jackson, ed. *Criticism: the Major Texts*. Enlarged ed. New York: Harcourt Brace Jovanovich, 1970.

Bradley, Sculley, et al., eds. *The American Tradition in Literature*. 3rd ed. Vol. I, New York: Norton, 1969.

Chi, Ch'iu-lang. "Liu Hsieh's View on Novelty and Russian Formalists' Concept of Defamiliarization." *Tamkang Review* (1980, Spring & Summer), Vol. X, No. 3 & No. 4.

Coleridge, S. T. *Biographia Literaria*. Ed. J. Shawcross. Oxford: Clarendon Press, 1907.

--------. *On the Principles of Genial Criticism*, Essay III, rpt. in Adams, 463-7.

Danziger M. K. & W. S. Johnson. *An Introduction to Literary Criticism*. New York: D. C. Heath, 1961.

Eliot, T. S. "Tradition and the Individual Talent," rpt. in Adams, 784-7.

Heidegger, Martin. *Poetry, Language, Thought*. Translated by Albert Hofstadter. New York: Harper & Row, 1971.

Johnson, Samuel. "Preface" to *Shakespeare*, rpt. in Adams, 329-336.

Liu, Hsieh. *The Literary Mind and the Carving of Dragon*. Translated by Vincent Yu-chung Shih. Taipei: Chung Hua Book Co., 1970.

Liu, Show-yi, ed. *Critical Essays on Western Literature*. Taipei: Lian-Ching Publishing Co., 1977.

Nithie, Elizabeth. *The Criticism of Literature*. New York: Macmillan, 1928.

Pope, Alexander. *An Essay on Criticism*, rpt. in Adams, 278-86.

Schopenhauer, Arthur. *The Art of Literature*. Ann Arbor: U of Michigan P, 1960.

Trawick, Buckner B. *World Literature*. Vol. II. New York: Barnes & Noble, 1955.

Trilling, Lionel. "The Sense of the Past." *Essays in Modern Literary Criticism*. Ed. Ray B. West. New York: Rinehart, 1960.

Young, Edward. "Conjectures on Original Composition." *The Art of Literary Criticism*. Ed. Paul R. Lieden & Robert Withington. New York: Appleton-Century-Crofts, 1941.

*This paper first appeared in 1987 in *JAH*, pp. 301-8.

The Magic Mirror with a Magic Lamp: Towards a Reconciliation of Mimetic and Expressive Theories of Literature

In his widely admired book, *The Mirror and the Lamp*, M. H. Abrams gives a well-documented tracing of the origins of many prominent romantic ideas which, constituting the so-called expressive theories, came to replace in vogue gradually during the Romantic Period a former set of classical or neo-classical ideas which make up the so-called mimetic theories. Now, as we understand from Abrams's own explication, the mimetic theories are all oriented towards the universe, seeking to explain art as essentially an imitation of aspects of the external world in which we live, whereas the expressive theories are author-oriented for its persistent recourse to the art producer to explain the nature and criteria of art. This tracing and this explication of Abrams's are indeed admirable as a piece of scholarship. However, I find Abrams himself did not seem to keep the different theoretical orientations clearly in mind when he made some statements. For example, in his Preface to the admirable book, he says: "The title of the book identifies two common and antithetic metaphors of mind, one comparing the mind to a reflector of external objects, the other to a radiant projector which makes a contribution to the objects it perceives" (Viii). The key word in this statement is *mind*, which we ordinarily take to be a word referring to the mental organ inherent in a person, be he an author or a reader, instead of referring to a work of art although an artist's mind will necessarily enter his work in some way. If we will remember, when Plato and Aristotle say that poetry is an imitation, they are referring to the concrete work, especially a dramatic work, not to the poet's or playwright's mind. Or even more accurately, the two initiators of mimetic theories are thinking especially of players imitating man's action and speech on the stage, who naturally represent the characters in the dramatic poet's text. If Plato and Aristotle compare anything at all to a mirror, it should be first and foremost the artifact (e.g., the painter's bed), not the artist. But, of course, even a wise man may get confused. When Plato states in *Republic* X that a mirror can create appearances and so can a painter, he seems to suggest indeed that an artist's mind is like a mirror. Now it is not that one's mind cannot be compared to a mirror. But we must understand that to claim the resemblance of a poet's mind to a mirror is not equal to saying his poem is like a mirror. In other words, the author's mind and the mind in the work should not be considered an identical one in the discussion of mimetic and expressive theories. And Abrams's explanation regarding the title of his famous book is obviously a betrayal of his neglecting the subtle distinction.

Nevertheless, Abram's explanatory statement is true in that man's mind does resemble both the mirror and the lamp in certain respects. And as I shall soon expound it below, every mind--the author's, that in the work, as well as the reader's--is capable of taking the two metaphors for a description of its nature and function in the literary world, which I think involves five co-ordinates (author, work, reader, language and the universe) in two basic actions (reading and writing).[1] And furthermore, I shall argue that no literary mind can possibly function well without its lamp quality and mirror quality working together. Thus, a reconciliation of mimetic and expressive theories is all but indispensable.

First, let us consider the author's mind. An author is fairly like anybody else in one respect, no matter what people have said about his talent or genius, sensibility or madness. That is, he lives in the universe, he experiences whatever comes to him in it, and thus there may be times when he thinks he "knows" something about it. This cognitive process is not possible without both the universe and the author's mind. But how come one can "know" or claim to "know" something? Here philosophers have differed in their interpretations. But fundamentally the various interpretations are of two groups: rationalism and empiricism. The former, variably called intuitionalism or apriorism and with such adherents as Descartes, Spinoza, Leibniz and Wolff, holds that genuine knowledge cannot come from sense perception or experience, but must have its foundation in thought or reason: certain truths are natural or native to reason and these innate or inborn truths are valid truths. The latter, also called sensationalism and followed by such thinkers as Hobbes, Locke, Berkeley and Hume, asserts instead that there are no *a priori* truths: all knowledge springs from sense perception or experience, and *pure* thought, or thought absolutely independent of sense perception, is impossible.[2] Now, when we talk of an author acquiring his knowledge from the outside world, we do emphasize the empirical viewpoint. Yet, if we admit the existence of inspiration, of the time when a literary genius penetrates the outside world and "sees into the life of things," the time indeed when imagination so possesses us that we lose consciousness of ourselves while a vision, a transcendental truth, an intuited meaning of life catches us unawares; then we must admit also the rationalist point of view.

In fact, in its cognitive process, an author's mind is indeed like a lamp and a mirror at once. It is like a lamp in that it throws light on that part of the external world which the eye is to see. Without one's mind ("absent-minded"), one may look at something without seeing anything. With one's mind (fully attentive), then, one can perceive what otherwise will be overlooked in one's sight. The mind is the source of will, desire, or impulse; the headspring of emotions; the projector that spotlights the empirical world with its possessor's will, desire, impulse or emotions so as to render different colors or shapes to whatever is under scrutiny, and to focus the eyes' attention for a clear sight or an extraordinary insight. The world is all darkness itself without "the lamp of Heaven, the sun." It is likewise all darkness without "the lamp of man, the mind." "I think, therefore I am"; and therefore everything is, as it is perceived.

On the other hand, however, the mind is really like a mirror, too. It is so because no mind can perceive anything without taking in images of the perceived. When the images come in and register themselves in the mind (become what we call memory or ideas), they are like images reflected in the mirror. They are never "the real thing"; they are only "images," appearances, of certain reality.[3] But however unreal these mirrored images may be, they are nonetheless crucial to man's understanding. Man never knows or understands directly through things themselves, but indirectly through images of things reflected or staying in the mind's mirror. That is why some philosophers come to affirm that no real understanding of the universe is possible. If reality is not a pre-existing Platonic Idea located in a special realm beyond our physical world, nor an *a priori* idea in one's mind, it is then only something perceived as an image from the empirical world; that is, it is only a phantom, an illusory or delusive phantom. Hence, all understanding is misunderstanding.

Now, it is not just the images as insubstantial phantoms that make man forever detached from reality. Man is willfully determined not to see the spade as a spade; he prefers to construct a spade of his own by means of his "imagination." This is especially true of an artist. A poet's reality, we may say, is more the images he himself creates than the mere images reflected instantly from outside into his mind's eye.[4] Various descriptions have been given of the imaginative faculty of mind, ranging from Dryden's "conjunction of two natures, which have a real separate being"[5] to Coleridge's "esemplastic" or "synthetic and magical power" (XIII) or the "shaping spirit."[6] All descriptions, however, just go to show that the mind is not just an ordinary mirror reflecting images of things from outside; it is rather a magic mirror capable of magnifying, minimizing, dissecting, rearranging, adding, and deleting images. And this unusual mental power has been explained in the light of association theories since Hume and Hartley and in the light of creative thinking, a subject much studied in relatively more modern times. But as such explanations need not concern us here, suffice it to say that all psychologists, past and present, agree that man's perception is a "plastic perception,"[7] that the human mind with its molding power is a creative, inventive, or innovative organ.

This understanding, however, should not blind us to the fact that the mind never really creates anything out of nothing; its invention is always based on certain already existing things; its innovation is often a mere remolding of the old material. To be brief, one can imagine only the imaginable. A chimera, as often adduced as an example, is never a purely fictional being beyond our empirical understanding; it is in fact the composite of three ordinary images: the head of a lion, the body of a goat, and the tail of a serpent. Likewise, any fantastic idea, abstract or concrete, that occurs in the mind is never so fantastic as to lose its root in the practical world of sense. So, we can say that the inventive mind is still imitating other things in its course of invention. Our mental mirror never ceases to reflect the external universe despite its strong creativity. That is why Edmund Burke says that our creative power cannot produce absolutely new things.[8]

Here mention can be made of the magic mirrors prevailing in ancient China and Japan. It is reported that such mirrors are hand mirrors of metal, with polished faces slightly convex in form, and with backs occupied with ornamentation and inscriptions in bold relief. They are known as magic mirrors from the fact that when a strong beam of light is reflected from their smooth and polished surface, and thrown on a white screen, an image of the raised ornaments and characters on the back of the mirror is formed with more or less distinctness in the disk of light on the screen. And it is observed that a mirror of this kind is so made that the irregularity of its surface is inconspicuous in ordinary light and does not visibly distort images, but when the mirror reflects a bright light on a screen the unequal radiation renders the minute differences of surface obvious.[9]

Now it occurs to me that this magic mirror is the best symbol of our mind.   Our usual mind naturally can reflect images of outward entities without visible distortion, that is, in a manner of sheer copying or imitation. But this mind of ours is not without something of its own.   What compose our memory, call them thoughts or ideas, are just like the ornaments or inscriptions on the back of the magic mirror.   If only there comes a strong beam of light to work on the surface of the mirror, then such things in the memory (thoughts or ideas) will appear, though somehow distorted, on the screen.   But the questions are: where does the strong beam come from? And what is the screen in our comparison?

We are all familiar with the story of Aladdin.   It is related in *The Arabian Nights* that the youth gets a magic lamp and ring, the rubbing of which brings two jinn, who do the owner's bidding.   I think this story is a good allegory for our present purpose.   No matter what the magic lamp and ring may represent, it is a tool used to fulfill one's wishes.   In our routine life, we use hammers, pencils, trains, computers and other material tools to fulfill many of our wishes.   But for an artist his tool is imagination.   Whatever he wants, he just imagines and then there it comes, just as the rubbing of the magic lamp and ring will surely bring about the jinn to do one's bidding.   So, we can say an author is an Aladdin with a magic lamp and ring in hand.   It is only that his magic lamp is equipped, as it were, with one of the above-mentioned magic mirrors.   Therefore, its working not only sets its own agents going but also provides a strong beam of light to set the magic mirror working too.   To speak plainly, imagination is a writer's magic lamp which makes possible the magic mirroring of his mind (the magnifying, diminishing, dissecting, rearranging, adding and deleting of images from within and without).   So, when we lose our imagination in our humdrum life, it is as if our soul's lamp-light has faded "into the light of common day" so that our magic mirror can no longer reflect anything extraordinary and fresh on our screen of life.[10]

Yet, an author is one who has not yet lost his magic lamp, who can still project a bright light on his magic mirror and thus reflect images from within and without onto the screen of writing, which is no more than a verbal transcription of the reflected images of his mentality.   But, of course, this transcription, as any transcription is, is never identical with the original copy. Besides, by the use of language, which is admittedly a poor medium for transmitting messages (not to say attitudes or moods), the author can never convey exactly what he has in mind, including his thoughts, ideas, feelings or whatever we choose to call it.   This is why Buddha prefers not to say anything and recognizes the impossibility of language.

To be sure, a true poet will also find himself tongue-tied in the face of an intuited truth, a truth (call it a vision) with such a happy arrangement of images as his bright magic lamp has caused his magic mirror to reflect miraculously on his mental screen.[11]   But, after all, a poet is not a Buddha. He cannot be content with silence.   He has to utter what is overflowing in his mind.   And the way to utter it is by language, spoken or written.   It is to be remembered that when Wordsworth, in his Preface to *Lyrical Ballads*, defines poetry as 'the spontaneous overflow of powerful feelings," he is referring to the state of poetic fullness in the mind.   It is not until the state is transcribed in human language (that is, when composition of a poem has truly begun) that a poet can be recognized as a poet.   In other words, a poet has to turn his mental screen into a linguistic screen before he can reach others for recognition.

But here we find a seeming division of opinion.   Benedetto Croce holds that expression presupposes impression (those who have never seen the sea can have no impressions of the sea and consequently cannot express the sea), and intuition co-exists with expression in the cognitive process (to intuit the sea is to express it).[12]   Therefore, for him art is intuition, is a "representation" in mind, is impressions reappearing in expression which is not necessarily verbal; in other words, there is no distinction between author and work, art is an act of intuition-expression, and what is external is not any more a work of art.[13]   In effect, Croce seems to identify our mental screen with the linguistic screen by asserting the strong bond between intuition and expression.   However, the fact is that by adopting language as the mode of expression, our mind must of necessity externalize our intuition and the process of externalization cannot but bring about dissimilarities (however subtle they may be) between intuition and expression.   One may disregard a sequence of sounds or a succession of printed words as the essence of poetry, but there is no perceivable poem without such external signs of linguistic entities.

Whereas Croce tries to eliminate the discrimination between intuition and expression and thus minimize the significance of artistic media, E. H. Gombrich, in contrast, tries to highlight the function of the media.   He says, "The forms of art, ancient and modern, are not duplications of what the artist has in mind any more than they are duplications of what he sees in the outer world."   For him, all art forms are "renderings within an acquired medium, a medium grown up through tradition and skill—that of the artist and that of the beholder" (1172).   This view, when applied to literary art, amounts to saying that literature is primarily a manipulation of language (an idea all Russian formalists will agree to); it has little to do with the writer's imitating the external world or expressing his internal world.   In other words, Gombrich seems to see the linguistic screen only, without caring much about its relationship to the mental screen where a writer's mind, with its magic lamp and mirror, first reflects images from outside and projects images from inside.

It is my contention that a literary text cannot be viewed as solely a pattern of unseen mentality nor solely as a tangible mode of linguistic system.

So long as the mental screen can be understood as distinguishable from the linguistic screen, a literary text should refer to both, which we may call internal and external texts respectively for convenience sake.   Then it becomes obvious that the external text (the linguistic screen) is the signifier while the internal text (the mental screen) is the signified, if we consider them in the light of a symbolic system.   It is of course difficult to maintain that language imitates or reflects reality (a three-letter word like *cat* never imitates or reflects the animal's appearance or action in any way), since, as de Saussure has told us, language is an arbitrary symbolic system.   However, there is no questioning that language does try to represent one's idea of something.   If one's idea of something is already an imitation or reflection of images from outside and a projection of images from inside, then language is, doubtless, a representation of these reflected and projected images.   In consequence, a literary work in its physical appearance as a linguistic entity is a representation of the author's mental reflection and projection.

Now, another question can be raised.   Is verbal representation a pure representation?   Does language merely represent ideas without shaping them in its own way?   To put it clearly, for example, does the word *cat* only denote the mewing animal or refer to the idea of that animal without adding something extra to it?   The answer is no, of course.   For at least the three-letter word has a sound, and a shape too if it is written or printed.   The sound and the shape of the word are the additives.   And in literature of all types, especially in poetry, the arrangement of sounds and shapes as well as the ideas of words strongly determines the "meaning" of the work.[14] Therefore, language as a symbolic system is also like the magic mirror with a magic lamp.   It at once represents (in a sense imitates or reflects) ideas and projects something of its own onto the linguistic screen.   So the linguistic screen (the external text) is never identical with the mental screen (the internal text).   An author's "intention" is never wholly equal to his "extention."   To see both as the same is to commit the "intentional fallacy."[15]

Talking of the intentional fallacy, we have stepped into the realm of reading. Reading, to be sure, is the reverse process of writing. While writing is the externalization of text through language, reading is the internalization. In reading one takes in the verbal text (the linguistic screen) and interprets or deciphers the textual codes or linguistic symbols by means of linguistic conventions (the set-up grammatical rules and lexical meanings). In ordinary reading it is expected that language remains the medium all the time, that it only enables the linguistic screen (the verbal or external text) to become in reverse order the mental screen (the imaginary or internal text), that it should only help the author's "extention" to be traced back to and tallied with his "intention."[16] In other words, in an ordinary sense to read is to imitate (or to reflect or to represent, if you like) what is being read (using the reader's voice to imitate the writer's voice, and the reader's ideas to reflect the writer's ideas). This idea of reading, however, is much challenged in recent phenomenological or psychological studies of the reading process.[17] It is commonly held nowadays that to read is to interpret, and to interpret is a subjective act, an act, we may see, no less than a self-expression. In other words, this new idea of reading holds that the reading process is not a passive course of reconstruction; it is rather an active course in which the reader is also a magic mirror with a magic lamp, always ready to project his own images onto the linguistic or mental screen. Hence, a reader reading is not very different from a writer writing; both are inventive to a high degree.

Indeed, there is some sense in equating the reader and the writer. After all, what makes them different is the material of their reading only: the reader reads books while the writer "reads" nature which is all the empirical world including man's books.[18] If, as we have argued in the early part of the paper, an author both imitates the outer world and expresses his inner world in his act of perception as well as in his act of writing, there is no reason to negate that a reader does pretty much the same thing. In fact, we can even equate reading with writing. For, if the linguistic screen is removed (language as a medium taken aside), what can be left of reading and writing? Only the presently-perceived images, and the created images which are but a new shaping of the already-existing images in the mind. If we will follow Croce to eliminate the boundary between intuition and expression, then there is practically no difference among author, work and reader. They are a Trinity. Reading is the beginning and end of writing, and writing is the end and beginning of reading.

If we cannot forget the difference, then the difference is only a *différance*, to use a helpful term of Derrida's. The universe cannot be understood directly by itself. It has to be understood through its images given to our senses. The sensually perceived images are also not final reality. They become our mental text with the aid of our imagination. Now the mental text has to be understood in turn through the linguistic text which stands for it. Then the linguistic text becomes another cluster of images to be perceived by the reader's senses (primarily those of sight and sound). And then the reader's perception of the linguistic text is to become another mental text in the reader's mind, which is again not understandable unless it is again changed into a linguistic text by the use of language. If to change perceived images into a mental text is an act of internalization and to change a mental text into a linguistic text is an act of externalization, then the process from author through work to reader is a process of internalization--externalization--internalization. At each stage, the text to be internalized or externalized is at once different from and similar to the text that has been internalized or externalized--a phenomenon much like the steps of a ladder (the lower step is always the same as, and different from, the higher step). In other words, the entire literary world from the universe through the author and the work to the reader is a symbolic system, using God's language (all things in the universe) and man's language (words representing all things in the universe) as the basic symbols. As a result, we have various texts--God's text (the arrangement of all things in the world), the author's text, which includes the arrangement of images or ideas of the world in his mind (the mental text) and the arrangement of images or ideas of the world in words (the linguistic text or what we commonly call "work"), and the reader's text (the arrangement of images or ideas of a linguistic text) which again can either stay a mental text or further become a linguistic text (as in the case of a written piece of criticism or translation)--and these texts are in a signified-signifier relationship, if we wish to borrow two semiotic terms. But as the two terms often suggest a relationship of arbitrary representation, it may behoove us to discard them in our consideration of writing and reading theories which, as we have tried to demonstrate so far, are all theories of the mind--the author's mind, the mind in the work, or the reader's mind--and the mind, viewed from any angle, is never a mere mechanic device for arbitrary representation. In point of fact, the mind, so long as it is a mind at all, always projects images of its own at the same time when it reflects images from outside. It is always a magic mirror with a magic lamp, to be metaphorical. Thus, mimetic and expressive theories should be reconcilably combined to describe it at any stage of creation, no matter whether it is experiencing life, writing a work, or reading a text.

Notes

1. Abrams sees only four co-ordinates, excluding the element of language, which I think is another focus of literary critics' theoretical thinking.
2. For a brief contrast of ideas like this, many books of philosophy can be referred to. See, for example, Frank Thilly's *A History of Philosophy,* pp. 282-3.
3. Cf. Hume's remark that ideas seem to be in a manner the reflexion of sense impressions. *Treatise*, p.2, quoted in Abrams, p.160.
4. Here let us not forget Wordsworth's "Tintern Abbey," 11. 106-7, with the comment that the natural scene observed is half-perceived and half-created (echoing Young's *Night Thought*, Night VI, 11. 425-6).
5. Originally said by Lucretius, but quoted by Dryden in his "Heroic Poetry and Heroic License," *Essays,* I , 186-7. Quoted again in Abrams, p. 161.

6. See his "Dejection: an Ode," 1. 86.
7. The phenomenon implied in this term is well illustrated in Irving A. Taylor, "The Nature of the Creative Process," pp. 66-72.
8. See his *The Sublime and Beautiful*, rpt. in Adams, p. 306.
9. See the entry "magic mirror" in *Encyclopedia Britannica*.
10. This is the philosophy embedded in Wordsworth's "Intimations of Immortality" from which I quote the line.
11. For an instance of this, see the famous passage about the crossing of the Alps in Wordsworth's *The Prelude*, Book VI, 1. 591 ff.
12. See his *Aesthetic*, rpt. in Adams, pp. 730-4.
13. For an explication of these ideas, see Wellek, *Four Critics*, p. 3ff.
14. What I. A. Richards calls the meanings of feeling, tone and intention, in addition to sense, in his *Practical Criticism*, all owe their existence largely to the shapes and sounds of words, not just to ideas.
15. I think this is the best way of explaining this often-confusing term invented by Wimsatt and Beardsley.
16. This is E. D. Hirsch's idea when he says in his *Objective Interpretation* that "hermeneutics must stress a reconstruction of the author's aims and attitudes in order to evolve guides and norms for construing the meaning of his text."
17. See, for example, Wolfgang Iser, *The Act of Reading* and Stanley Fish, *Is There a Text in This Class?*
18. Here we may well remember that nature has been considered the Great Book created by God or Heaven in both Western and Eastern worlds, and it is a common idea of many romantic nature poets.

Works Consulted

Abrams, M. H. *The Mirror and the Lamp.* New York: Oxford U. P., 1953.

Adams, Hazard, ed. *Critical Theory Since Plato.* New York: Harcourt Brace Jovanovich, 1971.

Burke, Edmund. *The Sublime and Beautiful.* Rpt. in Adams, 303-312.

Coleridge, S. T. *Biographia Literaria.* Ed. J. Shawcross. Oxford: Clarendon Press, 1954.

Croce, Benedetto. *Aesthetic.* Rpt. in Adams, 727-35.

Fish, Stanley. *Is There a Text in This Class?* Cambridge, MS: Harvard UP, 1980.

Gombrich, E. H. "From Representation to Expression," *Art and Illusion.* Rpt. in Adams, 1168-75.

Hirsch, E. D. "Objective Interpretation." Appendix to *Validity in Interpretation.* New Haven: Yale UP, 1973.

Hume, David. *Treatise of Human Nature.* Ed. L. A. Selby-bigge. Oxford: Oxford UP, 1978.

Iser, Wolfgang. *The Act of Reading.* Baltimore: Johns Hopkins UP, 1978.

Richards, I. A. *Practical Criticism.* London: Routledge, 1929.

Taylor, Irving A. "The Nature of the Creative Process." *Creativity: An Examination of the Creative Process.* Ed. Paul Smith. New York: Hastings House, 1959.

Thilly, Frank. *A History of Philosophy.* Revised ed. New York: Henry Holt & Co., 1951.

Wellek, René. *Four Critics: Croce, Valéry, Lukács and Ingarden.* Seattle & London: U of Washington P, 1981.

Wimsatt, W. K. Jr. & M. Beardsley. *The Verbal Icon: Studies in the Meaning of Poetry.* Kentucky: U of Kentucky P, 1954.

Wordsworth, William. *The Prelude.* Ed. Ernest de Selincourt. Oxford: Oxford UP, 1979.

Wordsworth, William & S. T. Coleridge. Preface to the second edition of *Lyrical Ballads.* Ed. R. L. Brett & A. R. Jones. London: Methuen, 1978.

*This paper first appeared in 1988 in *JLA*, pp. 17-25.

When Comparative Literature Ceases to Compare

Since our first program of comparative literature was launched at National Taiwan University in 1970, development in that field of study has been conspicuous in this country. National or international conferences have been held year after year on this island; an increasing number of comparative literary studies written in English or Chinese have been published in our chief organs for them (*Tamknag Review* and *Chung Wai Literary Monthly*) or elsewhere; and more and more of our literary scholars have become comparatists doing their own research or teaching their learning to the younger generations. This conspicuous development, however, has not rendered the nature of this new academic discipline conspicuous in our literary circles. It seems that the confusion which goes with the unhappy choice of name for the discipline has spread from the West to the Far East. And I find this confusion has raised a special problem worthy of our special attention here.

I have often heard it rumored, from the mouths of our comparatists, that comparative literature actually does not compare at all. I say *rumored* because I know it is not a verifiable fact. But there are people, indeed, who take the rumor for a truth and are so daunted by its implied attitude that they no longer dare to couple two pieces of literature for comparison when they mean to make a comparative study of them.

A rumor is never without its source. I think our comparatists' rumor has very much to do with their attempt to set up a Chinese School of comparative literature here in Taiwan. This School, as clearly declared in Professor John J. Deeney's *Pi-chiao wen-hsü yen-chiu chih hsin fang-hsiang* (*A New Orientation of Comparative Literary Studies*), is based on the Chinese Doctrine of Mean, being an eclectic school between the French School of influence studies and the American School of affinity studies (265-6).[1] Our comparatists, in other words, try to avoid making comparative literature a mere positivist science of establishing literary sources and influences or making it a mere subjective revealing of literary parallels by the method of *rapprochement*. This aim of theirs is indeed a noble one. However, in trying to achieve this aim, our comparatists have in fact channeled their attention mainly towards one restricted subject of study, that is, the adaptability of Western literary theories and methods to the study of our national literature. This tendency is testified by the statement in the "Preface" to an edition of our earlier comparative literary studies: "We may well declare boldly that this adoption of Western literary theories and methods for them to be tested and adjusted and finally used in the study of Chinese literature is characteristic of the Chinese School of comparative literature."[2] And this tendency is further testified by the fact that currently our most active comparatists are in actuality literary theorists or, more accurately, followers of Western literary theories (since they seldom, if ever, postulate theories of their own). They devote most of their time and effort to the study and introduction of Western theories of literature, especially the "new" ones (e.g., structuralist theories or poststructuralist theories).

Now, there is no reason why we should not establish a Chinese School of comparative literature. And there is no denying that the application of Western theories to our studies of native literature can yield unexpected fruitful results. But the question is, to what extent can we call such an application a comparative study of literature?

To be sure, such an application involves Chinese literature and Western theories of literature. If Western literary theories are undoubtedly derived from Western literatures (Greek, Roman, Italian, Spanish, French, English, German, Russian, American, etc.), then such an application is certainly, in a sense, an indirect study of two or more than two national literatures. If Western literary theories, on the other hand, are partly derived from other areas of human knowledge than literature (painting, sculpture, architecture, music, philosophy, history, politics, economics, sociology, religion, psychology, philology, natural sciences, etc.), as some of them obviously *are* (e.g., mimetic theories draw a lot on ideas of painting, and structuralist theories are closely related to linguistic ideas), then such an application is again, in a sense, an indirect study of literature in connection with other branches of knowledge. Thus, such an application does not fail our comparatists' definition of comparative literature: "a study of two or more than two national literatures, or of literature in connection with other areas of human knowledge."[3]

Our comparatists' definition is in fact a very close version of Henry Remak's: "In brief it is the comparison of one literature with another or others, and the comparison of literature with other spheres of human expression" (1). One notices here, however, that our comparatists have played down the idea of comparison by substituting the word *study* for Remak's *comparison*. They do so, I believe, because they feel they cannot very well emphasize the application of Western literary theories to the study of Chinese literature and call it comparative literature at once. For to compare (if we stick to the ordinary sense of the word) is "to bring or place together [actually or mentally] for the purpose of noting the similarities and differences," to quote an O.E.D. definition of the word. In their applying Western theories to studies of Chinese literature, our comparatists have indeed brought together our literature and Western theories (or indirectly, our literature and Western literatures or other areas of knowledge). But they do so not for the purpose of noting similarities and differences between our literature and Western theories, but for the purpose of testing whether Western theory can suit Chinese practice and for the purpose of adjusting Western theory to Chinese practice in case of unsuitability.

This testing and adjusting work, nevertheless, does have an implied sense of comparison. If Western theory suits Chinese practice perfectly well, Western literatures (which beget the theory) can naturally be said to be like Chinese literature. If Western theory somehow has to be adjusted before its application to Chinese practice, then Western literatures must somehow be different from Chinese literature. However, our comparatists' work of testing and adjusting can hardly be called comparative if Western theory is understood as a body of knowledge other than the knowledge of literature. For instance, when Roman Jokobson's ideas of "metaphor" and "metonymy" are applied to the reading of T'ang Poetry, can we say T'ang Poetry is being compared with anything at all in the course of the application? Are we assuming that T'ang Poetry is like children's language in having the two basic types of "aphasia"? This sense may indeed exist, though ever so unnoticeably. But I do not think our comparatists are ever quite aware of this "deep comparison."

Facing a case like this, a comparatist has always two easy ways to escape trouble arising from the question: Is it comparative literature? One way is simply to say No. The other way is to try to tell people that the word *comparative* means more than pairing together to see similarities and dissimilarities; it covers in fact all yoking together of two or more things; and so a linguistic study of literature is a comparative study, as it involves two things: linguistics and literature.[4] (In this broad sense, then, all literary studies are comparative studies.)

Yet, facing a case like this, our comparatists seem not to take either easy way out. Instead, they prefer to hazard the dangerous path of proclaiming that comparative literature actually does not compare at all. And since unfortunately this proclamation is often not accompanied by any satisfactory explanation, it has become a very queer "theory" to those who hear it and cannot guess what it really means.   But even such a queer "theory" is not without a seeming precursor in the West.   (Please do not accuse me of being sarcastic if I say I think it a pity that we are often more bad followers of Western theories than good inventors of our own theories.)   In the "General Introduction" to his *Comparative Literature: Matter and Method*, A. Owen Aldridge thus begins his second paragraph:

> *It is now generally agreed that comparative literature does not compare national literatures in the sense of setting one against another.   Instead it provides a method of broadening one's perspective in the approach to single works of literature – a way of looking beyond the narrow boundaries of national frontiers in order to discern trends and movements in various national cultures and to see the relation between literature and other spheres of human activity. (1)*

I quote this passage, however, not so much to prove that our comparatists are influenced by an American comparatist or vice versa,[5] as to point out that before our first comparative literature program was launched here in Taiwan, there was already such opinion in the West as to say that "comparative literature does not compare national literatures in the sense of setting one against another."   And I presume to question this statement and thereby the aforesaid rumor of our comparatists.

I have no idea how "generally agreed" upon Aldridge's statement now is. But as far as I am concerned, I just cannot agree with that statement.   I admit that comparative literature is not just setting one literature against another. But I just cannot conceive that there is any comparative literature without using the comparative method, nor, in case of two national literatures, that there is any comparative literature without "setting one against another." It is well to say that comparative literature "provides a method of broadening one's perspective in the approach to single works of literature – a way of looking beyond the narrow boundaries of national frontiers. ..." But what is the method, after all? And what is the way? Is it other than "setting one thing against another" and then see them at once for a better understanding?

In Aldridge's book, five categories of comparative literature are edited: Literary Criticism and Theory, Literary Movements, Literary Themes, Literary Forms, and Literary Relations. Is there any one of them, we may ask, that does not compare by setting one literature against another? Is not literary criticism or theory, for instance, the result of reading this author and that author and then comparing them in mind (if not on paper) by setting one against another or against something else? Likewise, how can a literary movement, or theme, or form, or relation be better understood without comparing the elements that make up the movement, theme, form, or relation, or without comparing this movement with that movement, this theme with that theme, etc.? It is often not necessary, of course, to show one's comparing process (which is essentially a process in mind) on paper or anywhere else. But the task of "setting one thing against another" is almost indispensable to any serious study of things.

But, of course, when Aldridge says that "comparative literature does not compare national literatures in the sense of setting one against another," he is not trying to negate the value of the comparative method, but trying perhaps to discourage a sort of comparative practice: namely, the mere setting one thing against another without further work for a meaningful result. And I believe our comparatists are also merely trying to discourage that sort of comparison when they say that comparative literature actually does not compare at all. The question, then, becomes: Do we need to discourage that sort of comparison?

It has been my notion that literature, like anything else, is but a body of facts, and serious readers of literature are interpreters of those facts. But before any work of interpretation can be done, the facts have to be selected and set forth for special attention. Now, one way to select and set forth literary facts is to set one group of facts against another, that is, to do the preparatory work for further comparison. This preparatory work may indeed provide only some collated data, showing at best an arid erudition or at worst a laughable shallowness. However, such work with such data is the basis for further analysis and therefore is indispensable. One may laugh, for instance, at a person who calls his paper a comparative study of *Ching Hua Yüan* (鏡花緣) and *Erewhon*, when we find in it nothing but a compilation of facts found in both books. But still that compilation is not without its effort and value. Another person with enough critical insight, maybe the very one who is laughing, can always make use of the data and come up with some meaningful interpretation.

At this point, it occurs to me that comparatists may be of two types: one more suitable for the initial stage, the other for the final stage, of the work, the two stages being the gathering of comparable material (setting one thing against another, or comparison in its mechanical sense) and the interpretation of the phenomena manifested by the material (critical analysis for a new finding, or comparison in its organic sense). It is clear that such critics as Benedetto Croce and René Wellek will have higher opinion of the second type of comparatists, [6] and so will many of us who favor aesthetic criticism. But let us not forget that the first type of comparatists can also render good service. In his conclusion of a perceptive essay, John Fletcher quotes T. S. Eliot's often-quoted statement that "comparison and analysis are the chief tools of the critic," and adds as his own last word for the essay: "In giving proper weight to the second, we should not allow ourselves to neglect the first" (129). I think Fletcher has fully expressed what I mean to say here.

But what makes the first type of comparatists so contemptible is often not the fact that he only provides comparable material, but the fact that he often tries beyond his ability, attempting to interpret as the second type of comparatists do but ending up with a wrong interpretation. This is the case mentioned by Professor Yüan Ho-hsiang (袁鶴翔) of those who, upon seeing that T'ao Yüan-ming (陶淵明) and Wordsworth are both poets of nature, jump quickly to the conclusion that both are romantic poets.[7] Yet, this is the fault of the man, not the fault of the method. I cannot see why the two nature poets should not be compared. Professor Yüan points out that T'ao's nature is Taoist nature (the natural, effortless way) while Wordsworth's nature is the Great Nature with its simple beauty. But will this great difference, then, prevent us from comparing the two great poets? Besides, how can Professor Yüan know the difference without comparing them?

H. M. Posnett, the New Zealand scholar who is often claimed to have first used the name "Comparative Literature" for a book title, has rightly said, "The comparative method of acquiring or communicating knowledge is in one sense as old as thought itself" (73).[8] For what thought is there that does not cover a view of something associated with something else? If we understand this, we may go on to assert that all Western literary studies, from Plato's *Dialogues* and Aristotle's *Poetics* onward, are nothing but comparative studies, and so are all literary studies ever made in the East. However, when we wish to establish comparative literature as a formal discipline, we naturally cannot make it cover all literary studies. In order to distinguish it from other literary studies, we naturally have to define its scope of study workably, that is, to make its scope neither too meaninglessly comprehensive nor too meanly restricted.

Now, as we know, the scope of comparative literature is often defined in terms of nationality or geographical area. The most popular notion is that comparative literature studies literatures of two or more nations. Under this notion, a comparison of Hsü Chih-mo (徐志摩) and Hardy (or of Kamban and

Milton, to use an Indian scholar's example) is comparative literature; but, regrettably, a comparison of Li Po (李白) and Tu Fu (杜甫) (or Kamban and Ilango) is not.[9]   Another popular notion is that comparative literature compares literatures of two or more languages.[10]   But this notion also has its difficulty.   For example, India is a nation with many languages.   Can we then call it comparative literature to compare two writers of the same nation who write in two different languages (e.g., Tagore and Bharathi)?   Or conversely, can we compare Dickens and Mark Twain and call it comparative literature when we know they speak the same language but belong to two different countries?[11]   Regardless of such trouble, however, the scope of comparative literature can really start from a clan within a small area or a city commonwealth and then enlarge it through a nation or country towards the whole world – a process Posnett has plainly adopted.   And what Robert J. Clements calls the three major "dimensions" of American or European comparative literary studies – Western Heritage (or Western Literature), East-West, and World Literature – are in fact scopes in the sense.

The various scopes of comparative literature are further complicated by its concerns.   The French School, as often pointed out, is primarily concerned with "modes of transmission," "reception, success and influence," "sources," "foreign travel," and "the image of a country in the literature of another country," etc.[12]   The American School, on the other hand, is mostly concerned with "analogies without contact," or "typological affinities."[13] The different concerns have then made scholars focus their attention on various literary problems: themes or motifs, movements or schools, genres, stylistics, forms, techniques, traditions, and other literary "relations," which in fact are part and parcel of literary theory or criticism.   Yet all concerns and all focuses are governed by the aims of study.   The aim may tend towards a chauvinistic glorification of one's national literature as an "influential" literature or as a genetic headspring of other literatures.   The aim may also tend towards an idea of "General Literature" or "World Literature," though the two terms have raised very much controversy as to what they really mean and are still to be debated for their use.[14]

But no matter what scope, concern, focus, or aim it may have, comparative literature, as its name suggests, cannot but take literature as its main object of study and cannot do without the comparative method. It has been my belief that there are always three basic ways to study an object: first, to study it in isolation; second, to study it in relation to something else; third, to study it in comparison with some other object. For instance, if we want to study a person, we can first study him in isolation by focusing our attention on his hair, eyes, complexion, body build, mentality, personality, etc. – all those elements we think intrinsic to the man. Secondly, we can study him by relating him to his birth (date, place, ancestral lineage, etc.), his educational background, his family or social circle, and all other circumstances in which he lives. Thirdly, we can also study him by comparing him with somebody else (his wife, his friend, his boss, etc.) or even with something (a dog, a wooden statue, a bottle of wine, or an unseen ghost, if you like). The relational study and the comparative study are both studies involving two or more things at once. But the relational study concentrates on factors of contiguity involved in the objects studied. Time contiguity, for instance, results in historical relationship; place contiguity, geographical relationship; blood contiguity, genetic relationship, etc. Since there is no contiguity without some sort of contact between the objects considered contiguous, all contiguous relationships are contactual relationships, too. On the other hand, the comparative study concentrates on factors of similarity involved in the objects studied. The factors of similarity may exist among things with contiguous relationship (e.g., complexion between parents and children); they may also exist among things without such relationship (e.g., the golden color between a girl's hair and a piece of gold). But all the same, the comparative study is as useful to our understanding of objects as the relational study or the isolationist study. By looking at a girl's hair, by relating her hair to her parents', and by comparing her hair with a piece of gold, we can all come to a better understanding of the fact that her hair is golden in color.

It follows then that as literature is an object of study, it can also be studied in isolation or in connection with something else by the relational or comparative method.   When we study Wordsworth's "Tintern Abbey," for instance, we can treat it as an isolated text and analyze its rhythm, diction, imagery, tone, etc., without connecting it with anything outside the text.   But we can also relate the poem to the tradition of "conversation piece," thus bringing the poem in contact with Horace's *Epistles* and *Satires* and with Coleridge's "This Lime-tree Bower My Prison" and other similar poems, or even with Auden's "Letter to Lord Byron."[15]   Or we can also compare it with Wang Wei's (王維) "Niao Ming Chien" ("鳥鳴澗"), as Wai-lim Yip (葉維廉) has done,[16] in order that we may gain some insight into the difference in developing aesthetic consciousness between Chinese and Western poetry.

In fact, the French School of comparative literature is a school using primarily the relational method, as it is devoted to the tracing of genetic or historical relationships among literary works.   Nevertheless, their method is never purely relational.   For in tracing how a work influences another, the relational scholar cannot but compare the two works and make his conclusion on the basis of similarities and dissimilarities found between both works.   In other words, the French School in fact uses the comparative method and the relational method at once.   Or to put it even more accurately, the French School in fact uses the comparative method for a relational purpose.   So it can legitimately call itself a school of comparative literature.

How about the American School, then?   "Of course, it is a real school of comparative literature, too," one may reply.   One may even be tempted to say, "It is the most really comparative of all schools of comparative literature."   For, as we know, it compares all literatures on the same level, without caring whether they have contactual relationship or not.   But does this School, then, have no relational purpose of and kind?   The answer is Yes.

One seldom compares two things without a purpose. In comparing two literatures, a serious scholar often hopes to see the reason lurking behind his analogical findings. In comparing Chinese and Western knights, for instance, James J. Y. Liu can always see the source of dissimilarities in mankind's universal aspirations.[17] Thus, this type of comparative literature has also a final relational purpose. So both, the French and the American Schools of comparative literature, are similarly searching unity in variety, though the latter with its location in a continent of more cosmopolitan culture naturally tends more towards the idea of World Literature.

Then what can we say about our professed school of comparative literature? As I have discussed it above, to apply Western theories to the study of Chinese literature is "comparative" only in a remote sense. Such an application, I may add here, is "relational" all right, but relational not so much in the sense of relating one literature to another or relating literature to other spheres of human knowledge as in the sense of relating literary theory to literary practice. (In establishing a psychological approach to literature, one is relating psychology to literature. But in applying such an approach to a literary work, one is relating a theory to a particular piece of literature.) When Western comparatists go one step forward to include literary theory and criticism within the sphere of comparative literature, they are still seeking unity in variety directly in their connecting literature with other arts or with various social and natural sciences, thus working towards an idea of "General Knowledge," so to speak. But when our comparatists try to test or adjust Western literary theories for the use of studying our national literature, they are not seeking directly any unity in variety; they are working at most only very indirectly towards an idea of either "World Literature" or "General Knowledge." So our School is in effect neither "comparative" nor "General Knowledge." So our School is in effect neither "comparative" nor "relational" in an obvious manner.

This fact, however, should not be used to doubt the value of our School. No matter whether our School is obviously comparative and relational or not, our comparatists still have the right to carry on their proposed studies and make contributions to our better understanding of Western literary theories and our national literature. What can be disparaged is perhaps their awkward or incompetent use of Western theories and methods (using Freudian terms everywhere, seeing Carnival Literature everywhere, reading archetypes or myths into everything, writing nonsensical papers based on inadequate knowledge of semiotics, phenomenology, feminist criticism, deconstruction theories, etc.). But this weakness, as I have said of the incompetent comparatists who make wrong interpretations on the basis of their comparable material, is to be blamed on the man, not on the method. In my opinion, if we want to blame our School of comparatists, we can only blame them for their inadvertent spreading of the rumor I have mentioned in the beginning of this essay.

After referring to Wellek's "The Crisis of Comparative Literature" to explain the difficulty of defining the new discipline's subject matter and methodology, John Fletcher once remarks: "Comparative literature, of course, *compares*; but what?" (108). I believe the "what?" is never to be answered for certain nor for all. Every literary comparatist, I further believe, should be allowed the freedom to choose his "what," so long as he is comparing and is dealing with literature. He may choose, if he likes, to compare two authors or two works (or even only parts of two works), two literary schools or movements, two versions of translation or two pieces of criticism; he may concern himself with a special genre, style, form, theme, motif, tradition, or any other topic; he may study literature in connection with another art, with sociology, anthropology, psychoanalysis, linguistics, religion, philology, or with any other branch of human expression; he may cross the frontier of his clan, his nation, his continent, or his hemisphere; and he may also cross the boundary of one period, one dynasty, one age, one century or one bigger section of time. And if some scholars should choose to establish another school of comparative literature anywhere in the world, they, too, must be given this freedom to choose their "what." But once they have chosen their subject matter, let them be prepared to *compare*, directly or indirectly, what they think is comparable if they want earnestly to become comparatists. In their course of comparison, they may be deplorable for their failure to achieve their aim of comparison (to solve a critical problem thereby, for instance) or for the unworthiness of their aim. Yet they will thus leave us no occasion to blame them for lying, for not doing what they have professed to do. However, since no comparatist can really do without comparing,[18] let no scholar and no school of comparative literature dare to rumor again that comparative literature actually does not compare at all, if it so happens that their methodology is obviously not "comparative" enough. For, when comparative literature ceases to compare, literary comparatists cease, too, to exist, and with that, alas, is gone an innate and important faculty of man for acquiring knowledge!

Notes

1. The Chinese title of this work is 《比較文學研究之新方向》.
2. See *Pi-chiao wen-hsüeh te k'en-t'uo tsai T'ai-wan* 《比較文學的墾拓在台灣》, ed. Ku T'ien-hung (古添洪) & Ch'en Huei-hua (陳慧樺), p. 2. The English translation is mine.
3. See Deeney, p. 201. The English translation is mine.
4. This is the argument implied in many etymological studies of the word. See, for instance, Clements's *Comparative Literature as Academic Discipline*, pp. 10-11.
5. Yet one can suspect that Aldridge may have some sympathy with the Chinese School of comparative literature, as he has several times been to Taiwan to attend international comparative literature conferences there.
6. See Croce's "Comparative Literature," rpt. in Schulz & Rhein, eds., *Comparative Literature*, pp. 219-23. Also see Wellek's "The Name and Nature of Comparative Literature" in his *Discriminations: Further Concepts of Criticism*, pp. 1-36.

7. See his "Lüeh-t'an pi-chiao wen-hsüeh" 〈略談比較文學〉 in Ku & Ch'en, p. 14.
8. See his *Comparative Literature*, p. 73.　This statement is often quoted not very accurately.
9. See S. Ramakrishnan, "The Name and Nature of Comparative Literature," in G. John Samuel & R. Shanmugham, eds., *Comparative Literature*, Vol. I, p. 14. Also see Deeney, p. 202.
10. S. S. Prawer thinks this is a better definition.　See his *Comparative Literary Studies: An Introduction*, p. 3.
11. These examples are also Ramakrishnan's.
12. See Naresh Gula, "Comparative Literature: Meaning and Scope," in Nagendra, ed., *Comparative Literature*, p. 33.
13. A clear chart showing the study concerns is made in Dioný Ďurišin, *The Theory of Literary Comparatistics*, p. 334.
14. Personally, however, I would refer to "General Literature" as a body of universal phenomena and laws of literature, and make "World Literature" stand for mankind's literary expression of cultural commonalities.
15. See J. A. Cuddon, *A Dictionary of Literary Terms*, p. 154.
16. See Ku & Ch'en, p. 21 ff.
17. See his *The Chinese Knight-Errant*, pp. 195-208.　A book of similar nature is T'ien Yü-ying's (田毓英) *Spanish Ch'i-shih and Chinese Hsia* 《西班牙騎士與中國俠》.
18. In the book in which they declare the Chinese School of comparative literature, Ku and Ch'en themselves each present a paper involving real comparison between Chinese and Western theories of literature, not just applying Western theory to Chinese practice.　See their *Pi-chiao wen-hsüeh te k'en-t'uo tsai T'ai-wan*, pp. 61-118.

Works Consulted

Aldridge, A. Owen.　*Comparative Literature: Matter and Method.*　Urbana, Chicago, & London: U of Illinois P, 1969.

Clements, Robert J.　*Comparative Literature as Academic Discipline.*　New York: Modern Language Association of America, 1978.

Croce, Benedetto.　"Comparative Literature," translated from *La Critica*, I (1903), 77-80, rpt. in H. J. Schulz & P. H. Rhein, eds., *Comparative Literature: The Early Years.* U of North Carolina P, 1973.

Cuddon, J. A. ed. *A Dictionary of Literary Terms.* New York; Doubleday & Co., 1977.

Deeney, John J. *Pi-chiao wen-hsü yen-chiu chih hsin fang-hsiang* 《比較文學研究之新方向》. Taipei: Lien Ching Publishing Co., 1978.

Ďurišin, Dioný. *The Theory of Literary Comparatistics.* Bratislava: Veda Publishing House of the Slovak Academy of Science, 1984.

Fletcher, John. "The Criticism of Comparison: The Approach through Comparative Literature and Intellectual History," *Contemporary Criticism.* Ed. Malcolm Bradbury & David Palmer. New York: Edward Arnold, 1970.

Ku, T'ien-hung (古添洪) & Ch'en Huei-hua (陳慧樺), eds. *Pi-chiao wen-hsüeh te k'en-t'uo tsai T'ai-wan* 《比較文學的墾拓在台灣》. Taipei: Tung Tah Book Co., 1976.

Liu, James J. Y. *The Chinese Knight-Errant.* London: Routledge & Kegan Paul, 1967.

Naresh Gula, "Comparative Literature: Meaning and Scope." *Comparative Literature.* Ed. Nagendra. Delhi: Delhi University Extension Service, 1977.

Posnett, H. M. *Comparative Literature.* New York: D. Appleton & Co., 1886.

Prawer, S. S. *Comparative Literary Studies: An Introduction.* London: Duckworth, 1973.

Ramakrishnan, S. "The Name and Nature of Comparative Literature," *Comparative Literature.* Vol. I. Ed. G. John Samuel & R. Shanmugham. Madras: Academy of Comparative Literature, 1980.

Remak, Henry. "Comparative Literature; Its Definition and Function." *Comparative Literature: Method and Perspective.* Ed. Newton P. Stallknecht & Horst Grenz. Southern Illinois UP, 1971.

T'ien, Yü-ying's (田毓英). *Spanish Ch'i-shih and Chinese Hsia* 《西班牙騎士與中國俠》. Taipei: Sang Wu, 1980.

Wellek, Rene. "The Name and Nature of Comparative Literature." *Discriminations: Further Concepts of Criticism.* New Haven: Yale UP, 1970.

Yüan, Ho-hsiang (袁鶴翔). "Lüeh-t'an pi-chiao wen-hsüeh" 〈略談比較文學〉, in Ku, 13-15.

*This paper first appeared in 1988 in *Tamkang Review*, Vol. xviii, No. 2 (Winter 1986), 109-120.

The Nature and the Locus
of "Literariness"

It is said that Roman Jakobson is the linguist to bear the responsibility for popularizing the idea of "literariness" (*literaturnost*) as the legitimate subject of literary scholarship.[1] And it is asserted that the bulk of Russian Formalist theoretical pronouncements deal directly or indirectly with the problem, *What is the nature and the locus of "literariness"?*[2] But after all the strenuous dealings of Jakobson and other fellows of his linguistic circle with the problem, do we have a much clearer understanding of what and where "literariness" is? The answer is no, of course. Today we may agree that to study literature is to know "literariness." But what exactly is this *sine qua non* ingredient in any literary work? And where exactly are we to find it? We seem not to have overcome the moot questions yet. Hence my justification for following up the issues here.

As we know, the Russian Formalists do have their definite idea of "literariness." In their effort to reduce art to mere device, they have chosen to promote the idea of "defamiliarization" (*ostranenie*) as the all sufficient feature of any literary composition. For them, especially for such earlier propounders of their theories as Viktor Shklovsky and Boris Tomashevsky, art is just the "laying bare" of one's technique; literature is just a special use of language which achieves its distinctness by deviating from and distorting "practical language."[3] Thus, their probing into the nature of "literariness" leads them to a rigorous (and vigorous) attempt to clarify, as linguists supposedly need to do, the differences between literary or poetic language and nonliterary or ordinary (or practical, standard, utilitarian, prosaic, scientific, everyday, communicative, referential, etc.) language. Such an attempt, however, has not succeeded. Jan Mukarovsky, for instance, has not really clarified the typological boundary between standard language and poetic language, although his essay devoted to such a study can be regarded as a sensible attempt of its kind.

In his "Standard Language and Poetic Language," Mukarovsky postulates the idea of "foregrounding," which, as the opposite of "automatization," is related to the idea of "defamiliarization" (to estrange something is to foreground it). "The function of poetic language," he says, "consists in the maximum of foregrounding of the utterance." Then he explains:

> *In poetic language foregrounding achieves maximum intensity to the extent of pushing communication into the background as the object of expression and of being used for its own sake; it is not used in the services of communication, but in order to place in the foreground the act of expression, the act of speech itself.*[4]

Here lies a common misconception that all Formalists have.[5] They delude themselves with the belief that there is such a language as "not used in the services of communication" but "used for its own sake." In point of fact, unless we can deny that poetic lines like Shakespeare's "Shall I compare thee to a summer's day,/Thou art more lovely and more temperate" do not convey any feeling or thought or attitude to anyone, or unless we can deny that such lines are poetic lines, I really cannot see why anyone can aver that poetic language can be used *not* in the services of communication. To say a language is used for its own sake is, in effect, to deny the basic fact that any use of language is to communicate, to convey the user's ideas to his intended object. "Language for language sake" may sound magnificent, just like the slogan "art for art sake." Yet, it only rings with a bogus truth.

We can understand, of course, that Mukarovsky is primarily asserting here that the reception of message, in poetry or literature, is assured by stylistic devices whose function it is to compel attention.[6] And indeed the foregrounding of utterance is a display of "artfulness," a way of creating verbal pleasure. And literature, as an art, is surely to arouse "the excitement of emotion for the purpose of immediate pleasure, through the medium of beauty" (Coleridge 365). Nevertheless, we still cannot verify that there is any speech spoken by a real person or by an imaginary character that provides pleasure alone, like pure music, without delivering any message. Algernon Charles Swinburne's sumptuously melodious lines, for instance, still communicate the poet's import, though their inherent orchestral music tends to carry the reader away from their embedded sense. In most literary cases, in fact, to place the act of expression in the foreground is to express the content more effectively than otherwise, or (to quote Pope) to make us realize "what oft was thought, but ne'er so well expressed."

Defamiliarization or foregrounding is indeed not a necessary device of poetry, nor is it a pertinent idea for distinguishing literary language from nonliterary language. Why? Because, for one thing, we do find acknowledged poetic lines sounding as familiar and unforegrounded as ordinary utterances. Wordsworth's *Lyrical Ballads,* for example, are rich in lines which can demonstrate his assertion that "a large portion of the language of every good poem can in no respect differ from that of good prose" (253). Therefore, for Wordsworth the poet is only "a man speaking to man"(255). In fact, Mukarovsky himself admits that "the writer, say a novelist, may either not distort the linguistic components of his work at all … or he may distort it, but subordinate the linguistic distortion to the subject matter"(54).

If to foreground a linguistic component by defamiliarizing it is a sufficient device of creating poetry or literature, then it would be rather easy to become a man of letters. For it is rather easy to invent a radically new text by making strange the verbal structure contained in it without having to care about its aesthetic effect. That is why one will find it much easier to compose a "surrealist" poem than a traditional sonnet.

When we consider the source of the pleasure which the reader experiences in reading a literary work, we will find that it lies as much in the familiarity as in the unfamiliarity of the work's linguistic components to the reader. A lover of chivalric romance, for instance, may find pleasure in any conventional diction and devices pertaining to that genre, just as a Peking-opera fan will enjoy seeing each detail of the opera performed on the stage according to expected modes although, we must grant, an occasionally original (and thus defamiliarized) touch in a work or performance may be pleasing, too.

It follows then that the defamiliarization or the foregrounding of certain linguistic components is indeed not equal to "literariness." A literary work, we must understand, is more than its linguistic style, be it normal or abnormal. To view it properly in the light of language, we must understand that a literary work is also a speech act or speech event like a conversation or a natural narrative; it therefore involves, like any verbal message, a message-sender, a message-receiver, the medium through which the message is sent and received, and the world in which message, sender, receiver, and medium exist. Thus, to seek "literariness" in a work is to explore all the factors of that work: its author, reader, universe, etc., as well as its language.

In his *Semiotics and Interpretation*, Robert Scholes accepts Jakobson's idea of "literariness." He agrees that literariness is found in all sorts of utterances; a literary work is simply one in which literariness is dominant (19). But unlike other formalist-semioticians, he does not locate literariness merely in the formal structure of a work's message. He thinks all the six factors of a communicative act as pointed out in Jakobson's schema (i.e., sender, receiver, contact, message, code, and context) are to be considered in any search for literariness. And he believes that "we sense literariness in an utterance when any one of the six features of communication loses its simplicity and becomes multiple or duplicitous"(21). For him literariness is found where a communicative act encourages us to sense a difference between maker and speaker (e.g., when the author uses a "persona" to tell his story), where the words of an utterance seem to be aimed not directly at us but at someone else (e.g., when a lyric is, as John Stuart Mill has suggested, overheard rather than heard), where spoken words are presented to us not in speaking but in another form of contact (e.g., all literature transmitted through writing or print), where the form of the message becomes more complicated than usual (e.g., the sound effects and syntactic patterning of verse), where the doubling of contexts is seen (e.g., when, reading a novel, we are led into a fictional world other than the world surrounding us immediately), and where the code of the message points to other communicative acts (e.g., in quoting from, alluding to, or parodying a previous text). To tidy things up, Scholes gives us the following list as a finder of literariness:

1. Duplicity of sender—role-playing, acting
2. Duplicity of receiver—eavesdropping, voyeurism
3. Duplicity of message—opacity, ambiguity
4. Duplicity of context—allusion, fiction
5. Duplicity of contact—translation, fiction
6. Duplicity of code—involved in all the above   (31)

Scholes is right here to remind us that literariness may occur anywhere in the entire process of verbal communication from the encoding to the decoding of message. But his idea of duplicity still leaves us room to question. I suspect that his duplicity is also a form of defamiliarization, not just an opposing term to simplicity. It seems to him that anything indicating a deviation from the normal speech situation is a mark of literariness.

Therefore, he says, "The more an essay alludes or fictionalizes, the more the author adopts a role or suggests one for the reader, the more the language becomes sonorous or figured, the more literary the essay (or the letter, the prayer, the speech, etc.) becomes"(34).

"Duplicity," as a term, also suggests a quantitative idea.   I cannot deny that literature has numerical matters in itself.   But I must deny that anything literary must be more than simple.   For me an artful element can be either simple or complicated, depending on the context in which it occurs.   If "literariness" is an artful quality, it need not always involve "duplicity."   To put it clearly, a literary message can be very simple and normal in regard to its sender, receiver, context, etc.   For me, for instance, the most moving (and thus most artful) lines in *King Lear* are the two simple lines: " . . . You think I'll weep;/No, I'll not weep" (II , IV, 280-1).   The two lines are spoken by King Lear to his two elder daughters when they have deprived him of all his privileges and ill-treated him very "unnaturally."   The two lines contain only a very "natural" (and therefore sincere and truthful) reply out of a heart-broken father's mouth.   Their "naturalness," in fact, forms a natural contrast to his two daughters' "unnatural" (and therefore false and unfilial) speech and manners.   And we know the theme of "natural vs. unnatural" is a dominant theme of the play.[7]

Here we must clarify a point.   That is, to bring about duplicity as well as to defamiliarize or to foreground a linguistic component is at best a mere device of creating "literariness," not the quality of literariness itself.   If we want to define "literariness" as a *sine qua non* quality of literature, we must consider not only the means but also the end of producing that quality.   For me the end of "literariness" is equivalent to the end of literature, which is to delight and to instruct (to delight instructively or to instruct delightfully) through the proper (or artful) use of language.[8]   To defamiliarize, to foreground, and to make duplicity are but three means to the same literary end.

In actuality, if we want to postulate an idea that can best cover all literary devices which serve to make up the quality of "literariness," the idea, I think, is "verbal artfulness." Literature is indeed a verbal art. Literariness therefore lies in the artful use of language. The term "artful" is better than the term "special." When the Formalists hold that literature is just a special use of language, they are right in pointing out the verbal nature of all literature, but the term "special" has limited their views to such ideas as defamiliarization and foregrounding. In fact, any artist's "special" device or skill or technique or anything one may choose to call it is "special" in that it aims to achieve his intended artistic purpose. The word "artful" thus can point more directly to the true nature of literature than "special."

For me, art is forever a matter of proper choice and good arrangement. Jonathan Swift says, "Proper words in proper places, make the true definition of a style."[9] S. T. Coleridge defines prose as "words in their best order," and poetry as "the best words in the best order."[10] I hold, in accordance with their views, that literature is just the artful (i.e., proper and best) selection and combination of all linguistic components (phonological, morphological, syntactical, semantic, pragmatic, etc.) for an aesthetic end (i.e., beauty with truth and goodness).

In their *Linguistics for Students of Literature*, Elizabeth Closs Traugott and Mary Louise Pratt discuss the concept of style as deviance in contrast with the concept of style as choice, and they make this comment: "In the end, the idea of style as deviance always leads back to the broader view that style is choice, where choice includes selecting or not selecting deviant structures. Style as choice subsumes style as deviance, for deviance is only one aspect of the language of literature"(33). The points they are making here are quite right. And I think these statements are still true if we substitute the word "literariness" for the word "style." And if we can make the word "choice" cover the idea of arrangement or combination (i.e., choice as including choosing to arrange or combine this way or that way), then I think literariness is really just a matter of choice.

The most famous statement in Jakobson's "Closing Statement: Linguistics and Poetics" is : "The poetic function projects the principle of equivalence from the axis of selection into the axis of combination."[11] This often-quoted statement is often taken to explain the literary phenomenon of cohesion. "What he means by this is that, in poetry, structures which are roughly equivalent in sound, or sentence structure, or grammatical category, or some other aspect tend to be combined in a linear order or sequence"(Traugott 22). Cohesion, in fact, is more than the combination of "roughly equivalent" elements. A more inclusive explanation of the same statement is Elmar Holenstein's: "A poetic sequence is characterized on all levels of language by the reiteration of the same and similar elements (alliteration, rhythm, homonymy, synonymy) and by their contrastive variations (rhythm, antonymy, negative parallelism). In the case of contrast, the antecedent link of the combination is repeated in an implicit (i.e., negative) manner"(145).[12]

The selection of similar or contrastive elements is of course a choice, and so is the way, indeed, of combining selected elements. So, broadly interpreted, Jakobson's famous statement does define "literariness" (for the Formalists, "literariness" and "poeticalness" are synonymous) as a matter of choice. His idea, however, is restricted to a Formalist concern. Like other Formalists, he focuses his attention exclusively on the form, that is, on the intrinsic patterning of the work under examination, ignoring, meanwhile, the origin and the destination of the work (that is, ignoring the author and the reader). We know this Formalist propensity has given rise to the American New Criticism, which in attacking the "intentional fallacy" and the "affective fallacy" has narrowed its view of literature to a mere idea of "unity" or "organic form" seen in the perspective of "tension" or "paradox" or "irony" or "ambiguity."

In his *The Mirror and the Lamp*, M. H. Abrams points out four co-ordinates of art criticism: namely, universe, artist, audience, and work. For him, thus, four theoretical groups are possible: those viewing work in relation to universe (e.g., mimetic theories), those viewing work in relation to artist (expressive theories), those viewing work in relation to audience (pragmatic theories), and those viewing work *per se* (objective theories). For me, the essential co-ordinates of art are five: universe, artist, audience, work, and medium. Within the domain of literature, the five co-ordinates are in fact work, author, reader, universe, and language. And for me all theories are but partial truths. Consequently, there is no theory but has its limitation or its "fallacy," if you like. If the New Critics do not commit the author-oriented "intentional fallacy" nor the reader-oriented "affective fallacy," they have instead committed the "objective fallacy," so to speak, by isolating the work from the universe in which it exists. By the same token the Formalist School, we might say, have committed the "linguistic fallacy" by concentrating on the medium (i.e., language) alone in their consideration of "literariness."

Roman Jokobson, as we know, is the first to point out the six elements involved in any communicative act: sender, receiver, contact, message, code, and context. And he assigns six corresponding functions to them: emotive, conative, phatic, poetic, metalingual, and referential. Within that schema, however, most Formalists have unfortunately confined their idea of "literariness" to the formal features of encoded message (the selection and combination of formally visible linguistic components), forgetting that "literariness" is never a mere objective quality inherent in a literary work.

"Literariness," to be sure, can be an objective quality in the sense that it can be observed or felt by more than a single individual. But that agreed-upon objective quality must first get into the author's mind consciously or unconsciously when he creates his work, and it ought to be able to emerge again in the reader's mind consciously or unconsciously when he reads it. In other words, "literariness" as an objective quality lies in effect in the subjective psyche of the man in contact with its formal embodiment (i.e., the work) through the medium of language.

In a literary man's (i.e., author's or reader's) subjective psyche, nevertheless, "literariness" is still a matter of proper choice and good arrangement. It may manifest itself in the proper choice and good arrangement of such obviously linguistic components as rhyme, rhythm, diction, sentence structure, and paragraph organization, or of such seemingly extra-linguistic components as images, motifs, and plot details.[13] In actuality, all that a literary work contains can be reduced to three things: sound, shape, and sense. That is, every literary work has three aspects: the audial, the visual, and the mental. The audial and the visual aspects are what make up the form of the work, while the mental aspect is what makes up the content of the work. When a work is heard (as in a recitation), the audial aspect alone will assume the form. When the work is seen in its written or printed form, the visual aspect will then be added to it. But all the three aspects are working together when one is reading, for reading is an act of the eyes, the ears and the brain. In any aspect, however, what the author or the reader imagines in mind is a structured text, which is no other than the meaningful detail of selection and combination.

With this understanding, we can then conclude that "literariness" is indeed "verbal artfulness," which is in turn nothing but proper choice and good arrangement of all linguistic components (phonological, morphological, syntactical, semantic, and pragmatic). But since the judgments of propriety or goodness rests with the author who creates the work and with the reader who responds to it, the quality of "literariness" is realized only in a person's mind; the true locus of "literariness" is not the work, but the author and the reader. And since both author and reader are subject to external influences from the ever-changing universe in which they live, "literariness" is never a stable quality that can be fixed once for all. It is rather a changeable quality that can vary with times, places, persons, and generic types of the work. That is why even the theoreticians of defamiliarization and foregrounding must, ultimately, also talk of the dynamic principle of literariness.[14]

When I talk of literariness as verbal artfulness, I also suggest that it is an indeterminate quality. For different people in different times and places can indeed see artfulness in different things. An eighteenth-century neo-classicist like Pope, for instance, would see artfulness in witty phrasings while a nineteenth-century realist like Henry James would see artfulness in all instances of faithful character portrayal. In fact, all literary theorists and practitioners have their own standards of verbal artfulness. The Russian Formalists, as we have discussed so far, are those who take such formal features as similarity and parallelism for verbal artfulness, thus privileging only those kinds of writing most explicable to their critical method.[15] Today a postmodernist, we might presume, would claim that verbal artfulness is just anything that comes by chance, something that depends on "aleation," not on any artistic order, formal or psychological—a definition diametrically opposed to our "normal" or "traditional" idea of art. Hence literariness or literature can be anything one likes it to be.

But does an individual really have a full right to decide his own idea of "literariness"? I say "yes" if he is to live entirely secluded from his fellow men or if he is determined not to care a fig about others' opinions. Yet, if he cannot do so, if he has to lead a social life and, thus, if he must rely somehow on "cooperative principles" for his happy existence in this "all too human" a world, I believe he can never really let the nature and the locus of "literariness" fall entirely on his own whim. In other words, one must see "literariness" as something determined collectively by the entire speech community to which one belongs. For, as one critic said recently, "So long as the concept of the object of study remains inadequately historicized in terms of specific reader communities at specific times … so long will searchers for literariness miss the point"(Colomb 313). "Literariness," or verbal artfulness, must eventually be a functional variable in the public mind.

Notes

1. In his *Novejsaja russkaja poezija, viktor Xlebnikov* (Prague, 1921), p. 11, Jakobson claims that "The subject of literary scholarship is not literature in its totality, but literariness, i.e., that which makes a given work a work of literature."
2. See Erlich, *Russian Formalism: History-Doctrine*, 3rd Edition, p. 172.
3. See Selden, *A Reader's Guide to Contemporary Literary Theory*, p. 8.
4. See Freeman, ed., *Linguistics and Literary Style*, pp. 43-44. This is reprinted from *A Prague School Reader on Esthetics, Literary Structure, and Style*, selected and translated by Paul L. Garvin, (Georgetown Univ. Press, 1964).
5. Compare the statement in the Prague Linguistic Circle's "Theses": "In its social role, language must be specified according to its relation to extralinguistic reality. It has either a communicative function, that is, it is directed toward the signified, or a poetic function, that is, it is directed toward the sign itself." (Translated and quoted by Mary Louise Pratt in her *Toward a Speech Act Theory of Literary Discourse*, p. 8.) Compare also Boris Tomasevskij's statement: "The chief trait of poetry is that it no longer presents an expression merely as a means or the action of an automatic mechanism, but as an element which has gained an original aesthetic value and has become an end in itself of the discourse." (Translated and quoted in Pratt, p. 12.) This same idea is seen of course in Jakobson's assigning "poetic function" to that which has its linguistic message oriented toward "the message as such."
6. Michael Riffaterre has the same idea in his "Criteria for Style Analysis," in *Essays on the Language of Literature*. But Stanley Fish takes it for a strong form of Pope's "What often was thought, but ne'er so well expressed." See Fish's *Is There a Text in This Class?* pp. 103-4.
7. The word "nature" and its cognates ("natural," "unnatural," "disnatured," etc.) recur throughout the play, producing ambiguity of the term and complexity of the play's theme.
8. In his "Art of Poetry," Horace asserts that the aim of the poet is either to benefit, or to amuse, or to make his words at once please and give lessons of life. I think that to delight and to instruct are often inseparable. Whatever pleases will also teach, directly or indirectly; whatever teaches will likewise please. And I think that all

other functions of literature one can think of (e.g., to move, to console, to express oneself, to reflect truth, to react to reality, etc.) can be incorporated into these two aims.

9. See his Letter to a Young Clergyman, January 9, 1720.

10. See his Table Talk, July 12, 1827.

11. This statement is reprinted in Thomas A. Sebeok, ed., *Style in Language*, p. 358.

12. Michael Shapiro, in his *Asymmetry: An Inquiry into the Linguistic Structure of Poetry*, argues that poetry is based on contrast rather than on similarity and parallelism. But Elizabeth Closs Traugott & Mary Louise Pratt hold that either parallelism or contrast can be considered an example of cohesiveness. See their *Linguistics for Students of Literature*, p. 39, Note 23.

13. These "seemingly" extralinguistic components are after all linguistic components since such things as images, motifs, and plot details must needs appear as visible or invisible linguistic entities (words in print or words in mind).

14. The dynamic principle is seen in the late Formalist concept of "the dominant." Jacobson and others, in their later phase, began to see poetic forms as something changing and developing not at random but as a result of the "shifting dominant." This idea finally cooperates with the Marxist idea of dialectical materialism to give rise to the Bahktin School of criticism.

15. In his "Closing Statement: Linguistics and Poetics in Retrospect," Derek Attridge says that Jakobson's method privileges poetry over prose, the short poem over the long poem, the lyric over the narrative, the formally patterned over the freely varying, etc. And he cites Jakobson's comments on Pushkin, Yeats, e. e. cummings, etc., for examples. See Nigel Fabb, et al., eds., *The Linguistics of Writing: Arguments between Language and Literature*, pp. 24-25.

Works Consulted

Abrams, M. H. *The Mirror and the Lamp.* New York: Norton, 1958.

Attridge, Derek. "Closing Statement: Linguistics and Poetics in Retrospect." *The Linguistics of Writing: Arguments between Language and Literature.* Ed. Nigel Fabb, et al. New York: Methuen Inc., 1987.

Coleridge S. T. "On the Principles of Genial Criticism Concerning the Fine Arts." *Criticism: The Major Text.* Ed. Walter Jackson Bate. New York: Harcourt, 1970.

Colomb, Gregory. "The Semiotic Study of Literary Works." *Tracing Literary Theory.* Ed. Joseph Natoli. Chicago: U of Illinois P, 1987.

Erlich, Victor. *Russian Formalism: History-Doctrine.* 3rd Edition. New Haven & London: Yale UP, 1965.

Fish, Stanley. *Is There a Text in This Class?* Cambridge, MS: Harvard UP, 1980.

Freeman, Donald C. ed. *Linguistics and Literary Style.* New York: Holt, Rinehart & Winston, Inc., 1970.

Garvin, Paul L. *A Prague School Reader on Esthetics, Literary Structure, and Style,* Washington, DC: Georgetown UP, 1964.

Holenstein, Elmar. *Roman Jakobson's Approach to Language.* Translated by Catherine Shelbert & Tarcisius Shelbert. Bloomington & London: Indiana UP, 1976.

Horace. "Art of Poetry." *Criticism: The Major Text.* Ed. Walter Jackson Bate. New York: Harcourt, 1970.

Jakobson, Roman. "Closing Statement : Linguistics and Poetics." *Style in Language.* Ed. Thomas A. Sebeok. Cambridge, MS: MIT Press, 1960.

Mukarovsky, Jan. "Standard Language and Poetic Language." *Linguistics and Literary Style.* Ed. Donald C. Freeman. New York: Holt, Rinehart & Winston, Inc., 1970.

Pratt, Mary Louise. *Toward a Speech Act Theory of Literary Discourse.* Bloomington: Indiana UP, 1977.

Riffaterre, Michael. "Criteria for Style Analysis." *Essays on the Language of Literature.* Boston: Houghton Mifflin Co., 1967.

Scholes, Robert. *Semiotics and Interpretation.* New Haven: Yale UP, 1932.

Sebeok, Thomas A., ed. *Style in Language.* Cambridge: MIT Press, 1960.

Selden, Raman. *A Reader's Guide to Contemporary Literary Theory.* Brighton, England: The Harvester Press, 1985.

Shapiro, Michael. *Asymmetry: An Inquiry into the Linguistic Structure of Poetry.* Amsterdam & New York: North-Halland Pub. Co., 1976.

Traugott, Elizabeth Closs & Mary Louise Pratt. *Linguistics for Students of Literature.* New York: Harcourt Brace Jovanovich, Inc., 1980.

Wordsworth, William. Preface to *Lyrical Ballads.* Ed. R. L. Brett and A. R. Jones. London: Methuen & Co., 1971.

* This paper first appeared in 1990 in Taiwan Normal University's *Studies in English Literature and Linguistics,* pp. 113-22.

The Dichotomy of Imagination

In the West, the imagination as an image forming faculty has been variously dichotomized. Plotinus, for instance, distinguishes between a higher and a lower phantasy (i.e., imagination).[1] For him the lower is dependent on sense while the higher is reflective of ideas. By this distinction he is making his Neoplatonic assertion that the World of Ideas is truer and thus higher than the World of Senses. This distinction, however, also suggests that imagination is, for Plotinus, a mediatory power between the material and the form of art, because in his ideology to create art through imagination is to invest matter with form, and that, in turn, is to unify sense with ideas.

After Plotinus, the next significant dichotomy of imagination was made by Hobbes. In his *Leviathan* Hobbes divides imagination into the simple and the compounded types. The former refers to "the imagining the whole object, as it was presented to the sense," as when one imagines a man or a horse he has seen before. The latter refers to the imagining of a compounded object whose parts have been perceived before at several times, as when "from the sight of a man at one time, and of a horse at another, we conceive in our mind a Centaure." This latter type also includes the compounding of the image of one's own person with the image of the actions of another man, as when "a man imagines himself a Hercules, or an Alexander."[2]

Hoboes' division of imagination into simple and compounded types does not transgress the bounds of experience, which is for him simply "much memory" or "memory of many things." However, contrary to many people's concept of Hobbes' empirical tradition, this division of his does not describe imagination as a faculty entirely passive and devoid of invention. To be sure, his "simple imagination" is not creative at all. Yet, his "compounded imagination" is, as he says, capable of "a fiction of the mind."[3] It explains, in fact, that imaginative creation is the work of dissection and recombination, or of relocational displacement of one sense impression with another, not that of producing something absolutely new--an idea to be directly uttered later by Edmund Burke in his *The Sublime and Beautiful*.

In the 18th century, Joseph Addison talked of primary and secondary pleasures of the imagination in his *Spectator* articles. The basis for such a classification is the source of pleasures to be derived from imagination. The source of the primary is really-seen objects while that of the secondary is remembered absent or fictitious objects. This assortment serves to explain people's difference of taste, besides calling our attention to the fact that imagination works not only in the writer but also in the reader--a fact the reader-oriented critics of our time have given special heed to.

The Scottish philosopher Dougald Stewart is one of the first to use *fancy* and *imagination* to designate two related sorts of the same image-forming faculty. He ascribes imagery wholly to "fancy," saying that it is the power which "supplies the poet with metaphorical language," while, freeing "imagination" from its close association with the image, he calls the imagination the power that "creates the complex scenes he [the poet] describes and the fictitious characters he delineates," as illustrated in Milton's Eden, Harrington's Oceana, and Shakespeare's Falstaff or Hamlet.[4] This differentiation between fancy and imagination is in essence little different from Hobbes' division of simple and compounded imagination. Yet, Stewart is here confined to the realm of literature, as he talks solely of metaphorical language and scenes and characters, instead of just the image of a man or a horse and the image of a Centaur or a Hercules in a scene. More importantly, he makes us realize that the image-forming faculty can deal with either linguistic or extralinguistic matters (arranging scenes and delineating characters are extralinguistic imagination).

The most impressive Romantic who dichotomizes the image-forming faculty by using the names of *fancy* and *imagination* is of course S. T. Coleridge. But before Coleridge's dichotomy appeared in *Biographia Literaria* (1817), his friend Wordsworth had made his own dichotomy in his Preface to *Poems* (1815). The two Romantics' ideas of fancy and imagination are quite different and their respective points have been subject to various interpretations and ample arguments. To speak summarily, for Wordsworth "Fancy is given to quicken and to beguile the temporal part of our nature, Imagination to incite and to support the eternal.--Yet is it not the less true that fancy, as she is an active, is also, under her own laws and in her own spirit, a creative faculty."[5] In contrast, regarding imagination as the only creative power, Coleridge thinks of fancy as merely a passive, associative, rather than creative, faculty, for, as he says, it is "indeed not other than a mode of Memory emancipated from the order of time and space" and it must needs "receive all its materials ready made from the law of association."[6]

Actually, neither Coleridge's nor Wordsworth's distinction between fancy and imagination makes any great sense in terms of literary creation. What really counts is Coleridge's further dichotomy of imagination into the primary and the secondary types:

The primary IMAGINATION I hold to be the living Power and prime Agent of all human Perception, and as a repetition in the finite mind of the eternal act of creation in the infinite I AM. The secondary Imagination I consider as an echo of the former, co-existing with the conscious will, yet still as identical with the primary in the kind *of its agency, and differing only in* degree, *and in the* mode *of its operation. It dissolves, diffuses, dissipates, in order to recreate; or where this process is rendered impossible, yet still at all events it struggles to idealize and to unify. It is essentially vital, even as all objects (as objects) are essentially fixed and dead. (Biographia Literaria,* chpt. 13)

This famous passage is indeed charged with philosophical depth, hence giving rise to difficulties of interpretation. In my book *Imagination and the Process of Literary Creation* (1991), I have given some critics' explications which may or may not be right. And I have given my own explication, which I dare to deem very sensible. Basically I agree with most critics that Coleridge's primary and secondary imagination ought to refer to the powers of human perception vs. artistic creation. Nevertheless, I think the primary imagination can be exercised in two modes: either with or without the user's conscious will. And it can result in either ordinary or extraordinary human perception, related respectively to what some psychologists call "R-thinking" (reality-adjusted thinking) and "A-thinking" (autism).[7]

In reality, the above-quoted passage of Coleridge's is a description of two crucial stages in the process of artistic creation. The first stage is a pre-composition stage. It is the stage when the poet is experiencing the world with his senses. In doing so the poet is actually perceiving something all the time with his primary imagination. If he is perceptive enough, he may have the so-called insight or vision. But to beget an insight or vision, the primary imagination may need to become extraordinary. A gifted poet may easily get his primary imagination into an extraordinary state, because he is "sensitive" or has great sensibility. At times, the poet may even seek the aid of alcohol, opium, or any other stimulant to have his insightful or visionary imagination. Anyway, the primary imagination is, doubtless, a pre-composition power employed to "see into the life of things," or, to use a common phrase, to "get ideas for writing."

The second crucial stage of artistic creation is the stage when the poet sits down at his desk, using his secondary imagination together with his conscious will to "recreate" the insight or vision or "idea" his primary imagination has obtained for him.   The work of this stage, as described in Coleridge's famous passage, is clearly both analytic and synthetic.   So, the secondary imagination is a composition power, with which the poet actualizes his idea or composes his poem.   Without this imagination the poet is only a half poet, or only a poet to himself since he has not yet expressed his poetry in words.

If we read Coleridge's famous definitions of the two sorts of imagination along with Wordsworth's famous definition of poetry, my argument above will sound even more convincing.   As we know, in his Preface to *Lyrical Ballads*, Wordsworth defines poetry as "the spontaneous overflow of powerful feelings," and says "it takes its origin from emotion recollected in tranquility."   Now, when does the spontaneous overflow of powerful feelings occur?   And when is emotion recollected in tranquility?   The poet's powerful feelings overflow spontaneously when he is excited by the workings of his primary imagination, of course.   And when the emotion is recollected in tranquility, the poet has somehow settled down working with his secondary imagination, to be sure.   So, Wordsworth's definition of poetry also comprises two crucial stages of poetic creation, echoing Coleridge's definition of primary and secondary imagination.

After Wordsworth and Coleridge, no epoch-making dichotomy of imagination has been found again.   But John Ruskin's three modes ("Imagination Associative," "Imagination Penetrative," and "Imagination Contemplative"), Irving Babbitt's two classes (the ethical vs. the Arcadian or dalliant imagination), Samuel Alexander's two types (the passive and the creative imagination), and Ernst Cassirer's three kinds ("the power of invention, the power of personification, and the power to produce pure sensuous forms") are among those recent classifications of imagination which may have uses of their own.

In my opinion, if we want to construct a system of dichotomies to fully explain the role of imagination in the entire process of literary creation, we must take into account at least the following points. First, we must distinguish the imagination used to beget ideas for writing from that used to express the ideas. Second, we must differentiate the imagination used to beget ordinary ideas from that used to beget insightful or visionary ideas. Third, we must tell apart the imagination used to deal with linguistic elements and that used to deal with extralinguistic elements. And finally, we must discriminate between the imagination used in direct contact with life and the imagination used in vicarious contact with life such as in reading a novel or in watching a movie. According to this scheme, then, we have ideational vs. technical imagination (corresponding to Coleridge's primary vs. secondary imagination); ordinary or plain imagination vs. extraordinary or visionary imagination; linguistic vs. extralinguistic imagination (dealing, respectively, with the sound, sense, and shape *in* language, and with such things as plot, characterization, setting, theme, motif, and imagery which are expressed *through* language); and direct vs. indirect imagination.

Obviously, the four dichotomies of imagination I make above are not purely my own thinking. They have in fact been considered directly or indirectly by previous thinkers, poets, or critics. I have said that Coleridge's primary and secondary imagination is equivalent to my ideational and technical (or pre-compositional and compositional) imagination. The same dichotomy is in effect implied in James Russell Lowell's assertion that "The poet is he who can *best see* and *best say* what is ideal--what belongs to the world of soul and of beauty"[8] (italics mine). Likewise, my assumed contrast between ordinary and extraordinary imagination is implied in Leslie Stephen's (not to say Wordsworth's) distinction between fancy and imagination: "fancy deals with the superficial resemblances, and imagination with the deeper truths that underlie them."[9] As to my idea of linguistic vs. extralinguistic imagination, it is already foreshadowed in Dougald Stewart's ideas of fancy vs.

imagination, as mentioned above. And finally in Addison's differentiating primary from secondary pleasures of imagination is already seen my concept of direct vs. indirect imagination.

My ways of dichotomizing imagination are in truth influenced by some classical Chinese critical ideas, too. In classical Chinese criticism, the term 神思 *shen-ssu* (literally, "divine thinking") and the term 比興 *pi-hsing* (literally, "comparing and exalting") are roughly equal to what I call visionary imagination and technical imagination here.[10]

But no matter from what sources I have drawn my dichotomies of imagination, I hope it is clear now that in the process of literary creation we do need various sorts of imagination to "read" life and "write" out our readings.

Notes

1. This distinction is mentioned in Alex Preminger, ed., *The Princeton Handbook of Poetic Terms*. But I can find only some hints of this distinction in Plotinus's work. See *Plotinus: The Six Enneads*, tr. Stephen Mackenna & B. S. Page, (Chicago & London: Encyclopaedia Britannica Inc., 1952).
2. *Leviathan*, part I, chapter 2. In the edition by C. B. Macpherson (Harmondsworth, Middlesex, England: Penguin Books, 1968), p. 89.
3. *Ibid.*
4. *Elements of the Philosophy of the Human Mind*, I, pp. 3, 5, & 8. Quoted in Preminger, p. 100.
5. See John Spencer Hill, ed., *The Romantic Imagination* (London: The MacMillan Press, 1977), p. 66.
6. See J. Shawcross, ed., *Biographia Literaria* (Oxford: Clarendon Press, 1954), p.202.
7. See Peter McKellar, *Imagination and Thinking: A Psychological Analysis* (New York: Basic Books Inc., 1957), p. 4 ff.
8. "The Function of the Poet," in *Literary Criticism: Pope to Croce*, eds., G. W. Allen & H. H. Clark, (Detroit: Wayne State U. P., 1962), p. 421.

9. *Hours in Library*, quoted in Frederick Clarke Prescott, *The Poetic Mind* (Ithaca, N. Y.: Great Seal Books, 1922), p. 142.

10. See Liu Hsieh, *The Literary Mind and the Carving of Dragons*, tr. Vincent Yuchung Shih, (Taipei: Chung Hua Book Co., 1975), pp. 216, 217, 276 & 278. There have been various interpretations of the meanings of *pi* and *hsing*, but they do not affect the basic fact that they are technical matters used in imaginative writing.

*This paper first appeared in 1991 in ICLA's *The Force of Vision*, Vol. 3, 355-62.

"The Intentional Fallacy" Reconsidered

Today "the intentional fallacy" has apparently become an established critical term, for we can find it in almost all books of literary terms. Its meaning, however, has often been misunderstood since W. K. Wimsatt and Monroe C. Beardsley first introduced it in their famous essay bearing the same name as its title. [1]   In fact, there seems to be more and more people getting confused about its usage.   And many fallacious ideas about this particular "fallacy" have poured into the present-day "trade market" of literary criticism.

Evidence of this term's confusing usage can be found in the various ways it is defined or explicated in some glossarial books.   For instance, in M. H. Abrams' *A Glossary of Literary Terms*, it is simply stated that the term is "sometimes applied to what is claimed to be the error of using the biographical condition and expressed intention of the author in analyzing or explaining a work" (22).   In C. Hugh Holman's *A Handbook to Literature*, it is similarly said that in contemporary criticism the term is "used to describe the error of judging the success and the meaning of a work of art by the author's expressed or ostensible intention in producing it."   But it is also noted therein that "Wimsatt and Beardsley say, 'The author must be admitted as a witness to the meaning of his work.'   It is merely that they would subject his testimony to rigorous scrutiny in the light of the work itself" (242). Under the entry of *intentional fallacy* in J. A. Cuddon's *A Dictionary of Literary Terms*, we read: "The error of criticizing and judging a work of literature by attempting to assess what the writer's intention was and whether or not he has fulfilled it rather than concentrating on the work itself" (330). When the same entry appears in Northrop Frye and others' *The Harper Handbook to Literature* we are told that it refers to "the idea that the meaning of a work can be explained by considering the author's intention, a fallacy according to the New Criticism." And we are told that critics who emphasize the intentional fallacy "are attempting to minimize the effect of too much reliance on Alexander Pope's advice, long standard in criticism: 'In every work regard the writer's end,/Since none can compass more than they intend'" (243-44).

With these different explanations we are really confused as to when "the intentional fallacy" may occur. Does it occur when we use biographical data to analyze or explain a work, or when we use the author's expressed intention to judge the success or meanings of his work, or when we attempt to assess what the author's intention was, or when we believe we cannot disregard the author's intention in any critical process?

In effect, it should not be too difficult to understand Wimsatt and Beardsley's own intentions in writing the essay and attacking the "intentional fallacy." From their biographical data and the essay itself we can clearly see that they are posing as "New Critics," are positing the "objective theory" that a literary work has an independent public existence, are encouraging "intrinsic studies" while discouraging "extrinsic studies" of literature, are trying to replace a system of values (covering the ideas of sincerity, fidelity, spontaneity, authenticity, genuineness, originality, etc.) with another system (integrity, relevance, unity, function, maturity, subtlety, adequacy, etc.), and are disputing the Romantic view of the author as an important source of meaning for works and they are doing all these by arguing that the author's intentions are not the proper concern of the critic.

However, not all critics agree that Wimsatt and Beardsley's intentions can rest at that. There are those who carry their propositions to extremes and assert that poems are strictly autonomous or autotelic, that works are discontinuous from language and each other, that any external evidence is critically inadmissible, that we cannot talk about an author's intention even in terms of the internal evidence of his work, etc., tec.[2]   In brief, in attacking "the intentional fallacy," Wimsatt and Beardsley have begot, ironically, a number of fallacies about their intentions.

Many fail to comprehend Wimsat and Beardsley's real intentions, I believe, because they never bother either to investigate the authors' life in question nor to examine their work closely.   (They are neither traditional critics nor "New Critics.")   Some of them may interpret the term merely by surmise or by free association of the term.   Others may prefer imposing their own ideas on the term, thus asserting the authority not of the author, not of the work, but of the reader.   (They are Humpty Dumptys, who want to be masters of words.)

We know Wimsatt and Beardsley attack not only "the intentional fallacy" but also "the affective fallacy"; they disapprove of any attempt to derive the standard of criticism from the psychological effects as well as causes of the pocm.   They preach for a critical objectivism stemming from looking at the work itself while opposing any relativism coming from considering the author's intentions or the reader's impressions.[3]   This New Critical stance, I think, is basically sound and firm in that it stresses the priority of the work as the basis of critical judgment.   No one, I believe, would deny that one's reading of "To His Coy Mistress" should be done first and foremost on the text itself, and Andrew Marvell's politics, religion, and career as well as the responses or reactions of other readers to the work can only serve as an accessory guide to one's interpretation.

Nevertheless, the New Critical stance is not without its weak aspect.   It has been pointed out that art does not exist in a vacuum.   Any artifact is a creation by someone at some time in history.   Many literary classics are admittedly autobiographical, propagandistic, or topical.   Hence it would be dangerous to assume that a work of art must always be judged or looked at or taught as if it were disembodied from all experience except the strictly aesthetic.[4]

But my aim here is not to reiterate this frequently-pinpointed weakness of the New Criticism. My intention is to point out that the New Critical idea of "intentional fallacy" is itself a fallacy in that it is a sort of separatism like the idea of those who are accused of "the intentional fallacy" or "the affective fallacy." In my mind a literary work is hardly separable from the intention of the author who creates it, nor from the intention of the reader who reads it. It is only when it is viewed as a pure physical object, a mere construct of black spots with blanks on paper entirely detached from author and audience alike, that we can say it has an "impersonal" or "objective" existence. Otherwise, we must admit that the work, the author, and the reader are a trinity, bound each to each with a common "intention"; therefore, no critical effort can manage to separate them without committing a sort of "intentional fallacy," and to assert the absolute authority of any one of them is impractical if not impossible.

This idea of mine bears largely on the meaning of the word "intention."[5] I think we must first understand that any object that comes into one's mind is an intended object. If a perceived object has any meaning at all, the meaning is never intentionless.[6] Actually, to intend is to "in-tend," to turn an external object into an internal object by our mental activity. Hence an "intention" is just an internalized version of an external object. Before an author writes a text, he usually has to "intend" a lot of things. (In our common language, we say he has to have a lot of life experience.) The things he "intends" include natural objects (mountains, waters, flora and fauna, etc.) and man-made objects (all practical inventions and devices as well as artifacts). After he "intends" these objects for some time, some developed "intentions" will arise in his mind to direct his outward action. (The developed "intentions" are commonly called "ideas.") If he is an ordinary man, the "intentions" may cause him to live an ordinary man's life. If he is a wit (in the neo-classical sense) or a genius (in the romantic sense), however, his "intentions" may lead him to create artistic works. When creating an artistic work, he is then an author. And in the process of artistic creation, he is in fact turning his "intentions" again into an external object by the use of is tool (language is a writer's tool). If we can coin the word "extention" as the antonym of "intention" and make it mean the external object resulting from externalizing one's "intention," then we can hold that to read is to "in-tend," to form "intentions" in the mental world while to write is to "ex-tend," to form "extentions" in the physical world.[7]

It follows then that our most important problems are whether or not an author's "intention" is identical with his "extention" and whether or not the author's "extention" is identical with his reader's "intention" of it. As we know, in the long past very few critics ever doubted the identity of an author's "intention" with his "extention." That is why people could comfortably resort to studies of authors' lives and freely connect their discovered authorial intentions with works, thus committing the so-called "intentional fallacy." After the Anglo-American New Criticism, however, people seem to become gradually aware of the discrepancy between an author's "intention" and his "extention." In Rène Wellek and Austin Warren's *Theory of Literature*, for instance, it is said that

> *"Intentions" of the author are always "rationalizations," commentaries which certainly must be taken into account but also must be criticized in the light of the finished work of art. The "intentions" of an author may go far beyond the finished work of art: they may be merely pronouncements of plans and ideals, while the performance may be either far below or far aside the mark. If we could have interviewed Shakespeare he probably would have expressed his intentions in writing* Hamlet *in a way which we should find most unsatisfactory. We would still quite*

> *rightly insist on finding meanings in* Hamlet *(and not merely inventing them) which were probably far from clearly formulated in Shakespeare's conscious mind.* (136)

What Wellek and Warren mean by "intentions" here does not much accord, of course, with my definition. Nevertheless, the above quotation makes it clear that they do think an author's "extention" can become very different from his "intention." And I think they are right in suggesting that. For a work certainly can be either above or below or even far aside the mark because of conscious or unconscious factors on the part of the author. Consequently the New Critics have reason to warn us not to rely on the author's expressed intentions for judgment of his work. (If we should stubbornly do so, we will be laboring under the "intentional fallacy," according to their belief.)

I think the discrepancy between "intention" and "extention" can be best clarified with the idea of *différance*. As we know, when Jacques Derrida coined the word, he was playing on two meanings of the French word *différer*: difference—between signs as the basis of signification, and deferment—of presence by the sign which always refers to another sign, not to the thing itself.[8] Now we can say an author's "extention" (i.e., written text or work) is a version (or copy, or transcription, or expression, or code, or record, or embodiment, or whatever else you think fit to use) of his "intention" (i.e., idea). Between these two terms, there is also a semiotic relationship: the author's "extention" is the signifier and his "intention" is the signified. So if here we can apply the Derridean idea of *différance*, we can say there is always difference between an author's "extention" and his "intention," though the difference may be hard to specify.

As a matter of fact, an author's entire creative process includes both the stage of reading and the stage of writing. No one can write anything without reading something. And for an author, to read is to "read" life, which includes the experience of reading books and other experiences.

When an author "reads," he is building up his "intention"; when he writes, he is then turning his "intention" into "extention," which as an external entity can be further read by others, whom we call readers. If one of the readers becomes a critic, that is, becomes one who expresses his idea in oral or written language about an author's work, then he will indeed undergo the process of turning his own "intention" of the author's "extention" into his own "extention," which is again readable by others. (Critics' criticism can be criticized again just as a translation can serve as the basis for another translation.) Thus, if we think of the universe as a composite of things each of which is a text, then the universe is full of texts which are created, that is "read" and "written" all the time by various authors including God and man. When we make "textual analysis," we are interpreting, which often involves "the hermeneutic circle" of repeatedly beginning with "reading" and ending with "writing."[9] And, we must remember, to "read" is to "in-tend"; to "write" is to "ex-tend." Yet, in this hermeneutico-semiotic system, no single "reading" ("intention") or "writing" ("extention") has an absolute determinate "presence," though it is always supplementarily present in one form or another in the mental or physical world. The definite "meaning" we seek in any text is always deferred by the alternate acts of "reading" and "writing," or by the constant interchange between "intention" and "extention." If we understand this, can we accuse any reader of having "the intentional fallacy"? Can we say someone has a wrong idea when we know no idea, be it the reader's or the author's, ever exists as absolute truth or determinate presence?

A moot question of modern criticism is whether or not an objective interpretation of the text is possible. In approaching that problem, E. D. Hirsch, Jr., says that there is no objectivity unless meaning itself is unchanging.[10] And for him the one underlying meaning of the work which does not change is the author's willed meaning, that is, his intention. For he believes that the meaning of a text "is determined once and for all by the character of the speaker's intention" (214). If Hirsch's position is right, then any mode of reading is but a way of approaching the authorial intention; any study of the text, be it intrinsic or extrinsic, is but an attempt to reconstruct the unchanging intention of the author. Thus, the "intentional fallacy" as the Anglo-American New Critics conceive it is out of the question with Hirsch.

We know Hirsch's position has been devastatingly criticized by David Couzens Hoy. In the latter's *The Critical Circle*, Hirsch is said to have committed the Cinderella fallacy (a fallacy which grows out of the dogmatic belief that if we think a thing must be there, then it is in fact there, even if it can never be seen), because he "begins by noting that there cannot be reproducibility without determinate meaning and goes on to assert that since there is reproducibility, it follows that there must be determinate meaning" (18). I agree that Hirsch has committed the Cinderella fallacy in doing that logical reasoning. Nevertheless, I still think Hirsch is right in postulating the idea of a determinate meaning which is tied up closely with the authorial intention. Although it is theoretically true that there is no dependable glass slipper we can use as a test, since the old slipper will no longer fit the new Cinderella, yet, we can suppose that a short lapse of time should not bring about change appreciable enough in Cinderella's feet to render impossible our recognition of the true girl. Paradoxically, our senses are not keen enough to perceive any minute change in objects so as to hinder seriously our sense of identity. Theoretically, the idea of *différance* is right: the author's "intention" is never identical with his "extention," and his "extention" is never identical with the reader's "intention" of it. Yet in practice the author often so succeeds in making his "extention" accord with his "intention" that we can say what a text means and what its author intends it to mean are identical. And the reader often so succeeds in "in-tending" the author's "extention" that he can feel his "intention" of it is equivalent to, if not identical with, the author's "intention." Theoretically it is true that every interpretation is a misinterpretation.[11] Yet, in practice every interpreter believes he has made a right interpretation and his belief is often justifiable in terms of our common understanding or consensus. The truth is, understanding literature is like understanding life: no one can claim his understanding is the only true understanding, but all can agree on an understanding as the valid understanding within a certain space and time. In other words, reading (and writing as well) is a social behavior. And any social behavior is a matter of common agreement, not a matter of scientific truth.

In his "The Deconstructive Angel," M. H. Abrams grants that Jacques Derrida's and J. Hillis Miller's conclusions are right, but he still believes in the three premises of traditional inquiries in the human sciences.

1. The basic materials of history are written texts and the authors who wrote these texts (with some off-center exceptions) exploited the possibilities and norms of their inherited language to say something determinate, and assumed that competent readers, insofar as these shared their own linguistic skills, would be able to understand what they said.

2. The historian is indeed for the most part able to interpret not only what the passages that he cites might mean now, but also what their writers meant when they wrote them. Typically, the historian puts his interpretation in language which is partly his author's and partly his own; if it is sound, this interpretation approximates, closely enough for the purpose at hand, what the author meant.

3. The historian presents his interpretation to the public in the expectation that the expert reader's interpretation of a passage will approximate his own and so confirm the "objectivity" of his interpretation. The worldly-wise author expects that some of his interpretations will turn out to be mistaken, but such errors, if limited in scope, will not seriously affect the soundness of his overall history.

If, however, the bulk of his interpretations are misreading, his book is not to be accounted a history but an historical fiction.[12]

For me these premises are correct and I think their rationale can hardly be challenged. Furthermore, I think the premises can dovetail perfectly into the three conclusions reached by Stanley Fish, who as we know is one of the "New readers" Abrams accused of being apostles of indeterminacy and undecidability. In the end of his *Is There a Text in This Class?* Fish says:

> *We see then that (1) communication does occur, despite the absence of an independent and context-free system of meanings, that (2) those who participate in this communication do so confidently rather than provisionally (they are not relativists), and that (3) while their confidence has its source in a set of beliefs, those beliefs are not individual-specific or idiosyncratic but communal and conventional (they are not solipsists). (321)*

And then he ads that "the condition required for someone to be a solipsist or relativist, the condition of being independent of institutional assumptions and free to originate one's own purposes and goals, could never be realized, and therefore there is no point in trying to guard against it." And so he thinks it unnecessary for Abrams, Hirsch, and company to "spend a great deal of time in a search for the ways to limit and constrain interpretation" (321).

Here we have arrived at the point where we can summarize the "intentional fallacies" we have discussed so far. The traditional critics commit "the intentional fallacy" because they rely too much on the author's intention (especially the expressed intention) for interpretation or judgment of his work. The New Critics try to rectify this "fallacy" by calling our attention to the fact that the work is the primary and ultimate ground on which we can base our interpretation or criticism. They forget, however, that no work can be really detached from either the author's intention or the reader's. They do not admit that a poem in fact cannot have a really independent public existence. To think that one can ignore the author's or the reader's intention in criticizing works is itself an "intentional fallacy." More recent critical theories have tried again to modify and correct the New Critical position. From that effort, however, two new types of "intentional fallacy" have arisen. On one hand, we have such critics as Hirsch, who try to bridge the author and the work by locating the work's meaning again in the author's intention (both explicit and implicit). These new author-oriented critics are right in pointing out a determinate ground for readings. But they overlook the fact that the meaning of a work is decided not by the author's intention alone; it is equally if not chiefly decided by the reader's intention as well. So they also have some "intentional fallacy" of their own. On the other hand, we have such reader-oriented critics as Fish, who in attacking "the affective fallacy fallacy" and trying to see literature only in the perspective of the reader, have themselves committed the "intentional fallacy" of neglecting the authorial intention. As I have suggested above, the author, the work, and the reader are a trinity hardly separable. The work is only an "extention" where the author's intention and the reader's meet. We cannot assert that the author's intention is completely identical with the reader's intention through the "extention." Still we must agree that insofar as communication is possible, there should be a considerable amount of sameness remaining between the author's intention and the reader's through the medium of the "extention." To emphasize the difference (as Derrida and others do) may be logically or metaphysically correct; it is, however, impractical as Abrams has feared. The deconstructionists, in fact, have committed an "intentional fallacy" as well: they turned intended objects into intentionless objects by reducing all things to signs and accounting for an intentional process in terms of non-intentional semiotic relationship.

In their "Against Theory," Steven Knapp and Walter Benn Michaels conclude that the theoretical impulse

> *always involves the attempt to separate things that should not be separated: on the ontological side, meaning from intention, language from speech acts; on the epistemological side, knowledge from true belief. Our point has been that the separated terms are in fact inseparable. ... Meaning is just another name for expressed intention, knowledge just another name for true belief, but theory is not just another name for practice. It is the name for all the ways people have tried to stand outside practice in order to govern from without. Our thesis has been that no one can reach a position outside practice, that theorists should stop trying, and that the theoretical enterprise should therefore come to an end.* (29-30)

I think these conclusions are true in their own right, especially when, as we know, they are directed against such "objectivists" as Hirsch on one hand and such proponents of indeterminacy as Paul de Man on the other. However, as people cannot stop "in-tending," it is of no avail to try to stop them from theorizing. For a "wise" man, to "in-tend" is to theorize.

Some twenty years before the publication of "Against Theory," Susan Sontag brought forth her essay "Against Interpretation." In it she proposes that the function of criticism "should be to show *how it is what it is,* even *that it is what it is,* rather than to show *what it means.*" And her famous conclusion is: "In place of a hermeneutics we need an erotics of art" (660). I think Sontag, in making the statements, has probably understood, like an existentialist, that we are forever living in a meaningless absurd world where to interpret (i.e., to seek meaning) is always vain. Yet, I presume she has not understood that from time immemorial wise men have been interpreting and theorizing (to interpret is also to theorize); they think only vulgar men can be content with living an "erotic" life. To forbid people to interpret is tantamount to forbidding them to think, to "in-tend." And that is morally the biggest "intentional fallacy."

In his *The Critical Path*, Northrop Frye wishes we could avoid "two uncritical extremes": the "centrifugal fallacy" which feels that "literature lacks a social reference unless its structure is ignored and its content associated with something non-literary," and the "centripetal fallacy" where we "fail to separate criticism from the pre-critical direct experience of literature" (32-33). In the critical path, in fact, we are perpetually making fallacies of all kinds. We are so many blind men feeling the same elephant. Our insight indeed comes from our blindness.[13] But all fallacies can be reduced and traced to a single fallacy, namely, "the intentional fallacy," which is the necessary result of "in-tending" anything. When we understand this, we may be willing, then, to forgive anyone who fails to understand others' "intentions," including those who we know have distorted Wimsatt and Beardsley's idea of "the intentional fallacy." For "to err [through intention] is human; to forgive [with intention], divine."

Notes

1. They first published "The Intentional Fallacy" in 1946. The essay was later included in their *The Verbal Icon* (Lexington, Kentucky: U of Kentucky P, 1954).
2. The first three "misconceptions" are pointed out in Roger Fowler, ed., *A Dictionary of Modern Critical Terms*, revised & enlarged, (London & New York: Routledge & Kegan Paul, 1987), p. 127.
3. See the beginning paragraph of their "The Affective Fallacy."
4. See Wilfred L.Guerin et al. *A Handbook of Critical Approaches to Literature* (New York & London: Harper & Row, 1966).

5. As will become clear below, I am here influenced by Franz Brentano's "intentional psychology," Alexius Meinong's theory of objects, and their subsequent phenomenologists.

6. Steven Knapp and Walter Benn Michaels argue for this point in their "Against Theory." See W. J. T. Mitchell, ed., *Against Theory* (Chicago: U of Chicago P, 1985), pp. 11-30.

7. I have discussed the same ideas elsewhere in terms of "the Great Text," "the small texts," "the internal text," and "the external text." See my essay "Reading and Writing as Text Changes," in *Journal of the College of Liberal Arts*, Chung Hsing University, Taichung, Taiwan, 1989.

8. See Roger Fowler, ed., *Modern Critical Terms*, p. 55. For Derrida's own discussion of the term, see his "différance," translated by Alan Bass, and reprinted in Hazard of Adams & Leroy Searle, eds., *Critical Theory Since 1965* (Tallahassee: Florida State University Press, 1986).

9. "The hermeneutic circle" as understood by Friedrich Schleiermacher refers to the fact that in trying to understand any hermeneutic object –a sentence or a text –the interpreter has to approach the parts by reference to the whole, yet cannot grasp the whole without reference to the parts, therefore, the interpreter is always running in the circle (or, rather, the chain) of parts-and-whole. This circle occurs indeed in both reading and writing. For each act of reading is the implicit beginning of an interpretation while each act of writing is the explicit end of it. As I conceive it, to read and to write constitute a larger "hermeneutic circle" which makes possible the existence of infinite texts in our world.

10. See his *Validity In Interpretation* (New Heaven: Harcourt, 1949), p. 214

11. This is an idea discussed in Harold Bloom's *The Anxiety of Influence* and *A Map of Misreading*. But Bloom uses the word "misprision" instead of "misreading" or "misinterpretation." The notion is also discussed in Paul de Man's *Blindness and Insight*.

12. "The Deconstructive Angel," in David Lodge, ed., *Modern Criticism and Theory* (London & New York: Longman, 1988), p. 266. This paper was originally delivered at a session of the Modern Language Association in December 1976 and was later published in *Critical Inquiry* 3 (1983).

13. Paul de Man says, "All language is, to some extent, involved in interpretation, though all language certainly does not achieve understanding." He also says, "And since interpretation is nothing but the possibility of error, by claiming that a certain degree of blindness is part of the specificity of all literature we also reaffirm the absolute dependence of the interpretation on the text and of the text on the

interpretation." See his *Blindness and Insight* (Minneapolis: U of Minnesota P, 1971), p. 31 & p. 141.

Works Consulted

Abrams, M. H., ed. *A Glossary of Literary Terms.* New York: Holt, Rinehart & Winston, 1957.

--------. "The Deconstructive Angel." *Modern Criticism and Theory.* Ed. David Lodge. London & New York: Longman, 1988.

Bloom, Harold. *The Anxiety of Influence.* New York & London: Oxford UP, 1973.

--------. *A Map of Misreading.* New York: Oxford UP, 1975.

De Man, Paul. *Blindness and Insight.* Minneapolis: U of Minnesota P, 1971.

Derrida, Jacques. "Difference." *Critical Theory Since 1965.* eds. Hazard Adams & Leroy Searle, Tallahassee: Florida State U P, 1986.

Fish, Stanley. *Is There a Text in This Class?* Cambridge, MS: Harvard U P, 1980.

Fowler, Roger, ed. *A Dictionary of Modern Critical Terms.* London & New York: Routledge & Kegan Paul, 1987.

Frye, Northrop. *The Critical Path.* Bloomington & London: Indiana U P, 1971.

--------. *The Harper Handbook to Literature.* New York: Harper & Row, 1985.

Guerin, Wilfred L. et al. *A Handbook of Critical Approaches to Literature.* New York & London: Harper & Row, 1966.

Hirsch, E. D. Jr. *Validity in Interpretation.* New Haven: Yale U P, 1967.

Holman, C. Hugh, ed. *A Handbook to Literature.* Indianapolis: The Hobbs-Merrill Co., 1972.

Hoy, David Couzens. *The Critical Circle.* Berkeley: U of California P, 1978.

Knapp, Steven & Walter Benn Michaels. "Against Theory." *Against Theory.* Ed. W. J. T. Mitchell. Chicago: U of Chicago P, 1985. 11-30.

Sontag, Susan. "Against Interpretation." *20th Century Literary Criticism.* Ed. David Lodge. London & New York: Longman, 1972.

Tung, C. H. "Reading and Writing as Text Changes." *Journal of the College of Liberal Arts.* Taichung, Taiwan: Chung Hsing U, 1989.

Wellek, Rène & Austin Warren. *Theory of Literature.* New York: Harcourt, 1949.

Wimsatt, M. K. & M. C. Beardsley. *The Verbal Icon.* Lexington, Kentucky: U of Kentucky P, 1954.

* This paper first appeared in 1991 in *Tamkang Review*, Vol. XXI, No. 4, 377-89.

The Circle of Textualization

In the West, hermeneutics was originally limited to Biblical exegesis, but since the nineteenth century it has been extended to any theory or procedure in interpreting literary, legal, or social science texts. Today this "science" has developed to such an extent that it is impossible to discuss the subject of textualization without reference to it. However, despite its modern development, some basic hermeneutic issues still remain to puzzle us and leave us room for hot dispute. The problem of the "hermeneutic circle," for instance, is itself still subject to various interpretations.

As we know, the "hermeneutic circle" was first described in the early nineteenth century by the German theologian Friedrich Schleiermacher, and was so named later in the same century by the philosopher Wilhelm Dilthey.[1] It describes this paradoxical fact: the meaning of constituent parts of a whole can be understood only if the whole has prior meaning, but only when those constituent parts are understood can the full meaning of the whole be grasped. Thus, in trying to understand a text, we must approach its parts by reference to its whole and at the same time grasp its entirety by reference to its parts. This, then, involves a progressive clarification of mutually conferred meanings. And the interpreter, according to Schleiermacher, cannot but "leap" intuitively into the circle, like the leap of faith.

In our century, Martin Heidegger has a different formulation of the hermeneutic circle, though. For him the paradoxical problem is to be solved not by an intuitive leap into the circle, but in terms of interplay between an interpreter and a tradition which is encountered, understood and remade in an open dialect. This position of Heidegger's is maintained and further described by his disciple Hans-Georg Gadamer, who believes that the interpreter is always situated in relation to the tradition "out of which the text speaks." For Gadamer, the effect, or *Wirkung*, of a text is an important constituent of its meaning. Since this *Wirkung* differs for different ages, it has a history and tradition (*Wirkungsgeschichte*) which necessarily conditions any contemporary interpreter's understanding of the text.[2]

To "leap" into Schleiermacher's hermeneutic circle and thus concentrate on the relationship between the constituent parts and the whole of a text is an objectivist gesture of interpretation. On the other hand, to emphasize the interplay between an interpreter and a tradition as Heidegger and Gadamer did, is to adopt a historicist view of the text by placing the interpreter as well as the text in the context which time is always developing with new interpreters and new texts of all sorts. These two hermeneutic positions, however, are not incompatible. They are, rather, mutually complementary. And I think E. D. Hirsch, Jr., has justified this claim by postulating the distinction between the idea of *meaning* and that of *significance*.

According to Hirsch, "*meaning* is that which is represented by a text; it is what the author meant by his use of a particular sign sequence; it is what the signs represent. *Significance*, on the other hand, names a relationship between that meaning and a person, or a conception, or a situation, or indeed anything imaginable" (8). Thus, to leap into Schleiermacher's hermeneutic circle is to explore the "meaning" of a text while to plunge into Heidegger's is to investigate a textual "significance."

However, Hirsch's position is often questioned. The reader-oriented critics such as Stanley Fish, for instance, will doubt that there is any invariable authorial meaning going with the text. For Fish, "the obviousness of the utterance's meaning is not a function of the values its words have in a linguistic system that is independent of context; rather, it is because the words are heard as already embedded in a context that they have a meaning that

Hirsch can then cite as obvious" (309). In his view of the instability of the text and the indeterminacy of textual meaning, Fish simply regards everything in the text – its grammar, meanings, formal units – as a product of "interpretative strategies" adopted by an "interpretative community."

I am not here to judge, once for all, which school of hermeneutics is correct. For me all theories are partially right and partially wrong, and that is why disputes can arise among them. To be sure, to theorize is itself to interpret. And to interpret is to set in motion a "circle of textualization" which comprises two basic human activities: namely, reading and writing. This argument of mine needs further explication, of course. But after my explication I believe such hermeneutic problems as the meaning of "meaning" and the indeterminacy of meaning will be clarified.

For me, we human beings (and all those things which can be said to have consciousness) are forever interpreting: the moment we cry at birth, we begin to interpret; and we keep interpreting our environment (context) until we die. Each time we are in contact with anything, our senses will turn the perceived object into an image, and the image will then be sent to our mind to be kept and processed there in various ways and turned into our feelings or ideas, giving rise at the same time to our reaction to the perception. Now, as to perceive is to internalize images of external objects, it is similar to the activity of reading, for to read is also to internalize an external object. It is only that reading always involves a particular human language, but perception does not. However, we can think this way: in perceiving things we are using a primary language, that is, our intuition, with which God has endowed every one of us; whereas in reading a written word we are using a secondary language, which our culture obliges us to learn. In other words, what we normally call "reading" is but a secondary interpretation while perception is a primary one. To read a book, for example, is to perceive the book first (interpreting its "natural code," i.e., page texture in terms of color, shape, etc.) and then to read it (interpreting its contained linguistic code).

But perception or reading is only the beginning of interpretation. The entire process of an interpretation always ends with a sort of reaction. To perceive a fire, for instance, may cause the perceiver to utter "Fire!" or go and get some water to extinguish it. Now, to utter a word or to perform a deed is to externalize a feeling or idea (an internal text) which comes from perception or reading. Since writing is similarly an act of externalizing feelings or ideas, we may well suggest that writing is a particular kind of reaction.

Indeed, if we regard every physical object as an external text and every mental object as an internal text, and if we consider every internalizing act as reading and every externalizing act as writing, then we will reach the conclusion that as long as one lives, one is "reading" and "writing" every minute. To perceive external texts (including God's texts like mountain, water, tree, insect, etc., and man's texts like building, furniture, road, book, etc.) is to "read" them, and to react in consequence of the perception by expressing one's internal texts (feelings or ideas about the perceived external texts) is to "write" them. This thinking naturally presupposes that all natural objects are signs of God's language, just as all artificial objects are signs of man's language.

It follows, therefore, that as the world is full of God's texts and man's texts, every conscious mind is forever interpreting them by a never-ending repetition of reading and writing, that is, constantly internalizing them and then externalizing them again and again. To live is to experience. To experience is to interpret. To interpret is to perceive and react, or simply to read and write. A writer is just someone who leads a particular life, who spends much of his time reading both God's texts and man's texts and then creating his own texts by employing human language to externalize his experience of life. A person may never write anything in a conventional language such as English, French, or Chinese. Nevertheless, the moment he is walking or doing anything else, he is "writing" in his own personal language, thus expressing his own style of life.

Indeed, we are every one of us a "reader" and "writer" at every moment. It is only that at a particular moment we may be "reading" not an ordinary book or text but something which we usually do not regard as a book or text (a natural object – a tree, for example), nor may we be "writing" an ordinary book or text but something which we seldom call so (an artificial but nonlinguistic work – a table, for example). But all the same. No matter whether it is an ordinary book (text) or not, "reading" is the beginning of an interpretation and "writing" is the end. As long as we live, we are engaged in an endless circle of interpretation: we "read" and "write," "read" and "write," "read" and "write,"... all the time. That is, we never cease to internalize God's or man's texts and then externalize them again and again. We are, in a word, forever existing in a "circle of textualization," forever changing external texts into internal ones and vice versa.

There is no writer but has read something. A rude mender of pots and kettles like John Bunyan might really be able to produce one of the three greatest allegories of the world's literature "without learning or literary example" except the Authorized Version of the Bible.[3] Yet, he had "read" much of his world, in addition to what his meager "school education" had provided him with. When a romantic poet turns to "the Book of Nature," he is not just finding consolation in it but also reading or interpreting it. Surely, a classical writer may be better versed in his predecessors' works than a romantic writer while the latter may be better "versed in the country things" than the former; yet, both types of writers must of necessity have read both God's and man's texts in order to write in man's conventional language. Wordsworth, for instance, had read Pope and other writers before he could compose his romantic poems preaching the gospel of "wise passiveness": "One impulse from a vernal wood/May teach you more of man;/Of moral evil and of good,/Than all the sages can."[4]

Emerson has a wise dictum: "We are symbols, and inhabit symbols." To regard the whole universe as a Great Text created by God is to regard all objects therein as symbols and presuppose that such symbols, together with their ever-changing ways of combination, constitute the Divine Language of God (or gods, if you like).   Thus, every literary man is a user of at least two languages: he uses God's language (let us call it the language of nature) to "read" and "write" sensually and intuitively, and uses man's language (the language of culture) to read and write intellectually.

Now, what we normally call a writer is someone who has an intensive use for man's language or the language of culture.   A poet, a novelist, a playwright, or an essayist is such a person.   But there are other people who also read and write very much in man's language of culture although as a rule they are not called "writers."   A critic who reads a literary work and then writes a critical essay, or a reviewer who writes a book review, for instance, is not a "writer" in the usual sense of the word; but like a writer he certainly makes an intensive use of his acquired language of culture. Likewise, when a translator translates or when an editor edits a work, it is again primarily a business of using man's conventional linguistic systems.

To use any linguistic system seriously is always to interpret something. An English writer (poet, novelist, essayist or playwright) may use English to interpret his world or his life experience by writing a text.   A critic, reviewer, translator, or editor may in turn use his own language to interpret the English writer's text.   To "interpret" means here a variety of intellectual activities, of course.   It includes the act of criticizing, commenting, evaluating, judging, explaining, explicating, etc.   And to be sure, we may easily accept a piece of criticism or a review as the result of the critic's or reviewer's interpretation of the text he has read.   But many may not so easily accept a translation or edition of some work as the result of the translator's or editor's interpretation of that work.   Yet, if we are willing to consider the matter thoroughly, we must admit that no translator can translate, nor can any editor edit, anything without first making a critical reading (i.e., interpretation) of his target text. A translation or an edition is, doubtless, an implicit interpretation.

Recently G. Thomas Tanselle has argued convincingly that a textual scholar's effort is a critical effort. He says, "any text that a textual critic produces is itself the product of literary criticism, reflecting a particular aesthetic position and thus a particular approach to what textual 'correctness' consists of" (35). If we wish to push the matter a bit further, indeed, even a printer or a publisher is also an interpreter of texts. A printer's concern is of course about the way of printing texts while a publisher's is about the commercial, educational, or political values of texts. But when a printer decides to print a text in a particular way, is the decision not made on the basis of his understanding and interpretation of the text? Likewise, when a publisher decides to publish a book, he must already have a sort of understanding or interpretation of the book, too. Certainly, a printer or a publisher may not bother to read carefully in person the text to be printed and published; he may gain his understanding or interpretation of the text from someone else (e.g., an editorial board or a literary agent). Nevertheless, no one can deny that he has, to a certain degree, his own interpretation of the text after he reads it himself or hears about it from others.

In this connection, we may note in passing that like any ordinary reader, a minstrel is an interpreter of literary texts, too. When a scop moved from court to court reciting his versions of *Beowulf* or other epic stories, was he not interpreting the texts he had in mind? Similarly, when a scanner scans a poem, he is (much like a musician playing or directing music) also interpreting the poem's text.

In his "The Discourse on Language," Michel Foucault distinguishes between two categories of discourse: "There is no question of there being one category, fixed for all time, reserved for fundamental or creative discourse, another for those which reiterate, expound and comment" (220). For him, "a single work of literature can give rise, simultaneously, to several distinct types of discourse." "The *Odyssey*, as a primary text," for example, "is repeated in the same epoch, in Berand's translation, in infinite textual explanations and in

Joyce's *Ulysses*" (221).   Here Foucault says as much as that the writer's text is the primary text, and it is the "fundamental or creative discourse," while the translator's, critic's, reviewer's, editor's, and all other readers' texts are secondary texts insofar as they are based on, related to, or influenced by, the writer's primary, creative text.

Basically, I think, Foucault is right in making this distinction.   However, I must point out two inadequacies connected with this distinction.   First, it is hardly all satisfactory to impute creativeness wholly to the writer's text, suggesting that the translator's or critic's or any other reader's text is not creative in nature.   As we know, Matthew Arnold has already told us that criticism is not to be denied its "sense of creative activity": "it may have, in no contemptible measure, a joyful sense of creative activity; a sense which a man of insight and conscience will prefer to what he might derive from a poor, starved, fragmentary, inadequate creation" (1423).   Today, in fact, many have agreed that no criticism is without creativeness even though the degree of its creativeness may not be as great as that of a "creative work."

For me, a piece of criticism and a "creative work" differ actually not in their degrees but in their kinds of creativeness.   A piece of criticism, it is true, is explicitly and chiefly derived from a criticized work.   I say "explicitly" because one can see clearly, for instance, that Erich Auerbach's "Odysseus' Scar" stems from the reading of Homer's epic.[5]   And I say "chiefly" because one can also understand that Auerbach, to use the same example, does not base his criticism of the epic entirely on his reading of it: he has in truth read other things (e.g., the Bible) and based his idea not only on his readings but also on his common sense which originates largely from other life experiences. Anyway, whereas we admit that a piece of criticism is explicitly and chiefly derived from a criticized work, there is no guarantee that the criticized work is therefore more creative than the critical work.   For all the originality imputed to Homer, we must grant that Auerbach is original and creative, too, in writing that famous essay.   For me, indeed, a piece of criticism and a "creative work" are equally creative in the sense that both are similarly the result of readings--readings of literature and "readings" of life. It is only that the former is conspicuously grounded on the latter in most cases. (There are indeed exceptional cases. For example, criticism of criticism is possible. And how about criticism of a translation of a "creative work"?)

In fact, we have really become accustomed to the idea that criticism is also creative in nature. Meanwhile, however, we seem not to have noted duly that creative writing is also critical writing. When an author parodies another author, a literary tradition, or a particular style (e.g., Aristophanes parodies Aeschylus and Euripides in *Frogs*, Cervantes parodies the whole tradition of medieval romances in *Don Quixote*, or Shakespeare parodies John Lyly's euphuism in *Henry IV*, Pt. I), is he not obviously critical of what he is parodying? By the same token, when an author writes "under the influence of another author, a literary movement, or a literary school (e.g., Milton under the influence of Virgil, William Morris under the influence of Pre-Raphaelitism, or T. S. Eliot under the influence of the Metaphysicals), is he not also critical in the sense that he either accepts or rejects certain elements of that influence? And, furthermore, when any writer writes of anything on the basis of his experience, is he not critical of that thing or that experience? Indeed, whatever we do, we are criticizing in a broad sense.

After considering the closeness between creative writing and critical writing, we are next in a position to relate translation to both types of writing. In the Preface to his *Ovid*, John Dryden distinguishes three grades of translation thus:

> *First, that of metaphrase, or turning an author word by word, and line by line, from one language into another. ... The second way is that of paraphrase, or translation with latitude, where the author is kept in view by the translator, so as never to be lost, but his words are not so strictly followed as his sense; and that too is*

> *admitted to be amplified, but not altered. ... The third way is*
> *that of imitation, where the translator (if now he has not lost that*
> *name) assumes the liberty, not only to vary from the words and*
> *sense, but to forsake them both as he sees occasion; and taking*
> *only some general hints from the original, to run division on the*
> *groundwork, as he pleases.*[6]

Now, is the third way of translation as expounded here far different from creative or critical writing? By no means. In effect, every instance of translation is as much the result of reading or interpreting some other text as the act of creative or critical writing. And if we are willing to broaden the sense of "translation," we might claim, too, that to paint a picture, to compose a piece of music, or even to build a house is a sort of creative and critical "translation"--all these activities, like any other activity, necessarily "translate" ideas (internal texts) into concrete works (external texts). Thus, to live is to create, to criticize, and to translate.

But in creating, criticizing, and translating, we are also editing if by "editing" we simply mean the action of altering, adapting, and refining. And, conversely, since to edit is to alter, adapt and refine, we cannot but admit that it is, to a high degree, creative and critical by nature; and somewhat translative, too.

Thus far, in criticizing Foucault's distinction between the fundamental, creative discourse and the derivative, commentary discourse, I have tried to make it clear that in truth there is no big difference between them. To my mind, the writer's text, the critic's, the reviewer's, the translator's, the editor's, the printer's, the publisher's, or indeed everyone's text is at once creative, critical, commentary, translative, editorial, evaluative, and interpretative. They are all immersed in the hermeneutic circle or the "circle of textualization." They all involve the two basic human activities: reading and writing, or the internalizing and externalizing of texts.

After we understand this, it becomes apparent that there is no sense in claiming, as Foucault does, the writer's text to be primary and considering every reader's as secondary. In point of fact, everyone's text can be primary or secondary, depending on whether it serves as the original or comes as the derivative. When *Odyssey* is criticized, translated, reviewed, edited, recited, printed, or published, it is primary because it is now the original in people's minds. But, as Edward Young has pointed out, Homer is only an "accidental original." There is every reason to believe that *Odyssey* must have been modeled on some earlier works, like any other masterpiece in the world. If it had not imitated any known work, it must, at least, have imitated life or nature, which, as we have repeatedly emphasized, is full of God's texts and man's texts. In this sense, then, we can say this epic of Homer's is also derived from other texts and therefore can be called secondary, like a critical essay or a translation of the work.

Personally I feel that a large quantity of the so-called modern or postmodern work owes its birth to the development of critical theory. Now, suppose a creative work is really created out of a critical essay, can we still call the creative work primary and the critical essay secondary? For example, we know Bertolt Brecht's many plays belong definitely to the genre of "epic theater." And it is certified that the name as well as the idea of "epic theater" comes from a famous essay "On Epic and Dramatic Poetry" by Goethe and Schiller.[7] Given this situation, can we say *Mother Courage and Her Children* is the primary text while "On Epic and Dramatic Poetry" is the secondary?

Many of our contemporary French critics have been persistent in underscoring the point that there is no origin for texts. The truth is: every text has its origin in some other text or texts. It is only that the origin is not often immediately identifiable. Foucault himself says that a primary text will allow us o create new discourse *ad infinitum* (221). Now I add that anyone's text can be the primary text.

Yet, logically speaking, there is a linear pattern among the kinds of texts we have discussed.   In the process of publishing a literary text, for instance, we first have the writer's text, which may then be edited and printed before it is published.   Normally, after the writer's text is published, we then have the translator's or critic's text, which may also be edited and printed before it is published.   But the translator's or critic's text can be again translated or criticized.   It can also be so read by a creative writer that a new creative work results from it.   Now, the creative work or translation or criticism originated from any other creative work or translation or criticism is forever capable of being read and interpreted for creating yet new creative or translative or critical texts.   Therefore, to trace the true history of a single text--be it creative, critical or translative--is often to betray a very long and very complicated line of intertextual relationships.   A biographer of an author, as so many biographers can bear testimony, is often one who sees only some obvious relationships among texts concerned.   Take T. S. Eliot's *The Waste Land* for example.   How many texts have "influenced" (i.e., helped to make possible) this modern text?   Only the works alluded to?   I think all previous texts of the world--not just the Western literary tradition--have either closely or remotely "influenced" it.   One may not say our Four Books have directly inspired Eliot into writing the poem.   Yet, can we not say that our Four Books have indirectly and remotely affected Eliot since they do affect Western thinking in some way?

I am not here to trace any line of intertextual relationships.   My point is: what we call intertextuality is in fact a very complicated network of textualization.   As Paul Ricoeur conceives it, each text is indeed free to enter into relation with all the other texts (334).   And as Julius Kristeva and others conceive it, each text is indeed like a mosaic work, or a series of quotations.[8]

But no matter how complicated the pattern of an intertextual relationship may be, it is forever the relationship of alternation between internal and external texts, or between reading and writing, which makes what I call the "circle of textualization." And it is this phenomenon of alternation that ushers in the moot issues of textual meaning and textual indeterminacy.

To talk about the problem of textual meaning, we must first acknowledge that meaning is always a mental entity, and as such it cannot but exist in someone or other's mind, although we often tend to believe that it is embedded in physical objects. In other words, meaning is but a sort of internal text, which is never identical with the external text, though representable by it. Now, who can claim to have the authority to decide the meaning of a literary text? This question easily brings us to the consideration of the "intentional fallacy."

As we know, "the intentional fallacy" was a term popularized by W. K. Wimsatt and Monroe C. Beardsley.[9] From the two critics' biographical data, we know they are posing as "New Critics" when they attack the fallacy in an essay with the very term as its title. They are, in fact, advocating the "objective theory" that a literary text has an independent public existence. Consequently, they are encouraging "intrinsic studies," while discouraging "extrinsic studies," of literature by replacing the Romantic system of values (covering the ideas of sincerity, fidelity, spontaneity, authenticity, genuineness, originality, etc.) with the scientific one (integrity, relevance, unity, function, maturity, subtlety, adequacy, etc.). They simply dispute the Romantic view of the author as an important source of meaning for texts.

We know Wimsatt and Beardsley attack not only "the intentional fallacy" but also "the affective fallacy." For them, the reader's impressions and the author's are equally unreliable as the standard for determining textual meanings. This New Critical stance, I think, is basically sound and firm in that it stresses the priority of the work as the basis of critical judgment. No one, I believe, would deny that one's reading of "To His Coy Mistress" should be done first and foremost on the text itself, and Andrew Marvell's politics, religion, and career as well as the responses or reactions of other readers to the work can only serve as an accessory guide to one's interpretation. However, art does not exist in a vacuum. Any artifact is created by someone at some time in history, and it is received by certain people at certain times, too. Hence, if it has any meaning at all, it cannot but be connected with the creator or receiver's mentality.

In my mind, a literary text is hardly separable from the intention of the author who creates it, nor from the intention of the reader who reads it. It is only when a work is viewed as a pure physical text, a mere construct of black spots with blanks on paper entirely detached from author and audience alike, that we can say it has an "impersonal" or "objective" existence. Otherwise, we must admit that the work, the author, and the reader are a trinity, bound each to each with a common "intention"; therefore, no critical effort can manage to separate them without committing a sort of "intentional fallacy," and to assert the absolute authority of any one of them is impractical if not impossible.

This idea of mine bears largely on the meaning of the word "intention."[10] I think we must first understand that any object (i.e., any external text) that comes into one's mind is an intended object. If a perceived object has any meaning at all, the meaning is never intentionless.[11] Actually, to intend is to "in-tend," that is, to turn an external text into an internal text by our mental activity (which is no other than the act of "reading"). Before an author writes a text, he usually has to "intend" a lot of things. (In our common language, we say he has to have a lot of life experience.) The things he "intends" include such natural objects as mountains, waters, flora and fauna, and such man-made objects as practical inventions, devices, and artifacts. After he "intends" these objects for some time, some developed "intentions" will then arise in his mind to direct his outward action. (The developed "intentions" are commonly called "ideas.") If he is an ordinary man, the "intentions" may cause him to live an ordinary man's life. If, however, he is a wit (in the neoclassical sense) or a genius (in the romantic sense), his "intentions" may lead him to create artistic works.

When creating an artistic work, he is then an "author" in the usual sense of the word. Now, in the process of artistic creation, he is in fact turning his "intentions" (internal texts) again into an external object (text) by the use of his tool (and language is a writer's tool). If we can coin the word "extention" as the antonym of "intention" and make it mean the external object or text resulting from externalizing one's "intention," then we can hold that to read is to "intend," or to form "intentions" in the mental world while to write is to "ex-tend," or to form "extentions" in the physical world.

It follows then that our most important problems are whether or not an author's "intention" (internal text) is identical with his "extention" (external text), and whether or not the author's "extention" is identical with his reader's "intention" of it. As we know, in the long past very few critics ever doubted the identity of an author's "intention" with his "extention." That is why people could comfortably resort to studies of authors' lives and freely connect their discovered authorial intentions with works, thus committing the so-called "intentional fallacy." After the Anglo-American New Criticism, however, people seem to become gradually aware of the discrepancy between an author's "intention" and his "extention." In Rène Wellek and Austin Warren's *Theory of Literature*, for instance, it is said that

> *"Intentions" of the author are always "rationalizations," commentaries which certainly must be taken into account but also must be criticized in the light of the finished work of art. The "intentions" of an author may go far beyond the finished work of art: they may be merely pronouncements of plans and ideals, while the performance may be either far below or far aside the mark. If we could have interviewed Shakespeare he probably would have expressed his intentions in writing* Hamlet *in a way which we should find most unsatisfactory. We would still quite rightly insist on finding meanings in* Hamlet *(and not merely*

inventing them) which were probably far from clearly formulated in Shakespeare's conscious mind. (136)

What Wellek and Warren mean by "intentions" here does not much accord, of course, with my definition.   Nevertheless, the above quotation makes it clear that they do think an author's "extention" can become very different from his "intention."   And I think they are right in suggesting that.   For a work certainly can be either above or below or even far aside the mark because of conscious or unconscious factors on the part of the author.   Consequently, the New Critics have reason to warn us not to rely on the author's expressed intentions for judgment of his work.

I think the discrepancy between "intention" and "extention" can be best clarified with the idea of *différance*.   As we know, when Jacques Derrida coined the word, he was playing on two meanings of the French word *differer*: difference--between signs as the basis of signification, and deferment--of presence by the sign which always refers to another sign, not to the thing itself.[12]   Now we can say an author's "extention" (i.e., external text) is a version (or copy, or transcription, or expression, or code, or record, or embodiment, or whatever else one thinks fit to use as a term) of his "intention" (i.e., internal text).   Between these two terms, there is also a semiotic relationship: the author's "externtion" is the signifier and his "intention" is the signified.   So according to the Derridean idea of *différance*, there is always difference between an author's "extention" and his "intention," though the difference may be hard to specify.

As a matter of fact, an author's entire creative process includes both the stage of reading and the stage of writing.   No one can write anything without reading something.   And, for an author, to read is to "read" life, which includes the experience of reading books and other experiences.   When an author "reads," he is building up his "intention" (internal text); when he writes, he is then turning his "intention" into "extention" (external text), which as an external entity can be further read by others, whom we call readers. If one of the readers becomes a critic, that is, becomes one who expresses his idea in oral or written language about an author's work, then he will indeed undergo the process of turning his own "intention" of the author's "extention" into his own "extention," which is again readable by others. (Critics' criticism can be criticized again just as a translation can serve as the basis for another translation.) Thus, if we think of the universe as a composite of things each of which is a text, then the universe is full of texts which are created, that is, "read" and "written" all the time by various authors including God and man. When we make "textual analysis," we are interpreting, which often involves "the hermeneutic circle" or "circle of textualization" because we are repeatedly beginning with "reading" and ending with "writing." Yet, in this hermeneutico-semiotic system, no single "reading" ("intention") or "writing" (extention") has an absolute determinate "presence," though it is always supplementarily present in one form or another in the mental or physical world. The definite "meaning" we seek in any text is always deferred by the alternate acts of "reading" and "writing," or by the constant interchange between "intention" and "extention." If we understand this, can we accuse any reader of having "the intentional fallacy"? Can we say someone has a wrong idea when we know no idea, be it the reader's or the author's, ever exists as absolute truth or determinate presence?

We may recall now that E. D. Hirsch, Jr., maintains that it is impossible to have any objective interpretation unless meaning itself is unchanging (214). And for him the one underlying meaning of the text which does not change is the author's willed meaning, that is, his intention. For he believes that the meaning of a text "is determined once and for all by the character of the speaker's intention" (214). If Hirsch's position is correct, then any mode of reading is but a way of approaching the authorial intention; any study of the text, be it intrinsic or extrinsic, is but an attempt to reconstruct the unchanging intention of the author. Thus, the "intentional fallacy" as the Anglo-American New Critics conceive it is out of the question with Hirsch.

Hirsch's position has been devastatingly criticized by David Couzens Hoy. In the latter's *The Critical Circle*, Hirsch is said to have committed the Cinderella fallacy (a fallacy which grows out of the dogmatic belief that if we think a thing must be there, then it is in fact there, even if it can never be seen), because he "begins by noting that there cannot be reproducibility without determinate meaning and goes on to assert that since there is reproducibility, it follows that there must be determinate meaning" (Hoy 18). I agree that Hirsch has committed the Cinderella fallacy in doing that logical reasoning. Nevertheless, I still think Hirsch is right in postulating the idea of a determinate meaning which is tied up closely with the authorial intention. Although it is theoretically true that there is no dependable glass slipper we can see as a test, since the old slipper will no longer fit the new Cinderella, yet we can suppose that a short lapse of time should not bring about change appreciable enough in Cinderella's feet to render impossible our recognition of the true girl. Paradoxically, our senses are not keen enough to perceive any minute change in objects so as to hinder seriously our sense of identity. Theoretically, the idea of *différance* is right: the author's "intention" is never identical with his "extention," and his "extention" is never identical with the reader's "intention" of it. Yet, in practice the author often so succeeds in making his "extention" accord with his "intention" that we can say what a text means and what its author intends it to mean are "the same." And the reader often so succeeds in "in-tending" the author's "extention" that he can feel his "intention" of it is equivalent to, if not identical with, the author's "intention." Theoretically, it is true that every interpretation is a misinterpretation.[13] Yet, in practice the majority of interpreters believe they have made the right interpretations and their belief as such is often justifiable in terms of our common understanding or consensus. The truth is: understanding literature is like understanding life: no one can claim that his understanding is the only true understanding, but all can agree on an understanding as the valid understanding within a certain space and time.   In other words, reading (and writing as well) is a social behavior.   And any social behavior is a mater of common agreement, not a matter of scientific truth.

Mention can be made here of Luigi Pirandello's *Six Characters in Search of an Author*.   The play, as we know, is a vivid presentation of a relativist theme: the difficulty of presenting "truth."   The six characters' reality of life is incapable of being staged satisfactorily after they have found the author.   But why?   Because the characters feel that as soon as the actors begin to act their story, the cheap conventions of the stage have intruded and their "truth" is distorted (reality becomes artificiality).   Judging from this response, we know the characters' "intention" is not well understood by the author.   But whose fault is it?   I say nobody's.   For there is unavoidably some disparity between the characters' "intention" (their idea about their family tragedy) and their "extention" (their verbal description of their family tragedy), and so is there between the actor's "intention" (idea about the characters' tragedy) and their "extention" (their presentation of the tragedy).   That is to say, the "truth" or "reality" contained in the characters' internal text is thrice distorted in the alternation of intentions and extentions, which finally becomes the actors' stage presentation.

Since a gap always exists between one's "intention" (internal text) and "extention" (external text), and between one's "extention" and another's "intention" of it, it is no wonder that many people feel it difficult to express themselves at times, and still more people feel it impossible to make themselves understood.   Facing this situation, shall we give up any hope of communication, then?

A serious writer will answer "No" to the question.   He may understand that every reading is a misreading, every writing a miswriting, every understanding a misunderstanding, every interpretation a misinterpretation, etc.   Yet, he knows, too, that communication is not for complete or perfect understanding. In the course of reading, writing, or interpretation, we can always give heed to some determinate, shared meaning rather than to the indeterminate, unshared sense. The hermeneutic circle or the circle of textualization is built on the basis of sameness rather than difference. That is why even Stanley Fish, who is one of the "New Readers" M. H. Abrams accused of being apostles of indeterminacy and undecidability, concedes that "communication does occur, despite the absence of an independent and context-free system of meanings" (321).

But how on earth does communication take effect in the realm of literature? This bears largely on the problem of the nature of reading. And regarding this problem many modern reader-oriented critics have their own opinions. Roman Ingarden, for instance, presumes that literary works form organic wholes, but every text is readily equipped with its indeterminacies, and therefore it is the reader's function to concretize the text correctly by rendering it internally consistent. Similarly, Wolfgang Iser suggests that the reader's journey through the text is a continuous process of adjusting his viewpoints based on his formerly expected textual meanings, and, besides such adjustments, to read is to actualize the text by filling up the "blanks" or "gaps" (of meaning) necessarily existing in it. Somewhat different from Ingarden and Iser, Hans Robert Jauss uses the term "horizon of expectations" to describe the process of reading literary texts in a given period. For him, each text has its original "horizon of expectations" which tells us how it was valued and interpreted at its first appearance. When it is read later, however, the horizon is always already changed, and so (following Gadamer's argument that all interpretations of past literature arise from a dialogue between past and present) Jauss views the reader's understanding as a "fusion" of past and present horizons.[14]

Interpretations of the process and nature of reading do vary among critics. But all critics seem to agree that the actual reader can in fact carry on two types of reading. Ingardern, for example, distinguishes "ordinary, purely passive (receptive) reading" from "active reading" (37-40).   He grants that every reading is an activity consciously undertaken by the reader and not a mere experience or reception of something.   Nevertheless, he asserts that in many cases "the whole effort of the reader consists in thinking the meanings of the sentences he reads without making the meanings into objects and in remaining, so to speak, in the sphere of meaning."   Thus, this purely passive manner of reading is mechanical in the sense that the reader "is occupied with the realization of the sentence meaning itself and does not absorb the meaning in such a way that one can transpose oneself by means of it into the world of the objects in a work."   By contrast, in "active" reading one not only understands the sentence meanings but also apprehends their objects and has a sort of intercourse with them.   In other words, when a literary text is read actively, "we think with a peculiar originality and activity the meaning of the sentences we have read; we project ourselves in a co-creative attitude into the realm of the objects determined by the sentence meanings" (37-40).

Ingarden's distinction is close to Roland Barthes's.   According to Barthes, there are readings "which are mere acts of consumption: precisely the ones in which the 'significance' is censored all the way along."   "Full reading," he continues, "is the kind in which the reader is nothing less than the one who desires to write, to give himself up to an erotic practice of language" (42).   This distinction of Barthes's is fully appreciated by Mary Bittner Wiseman, who, in echoing Barthes's (and also Julius Kristeva's) idea, says: "What is ordinarily called reading is often passively consuming worlds and voices presented by culture and author; it is merely a kind of looking and listening.   The other sort of reading is operating a text, speaking to it as to the other as instigator, as Kristeva says" (54-55).

But closer to the real process of reading is Michael Riffaterre's distinction between heuristic reading and retroactive reading.   According to Riffaterre, each reading act comprises two stages of interpretation.   The reader first performs a sort of heuristic reading, during which textual meaning is apprehended through the reader's linguistic competence and literary competence.   After that, the reader performs a sort of retroactive reading:

> *As he progresses through the text, the reader remembers what he has just read and modifies his understanding of it in the light of what he is now decoding.   As he works forward from start to finish, he is reviewing, revising, comparing backwards.   He is in effect performing a structural decoding: as he moves through the text he comes to recognize, by dint of comparisons or simply because he is now able to put them together, that successive and differing statements, first noticed as mere ungrammaticalities, are in fact equivalent, for they now appear as variants of the same structural matrix.* (5-6)

Propounding a "transactional theory" of the literary work, Louise M. Rosenblatt believes that the same text can be read either efferently or aesthetically.   In efferent reading "the primary concern of the reader is with what he will carry away from the reading," while in aesthetic reading "the reader's primary concern is with what happens during the actual reading event."   Adopting the first stance, therefore, the reader "disengages his attention as much as possible from the personal and qualitative elements in his response to the verbal symbols; he concentrates on what the symbols designate, what they may be contributing to the end result that he seeks --the information, the concepts, the guides to action, that will be left with him when the reading is over."   In contrast, the second stance will permit the whole range of reading responses generated by the text to enter into the reader's center of awareness, and out of these materials he will then select and weave what he sees as the literary work of art (Rosenblatt, 1978, 22ff.).   Needless to say, Rosenblatt's two stances of reading are parallel in a way to all the other dichotomies just mentioned above.

In fact, all the dichotomies of reading so far covered can be related to Schleiermacher's hermeneutic distinction between two aspects of the act of understanding: speech is to be understood, first, as something carved out of language and, second, as a fact about a thinking subject. The first aspect, as Peter Szondi explains, is the study of speech in its relationship to the whole language; it thus employs the grammatical interpretation based on factual knowledge of language and history. The other aspect is the study of speech in its relationship to the mental process of an author; hence, it employs the psychological interpretation (Schleiermacher also calls it "technical" interpretation), based on empathy or psychological identification with the author on the part of the reader (Szondi 101-3).

But Schleiermacher's "psychological" interpretation has played down the active, productive, retroactive, operating, or aesthetic element involved in the course of reading. For it does not take into account the fact most modern critics are never tired of repeating: Reading actually refers to two "semiotic" (to use Robert Hodge's preferred term) acts--"one an act of interpretation that attempts to reconstruct the original act of production, the other a piece of writing which incorporates the text-as-read into a new text" (Hodge 110-1). In other words, Schleiermacher has indeed overlooked the creative quality contained in the act of reading.

Yet, creative or not, reading is always based on an external text, which is always part of a larger context or always an intertext to other texts. In consequence, reading can be focused mainly on the text itself or on its relationship with other texts; that is, on its own textual meaning or on its contextual or intertextual meaning. Paul Ricoeur calls these two different targets of reading *explanation* and *interpretation*:

> *We can, as readers, remain in the suspense of the text, treating it as a worldless and authorless object; in this case, we* explain *the text in terms of its internal relations, its structure. On the other hand, we can lift the suspense and fulfill the text in speech, restoring it to living communication; in this case, we* interpret *the text. These two possibilities both belong to reading, and reading is the dialectic of these two attitudes.* (338)   (emphasis mine)

This dichotomy of reading is somewhat similar to Szondi's division between grammatical and psychological readings, to be sure. But I think it is even more closely related to David Birch's classification of "relevance." According to Birch,

> *Relevance is determined for the most part in two ways: the first way looks at a number of rules of relevance that apply internally in a text, that is, the function and context of the text are not considered; I'll call this "text-in-itself relevance." The second way is the exact opposite: the text is considered as part of a much larger field of discourse and its relevance depends on social/historical institutions; I'll call this "institutional relevance."* (35)

These two types of "relevance" are in effect no other than what Hirsch calls meaning and significance, or what Ricoeur calls sense and meaning.

It is clear now that the passive, consumptive, grammatical, heuristic, or efferent reading tends more toward internal relevance or explanation to get at the text's relatively more stable semantic component which Hirsch calls meaning but Ricoeur calls sense, whereas the active, productive, psychological, retroactive, or aesthetic reading tends more toward institutional relevance or interpretation to get at the text's relatively more indeterminate semantic component which Hirsch calls significance but Ricoeur calls meaning. Now, is there any actual reading which belongs purely to one or the other class of reading? Certainly not. Every actual reading is understandably a combination of both. But owing to the reader's personal or situational differences, a particular instance of reading can be more characteristic of one or the other type.

If every reading is actually both passive and active, efferent and aesthetic, explanatory and interpretive, etc., we can conclude that it is more or less creative at any time it occurs. This creative quality in reading is best explained by Rosenblatt:

> *Through the medium of words, the text brings into the reader's consciousness certain concepts, certain sensuous experiences, certain images of things, people, actions, scenes. The special meanings and, more particularly, the submerged associations that these words and images have for the individual reader will largely determine what the work communicates to him. The reader brings to the work personality traits, memories of past events, present needs and preoccupations, a particular mood of the moment, and a particular physical condition. These and many other elements in a never-to-be-duplicated combination determine his response to the peculiar contribution of the text.* (Rosenblatt, 1976, 30)

This creative reading is indeed an interaction (or transaction, as Rosenblatt prefers it) between the text and the reader. And its result is: the reader forms an internal text (i.e., idea) from such an interaction. No wonder one can assert that "each time a reader reads a text, a new text is created" (Birch 21).

And Ricoeur can hold this: "To read is, on any hypothesis, to conjoin a new discourse to the discourse of the text. This conjunction of discourses reveals, in the very constitution of the text, an original capacity for renewal which is its open character. Interpretation is the concrete outcome of conjunction and renewal" (343).

We know Barthes is all for the "writerly text" and against the "readerly text," because the former, he believes, leaves more room for the reader to create his own text in reading it. In reality, Barthes's theory of the text not only "extends to infinity the freedoms of reading (authorizing us to read works of the past with an entirely modern gaze, so that it is legitimate, for example, to read Sophocles' 'Oedipus' by pouring Freud's Oedipus back into it, or to read Flaubert on the basis of Proust), but it also insists strongly on the (productive) equivalence of writing and reading" (42).

In view of its similarly creative or productive quality, reading can indeed be equated with writing. It is only that reading is creative at the stage of internalizing an internal text, while writing is creative at the stage of externalizing an internal text; the former produces an internal text, the latter an external one. And, indeed, one can never be sure which comes first in the "circle of textualization": Is it reading or writing? (Just as we can never be certain which comes first: the egg or the chicken?) It is only that in the hermeneutic process, we normally take reading for the beginning, and writing for the end, of a particular interpretation. Thus, a critic begins his criticizing in reading a text and ends it in writing a critical essay.

Now, both reading and writing (in their usual sense) are linguistic acts. They cannot do without language. What, then, is the role played by language in the circle of textualization? In his *Language, Truth and Poetry*, Graham Dunstan Martin convincingly argues that the semiotic triangle made up of word, concept and referent should be replaced by the rectangle with word-form, word-image, concept, and referent as its four sides (see Figure 1 below):

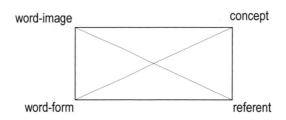

Figure 1

In the act of reading, to use this figure, we first have contact with the word-form (the word as we hear it pronounced or see it written or printed in any particular instance), then turn it into the word-image (our mental apprehension of it, and assimilation of it to other similar sounds or shapes all interpreted as "the same"), and then connect it to the concept (the meaning or sense of the word) before realizing it in terms of the referent (the external object represented by the concept of the word-image of the word-form).[15]   In fact, in reading a written or printed text, we must change the written or printed form into the written or printed image of the word first, and then connect the visual image with the representing sound (auditory image) before we can connect it with the concept of the word.   So in the seemingly simple act of reading a printed poem, we need to undergo a good series of linguistic changes in our mind before the poem as an external entity can be said to make sense (have connection with the outside world).   Now, every linguistic change in our mind is really an interpretation, and the change can be creative in the sense that the mind does participate actively in the making of the word-image and the concept, as well as in the perception of the word-form and the referent. (Perception, by the way, also involves an active transaction between the perceiver and the object perceived--according to Ulric Neisser, a prominent cognitive psychologist.[16])

In the act of writing, as we can conceive it, the order of the linguistic changes is reversed, of course. The writer begins with the referent, forms his concept of it, turns it into a word-image, and finally actualizes it in a word-form. The changes, needless to say, are also textual changes (internal and external), which bring about new texts each time and therefore are productively creative, and hermeneutically interpretative.

But, as I have repeatedly emphasized, reading and writing need not be performed on linguistic texts only. As all objects can be regarded as texts, so can our ordinary perception and reaction to anything be thought of as a sort of "reading" and "writing." Hence, all men, including reader and writer, are "reading" and "writing" all the time so long as they live. That is to say, we actually never for a moment step out of the "circle of textualization," so long as we still keep our consciousness and thus are still able to interpret the galaxies of texts (God's and man's) that come within our sensual contact.

Recently, Linda Flower used a conceptual map to highlight certain features of reading and writing as constructive processes. The map is as Figure 2 printed below:[17]

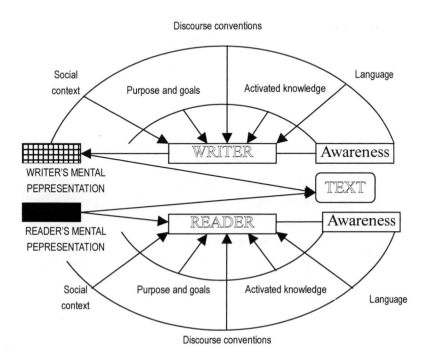

Figure 2

The above map shows that writing and reading are acted on by multiple forces: the outer circle in the figure denotes forces such as the social context, discourse conventions, and language, and the inner circle denotes the activated knowledge and purposes relevant to this particular act of reading or writing. The map also shows that writing and reading lead to the construction of mental representations of meaning--in the minds of reader and writer. But as it is explained, these internal representations (what I call internal texts) cannot be equated with the (external) text the writer writes down or the cues to meaning construction the reader perceives, or with any one reading of the text itself. However, we can think of these constructions as two related but different networks of information, which are not necessarily coded in words and sentences or even language (i.e., not necessarily linguistic texts). Indeed, this knowledge may take the form of abstract propositions, code words and pointers to schemas, or even images (i.e., nonlinguistic texts). Moreover, these representations of meaning are likely to go well beyond the propositional content of a text and to include both a reader/writer's own web of intentions and those they impute to the other players in the discourse.[18] Thus, a certain "fallacy" is likely to occur when any one inadvertently equates these representations of meaning (internal texts) with the propositional content of the (external) text, or with the reader/writer's own web of intentions, or with the intentions imputed to the other players in the discourse. The three kinds of fallacy are respectively the "objective fallacy," "intentional fallacy," and "affective fallacy," of course.

But to err is human. In our ceaseless life of interpretation, in the unending leap into "the hermeneutic circle," or in the perpetual engagement with "the circle of textualization," we really cannot avoid "reading" or "writing" inaccurately, because language is a medium and anything going through a medium is likely to be changed somehow, just as a ray of light is refracted, a sound is weakened, through the air or water. Perhaps we are unwilling to acknowledge it, but it is true that what we call creation or production is as much the result of misinterpretation as that of correct interpretation. The circle of textualization, in a word, is the circle of indeterminate reading and writing of texts correctly and incorrectly, as the "New Readers" will gladly pronounce it to be.

Notes

1. This and the following information concerning the term is based on the explication of the entry "hermeneutics" in Beckson & Ganz's *Literary Terms: A Dictionary,* and of the same entry in Fowler's *A Dictionary of Modern Critical Terms.*

2. See Hoy's *The Critical Circle*, pp. 41-2.

3. See Moody & Lovett's *A History of English Literature*, pp. 169-71.

4. See his "Expostulation and Reply" and "The Tables Turned."

5. This famous essay is the first chapter of his *Mimesis: The Representation of Reality in Western Literature.*

6. Quoted in Wimsatt & Brook's *Literary Criticism: A Short History*, p. 216.

7. See Maynard Mack, et al., eds., *The Norton Anthology of World Masterpieces*, vol. 2, p. 1276.

8. See Owen Miller, "Intertextual Identity," in Mario J. Valdes & Owen Miller, eds., *Identity of the Literary Text*, p. 24.

9. They first published "The Intentional Fallacy" in 1946. The essay was later included in their *The Verbal Icon.*

10. As will become clear below, I am here influenced by Franz Brentano's "intentional psychology," Alexius Meinong's theory of objects, and their subsequent phenomenologists.

11. Steven Knapp and Walter Benn Michaels argue for this point in their "Against Theory." See W. J. T. Mitchell, ed., *Against Theory*, pp. 11-30.

12. See Roger Fowler, ed., *Modern Critical Terms*, p. 55. For Derrida's own discussion of the term, see his "Différance," tr. by Alan Bass, rpt. in Hazard Adams & Leroy Searle, eds., *Critical Theory Since 1965*, pp. 120-30.

13. This is an idea discussed in Harold Bloom's *The Anxiety of Influence* and *A Map of Misreading*. But Bloom uses the word "misprision" instead of "misreading" or "misinterpretation." The notion is also discussed in Paul de Man's *Blindness and Insight.*

14. See Raman Selden, *A Reader's Guide to Contemporary Literary Theory*, chapter 5. Also See Terry Eagleton, *Literary Theory: An Introduction*, p. 80ff.

15. I have somewhat modified Martin's definitions of the terms. See his *Language, Truth and Poetry*, p. 26.

16. See his *Cognition and Reality: Principles and Implication of Cognitive Psychology*, esp., p. 54.

17. See her "Interpretive Acts: Cognition and the Construction of Discourse," in *Poetics*, 16 (1987), 109-130.

18. For this explanation, see Linda Flowers, et al., *Reading to Write: Exploring a Cognitive and Social Process*, p. 13.

Works Consulted

Arnold, Matthew. "The Function of Criticism at the Present Time." *The Norton Anthology of English Literature*. 4th edition. Ed. M. H. Abrams, et al., vol. 2, 1422-24.

Auerbach, Erich. *Mimesis: The Representation of Reality in Western Literature*. Trans. by W. R. Trask. Princeton UP, 1953.

Barthes, Roland. "Theory of the text." *Untying the Text*. Ed. Robert Young., London: Routledge & Kegan Paul, 1981.

Beckson, Karl & Authur Ganz. *Literary Terms: A Dictionary*. 3rd edition. New Your: The Noonday Press, 1989.

Birch, David. *Language, Literature and Critical Practice*. London & New York: Routledge, 1989

Bloom, Harold. *A Map of Misreading*. Reprint edition. Oxford UP, 1980.

--------. *The Anxiety of Influence*. 2nd edition. Oxford UP, 1997.

de Man, Paul. *Blindness and Insight*. 2nd edition. U of Minnesota P, 1983.

Derrida, Jacques. "Différance." Trans. by Alan Bass. Rpt. in Hazard Adams & Leroy Searle, eds. *Critical Theory Since 1965*. Tallahassee: Florida State UP, 1986. 120-30.

Eagleton, Terry. *Literary Theory: An Introduction*. Oxford: Basil Blackwell, 1985.

Fish, Stanley. *Is There a Text in This Class?* Cambridge, MS.: Harvard UP 1980.

Flower, Linda. "Interpretive Acts: Cognition and the Construction of Discourse." *Poetics*. 16 (1987), 109-130.

Flower, Linda et al. *Reading to Write: Exploring a Cognitive and Social Process*. New York & Oxford: Oxford UP, 1990.

Foucault, Michel. *The Archaeology of Knowledge*. Trans. by A. M. Sheridan Smith. New York: Pantheon Books, 1972.

Fowler, Roger. *A Dictionary of Modern Critical Terms*. London: Routledge & Kegan Paul, 1987.

Hirsch, E. D. *Validity in Interpretation*. New Haven & London: Yale UP, 1967.

Hodge, Robert. *Literature as Discourse*. Cambridge: Polity Press, 1990.

Hoy, David Couzens. *The Critical Circle*. Berkeley: U of California P, 1978.

Ingarden, Roman. *The Cognition of the Literary Work of Art*. Evanston: Northwestern UP, 1973.

Knapp, Steven & Walter Benn Michaels. "Against Theory." *Against Theory*. ed. W. J. T. Mitchell. Chicago: U of Chicago P, 1985. 11-30.

Mack, Maynard, et al., eds. *The Norton Anthology of World Masterpieces*. 4th edition. New York: Norton, 1979. Vol. 2.

Martin, Graham Dunstan. *Language, Truth and Poetry.* Edinburgh: At the UP, 1975.

Miller, Owen. "Intertextual Identity." *Identity of the Literary Text.* Ed. Mario J. Valdes & Owen Miller. Toronto: U of Toronto P, 1985.

Moody, W. V. & R. M. Lovett. *A History of English Literature.* Revised 7th edition. New York: Charles Scribner's Sons, 1964.

Neisser, Ulric. *Cognition and Reality: Principles and Implication of Cognitive Psychology.* San Francisco: W. H. Freeman, 1976.

Ricoeur, Paul. "What Is a Text? Explanation and Understanding." *Twentieth-Century Literary Theory.* Ed. Vassilis Lambropoulos & David Miller. Albany: State U of New York P, 1987.

Riffaterre, Michael. *Semiotics of Poetry.* London: Methuen & Co., 1978.

Rosenblatt, Louise M. *Literature as Exploration.* New York: The MLA of America, 1976.

--------. *The Reader, the Text, the Poem.* London & Amsterdam: Southern Illinois UP, 1978.

Selden, Raman. *A Reader's Guide to Contemporary Literary Theory.* Brighton, England: The Harvester Press, 1985.

Szondi, Peter. *On Textual Understanding and Other Essays.* Trans. by Harvey Mendelson. Minneapolis: U of Minnesota P, 1986.

Tanselle, G. Thomas. *A Rationale of Textual Criticism.* Philadelphia: U of Pennsylvania P, 1989.

Wellek, Rène & Austin Warren. *Theory of Literature.* New York: Harcourt, 1949.

Wimsatt, W. K. Jr. & M. C Beardsley. *The Verbal Icon.* Lexington, Kentucky: U of Kentucky P, 1954.

Wimsatt, William K. Jr. & Cleanth Brook. *Literary Criticism: A Short History.* New York: Alfred A. Knopf, 1959.

Wiseman, Mary Bittner. "Texts of Pleasure, Texts of Bliss." *Text, Interpretation, Theory.* Ed. James M. Heath & Michael Payne. London & Toronto: Association of University Presses, 1985.

* This paper is adapted from Chapter 5 of my book *The Scene of Textualization* (1992) and it was reprinted in 《國立中興大學台中夜間部學報》第三期 (1997), pp. 145-181.

The Four Linguistic Spaces of Poetry

Ⅰ. Poetry and Verbalization

Poetry has been variously defined in different cultures; however, as suggested in a handbook to literature, all definitions of poetry must have three parts: a particular content, a more or less specific form, and a particular effect (Thrall 366). It therefore follows that a poet is someone capable of conceiving a particular idea and expressing it in such a form as to achieve a particular effect.

The poetic content may be a poet's particular emotion or thought, such as what William Wordsworth called "the spontaneous overflow of powerful feelings," or in Thomas Carlyle's words, "musical thought" (Thrall 365). The particular emotion or thought may come from the poet's inspiration or meditation, imagination or wit, heart or head. Regardless of its source, it is often presumed to contain some worthy and/or pleasurable meaning, idea, or "truth." Therefore, if anyone at any moment possesses such an emotion or thought, in one sense he may be said to be momentarily full of poetry.

But to own such a poetic feeling or thought is not yet equal to being a poet. A poet is recognized through his work—be it oral or written—rather than through those unexpressed poetic feelings or ideas still stored in his psyche. One might be considered poetically inclined or feel oneself full of poetry at the moment, for instance, when one is captivated by the realization that man is born to grow like a tree, and then to decay and disappear like a piece of wood over the course of time. Yet, one cannot be called a poet for that before expressing this realization in a poem, just as Gerard Manley Hopkins did in composing his "Spring and Fall." In other words, poetry involves a verbalization stage in addition to the cognition (conceptualization) stage.

In my book, *Imagination and the Process of Literary Creation*, I propose a two-stage theory of literary creation: the "plastic perception" stage (i.e., the stage of receiving and forming the "idea" or "germ" for a piece of writing) and the "plastic communication" stage (i.e., the stage of finding and using the "technique" or "skill" to communicate the idea). I also suggest that these two stages, indeed, involve the use of what S. T. Coleridge respectively called "primarily imagination" and "secondary imagination"—which are, to me, simply ideational imagination and technical imagination. According to this theory, poets are indeed "both seers and makers, defined by characteristics of insight and language, which are often, in finished poems, inseparable" (Frye 357). In addition, poetry certainly "begins in the images of the preconscious or subconscious mind and is filtered through language toward the precise symbols and syntax of an imaginative construction at first glimpsed only dimly by the poet" (Frye 357).

Normally we cannot know for certain how a particular poet, with his particular primary or ideational imagination, comes to have a certain feeling or idea at the stage of plastic perception; neither can the poet himself understand this process. That is why we often ascribe this process to the so-called "inspiration." On the other hand, when a poet uses his secondary or technical imagination to compose a poem during the plastic communication stage, he knows what is transpiring, for the poet is now consciously employing language as a tool or medium to convey his feelings or ideas.

Certainly, when composing a poem, one may need to be concerned with such seemingly extra-linguistic matters as plot, characterization, setting, theme, motif, and imagery—all of which are expressed *through* language—as well as with such linguistic elements as the phonological, morphological, syntactical, semantic and other components of a language—all of which are expressed *in* the language itself.   Nevertheless, it is safe to say that, more than any other genre, poetry requires intensive care in using linguistic elements; in poetry, the act of verbalization matters most in expressing its sense or sensibility.

Ⅱ. The Art of Poetry

In his "Linguistics and Poetics," Roman Jakobson points out six "constitutive factors" observable in any speech event: addresser, context, message, contact, code, and addressee; he also assigns to them six corresponding verbal-communication functions: emotive, referential, poetic, phatic, metalingual, and conative (66-71).   For Jakobson, the poetic function is manifest when the message to be communicated becomes the focus for its own sake.   When discussing "What is poetry," he writes:

> *Poeticity is present when the word is felt as a word and not a mere representation of the object being named or an outburst of emotion, when words and their composition, their meaning, their external and inner form, acquire a weight and value of their own instead of referring indifferently to reality.* (378)

Jakobson also points out "two basic modes of arrangement used in verbal behavior, *selection* and *combination*," and he proposes that the poetic function "projects the principle of equivalence from the axis of selection into the axis of combination" (71).   This oft-quoted statement is frequently used to explain the literary phenomenon of cohesion.   "What he means by this is that, in poetry, structures which are roughly equivalent in sound, or sentence structure, or grammatical category, or some other aspect tend to be combined in a linear order or sequence" (Traugott 22). However, cohesion is, in fact, more than the combination of "roughly equivalent" elements; a more complete explanation of the same statement is written by Elmar Holenstein:

> *A poetic sequence is characterized on all levels of language by the reiteration of the same and similar elements (alliteration, rhythm, homonymy, synonymy) and by their contrastive variations (rhythm, antonymy, negative parallelism). In the case of contrast, the antecedent link of the combination is repeated in an implicit (i.e., negative) manner.* (145)

Jakobson is one of the leading Russian Formalists. His ideas on poeticity and the poetic function are therefore related to such key Formalist notions as "foregrounding" and "defamiliarization." His concept of poeticity, for instance, is in accordance with Jan Mukarovsky's postulate that the function of poetic language consists in the foregrounding of the utterance:

> *In poetic language foregrounding achieves maximum intensity to the extent of pushing communication into the background as the object of expression and of being used for its own sake: it is not used in the services of communication, but in order to place in the foreground the act of expression, the act of speech itself.* (43-44)

In addition, his "two basic modes of arrangement" (selection and combination) are said to be the basic modes used not only in an ordinary man's "verbal behavior," but also in a poet's attempt to defamiliarize words and phrases so that poeticity or literariness is achieved.

In a previous article, I argue against the idea of defamiliarization or foregrounding as being the only requirement for poeticity or literariness. [1]   I certainly agree that a poem involves the artful arrangement of linguistic components.   Yet, I also believe that defamiliarizing words or phrases is not the only way to create a poetic arrangement.   For me, a poetic arrangement comes from the proper selection and combination of words, and that makes people feel not only "strange," but also "wonderful."   What is strangest can be nothing but nonsense. And a common phrase put in the proper place can also produce the foregrounding effect of poetry.   Therefore, I believe that Jonathan Swift's definition of a style ("proper words in proper places") [2] or Coleridge's definition of poetry ("the best words in the best order") [3] are in effect clearer and more accurate descriptions of the art of making poetry.

Ⅲ. The Four Linguistic Spaces

I have mentioned above that the process of poetic creation is a two-stage process: the stage of cognition (or conceptualization) plus the stage of verbalization.   I have also suggested that the second stage is even more important to the poet's converting a feeling or idea into a perceivable poem. And I have made it clear that this process of actualization concerns the artful arrangement of all linguistic components (not just a defamiliatization or foregrounding of some components) in the poem.

Now, the question is: What are the essential linguistic components involved?   To answer the question, one usually must consider the units of language, from the smallest to the largest—namely, from the phonetic through the phonemic, morphological, and syntactical levels to the level of an entire discourse or text (in other words, from individual sounds through words, phrases, clauses and sentences to an entire composition).   At each level or unit, poets presumably must attempt to select the best elements and then combine them in the best order according to their imaginative judgments.

However, here I wish to suggest another way of considering the question. I believe that all modern poets work with four linguistic spaces—no matter at what level or unit and no matter at what moment they are dealing with the linguistic components. These four linguistic spaces are **sense, sound, shape,** and **situation**. Before I elaborate on these four spaces, however, I must explain why I say "modern poets." As one can infer from the history of language development, the world's writing systems are later human inventions which resulted from the necessity of representing the transitory speech in a more permanent form. Therefore, in a primitive culture where no writing system exists, its people can only have an oral tradition of literature. Within that tradition, the poet—or, more properly called, the bard or the scop—can only compose and recite poetry in sounds which have a particular sense in a particular situation, that is, without resorting to any visual representation of the sound. This pre-modern poet, therefore, worked artfully in only three spaces—**sound, sense,** and **situation**—as far as the stage of verbalizing or actualizing a poem is concerned. However, with the invention of writing systems (and later with that of printing), poets began to have a fourth space to work in—namely, **shape**—which is the visual aspect of language.

Today, of course, a poet can still circumvent the visual aspect by recording his poems on tape and having them *heard* rather than *seen*. However, as the great majority of poets publish their poems in books, one sees that **shape**—the visual aspect of language—is often additionally taken into consideration when a "modern" poet writes artfully.

The so-called "concrete poetry" is a good example of how **shape** has become a prominent aspect of poetry. The tradition of "shaped poems" (*carmen figuration*) is very old—dating from Hellenistic times. Concrete verse may be regarded as a graphic art, if it employs graphemes and typefaces in clusters, morphemes, words or phrases to create designs which emphasize pictures rather than words.   Nevertheless, so long as a poem's shape is used to intensify the sense of the verse, one can still deem it as being part of the poet's poetic imagination.   In truth, most of the best-known concrete poems (such as George Herbert's "The Altar," Dylan Thomas's "Vision and Prayer," Lewis Carroll's "Long and Sad Tail of the Mouse" in *Alice in Wonderland*, Edwin Morgan's "Siesta of a Hungarian Snake," Francois Rabelais's "epilenie," and Guillaume Apollinaire's "Il pleut") are famous not only for their interesting graphic designs, but also for their effect of making shape, like sound, echo sense and situation within the poems.[4]

To illustrate how a poet can make his poem more meaningful by exploiting the dimension of shape, let us consider, e. e. cummings's "L(a":[5]

l(a

le

af

fa

ll

s)

one

l

iness

In *The Princeton Handbook of Poetic Terms*, this poem is used as an example to show how, unlike an ordinary poem, a concrete poem will not "yield up its heart to oral reading because no picture will":

A haiku-*like evaded simile is here so arranged that the vehicle is literally troped into the tenor: "loneliness" contains the single leaffall, its emblem.   This might have been done in a single horizontal line, but the vertical format graphically represents the*

> *dropping, enforces a slow scanning (and hence, reading), discovers hidden "ones" in the words (with graphic puns based on the identity of the 12th letter of the alphabet with the first Arabic numeral in many typefaces), etc.*
>
> (Preminger 46)

Much more can be said about the graphic arrangement of the poem. In my opinion, the poem cannot be scanned or read as "loneliness, a leaf falls," nor as "1(a, le, af, fa, ll, s), one, 1, iness," nor as a sequence of all twenty constituent letters plus the two parentheses. The poem is hard to read out loud; this naturally suggests the feeling one has when one is lonely while watching a leaf fall. In addition, to tear apart the word "loneliness" and the sentence "a leaf falls" so that they become an unutterable sequence of letters is to suggest that unspeakable loneliness comes from the separation or tearing apart of relationships—just as a leaf falls from a tree. As to the graphic punning of "l," where each "l" resembles an individual, the vertical arrangement hints that at first, two persons in two families ("1(a" & "le") become associated, then after a time of mutual friendship or courtship ("af" followed by "fa"), the two become a pair or couple ("ll"). Yet afterward, over the natural course of time, the plural (the "s" in "s)")—becomes singular—as emphasized by the word "one" on the next line and graphically/numerically suggested by the "1" on the following line. Eventually, what one sees is only a small "l" with its own quality ("iness"), which appears to lie flat on the ground or on a bed—a state of pensive loneliness. Reading the poem this way, one sees the natural course of a human life hidden in the graphic arrangement of the poem.

Certainly, many other examples of "pattern poetry" (another name for "concrete poetry") are not nearly as complex or sophisticated as this poem of cummings's. Actually, since the first appearance of such bucolic Greek poets as Simiaš of Rhodes, pattern poems have often been simply considered as embodiments of false wit. Nevertheless, shaped verse—as seen in such modern sub-genres as "type poems," "type-writer poems," and "object poems," as well as in such movements as *Spatialisme* and *Lettrisme*—is enough proof that as language has incorporated the dimension of shape in modern times, poets have increasingly felt the need to exercise their imaginative power on the visual effects of graphic elements in their poems.[6]

Shape in poetry is not only apparent in typographical figures. In one written introduction to poetry, Laurence Perrine points out three broad external patterns which a poet may impose on a poem: fixed form, in which an entire poem follows a fixed, traditional pattern (e.g., rondeau, roundel, villanelle, triolet, sestina or ballade in French, and limerick or sonnet in English); stanzaic form, in which the poet uses either a series of self-invented stanza patterns or traditional stanzas (e.g., terza rima, ballad meter, rime royal, Spenserian stanza, etc.); and continuous form, in which the constraints of formal design are slight (e.g., free verse, blank verse, etc.).[7] While usually there is no meaningful connection between the content and the adopted form of a poem, in some cases poets do use form to express an idea. For example, in using the sonnet form for his "Piazza Piece," John Crowe Ransom successfully and ironically hints at the conventional content of sonnets—a gentleman keeps persistently pursuing a lady and complaining to her while the lady persistently rejects him. Likewise, in my own Chinese poem titled "The Assassin," I use stanzas containing three long lines plus two short ones to suggest the Chinese set expression *"san-ts'ang liang-tuan"* (literally, "three-long two-short"), which indicates "the state of being precarious"—one of the poem's themes.

However, a poem's shape is not necessarily visible. In ordering images, ideas, or any other materials in a poem, a poet is creating internal patterns which can only be perceived by "the inward eye." For instance, Walt Whitman's "When Lilacs Last in the Dooryard Bloomed" is a poem organized around three recurrent images (lilacs, Venus, and the thrush) that are further centered around the "thought of him I love"; the result is an elegy with a successful structure, fervor, and verbal rhythm. In this light, a good poet is one who is capable of creating internal forms rather than following outward patterns. In trying to appeal to our natural love of shape, the poet must launch his imagination into the realm of invisible shapes as well as that of the visible.

Next to shape, let us discuss the space of **sound**. When we talk of such poetic devices as rhymes, alliteration, assonance, consonance, paronomasia and refrain, we concern ourselves with ways of arranging sound via repetition and variation; when we find instances of onomatopoeia, euphony, cacophony, or other musical effects in a poem, we become aware of certain combinations of sounds. Indeed, prosody is an essential part of poetry in almost all cultures. Different languages offer different phonological features to be used as metrical bases: e.g., number of syllables in Hungarian folk poetry, syllabic length in classical Greek and Latin verse, heavier and lighter pulses in English and German verse, and the use of even or non-even tones in classical Chinese poetry—thus producing what John Lotz called purely-syllabic meter, durational meter, dynamic meter, and tonal meter (14). Yet, all poets have the same aim when working in the space of sound: they want their verses to have pleasant rhythms, or even better, to make their sounds appear as echoes to their senses—as Alexander Pope suggests they must in his *Essay on Criticism* (Part II, 364-373).

To make sound seem an echo to, and a shape of, sense is to admit that sense is the center of poetry. Indeed, sense is the space in which poets work hardest with all rhetorical devices. In using puns, malapropisms, or other devices, for instance, a poet focuses on both sound and sense; in using such devices as simile, metaphor, synecdoche, metonymy, oxymoron, conceit, personification, apostrophe, paradox, irony, allegory, symbol, hyperbole, understatement, and allusion, a poet focuses mainly on sense. In fact, in utilizing the denotations and connotations of certain words and in arranging certain images, motifs or themes, a poet is even more directly concerned with sense. Whatever a poet does in the realm of sense, he strives to create richness of meaning, or what William Empson calls "ambiguity,"[8] which, for the great majority of critics, is the most important attribute of poetry.

Sound, shape, and sense are the three basic elements of linguistic or poetic text; however, every text has its context, and is an intertext to other texts.[9] To place a text in its context and see its intertextuality is to take into account its social aspect, to pragmatically consider language or poetry not only as a locutionary act, but also—to borrow J. L. Austin's terminology—as an illocutionary and perlocutionary act.[10] Put simply, it is to consider the dimension of **situation** in addition to those of sound, shape, and sense.

I must emphasize that every poem involves at least two situations. One is when it is regarded as speech uttered by the speaker in a poem to the audience in the poem; the other is when the poem is regarded as speech of the poet addressing his audience. Of course, in some lyrics the speaker in the poem can be identified with the poet. However, it is safer to differentiate the two situations, since the situation of the speaker in the poem cannot logically be identical to that of the poet in the world. Matthew Arnold's "Dover Beach," for instance, can be viewed in two ways: first, as the poet's speech to his readers about faith in general in 19th-century England, and second, as the speech of an unidentified speaker in the poem to his sweetheart about the timelessness of lovers' faith.[11]

In his book on poetry and poets, T. S. Eliot says that there are three voices of poetry:

> *The first voice is the voice of the poet talking to himself—or to nobody. The second is the voice of the poet addressing an audience, whether large or small. The third is the voice of the poet when he attempts to create a dramatic character speaking in verse; when he is saying, not what he would say in his own person,*

but only what he can say within the limits of one imaginary character addressing another imaginary character. The distinction between the first and the second voice, between the poet speaking to himself and the poet speaking to other people, points to the problem of poetic communication; the distinction between the poet addressing other people in either his own voice or an assumed voice, and the poet inventing speech in which imaginary characters address each other, points to the problem of the difference between dramatic, quasi-dramatic, and non-dramatic verse. (96)

I wish to add that each voice represents a different speech situation—either real or imaginary—in which words are contextualized, thus gaining their illocutionary and perlocutionary force and perhaps assuming radical change in meaning.

Take, for example, two lines from A. E. Housman's "Terence, This Is Stupid Stuff." It has been suggested by Laurence Perrine that the poem contains an instance of verbal irony in the lines, "Pretty friendship 'tis to rhyme/Your friends to death before their time," since here we may actually "substitute the literal *sorry* for 'pretty' with little or no loss of meaning"(105). But how can we be sure? The answer is, of course, "from the context." In the verbal context, we know the speaker is talking sarcastically to his friend Terence. Likewise, we sense irony in a line from Shelley's "Ozymandia" ("Look on my works, ye Mighty, and despair!") because Shelly is depicting the King's vanity by pointing to the ruined statue on the boundless and bare sands. Indeed, as irony entails the perception of a clash between appearance and reality, it can only be detected through an understanding of a communicative situation—one which contains knowledge of who is speaking to whom under what circumstances.

Like irony, the detection of paradox is largely based on the understanding of a communicative situation. John Donne's lines, "Divorce me, … imprison me, for I/except you enthrall me, never shall be free,/Nor ever chaste, except you ravish me" are paradoxical partly because we know that the speaker has the idea that a sinful person is like one wedded to Satan. From this example one understands that paradox, as well as irony, is closely related to the so-called "point of view" in narration, for a person's point of view (e.g., Donne's or the speaker's depraved view of man in "Batter My Heart, Three-Personed God") is partly determined by his sense of the situation he is in.

Paradox and irony are also associated with "tone." As Hugh Kenner suggests, tone is determined "by the writer's or speaker's *sense of the situation*, perhaps an imagined situation" which includes "both his sense of the gravity of his subject, and his relationship, courtly, solemn. offhand, intimate, or whatever it is, with his audience" (17). In Robert Frost's "Stopping by Woods on a Snowy Evening," one may assert, the speaker is speaking in a meditative tone because we know from the context that he is pondering a conflict between instinctive enjoyment of beauty and rational fulfillment of duty.

So, judging from all facets (that is, all elements connected with sense or sound or shape), one can always conclude that there is no poetic utterance without its situation, since "all utterances are used to do things" (York 16). And, therefore, we may affirm that a good poet must have "pragmatic imagination" in addition to aesthetic imagination. Besides using all devices available to turn sound, shape, and sense into an organic sequence of beauty, the poet has to use all devices available to *situate* the whole of that sequence of beauty so well that it meets the standards of "proper words in proper places," "the best words in the best order," and "useful words in useful situations." After all, poetry is indeed "a form of language in which appropriacy—appropriacy of feeling to object, of character to setting, of *signifiant* to *signifie*, and perhaps most essentially of all, of utterance to situation—becomes itself the main focus of attention for author and reader alike" (York 26).

IV. Linguistics and Poetics

In *Linguistcs for Students of Literature*, Elizabeth Closs Traugott and Mary Louise Pratt present the idea of a "grammar of a text" (Traugott 24). In their view, every literary text has a "grammar," just as every language has one. But, previously, when attacking the "poetic language fallacy" of the Prague Linguistic Circle, Pratt mentioned the underlying analogy of the Circle's central idea: "Grammaticality is to linguistics what poeticality is to poetics, and the difference between the linguist's grammar and the poetician's grammar is the difference between literature and nonliterature" (Pratt 11).

In my view, if "grammar" means only a set of rules for selection and combination, then the Prague Linguistic Circle and the new American linguists are both correct in postulating a "grammar of a text" and an analogy between linguistics and poetics, since both linguists and poeticians are indeed searchers and researchers of the rules of language. However, I must stress that all linguistic rules stem from the four fundamental spaces—sound, shape, sense, and situation. Linguists may call their four fields phonology, graphology, semantics, and pragmatics, and poeticians may lack names for the same dimensions, yet they are all the same. Both are searching for rules concerning how sequences of sounds or shapes are selected and combined to make sense in certain situations so that effective communication is achieved.

However, communication through language is not always effective, since there are linguistic problems such as aphasia. Jakobson has discussed two basic types of aphasia: one due to a similarity disorder and the other due to a contiguity disorder—that is, disorders on the axes of selection and combination.   Besides, Jakobson has also related these two types of aphasia to the two poles of literary practice: metaphor and metonymy.   Although he understood that selection (the metaphoric relation of similarity) and combination (the metonymic relation of contiguity) appear at any verbal level—morphemic, lexical, syntactic, or phraseological—he asserted that different types of literature lean toward either the metaphoric or the metonymic.   For example, he asserted, lyric poetry tends toward the metaphoric while realistic prose tends toward the metonymic.[12]

In the end, there remains a paradox: poets are the most effective communicators *apparently* having both types of incurable aphasia.   Once inspired, a poet is sure to utter words which may appear to be in disorder paradigmatically and/or syntagmatically (or, if you prefer Jakobson's terms, metaphorically and/or metonymically).   However, upon closer examination one will find that so many sounds, shapes, senses, and situations are selected and combined so well that the poet's feelings and ideas are communicated perfectly.   The poet is, indeed, *divinely* mad; one may even claim that poets are born linguists and poeticians at the same time.

But, of course, a poet need not know any technically linguistic or poetic terms.   As a master of language, a poet knows instinctively all the phonological, graphological, semantic, and pragmatic features available, and is able to make good use of them in the process of composition.   A Chinese poet, for instance, will instinctively know how to utilize the Chinese tonal system in his or her prosodic imagination, how to use Chinese characters (with their pictograms, ideograms, and phonograms in roughly square shapes) for concrete designs, how to enrich the meanings of Chinese phraseology, and how to fit each and every character into its situation.   That is, the Chinese poet will be able to make the best use of the four linguistic spaces offered to him by his language when he composes his Chinese poem.   And similarly a poet of any other nationality writing in any other language will be able to make the best use of the four linguistic spaces that his own language offers him.

Notes

1. The article is "The Nature and the Locus of 'Literariness,'" *Studies in English Literature and Linguistics.* Taipei: Taiwan Normal University, 1990, No. 16, 113-122.
2. See his Letter to a Young Clergyman, January 9, 1720.
3. See his Table Talk, July 12, 1827.
4. For further examples and discussion of concrete poems, see Emmett Williams, ed. *An Anthology of Concrete Poetry* (1967), S. Bann, ed. *Concrete Poetry: An International Anthology* (1967), and Mary E. Solt, ed. *Concrete Poetry: A World View* (1968).
5. This is the first of cummings's *95 Poems* (1958).
6. For the modern varieties of shaped verse, see such books as John Hollander's *Types of Shape* (1969), May Swenson's *Iconographs* (1970), B. Bowler's *The Word as Image* (1970), and E. Gomringer's *Konkrete Poesie* (1972).
7. See Perrine's *Sound and Sense*, 5ᵗʰ edition, chapter 14, pp. 217-221.
8. On page 3 in his *Seven Types of Ambiguity,* Empson refers to ambiguity as "any verbal nuance, however slight, which gives room for alternative reactions to the same piece of language."
9. I have discussed this idea in my book, *The Scene of Textualization.*
10. See his *How to Do Things with Words*, Chapter VIII.
11. For a full discussion of the two views, see my article "A New Linguistic Analysis of Arnold's 'Dover Beach,'" pp.63-77.
11. See Roman Jakobson and Morris Halle, *Fundamentals of Language*. Part II , pp. 69-96.

Works Consulted

Austin, J. L. *How to Do Things with Words.* 2ⁿᵈ edition. Oxford: Oxford UP, 1975.

Bann, Stephen, ed. *Concrete Poetry: An International Anthology.* London: London Magazine, 1967.

Bowler, B. *The Word as Image.* London: Studio Vista, 1970.

Coleridge, S. T. *Biographia Literaria.* Ed. J. Shawcross. London: Oxford UP, 1907.

Eliot, T. S. *On Poetry and Poets.* New York: Farrar, Straus & Giroux, 1957.

Empson, William. *Seven Types of Ambiguity.* London: Penguin, 1961.

Gomringer, E. *Konkrete Poesie.* Bloomington: Indiana UP, 1972.

Holenstein, Elmar. *Roman Jakobson's Approach to Language.* Trans. by Catherine Schelbert & Tarcisius Shelbert. Bloomington: Indiana University Press, 1976.

Hollander, John. *Types of Shape.* New Haven: Yale UP, 1991.

Jakobson, Roman. "Linguistics and Poetics." *Language in Literature.* Ed. Krystya Pomorska & Stephen Rudy. Cambridge, MS: The Belknap Press of Harvard UP, 1987.

Jakobson, Roman & Morris Halle. *Fundamentals of Language.* The Hague: Mouton Publishers, 1980.

Kenner, Hugh. *The Art of Poetry.* 1959.

Lotz, John. "Elements of Versification." *Versification: Major Language Types.* Ed. W. K. Wimsatt. New York: Modern Language Association, 1972.

Mukarovsky, Jan. "Standard Language and Poetic Language." *Linguistics and Literary Style.* Ed. Donald C. Freeman. New York: Holt, Rinehart & Winston, 1970.

Northrop Frye, et al. *The Harper Handbook to Literature.* New York: Harper & Row, 1985.

Pratt, Mary Louise, *Toward a Speech Act Theory of Literary Discourse.* Bloomington: Indiana University Press, 1977.

Perrine, Laurence, ed. *Sound and Sense.* 5th Edition. New York: Harcourt Brace Jovanovich, 1977.

Preminger, Alex, ed. *The Princeton Handbook of Poetic Terms.* Princeton, NJ: Princeton UP, 1986.

Solt, Mary E., ed. *Concrete Poetry: A World View.* Bloomington: Indiana UP, 1968.

Swenson, May. *Iconographs.* New York: Scribner, 1970.

Thrall, William F.& Addison Hibbard. *A Handbook to Literature.* Revised by C. Hugh Holman. New York: Oddyssey Press, 1972.

Traugott, Elizabeth Closs & Mary Louise Pratt. *Linguistics for Students of Literature.* New York: Harcourt Brace Jovanovich, 1980.

Tung, C. H. "The Nature and the Locus of 'Literariness,'" *Studies in English Literature and Linguistics.* Taipei: Taiwan Normal University, 1990

--------. *Imagination and the Process of Literary Creation.* Taipei: Bookman Books, 1991.

--------. "A New Linguistic Analysis of Arnold's 'Dover Beach.'" *Studies in English Literature and Linguistics.* Taipei: Taiwan Normal University, 1992.

--------. *The Scene of Textualization.* Taipei: Bookman Books, 1992.

Williams, Emmett, ed. *An Anthology of Concrete Poetry.* New York: Something Else Press, 1967.

York, R. A.   *The Poem as Utterance.*   London & New York: Methuen, 1986.

*This paper first appeared in 1994 in *Proceedings of NSC,* Part C, Vol. 4, No. 1, 68-75.

Work, Text, Discourse:
Literary Problems, Old and New

It is often noted that Roland Barthes regards the movement from structuralism to post-structuralism as a movement from "work" to "text."[1] Indeed, as we enter the post-structuralist or postmodern era, the term "text" seems to come into vogue suddenly in the literary circle; it is often used to replace the term "work" wherever possible.   However, "text" is not the only word to enjoy critical popularity in our era.   Almost at the same time, or maybe somewhat later, the term "discourse" has begun to come into fashion, too.   Thus, today we frequently find instances of referring to a piece of literature as a literary "discourse," rather than as a literary "work" or "text."

The shift from "work" to "text" and to "discourse" has, of course, its reasons.   It may be due to some change in our entire critical climate.   Or it may be caused by some individual, influential critics (such as Barthes and Foucault) who popularized their preferred terms.   But we are not here to account for the reasons.   We are here, instead, to probe into the implications of this shift in terms.

To be sure, none of the three words are neologisms.   But the words "text" and "discourse" have obviously acquired new meanings as they are used to replace the word "work."   In a book of mine (*The Scene of Textualization*), I have explored the concept of the text.   And I have reached the following conclusion:

The text is not necessarily restricted to a literary or artistic text. All things, great and small, can in fact be viewed as texts. For everything must needs possess a structured pattern of its own, and the idea of structured pattern (or, web, network, fabric, etc.) is the essential quality of the text. But normally when we talk about the text, we refer to the structured pattern of words, that is, a discourse, or a linguistic/literary text, which can be either oral or written, long or short. The literary text is usually written or printed, though in modern times oral literature can be recorded and keep its auditory nature. Besides, a literary text normally does not stop at a sentence, as does a linguistic text. It usually refers to a work or part of a work of some length. Furthermore, the literary text is not limited to its physical appearance of sound and shape. It denotes, too, the structure of sense that goes with the sound and shape. Now, the structuring principle of the (literary) text is indeed unity—cohesion of form and coherence of content—which is ensured by paradigmatic and syntagmatic arrangements (selection and combination). However, in constructing such a unified text, various factors have entered it as necessary and concomitant influences. The factors include the text-producer's intentionality, the textual message or information, the text-receiver's responsive attitude and the situation in which the text with its producer and receiver lies. Finally, it is found that every text has its intertext and context. A text may be considered as lying independently of other texts. But actually it keeps a sort of relationship with all other texts. It is first of all one of the texts which constitute the context. It may contain smaller texts within itself and be their context. It may be just a small text interrelated with other small texts which are its intertexts (or sometimes confusingly called context) or related to its larger embedding text as a subtext. Anyway, the world is indeed a text replete with all sorts of texts, each of which again contain smaller texts, and so proceed ad infinitum. (Tung, 1992, 30-31)

How, then, is the text different from the work? In another book of mine (*Imagination and the Process of Literary Creation*), I have suggested that a work is to a text what a garment is to a piece of cloth (Tung, 1991, 156-7). There are a number of implications in this analogical comparison. First, it implies that a work is always a text, but not vice versa (just as a garment is cloth, but a piece of cloth is not necessarily a garment). The second implication is: both the work and the text are indeed like fabrics. Just as clothes and cloth are both woven materials, so are the work and the text both woven with sound, shape, and sense. However, we have the third implication: although both the work and the text have their respective boundaries or demarcations, the boundary or demarcation of the work is more conspicuously fixed and seen than that of the text, just as the boundary or demarcation of a garment is more plainly fixed and perceived than a piece of cloth. (Here we must admit that Barthes and many other critics are correct in suggesting the openness of the text in contrast with the closedness of the work, though Barthes's idea that the text is boundlessly open, while the work is tightly closed, is impractical.) This, then, leads to the fourth implication: the work is further designed than the text, just as a suit of clothes is further designed that a piece of cloth. And the final crowning implication is: the work is designed and used more consciously for ethical and aesthetic as well as practical purposes. Writers write works to teach and delight as well as to provide reading material. Similarly, tailors make clothes to appeal to our sense of decency and beauty in addition to providing us with a mass of warming material. In contrast, like a piece of cloth, the text is often thought of as a mere pattern of material waiting for further designing and utilization so that specific ethical and aesthetic purposes can be achieved in addition to its basic material use.

This last point brings us to the understanding that "work" is more an author-oriented concept than "text" while the latter concept contains a more objective view than the former. Traditionally, we believe God created the world and we regard the world as God's "work." We guess the Great Author had His intention in accomplishing this "work" although we may not know what intention it was. Then, as Romantics supposed, the poet is also a creator, a great author capable of producing a "work" through his genius. In contrast, when a formalist or structuralist speaks about the "text" of a work, he is concentrating on its components and the way they are organized—the so-called textuality or textual details. He is, in a word, treating the text as a mere object, regardless of its author.

What, then, is implied in the concept of "discourse"? Originally, "discourse" referred to the formal exposition (a dissertation, treatise, sermon, etc.) in speech or writing of a particular subject. In that sense it is, of course, a "work" or a "text" (as no one denies that Descartes' *Discourse on Method* is). But today this term has assumed a wider range of meaning than that. In linguistics it has come to stand for a unit of language larger than the sentence, stressing at the same time our "communicative competence," which enables us to say the right thing at the right time. Thus, one of the aims of discourse analysis is "to show how a knowledge of conventions for links between sentences and for links with context is a necessary condition of successful communication" (Fowler 62).

In his *How to Do Things with Words*, J. L. Austin distinguishes three types of speech act: locutionary act, which is to make an utterance with a certain sense and reference; illocutionary act, which is to accomplish some communicative purpose by making an utterance; and perlocutionary act, which brings about or achieves a certain effect by saying something (Austin, 94-120). According to this distinction, then, we can say that the idea of "text" is linked preeminently to literature as a locutionary act, the idea of "work" to literature as an illocutionary act, and the idea of "discourse" to literature as a perlocutionary act, as the three ideas suggest emphasis, respectively, on the objective, the genetic, and the affective nature of literature.

Our renewed reliance upon the term "discourse" is indeed related to the growth in importance of pragmatics (Hawthorn 46). However, the term owes its popularity in the critical circle primarily to the influence of Michel Foucault. In his *The Archaeology of Knowledge*, Foucault conceives discourse as "large groups of statements" which are rule-governed language terrains based not on a well-defined field of objects, nor on a definite, normative type of statement, not on a well-defined alphabet of notions, nor on permanence of a thematic, but on "rather various strategic possibilities that permit the activation of incompatible themes," or on "a system of dispersion" which allows the "discursive formation" (Foucault, 1972, 37-38). According to this concept, then, all societies have procedures by which to govern discursive practices, discursive objects, and discursive strategies so that discursive regularities may be produced to ward off certain "powers and dangers" (Foucault, 1981, 52).

No matter what nuances of meaning it may have, Foucault's notion of "Discourse" is obviously a situation-based or context-bound notion of language, a notion conducive to the development of the present ethos of cultural studies. Today, when we talk about feminist issues, postmodern conditions, or postcolonial problems; when we complain about "sexual politics," question about "grand narratives," or argue with "Orientalism," we are engaged in discourses in the Foucauldian sense, no matter what state of "hegemony," what sort of "ideology," or what kind of "otherness" we are concerned with, in this world of multiplicity, heterogeneity, and disintegrity.

In his Introduction to the third edition of *A Reader's Guide to Contemporary Literary Theory*, Peter Widdowson uses Roman Jakobson's famous diagram of linguistic communication to explain that literary theory can be oriented towards the writer, the context, the writing, the code, or the reader (Selden 3-4). And he suggests that the romantic-humanist, the Marxist, the formalistic, the structuralist, and the reader-oriented theories of our time correspond to those five orientations (Selden 4). This is all true. But I must add that the writer-oriented (Romantic-humanist) theories cling more to the idea of "work," and the context-oriented (Marxist) theories tend to favor the idea of "discourse" while the code-oriented (structuralist) theories mainly take to the idea of "text," if we cannot be certain what other theories prefer which term. Indeed, the whole *Reader's Guide* covers a history of how the three words "work," "text," and discourse" are variously adopted and adapted for use by Western contemporary literary theory.

Recently, in an international conference of literary theory, J. Hillis Miller presented a paper entitled "Black Holes in the Internet Galaxy: New Trends in Literary Study in the United State."[2] In that paper, Miller traces three periods of American literary study which make up the "new trends": the epoch of the New Criticism, which came after 1945; the heyday of theory ("theory structuralist, semiological, phenomenological, reader response, Marxist, Lacanian, or Foucauldian, but especially and quintessentially deconstructionist theory"), which superseded the New Criticism in the 'sixties, 'seventies, and early 'eighties; and the present era of cultural studies, which came around 1980. These three phases of literary study can in fact be represented by the three terms—work, text, discourse—respectively. For the American New Criticism, with its emphasis on the work as an organic form possessing in it "unity," "irony," "paradox," "tension," or "ambiguity," was still a humanist theory recognizing a great work of literature as something capable of promoting the values of human life, although it warns the reader not to commit "the intentional fallacy" or "the affective fallacy." Later, however, when the structuralist and some poststructuralist theories came to hold controversy over the nature of the text—to proclaim "the death of the author," to get into the "hermeneutic circle," to ask "Is there a text in this class?" and to probe into all sorts of "logocentrism"—the notion of the work as an embodiment of human values was replaced by the notion of literature as mere language, mere "tropes," mere signs devoid of origins and useful only as the object of scientific investigation or philosophical speculation.   In a word, the second new phase of literary study was concentrated on the text, not on the context.   To take the context into consideration is the concern of the cultural studies today.   The so-called "new historicism," for instant, is a fairly diverse body of scholarship dealing with, among other things, "the importance of local political and social contexts for the understanding of literary texts," based upon the assumption that "in a given historical moment, different modes of discourse ... are rarely if ever autonomous" (Wayne 793).

So far I have roughly defined the connotations of the three words "work," "text," and "discourse" in connection with the history of modern literary criticism.   Here with no scruple about oversimplification, I may say this: As literature is a way of language, a literary "work" stresses language in origin; a literary "text," language in code; a literary "discourse," language in use.   But does this shift in stress as evidenced by the use of the three key words merely occur in our age (after the New Criticism)?

The answer to the question is, of course, "No."   My contention is : ever since mankind had literature, literary problems have been essentially the same. New problems always take origin in old ones.   Thus, the problems associated with the modern ideas of "work," "text," and "discourse" can be traced back to very ancient times.

Take Plato's *Dialogues* for example.   When Socrates said that all good poets, epic as well as lyric, compose their beautiful poems not by art, but because they are inspired and possessed, he was seemingly answering the question: Where does poetry come from? Or what sort of person is a poet?[3] Plainly, for Socrates and Plato, poetry comes from the Muse, who possesses and inspires the poet, or from the poet, who is divinely possessed and inspired.

This theory (or belief) is, of course, challenged again and again throughout later Western history. In the neoclassical period, for instance, Pope asserted famously that "True ease in writing comes from art, not chance,/ As those move easiest who have learned to dance" (*An Essay on Criticism*, II. 362-3). For Pope and for many other neoclassical critics, the poet is but a craftsman, somewhat like a carpenter, who is not a divinely possessed and inspired person, but learns his art through much experience. So the issue becomes: Is the poet (the author) a divinely inspired person or a learned craftsman? Later, the Romantics apparently tended towards holding the former concept, because they believed the poet to be a genius, who, as Edward Young suggested, "differs from a good understanding, as a magician from a good architect."[4] Now, in our century people are still puzzling over this issue. When Sigmund Freud reduces a man of letters to a neurotic case, a daydreamer, who fantasies by creating literature to fulfill his repressed desire, he seems to believe that the author is indeed a "mad" person, but not "divinely mad." When in his "Tradition and the Individual Talent" T. S. Eliot compares the poet to a catalyst and holds that "the poet has, not a 'personality' to express, but a particular medium, which is only a medium and not a personality" (Adams, 786), is he negating the divine quality or the craftsmanship in a poet? He seems to be doing both, although we know his emphasis on tradition and the "historical sense" is an anti-romantic position leaning towards the idea of craftsmanship. Anyway, he is in line with the structuralists who proclaim "the death of the author" and try to forget the authorial origin of the work.

So, from ancient times up to the present, we are forever approaching the same literary problem: If literature comes from the literary man, what sort of person is he? As we try to provide the answer, we may, unknowingly perhaps, rely particularly on certain ideas. To be specific, those who believe that literature is created by a divinely possessed or inspired man, as well as those who believe that literature is made by a skillful craftsman, necessarily acknowledge that what is created or made is a "work," an achievement of power or effort.   In contrast, those who think of literature not as something accomplished through someone's power or effort—for example, those who think of literature as merely the composite of linguistic signs the code of which is "always already written," or those who think of it as a form of powerful language controlled by someone who need not be the author—will naturally consider literature not in terms of "work" but in terms of "text" or "discourse."

Whereas the idea of "work" is necessarily connected with the expressive theory of literature—which regards literature as a form of expression derived from the author who may be a divinely inspired prophet (*vates*) "possessed" by a muse or fundamentally a craftsman (*poeta*, "maker") who is fully conscious of what he is doing both at the moment of composition and afterwards—the idea of "text" is befittingly linked to the mimetic theory, which regards literature as a way of reproducing or recreating the experience of life in words, just as painting reproduces or recreates certain figures or scenes of life in outline and color.   And this theory also goes back to Plato although the term "text" did not prevail at his time.

In the *Republic*, we may remember, Plato tells us that reality is an ideal form, or the absolute One behind the many (the light whose shadows only are visible to mankind in its cave).   Anything in this world, therefore, is for him but an imitation or copy of the real.   If a chair or a bed made by a carpenter is at one remove from the real, a picture or a verbal description of a chair or a bed is then twice removed from reality, since the painter or the writer copies from the carpenter's chair or bed.   So, in Plato's mind literature is but a copy of a copy.   And that is one reason why he would not allow poetry a high place in his ideal state.

Plato's theory of imitation was repeatedly modified, of course, in subsequent times.   Aristotle first dropped out the negative sense of imitation in his *Poetics*.   When he called epic poetry, tragedy, comedy, dithyrambic poetry, and even the music of the flute and lyre "modes of imitation" (*mimesis*), he meant positively the representation or recreation of life—a sense taken over by Renaissance defenders of poetry like Sir Philip Sidney or neoclassical critics like Samuel Johnson. But is the literary representation of life a faithful copying like photographic reproduction? Some Realists or Naturalists seem to suggest that, though we know it is impossible. And does the literary recreation of life become a highly idealized version of it? Some Romantics seem to make it so, and thus cause some revolting outcries from Realists or Naturalists.

Today, one may not know it, but many contemporary theorists are again centering around the idea of imitation. When the structuralists talk of the distinction between *langue* (language) and *parole* (articulated speech), between system and syntagm, or between competence and performance, they are in fact implicitly echoing Plato's distinction between the Real World of Ideas and the unreal world of phenomenal objects. It is true that the stucturalists never say *parole* (syntagm, performance) is a copy or imitation or *langue* (system, competence), and they never assert which is the real and which is the unreal. Yet, by pronouncing that we must "use language as the norm of all other manifestations of speech" (Saussure, 9), any structuralist is suggesting indeed that *langue* is the stable and real from which *parole* derives. Hence, we can deduce from this structuralist idea that parole is derivatively a copy or imitation of *langue*.

For Jacques Derrida, as we know, there is no absolute "being as presence." He pointed out that we all tend to become logocentric, adopting terms to operate as centering principle and not knowing that all terms are but signs which exist in a state of "diffèrance" and which, therefore, cannot become a full presence though they can "supplement" one another. In actuality, these Derridean concepts are again related to Plato's concepts. While Plato believes in the existence of a transcendental world of Ideas which, being real, serves as the absolute being of stable and full presence, Derrida negates such an existence. What Derrida conceives is a world of endless copying, a world in which signs represent each other or terms "imitate" each other by a process of supplement (addition-substitution) and *différance* (differing in spatial quality of terms and deferring in temporal presence of meaning). Thus, nothing is "real" (has stable presence) and nothing is identical with any other thing, just as no copy is completely equal to its original.

The above discussion shows that structuralist and deconstructionist thinkers are in truth investigators, like Plato and other classical and neoclassical critics, who try to answer the same old philosophical questions: Is there reality? What is it? What stands for it? Within the confines of literary consideration, they evidently take all concrete literary texts for mere representations or imitations of something else, be it reality or not. And interestingly enough, the idea of representation/imitation is also embedded in a Marxist theory like Georg Lukàcs'. Lukàcs, as we know, considers literature as a special form of reflecting reality. For him, the truly realistic work possesses an "intensive totality" which corresponds to the "extensive totality" of the world itself (Selden, 76; Adams, 797).

No matter what school of critics propounds it in whatever way it prefers, any mimetic theory of literature is in essence a theory most favorable to the substitution of the idea "text" for "work." For when we mention imitation or copying, we cannot but have the idea of sameness in mind. And the idea of sameness links itself most easily, of course, to the shapes or structures of the objects compared. Now, as I have said in the earlier part of this essay, the term "text" is the very one that stresses the idea of patterning or structuring. No wonder people keep talking about "the plural text," the "readerly vs. writerly text," the "open vs. closed text," etc., when they draw their attention to the act of reading and writing as the creating/making/producing of various texts for further textualization.[5]

So far we have touched on the expressive and mimetic theories of literature and argued that, in considering the literary problems they are concerned with, they naturally favor "work" and "text," respectively, for their critical terms when they refer to concrete pieces of literature, no matter whether the theories are propounded in the remote past or in our present time. It remains now for us to deal with a third class of theories, the affective or pragmatic ones, which has much to do with the idea of "discourse."

Again, the third class of theories must go back to classical antiquity. Plato, it is well known, wanted to prohibit poetry in his ideal state of reason, because poetry "feeds and waters the passions instead of drying them up" (Trilling, 51). His disciple, Aristotle, did not prejudice against poetry as he did. But Aristotle's idea of *catharsis* also calls attention to the effect of literary art. So, from ancient times, people have been trying to answer the question: What does (or should) literature do to us? After Aristotle, Quintilian emphasized that literature aims to move the audience and thereby give pleasure. Horace, in his *Ars Poetica*, is best remembered for stating that poets either teach or delight, at their best combining the useful and the delightful. After Horace, critics have emphasized sometimes the useful, sometimes the delightful. A neoclassical critic like Samuel Johnson would underscore the moral (useful) principle of literature. In contrast, a 19th-centruty esthete like Edgar Allan Poe would stress the pleasure principle.

In our century, some Soviet Socialists have aligned themselves with Lenin's idea of "Party Literature" to make literature "useful" in the sense that it serves some political purposes. Bertolt Brecht, with his ideas of "epic theater" and "alienation effect," also proposes that dramaturgy should help educate the audience and move them to action, rather than let them indulge in passive emotional identification with characters in the play. In her *la revolution du langage poetique,* Julia Kristeva even believes that radical social change can be achieved through the disruption of authoritarian discourses: poetic language with its subversive openness of "the semiotic" can disrupt society's closed order of "the symbolic" (Selden, 142). And Michel Foucault, of course, is most impressive and influential in theorizing the close connection of literary discourse with power. Indeed, he has opened the way to a non-truth-oriented form of history study called "New Historicism." And he has assisted in giving rise to such postcolonial criticism as attacking any repressive ethnocentrism in literature.

Certainly, literary critics never cease to consider the function of literature and look into how literature works to affect people. And, certainly, in the course of postulating theories regarding the same old literary problems, the critics may not stick to the principle of referring to a body or bulk of literature as "discourse" rather than as "work" or "text." Nevertheless, it is undoubtedly true that those who take into account the social, political, and cultural aspects of literature, especially those who see literature not just as a "reflection" of reality but as a purposeful "refraction" or even "reaction" from socio-political reality, will necessarily resort to the word "discourse." For, as stated above, the word implies language in use, brings forth the "perlocutionary force," and best represents the critic's attitude towards the use of literature. Or, as Paul A. Bove has suggested, "discourse" provides a privileged entry into the poststructuralist mode of analysis precisely because it is the organized and regulated, as well as regulating and constituting, functions of language that it studies: its aim is to describe the surface linkages between power, knowledge, institutions, intellectuals, the control of populations, and the modern state as these intersect in the functions of systems of thought (Lentricchia, 54-55).

In conclusion, then, we have probed into the implications that go with the words "work," "text," and "discourse" which have been admitted into critical terminology and enjoyed different degrees of popularity in different ages. And we have associated the three words with three traditional classes of literary theories: expressive, mimetic, and affective. We have, furthermore, come to realize that actually the literary problems that accompany the theories—the origin, reference, and function of literature (What sort of person creates/makes/produces literature? How is literature related to reality? And what does literature do?)—have been approached from different angles with different solutions. Yet, all the same. New critics are not nearer to the "truth" (if any) than old ones. By using "text" or "discourse" to replace the old-fashioned "work," our contemporary theories are merely emphasizing their standpoints at best. After all, a new term is but a new trope, or a new "floating signifier," in the rhetoric of criticism. It has no full presence at any time.

Notes

1. This idea of Barthes', appearing in his *Image-Music-Text* (1977) and reprinted in Josue V. Harari, ed., *Textual Strategies* (1979), is noted in Eagleton's *Literary Theory: An Introduction*, p. 138.
2. The paper was presented on December 16, 1994, at National Sun Yat-sen University, in Kaohsiung, Taiwan.
3. In fact, of course, Socrates was explaining to Ion why a rhapsode could have the gift of speaking excellently about a poet like Homer. (See "Ion.")
4. Edward Young's *Conjectures upon Original Composition*, in Hazard Adams, ed., *Critical Theory Since Plato*, p.341. Although Wordsworth said that a poet is "a man speaking to men," he added that a poet is a man "endowed with more lively sensibility, ... and a more comprehensive soul, than are supposed to be common among mankind." For a good discussion of the development of the idea of genius, see Wimsatt and Brooks, pp. 283-312.
5. In my paper "Reading and Writing as Text Changes," I have discussed fully the ideas of reading and writing as merely changing external texts to internal texts and vice versa. See *Journal of the College of Liberal Arts*, Chung Hsing University, Vol. XIX (1989), 1-10.

Works Consulted

Adams, Hazard. *Critical Theory Since Plato.* New York: Harcourt Brace Jovanovich, 1971.

Adams, Hazard & Searle, Leroy, eds. *Critical Theory Since 1965.* Tallahassee: Florida State UP, 1986.

Austin, J. L. *How to Do Things with Words*, 2nd ed., Oxford & New York: Oxford UP, 1976.

Eagleton, Terry. *Literary Theory: An Introduction.* Oxford: Basil Blackwell, 1983.

Foucault, Michel. *The Archaeology of Knowledge and the Discourse on Language*, translated by A. M. Sheridan Smith. New York: Pantheon Books, 1972.

--------. "The Order of Discourse" in Robert Young, ed., *Untying the Text.* London & New York: Routledge & Kegan Paul, 1987, 48-78.

Fowler, Roger. *A Dictionary of Modern Critical Terms*, revised & enlarged ed. London & New York: Routledge & Kegan Paul, 1987.

Harari, Josue, ed. *Textual Strategies: Perspectives in Post- Structuralist Criticism.* Ithaca, N.Y.: Cornell UP, 1979.

Hawthorn, Jeremy. *A Concise Glossary of Contemporary Literary Theory.* London: Edward Arnold, 1992.

Lentricchia, Frank & Mclaughlin, Thomas. *Critical Terms for Literary Study.* Chicago & London: The U of Chicago P, 1990.

Lukacs, Georg. "Art and Objective Truth," in Adams & Searle, 791-807.

Saussure, Ferdinad de. *Course in General Linguistics.* Ed. Charles Bally, et al., translated by Wade Baskin. New York: McGraw-Hill, 1959.

Selden, Raman & Widdowson, Peter. *A Reader's Guide to Contemporary Literary Theory*, 3rd ed. New York & London: Harvester Wheatsheaf, 1993.

Tung, C. H. *Imagination and the Process of Literary Creation.* Taipei: Bookman Books, 1991.

--------. *The Scene of Textualization: A Genetic Consideration of Literature.* Taipei: Bookman Books, 1992.

Wayne, Don E. "New Historicism" in Martin Coyle, et al., eds. *Encyclopedia of Literature and Criticism.* London: Routledge, 1990. 791-805.

Wimsatt, W. K. Jr. & Brooks, Cleanth. *Literary Criticism: A Short History.* New York: Vintage Books, 1957.

* This paper first appeared in 1995 in *JAL*, pp. 31-44.

Is the Author "Dead" Already?

I. The Rhetorical Nature of Theory and Criticism

Our era is witnessing a booming market of literary theories and a flourishing business of critical trade. As commerce is practical, rather than theoretical, our critical industry tends naturally to meet competitions more by finding fault with others than by playing fair games. Thus, our theory-mongers or criticism-traffickers are often (intentionally) blind to their own shortcomings, and they often claim their insight, if any, to be the only valuable insight. They forget that any theory is but a partial truth at best, not a universal law. They also forget that any critical act is but a matter of sheer rhetoric, which is an art employed to persuade others by verbal means, not necessarily to lead them to a comprehension of any absolute truth.

Rhetoricians recognize two basic rhetorical devices: metaphor and metonymy. But the two devices are used not only by orators (as in the past) or authors of literature in the narrow sense of the word (poetry, drama, fiction, etc.) but also by literary theorists or critics, who theorize about literature or criticize literary works. Consider, for instance, the two statements below:

1. "The birth of the reader must be at the cost of the death of the Author." (Barthes, 148)
2. "The author-function is ... characteristic of the mode of existence, circulation, and functioning of certain discourses within a society." (Foucault, 148)

In the first statement, Roland Barthes talks about the "birth" of the reader and the "death" of the author. Yet, we know "birth" and "death" here are but metaphors: they do not refer to the acts of coming into existence and ceasing to be, respectively. From their context we know they refer, rather, to the fact that in determining the meaning of any text, the reader cannot gain his importance until the author loses his dominating place, just as the son must eventually replace the father in terms of authority in the natural course of birth and death. In the second statement, Michel Foucault is talking about the function of an author. Yet, here by "an author" he does not mean the *originator* of a literary work or some literary works. Instead, he means the author's *name*, which, according to his argument, "does not pass from the interior of a discourse to the real and exterior individual who produced it," but "manifests the appearance of a certain discursive set and indicates the status of this discourse within a society and a culture" (147). So, he is here talking about the author metonymically, using part of an object (the author's name) to represent the whole object (the entire author with his name, body, life, works, etc.).

The above two examples show clearly that literary theorists or critics, no less than creative writers of literature, must of necessity make use of tropes (figures of speech) from time to time to state their ideas. This fact naturally links theory and criticism, as well as literature, to the discipline of rhetoric—a fact Paul de Man has demonstrated convincingly in his *Allegories of Reading*.

II. The Historical Statuses of the Author in the West

Concerning the author, Western thinkers or writers have had all sorts of their say. But just as pointed out in the foregoing section, whatever they say about the author is always tinged with rhetorical purposes and devices. We may well divide those thinkers or writers into two camps: the detractors-plaintiffs and the extollers-defendants of the author, based on consideration of whether or not they talk about the author favorably. (In doing so, we are using tropes ourselves.) Furthermore, we may regard them as judges of the author's historical statuses, determining with their power of discourse the "birth, life, and death" of that species of men and women whom we most generally call "the author," "the artist," or "the writer," but sometimes more particularly call "the poet," "the playwright," "the novelist," "the essayist," or any other name pertaining to a specific genre of literature.

Now, let us discuss the matter in detail. As is well known, Plato was a great detractor of the poet. The poet in his mind was, of course, not exactly the kind of poet in our mind today. The poet, as he conceived, actually referred more to either an epic writer or a dramatist than to a lyricist. Anyway, the kind of author called "the poet" was for Plato not a trustworthy person. In *Ion* he records Socrates as saying that "the poet is a light and winged and holy thing, and there is no invention in him until he has been inspired and is out of his senses, and reason is no longer in him"(14-15). Although the poet is here regarded as a "holy thing," he is said to be "out of his senses" when he is inspired. Later, in *The Republic*, the poet is further disparaged as an inferior imitator (as he only imitates imitations), a liar (about gods), and a bad influence (whose poetry "feeds and waters the passions instead of drying them up"). Thus, the poet was for Plato a dangerous person pedagogically, metaphysically, ethically, and politically. He was therefore sentenced to be banished from the philosopher's ideal state, if not to "die" in it.

After Plato's sentence of banishment, there followed a succession of defendants trying to "legitimate" the poet's stay in any state. Plato's disciple Aristotle admits in his *Poetics* that "Epic poetry and tragedy, comedy also and dithyrambic poetry, and the music of the flute and of the lyre in most of their forms, are all in their general conception modes of imitation" (48). But, unlike Plato, he did not debase artistic imitation. He thought, instead, that

"Imitation … is one instinct of our nature" (50). And his analytical explanation of poetical genres, especially tragedy, implies that the poet is a creator of forms, an artist in the sense that he is able to make such "parts" as "plot, character, diction, thought, spectacle, and song" cohere into a form worthy of its genre.

The idea of imitation gains a second sense in Horace's *Art of Poetry*. For both Plato and Aristotle, imitation means "imitation of nature or real life." For Horace, however, a trained artist's imitation can mean not only "to take as his model real life and manners" (73), but also to "thumb well by night and day Greek models" (72). Thus, the author becomes an imitator of other writers as well as of life and nature. Besides, as Horace proposes that the aim of the poet is "either to benefit, or to amuse, or to make his words at once please and give lessons of life" (73), he is suggesting that the poet is both an entertainer and an instructor. And as the entire *Ars Poetica* is full of guiding principles for a writer's craft, it implies that Horace regarded the artist as a craftsman, rather than as a creator.

Longinus might be the first known expressive theorist of literature in the West. In his *On the Sublime*, he holds that "sublimity is the echo of a great soul," and that "the truly eloquent must be free from low and ignoble thoughts" (81). For him, therefore, a great poet is a person with elevation of mind and is capable of "forming great conceptions" and producing "vehement and inspired passion" (80). Thus, in his view the author is an expresser of his own soul, not a mere medium who utters the Muse's words when he is possessed.

The neo-Platonic philosopher Plotinus believes that the beauty of the artist's creation lies not in any physical object that it copies, nor in any matter that it shapes, but in what the artist imposes on his materials. The arts "give no bare reproduction of the thing seen but go back to the reason-principles from which nature itself derives, and, furthermore, that much of their work is all their own; they are holders of beauty and add where nature is lacking"

(106). In contrast to Plato, he considers the artist a creator of vehicles of valuable, spiritual insight into the One, which is "a unity working out into detail"(109).

Renaissance men were mostly defenders of the author. In defense of the poet, for instance, Boccaccio argues that "however he may sacrifice the literal truth in invention, [the poet] does not incur the ignominy of a liar, since he discharges his very proper function not to deceive, but only by way of invention" (131). Moreover, as fervid and exquisite inventors, poets are not merely apes of the philosophers, but "should be reckoned of the number of the philosophers, since they never veil with their inventions anything which is not wholly consonant with philosophy as judged by the opinions of the ancients" (134). Finally, Boccaccio even claims that the pagan poets of mythology are theologians since "they clothe many a physical and moral truth in their inventions" (135).

For Scaliger, "the poet depicts quite another sort of nature, and a variety of fortunes; in fact, by so doing, he transforms himself almost into a second deity" (139). Another Renaissance scholar, Castelvetro, does not regard the poet so highly as Scaliger does. Nevertheless, he also speaks for the poet because he concludes that "poetry is conceived and practiced by the gifted man and not the madman, as some have said, for the madman is not able to assume various passions, nor is he a careful observer of what impassioned men say and do" (152).

The Puritan Stephen Gosson reverted to Plato's unfavorable attitude towards poetry. In his *School of Abuse*, he treated the poet as one of "the caterpillars of a commonwealth," a waster of time, a mother of lies, and a nurse of abuse. It was to answer such attacks that Sidney wrote his *An Apology for Poetry*, in which besides rebuffing Gosson's points, he avers that the poet is in fact a moderator between the philosopher and the historian, "the food for the tenderest stomachs," and "indeed the right popular philosopher" (160-61).

In the Neoclassical Period, important literary figures such as Boileau and Pope followed basically the classical idea of the author as a craftsman whose art it is to imitate nature and classical writers and plan and polish his work with pains. This idea is of course refuted later by Romantic writers. Edward Young, for instance, thinks of the artist as an original or a man of genius, who has "the power of accomplishing great things without the means generally reputed necessary to that end" (341). William Blake also believes in the poet's genius. And for him genius is always connected with the power of arousing inspiration, imagination, or vision. In contrast, William Wordsworth tries to play down the idea of "genius." He tells us that the poet is but "a man speaking to men" (437). But with the addition that the man, however, is "endowed with more lively sensibility, more enthusiasm and tenderness, who has greater knowledge of human nature, and a more comprehensive soul, than are supposed to be common among mankind ..." (437), he actually maintains that the poet is an extraordinary man, if not a genius. In truth, Wordsworth carries not only the expressive theorist's view that "poetry is the spontaneous overflow of [the poet's] powerful feelings" (441), but also the pragmatic view that the poet is "the rock of defense for human nature; an upholder and preserver, carrying everywhere with him relationship and love" (439).

In 1820, Thomas Love Peacock published a satirical treatise titled "The Four Ages of Poetry," aiming to ridicule his romantic contemporaries. This satire, however, brings forth the idea that poetry has been evolving in a cycle of four ages: iron, gold, silver, brass. And this idea of evolution consequently suggests that the poet suffers historical changes, too. In the iron age, poets are only rude bards celebrating "in rough numbers the exploits of ruder chiefs ..." (491). In the golden age, poets are "the greatest intellects" such as Homer and Shakespeare. In the silver age, poets can be either imitative or original, but such figures as Virgil and Pope mostly try to recast the poetry of the age of gold by giving an exquisite polish to it. Then in the brass age, poets like Nonnus and Wordsworth are but semi-barbarians in civilized communities because they "take a retrograde stride to the barbarisms and rude traditions of the age of iron, professing to return to nature and revive the age of gold" (494). Such poets can be "splendid lunatics" or "puling drivellers" or "morbid dreamers" (496).

Peacock's satirical attack on poetry meets a vigorous answer in Shelley's *A Defense of Poetry*. In this vigorous defense, poets become institutors of laws, founders of civil society, inventors of the arts of life, good teachers, prophets, and unacknowledged legislators of the world. For Shelley, indeed, a poet is sometimes like a nightingale "who sits in darkness and sings to darkness and sings to cheer its own solitude with sweet sounds" (502). And sometimes a poet is like an Aeolian lyre, capable of making music in response to outward influences. But always a poet is more than a nightingale plus an Aeolian lyre: "as he is the author to others of the highest wisdom, pleasure, virtue and glory, so he ought personally to be the happiest, the best, the wisest, and the most illustrious of men" (512).

Across the Atlantic, Emerson joins with the English Romantics in extolling the kind of author called "the poet." He says that the poet "stands among partial men for the complete man, and apprises us not of his wealth, but of the common wealth" (545). "The poet is the sayer, the namer, and represents beauty" (546). Just because symbols, tropes, fables, oracles and all poetic forms have the effect of making us feel the power of emancipation and exhilaration, "poets are thus liberating gods" (551).

After the Romantic Movement, poetry seemed to yield gradually to fiction in importance. The succeeding movement, namely, Realism is in actuality more concerned with fiction writers than with poets. In his *The Experimental Novel*, for instance, Zola argues that the novelist is neither a mere copyist of nature, nor a photographer. The novelist is, instead, "equally an observer and an experimentalist" like a natural scientist (649). For Henry James, a novelist may not be such a scientist. Rather, a novelist may well be an utterer of personal impressions of life, since for him a novel is "in its broadest definition a personal, a direct impression of life" (664).   And since James emphasizes the stage of execution—"the execution belongs to the author alone; it is what is most personal to him, and we measure him by that" (664)—he seems to suggest that the novelist as an author is a great executer, who is able to finish his work artistically.

In the 20th century, the author is viewed from yet different angles.   In the mind of a psychoanalyst like Freud, a creative writer is merely a daydreamer, who fantasies just like a child at play.   For Jung, Freud's disciple, however, a creative writer becomes an expresser of "the collective unconscious" or racial memory, as the creative process "consists in the unconscious activation of an archetypal image, and in elaborating and shaping this image into the finished work" (818).   And for T. S. Eliot, "the poet has, not a 'personality' to express, but a particular medium, which is only a medium and not a personality, in which impressions and experiences combine in peculiar and unexpected ways" (786).   So, the poet is but a receptacle of tradition and a catalyst, whose mind is "the shred of platinum" with which to operate upon the experience of the man himself.

Ⅲ. The Author Facing Our Contemporary Theories

The second section above has given a general survey of how the author (often more specifically called the poet, the novelist, etc.) suffers continuous changes regarding his social status in the course of Western history.   In fact, the author's status suffers even more radical changes in our contemporary age when various literary theories swarm into our cultural market to compete for sales.   And this fact heats up the moot question of whether the author is "dead" or not.

Among our contemporary critical schools, the Anglo-American New Criticism can be counted as one of the most influential. With its sole concern with the "text in itself," as we know, this critical school (or movement) has purposely overlooked the importance of the author as the origin of the text. Such "New Critics" as Wimsatt and Beardsley even go so far as to warn us not to commit "the intentional fallacy" by caring about the author's original intention when we read a work. This position has indeed struck a chord with the poststructuralist notion of "the death of the author." However, since New Criticism sees the work as an organic form having in it "unity," "tension," "paradox," "irony," "ambiguity," etc., it implies that the author is a shaper, if not a creator, of that form.

Russian Formalism, it is said, helped to develop the Anglo-American New Criticism. It is like New Criticism in paying close attention to textual details. However, while New Criticism remains fundamentally humanistic, Russian Formalism has reduced literature to a purely scientific object fit only for the study of its method or devices in its linguistic aspect. Hence, no matter what content a work may have, it is supposed to owe its value to its form, to the fact that it can "defamiliarize" rather than "automatize" our perception by "laying bare" the formal devices or technique employed in the work. According to this doctrine, then, the author is a technician whose skill it is to bring about the artfulness or literariness of his product.

All Marxist theories agree that men's consciousness or ideology is determined by their social being or material existence. The great Marxist critic Georg Lukàcs, therefore, treats the work of art as a special form of reflecting reality, rather than as reality itself. For him, the truly realistic work possesses an "intensive totality" which corresponds to the "extensive totality" of the world itself. Accordingly, the author is overlooked, while the material world (especially in its socio-economic aspect) is highlighted, in this doctrine. It seems that the author is nothing but a bearer and presenter of a sort of ideology embodied somehow in his work.

Indeed, due to its material determinism, Marxist Criticism tends to slight the author's creativity or individuality. This tendency is even more manifest in the politically-controlled aesthetics of the Communist society. The Soviet socialist critics, for instance, want their writers to stick to the principles of *partinost* (partisanship), *narodnost* (popularity), and *Klassovost* (class nature). Consequently, in their view, writers are but supporters of party policies or class interests.

Literary structuralists or semioticians are of the opinion that literature is a cultural system, and any system, following its principles of structure or rules of signification, is composed of a definite number of selected elements or "signs" divisible into "signifiers" and "signifieds." A structuralist or semiotic critic like Vladimir Propp or A. J. Greimas, therefore, seeks to disclose the structural or signifying pattern (with its principles or rules) lying behind a bulk of literature (e.g., Russian fairy tales or all narrative stories). No matter whether this effort is worth while or not, it has led to the assumption that literature is "always already written"; any specific work (e.g., a Russian fairy story) is merely the result of applying some particular set of principles or rules already inherent in the genre or species of literature to which the work belongs. And this assumption, moreover, implies that the structural principles or signifying rules, rather than the author, are the real origin of the work. In consequence, the author is at best a mere applier of such principles or rules if he is not "dead" yet. In fact, those who support Roman Jakobson's theory of "metaphor and metonymy" are likewise suggesting that the author as such is a person who selects (paradigmatically) and combines (syntagmatically) textual elements into texts.

Roland Barthes, the critic who supposedly first proclaimed the death of the author is considered a structuralist at first and a poststructuralist at last. However, when he says, "The birth of the reader must be at the cost of the death of the author," he is a reader-oriented critic, too, besides being a structuralist negating the originality of the author and a poststructuralist asserting the multiplicity of reading. Like other reader-oriented theorists (e.g., Wolfgang Iser, Hans Robert Jauss, Jonathan Culler, etc.), Barthes actually focuses his attention on the reading process and emphasizes the importance of the reader in determining the meaning of the text. Therefore, the author is apparently "dead" to him indeed, as far as textual interpretation is concerned. It is only that whereas reader-oriented critics seldom specify the author's status (except, perhaps, suggesting that the author is a provider of texts for reading), Barthes has virtually reduced the author to nothing more than a scripter who draws a writing from "the immense dictionary" of culture. (147)

As a poststructuralist, Julia Kristeva relies much on Lacan's Freudian psychology for her distinction between "the semiotic" (the disorganized, irrational, pre-linguistic flux of material) and the "symbolic" (the regulated, rational, post-linguistic order of things). For her, poetic language is liberated from the unconscious. Thus, it is permeated with the semiotic and it has the power to subvert society's closed symbolic order. This theory consequently implies that the poet is a subverter of the social order (a "revolutionary" in that sense) through his poetic language.

Jacques Derrida's deconstructionist ideas (most importantly those of "logocentrism," "differance," and "supplementarity" have denied the real presence of any structural center, and viewed every human discourse as a sign "played" in an endless series of signification. Hence, for an author to write a work is for him to "play" with "floating signifiers" in the game of signification, never able to bring any determinate meaning to the performance. In this sense, the author is then a player in his artistic process, just as a musician is at his instrument.

The American deconstructionist Harold Bloom has evinced the theory that since Milton, poets have suffered an awareness of their "belatedness" and they are compelled to write belatedly, that is, to create an imaginative space by "misreading" their masters. Poets, thus, perform what he calls "poetic misprision" and bring forth revisionary texts.   According to this theory, then, the author becomes a revisionist, an intentional worker of "poetic misprision."

In his "What Is an Author?"   Michel Foucault tells us that an author's name "permits one to group together a certain number of texts, define them, differentiate them from and contrast them to others" (147).   Accordingly, as I have mentioned in the beginning of this essay, the author is for Foucault not an originator of works but a name functioning in social discourses.

In this postmodern era, image-creating communication technologies proliferate all sorts of self-mirroring images so much so that people like Jean Baudrillard envisage the appearance of the culture of "hyperreality" in which the real is lost while the depthless "simulacra" prevail.   In this world the best an artist can do seems to be mimic past styles without purpose or irony—an act called "pastiche" by Fredric Jameson.   In this view the author, then, is reduced to a practitioner of "pastiche," with his imagination, inspiration, and creativity all "dead."

Our era is also one in which sexual and racial problems become great critical issues.   Many feminist theorists have seen vast differences between both sexes in terms of biology, experience, discourse, the unconscious, and socioeconomic conditions.   As a result, female writing is said to be widely different from male writing.   And since our world has been dominated by "patriarchy," literature has easily become part of the male discourse which often regards women with bias or ignorance culminating in a sort of "phallocracy."   If this feminist theory is true, the author—especially the male author--is then a monomaniac obsessed with some partial views of both sexes.

Likewise, many postcolonialist critics have seen a repressive "ethnocentrism" in Western writing.   For them, therefore, literature is also biased through the author's ethnic identity.   Accordingly, the author is often a racist—another monomaniac, if only he is now obsessed with some partial views of certain races.

VI. **Is the Author "Dead" Already?**

In one book of mine (*The Scene of Textualization*), I point out that death is a universally compelling theme, but paradoxically it is not in the primeval time when we had little to guarantee our survival, but in the modern time when mass production promises our plenitude, that we have the keenest sense or, rather, fear of death. Today, this fear of death (or "moriphobia," as I choose to call it) has worsened to such an extent that we seem to see death everywhere. After Nietzsche proclaimed the death of God, our modern or postmodern men have proclaimed the death of man, of the author, of imagination, of literature, etc. But as I have pointed out in the beginning of this essay, when we talk of "death," we do not necessarily mean "the ceasing to function of a certain physical body" (as when we say a particular author—Shakespeare or Milton, for instance—died at a certain time). When we say "death," we are more often than not a rhetorician, using the term as a trope. When Nietzsche proclaimed "God is dead," he was trying to deprive Him of His authority, to deny His power of creation, to disown Him as the sole origin of Truth, and even to negate His omnipresence, rather than to assure us that God's body has ceased to function for Him in Heaven or anywhere. Similarly, when we ask "Is the Author dead already?" we do not mean to ask whether or not any particular author has died physically. We are, instead, interested in knowing whether or not the special group of writers called "the author" has lost its function or status in the human world.

This interesting question has been touched on by Richard Kearney. In his *The Wake of Imagination*, Kearney plausibly divides the whole (Western) world's cultural history into three major periods: the premodern, the modern, and the postmodern times. For him, the premodern world kept the *theocentric* quality of the icon; the modern world offers an *anthropocentric* trend, instead; and the postmodern world replaces both with an *ex-centric* paradigm of parody. As he further explains, the premodern cultures of

Jerusalem and Athens tended to construe the artist primarily as a *craftsman* who, at best, models his activity on the "original" activity of a Divine Creator. The modern movements of Renaissance, Romantic and Existentialist humanism, then, substituted the original *inventor* for the mimetic craftsman. But this anthropocentric figure is himself overturned in the postmodern time. All surprisingly, only a *bricoleur* comes to take his place. And this new artist, so called, is a "player" in a game of signs, an "operator" in an electronic media network.

Kearney obviously does not think that the author has ever "died" at any time in history. It is only that the author has *changed* his status or function from time to time—from a craftsman through an inventor to a *bricoleur*, for instance. I agree with Kearney on this point. In fact, in the second and third sections of this essay, I have discussed in even more detail how the author has been changing his status and function in the minds of different thinkers, critics, or writers. My discussion has also implied that the author really never dies; what has befallen him is only an endless series of "transformation." One can never gainsay that every literary work or text needs an author to come into being, no matter whether you call the author a poet, novelist, dramatist, essayist, imitator, artist, craftsman, inventor, liar, creator, genius, semi-barbarian, prophet, daydreamer, catalyst, subverter, monomaniac, or anything else you like. However, when people give the author an epithet other than "the author," they are often talking rhetorically of his changed status or function in a different social milieu. In that way, the history of the author is one of metamorphoses, rather than one of "being or not being." In that history, one kind of author is replaced by another from time to time as social and cultural conditions change in time. With this understanding, then, we can have this prospect: as computers become our daily necessity, in the foreseeable future the author may be no longer a "writer" who writes on book pages, but may become a "programmer" handling some kind of "software." At that time, we may of course declare that the *old kind* of author has fallen "dead." Yet, at the same time we must admit that a *new kind* of author has risen as successor. In that situation, the "race" of artists called "the author" certainly cannot be said to have become extinct. And our conclusion is: better than individuals, the author as a general species surely forever has "generations" to continue its life in this world, so long as men can breathe and eyes can see. As a consequence, "Is the author dead already?" proves to be merely a rhetorical question. Our answer is emphatically: "Of course not."

Works Consulted

Adams, Hazard, ed. *Critical Theory Since Plato.* New York: Harcourt Brace Jovanovich, 1971.

Aristotle. *Poetics.* Rpt. in Adams, 48-66.

Barthes, Roland. "The Death of the Author." Rpt. in *Image, Music, Text.* New York: Hill & Wang, 1977.

Baudrillard, Jean. *Simulations.* New York: Semiotext(e), 1983.

Blake, William. *Annotations to Reynolds' Discourses.* Rpt. in Adams, 402-12.

Bloom, Harold. *The Anxiety of Influence.* New York & London: Oxford UP, 1973.

Boccaccio, Giovanni. *Genealogy of the Gentile Gods.* Rpt. in Adams, 127-35.

Boileau-Despreaux, Nicolas. *The Art of Poetry.* Rpt. in Adams, 259-71.

Castelvetro, Lodovico. *The Poetics of Aristotle Translated and Explained.* Rpt. in Adams, 145-53.

Culler, Jonathan. *Structuralist Poetics.* London: Routledge & Kegan Paul, 1975.

de Man, Paul. *Allegories of Writing.* New Haven: Yale UP, 1979.

Derrida, Jacques. *Of Gramatology.* Baltimore: Johns Hopkins UP, 1976.

--------. "Structure, Sign, and Play in the Discourse of the Human Sciences." *Writing and Difference.* London: Routledge & Kegan Paul, 1978.

Eagleton, Terry. *Marxism and Literary Criticism.* London: Methuen, 1976.

Eliot, T. S. "Tradition and the Individual Talent." Rpt. in Adams, 784-90.

Emerson, Ralph Waldo. "The Poet." Rpt. in Adams, 545-554.

Erlich, Victor. *Russian Formalism: History-Doctrine*, 3rd ed. New Haven & London: Yale UP, 1981.

Foucault, Michel. "What Is an Author?" *Textual Strategies.* Ed. Josue V. Harari.. Ithaca, NY: Cornell UP, 1979.

Freud, Sigmund. "Creative Writers and Daydreaming." Rpt. in Adams, 749-53.

Gates, Henry Louis, Jr. *"Race," Writing and Difference.* Chicago & London: Chicago UP, 1985.

Gosson, Stephen. *The School of Abuse.* Ed. E. Arber. London: English Reprints, 1868.

Horace. *Art of Poetry.* Rpt. in Adams, 68-75.

Jacobson, Roman. *Language in Literature.* London & Cambridge, MS: The Belknap Press of Harvard UP, 1987.

James, Henry. "The Art of Fiction." Rpt. in Adams, 661-70.

Jameson, Fredric. *Postmodernism, or the Cultural Logic of Late Capitalism.* London: Verso, 1991.

Jung, Carl Gustav. "On the Relation of Analytical Psychology to Poetry." Rpt. in Adams, 810-18.

Kearny, Richard. *The Wake of Imagination.* London: Hutchinson Education, 1988.

Kristeva, Julia. *The Kristeva Reader.* Ed. Toril Moi. Oxford: Basil Blackwell, 1986.

Longinus. *On the Sublime.* Rpt. in Adams, 77-102.

Lukàcs, Georg. *Writers and Critic and Other Essays.* London: Merlin Press, 1970.

Millet, Kate. *Sexual Politics.* New York: Doubleday, 1970.

Peacock, Thomas Love. "The Four Ages of Poetry." Rpt. in Adams, 491-97.

Plato. *Ion* and *Republic.* Rpt. in Adams, 12-46.

Plotinus. "On the Intellectual Beauty." Rpt. in Adams, 106-13.

Pope, Alexander. *An Essay on Criticism.* Rpt. in Adams, 278-86.

Prop, Vladimir. *The Morphology of the Folktale.* Austin & London: Texas U. P., 1968.

Scaliger, Julius Caesar. *Poetics.* Rpt. in Adams, 137-43.

Selden, Raman & Peter Widdowson. *A Reader's Guide to Contemporary Literary Theory*, 3rd ed. New York and London: Harvester Wheatsheaf, 1993.

Shelley, Percy Bysshe. "A Defense of Poetry." Rpt. in Adams, 499-513.

Showalter, Elaine. *A literature of Their Own.* Princeton: Princeton UP, 1977.

Sidney, Sir Philip. *An Apology for Poetry.* Rpt. in Adams, 155-57.

Tung, Chung-hsuan. *The Scene of Textualization.* Taipei: Bookman Books, 1992.

Wimsatt, K. K. Jr. & Monroe C Beardsley. "The Intentional Fallacy." Rpt. in *The Verbal Icon.* London: Methuen, 1970.

Young, Edward. *Conjectures on Original Composition.* Rpt. in Adams, 338-47.

Zola, Emile. "The Experimental Novel." Rpt. in Adams, 647-59.

* This paper first appeared in 1996 in *JLA*, pp. 1-15.

From Romantic Movement to Postmodern Style: A Reflection on Our *Fin-de-Siècle* Art of Literature

I. A Dualistic History

The recorded history of Western literature has been generally assumed to begin with two separate traditions: Hellenism and Hebraism. This assumption is a dualism by nature, as it reduces all possible sources to two elements. This dualism, furthermore, implies the co-existence of two mutually opposing cultures: the Greek and the Judaic. Various differences between the two cultures have been pointed out. The Greek culture is said, for instance, to be secular, aesthetic and hedonistic while the Judaic culture is religious, ethic, and ascetic. But the differences are capable of being reduced to two contrasting terms indicating not only the characteristics of human societies but also the psychic components of human beings. Matthew Arnold in his *Culture and Anarchy*, for instance, attributes "spontaneity of consciousness" to Hellenism and "strictness of conscience" to Hebraism (chapters IV & V).

Reduction entails oversimplification, no doubt. But it also brings about clarity. All dualistic thinkers, including Arnold, seek to clarify matters by reducing all structural elements to two ultimate ones. Thus history is for them but a matter of changing the dominant, to use a later Russian Formalist idea, between the competing two. The nineteenth-century England, for instance, was for Arnold dominated by the strict moral code of Hebraism. Hence his call for more Hellenism.

Hellenism is sometimes equated to Classicism. Therefore, one can thus talk of Western history:

> *The reintroduction of Classical learning through the Moslem conquests in Spain is a partial explanation of the ensuing Renaissance when Classicism seemed to be dominant. The Reformation is explainable as a resurgence of Hebraic religious feeling. The Neo-Classic Age and the following period of the Enlightenment were inspired by Classical models, but the theories of the Romantic Movement and of many of the nineteenth century German philosophers emphasize the intuitive approach to knowledge upon which Hebraism was built.* (Horton & Hopper 4)

The quotation above embeds, in fact, another popular set of dualistic terms: Classicism vs. Romanticism. Here Romanticism is obviously linked to Hebraism while Classicism is associated with Hellenism. But, as we know, the Classic/Romantic dualism is popular only after the so-called Romantic Movement.

II. The Classic/Romantic Contrast

Western historians often regard the Romantic Movement as a reaction to Neoclassicism, and set the period of its triumph within the late eighteenth and early nineteenth centuries. But to replace the old binary opposition (Hellenism/Hebraism) with the new one (Classicism/Romanticism) is to further complicate the dualistic contrasts. Now it suggests not simply the contrasts between secularity and religiosity, aesthetics and ethics, or hedonism and asceticism. It also suggests many other contrasts, and some of the contrasts may not accord with the discriminations that go with the dichotomy of Hellenism vs. Hebraism.

One scholar, for instance, lists ten contrasting items between Romanticism and Classicism as follows:

ROMANTICISM	versus	**CLASSICISM**
1. emotional appeal	instead of	appeal to reason
2. the subjective point of view	instead of	the objective point of view
3. an individual approach	instead of	a normal and typical approach
4. dissatisfaction with the known	instead of	suspicion and horror of the unconventional and unknown
5. experimentation with musicality and color in expression	instead of	clear and ordered expression and form, a belief in beauty of measured precision
6. emphasis on feelings and emotional reactions	instead of	emphasis on content and idea
7. emphasis on the immeasurable and undetermined	instead of	emphasis on the measurable and the determined
8. importance of particular and individual thought	instead of	importance of universal thoughts and ideas
9. love of external nature in its wild and primitive state	instead of	love of man's accomplishments in taming and controlling the wild and rebellious in nature

10. rejection of tradition (except	instead of	acceptance of tradition (of
from earlier romantic		earlier classical
periods-in particular primitive		periods-particularly those of
folk cultures, Renaissance		ancient Greek and Roman
developments or idealized		cultures)
historical associations)		

Then he adds: "this list of contrasting qualities might be continued indefinitely, but a list of any length would show the same general desire of the romantic to escape from reality which seems to oppress his aesthetic expression, and to experiment with an ideal more satisfying to the individual, and the contrasting fear of the classic to depart from known and tried norms of form and theme established by settled and prosperous aristocratic groups" (Smith 40).

Indeed, we can gather from numerous literary dictionaries, handbooks, encyclopedias, etc., enough definitions, explanations, and commentaries to explicate the Classic/Romantic dichotomy and can be justified in further asserting that Neoclassicism stresses the general, the urbane, the sensual, the keen and sober while Romanticism stresses the particular, the rustic, the visionary, the dreamy and frenzied; that while Neoclassicism values sense, wit, intellect, decorum, restraint, laws, civilization, tight close form, etc., Romanticism values feeling, imagination, inspiration, sincerity, freedom, caprices, primitivism, loose open form, etc.; that whereas Neoclassicism is head, bright, Apollonian, mimetic, mechanic, static, satiric, and commentary, Romanticism is heart, melancholy, Dionysian, expressive, organic, dynamic, lyric, and prophetic; and finally even that the one is an artificer, a mirror, and a believer in stability and the sinful nature of man while the other is a creator, a lamp, and a believer in mutability and the natural goodness of man.

Yet, as a movement against Neoclassicism, Romanticism has now accumulated so many attributes that it becomes impractical to define it as a critical term.[1] Thus, A. O. Lovejoy suggests that the term Romanticism has come to mean nothing at all since it means so many things while Walter Raleigh and Arthur Quiller-Couch suggest abandoning the terms "romantic" and "classic" altogether.

III. The Modernist /Postmodernist Dichotomy

After the Romantic Period, Western literature is said to enter the period of Realism and Naturalism.   But the slogans "Realism" and "Naturalism" indicate mainly a new methodology of treating art materials.   Aiming at a truthful representation of contemporary life and manners, Realism or Naturalism is observational and objective in method, thus more affiliated to Classicism than to Romanticism.   Indeed, "truth, contemporaneity, and objectivity were the obvious counterparts of romantic imagination, of romantic historicism and its glorification of the past, and of romantic subjectivity, the exaltation of the ego and the individual" (Mack, et. al., 878). However, the contrast between Romanticism and Realism/Naturalism is not so keenly felt and widely discussed as that between Classicism and Romanticism.

After Realism/Naturalism, Western literature is sometimes said to turn to Symbolism, which is in a way a Romantic revival, as it emphasizes again the power of vision or imagination in its effort to use an image or a cluster of images to suggest ("symbolize") another plane of reality ("the essence of things") that cannot be expressed in more direct and rational terms.   Yet, the contrast between Symbolism and Realism/Naturalism is also not so widely discussed as that between Classicism and Romanticism.   In fact, Symbolism is sometimes regarded as a trend liable to be merged into the so-called Modernism.

"Modernism" is the usual term for the change in attitudes and artistic strategy occurring at the beginning of the twentieth century.   "Modernism is an attempt to construct a new view of the world and of human nature through the self-conscious manipulation of form" (Mack 1383).   In its broadest sense, Modernism embraces a great number of movements.[2]   Taken more narrowly, however, Modernism refers to " a group of Anglo-American writers (many associated with the Imagists, 1908-1917) who favored clear, precise images and 'common speech' and thought of the work as an art object produced by consummate craft rather than as a statement of emotion" (Mack 1383). Therefore, Modernism seems to be closer to Classicism than to Romanticism in essence.

But the trouble is: as Modernism continues to develop, it takes in so wide a variety of trends that people begin to find it inadequate to talk of "varieties of Modernism."   In actuality people have found it incumbent on them to discriminate the Postmodernist from the Modernist.   In recent years, as we know, many critics have engaged themselves in the hot dispute on whether Postmodernism is a continuity of or a break with Modernism.   But before the problem is settled, the Modernist/Postmodernist contrast is already keenly felt and widely discussed.

In his *The Dismemberment of Orpheus*, Ihab Hassan gives us a table showing the "schematic differences" between Modernism and Postmodernism, thus:

Modernism	Postmodernism
Romanticism/Symbolism	Pataphysics/Dadaism
Form (conjunctive, closed)	Anti-form (disjunctive, open)
Purpose	Play
Design	Chance
Hierarchy	Anarchy
Mastery/Logos	Exhaustion/Silence
Art Object/Finished Work	Process/Performance/Happening
Distance	Participation

Creation/Totalization	Decreation/Deconstruction
Synthesis	Antithesis
Presence	Absence
Centering	Dispersal
Genre/Boundary	Text/Intertext
Semantics	Rhetoric
Paradigm	Syntagm
Hypotaxis	Parataxis
Metaphor	Metonymy
Selection	Combination
Root/Depth	Rhizome/Surface
Interpretation/Reading	Against Interpretation/Misreading
Signified	Signifier
Lisible (Readerly)	*Scriptible* (Writerly)
Narrative/Grande Histoire	Anti-narrative/Petite Histoire
Master Code	Idiolect
Symptom	Desire
Type	Mutant
Genital/Phallic	Polymorphous/Androgynous
Paranoia	Schizophrenia
Origin/Cause	Difference-Différance/Trace
God the Father	The Holy Ghost
Metaphysics	Irony
Determinacy	Indeterminacy
Transcendence	Immanence

$$(267\text{-}8)^3$$

This table tells us that the Modernist/Postmodernist dichotomy is even more complicated than the Classic/Romantic dichotomy, although Hassan's further explanations try to convince us that all the schematic differences can be reduced to the last two listed items: the contrast of determinacy vs. indeterminacy and that of transcendence vs. immanence.

Hassan admits that the dichotomies his table represents "remain insecure, equivocal" (269). For me the first item in his table is already very puzzling. Why should he let Romanticism/Symbolism be incorporated into Modernism? And why should he think of Romanticism/Symbolism as the counterpart of Pataphysics/Dadaism? But I am not here to puzzle over Hassan's schematic table. My business is to argue that the Modernist/ Postmodernist dichotomy is essentially related to the Classic/Romantic contrast, which in turn is derived from the Hellenistic/Hebraic dualism.

IV. From Romantic Movement to Postmodern Style

Hassan once said: "Orpheus, that supreme maker, was the victim of an inexorable clash between the Dionysian principle, represented by the Maenads, and the Apollonian ideal which he, as poet, venerated. Orpheus is dismembered; but his head continues to sing, and where his limbs are buried by the Muses, the nightingales warble sweeter than anywhere else in the world. The myth of Orpheus may be a parable of the artist at certain times. The powers of Dionysos, which civilization must repress, threaten at these times to erupt with a vengeance. In the process energy may overwhelm order; language may turn into a howl, a cackle, a terrible silence; form may be mangled as ruthlessly as the poor body of Orpheus was " (*The Postmodern Turn*, 13). These statements prove that Hassan is also a dualistic thinker. His Apollonian/Dionysian clash reminds us naturally of Nietzsche's distinction between the Apollonian (the rational form and repose) and the Dionysiac (the irrational energy and ecstasy). This clash, moreover, can be connected with Freud's division of the conscious/unconscious human psyche, as it talks of the repression of civilization and the process of energy overwhelming order. But it is likewise justifiable to associate this clash with the Hellenistic/Hebraic dualism and the Classic/Romantic contrast as it is basically a clash between the aesthetic/hedonistic and the ethic/ascetic tendencies; and between the cult of reason /sense/ rationality and the cult of instinct/feeling/sentimentality.

In truth, Hassan's Apollonian/Dionysian clash also typifies the Modernist/Postmodernist conflict. In Hassan's mind, the Postmodern times are those when Orpheus is dismembered, form is mangled, and language turns into a howl, a cackle, a terrible silence, or those when Dionysos triumphs over Apollo. So they are akin to the Romantic period when emotional appeal predominates over the Classical appeal to reason or intellect. For me, in fact, the Postmodern style is no other than the result of pushing the Romantic Movement to its extreme. This postulate of mine can be verified through logical thinking and factual studies.

Our logical thinking can be plied on the spiritual shifts from Romanticism to Postmodernism. First, we all assume that love of freedom is a Romantic spirit. This spirit makes all Romantic heroes hate any restraint and seem rebellious at times. Now, we may ask: if one exercises one's freedom to an extreme, what is the result? Will freedom become waywardness? Indeed, the negating or subverting waywardness we find in the Postmodern style can be looked upon as the consequence of seeking extreme freedom.

Second, we all know Romanticism values spontaneity. Romantic artists wish to refrain from artifice. They hope poetry can come to them "as naturally as the leaves to a tree."[4] Now, what is the result of total spontaneity, of sheer natural impulse? Isn't it the same as the preclusion of any definite aim, reason or pattern, the same as simply letting things occur, the same as, in another word, letting randomness prevail--an apparent characteristic of Postmodern art?

Third, how about the Romantic emotionality? If one completely lets loose one's temper or emotions, will not one bring about perversity or absurdity, another apparent characteristic of the Postmodern style?

Fourth, we may think of Romantics' focus on change. What will be one's world view if one comes to recognize the truth that "Naught may endure but Mutability"?[5] Will it not approximate the Postmodernists' doctrine of indeterminacy?

Fifth, if we turn to Romantics' individualism, we will find it makes their works highly autobiographical, confessional, and subjective. In effect, their subjectivity often tinges their worlds so much so that it seems their mind has the capacity "to generate itself in the world, to act upon both self and world, and so become more and more, im-mediately, its own environment" (Bertens 29)[6]--that is, their mind seems to have reached the Postmodern state of "immanence."

Sixth, the democratic spirit of Romanticism naturally leads to the preference for rusticity and the commonplace. This preference, then, helps to level all artistic genres, making all hierarchical thinkings impossible and establishing the pop culture with its decenteredness, its emphasis on the marginal and the under-privileged, and its aim at mere popularity, which the Postmodern age typifies.

Seventh, we know Romantics tend to rely on their imagination or vision for their creative power. Now, let us imagine what may happen if one is entirely preoccupied with one's imaginings or visions? Will not one probably be living in a dreamy, unreal, even nightmarish world, a world fraught with nonreferential, Postmodern images?

Eighth, we know Romantics have a predilection for the loose, open form. Now, what form is the most loose and open? Isn't it a form without any shapes or bounds, an amorphous, boundless anti-form which some Postmodern works often assume?

Ninth, Romanticism extols originality. But can anybody or anything be truly original if to be so is to be entirely different from anybody or anything else, to be derived from nobody or nothing, and to have no trace at all of ever imitating anybody or anything? A truly insightful Romantic, in seeking originality, will soon find that no originality is ever possible. He will even come to the desperate conclusion that we are all too belated, we can no longer be the fountainhead, we can only imitate, revise, or parody--an understanding typical of the Postmodern mentality.

Tenth, it is found that Romanticism prefers complexity while Classicism prefers simplicity. What, then, is the most complex? Isn't it something that is polysemous, polyphonic, polylectic, multivalent, and multifarious--in short, something that can betray the Postmodern quality of plurality or heterogeneity?

Eleventh, Romantics are idealistic. But where is the ideal love, ideal beauty or ideal state? If one is extremely idealistic, one will find that everything is a deceiving elf like Keats's nightingale, and that no ideal is ever accessible. Therefore, an idealistic Romantic will soon become a nihilist, a Postmodern hero deconstructive in thought and action.

From the eleven points mentioned above, we can see that the Romantic Movement can logically lead to the Postmodern style, indeed. But this logical relationship needs to be strengthened by factual evidence. What follows, then, is a series of factual considerations based on the six factors of communication Roman Jakobson has pointed out.[7]

V. The *Fin-de-Siècle* Reflection

A. The World

The world today is, of course, not the antique world when Greek and Roman mythologies prevailed, nor is it the medieval world when Christian religion throve on the feudal system of life. Ever since the Renaissance, historians tell us, the world has entered the modern times. But the modern world has been becoming more and more modern period by period. If the Romantic spirit is to appreciate change, what changes has the spirit brought on our modern world today? To begin with, the world, as we know, has many more nations than it used to have. More nations with more people plus the domination of democratic ideologies have made our world highly individualistic. Each nation as well as every individual is constantly claiming its own right. Romantic individualism has reached its apogee indeed, for all the efforts of the United Nations to make our common wealth as well as common peace.

Economically, we have indeed entered what Fredric Jameson calls the late capitalist, consumer society. In this society, the boundaries between high culture and mass or popular culture are effaced, as products of all kinds are poured out to cater to all appetites. The Romantic ideal of equality has manifested itself in the much greater opportunities for the consumers to choose among the great plenitude of objects.

The diversity of merchandise is coupled with the diversity of knowledge. Today, all sciences and technologies have developed to such an extent that every small subject of study requires a specialist or expert. This tendency naturally makes a great multitude of individual authorities. But these individual authorities cannot help feeling solitude as Romantics do, since their expertise will of necessity limit their community to a small coterie of their peers.

The great number of experts as individual authorities is echoed in the great number of religious sects. Today, the world witnesses the booming of any marketable things, including branches of faith. Christians, Buddhists, Muslims, and what not have all sects of adherents. Clergymen are as variegated as laymen.

Indeed, even infidels have wide varieties. They do not believe in any formal religion. But they believe in all sorts of doctrines, academic or not. As a result, our world today is really full of -isms and -ists in all fields of knowledge. All the -ists are theorists. And all theorists are idealists like Romantics.

What, then, has become of the world with so many different believers producing so many different objects for so many different states of people? One big problem is the environmental one. As natural resources are dwindling under the exploitation and destruction of mankind, we are suddenly brought to an awareness that we need not only industrial revolution but also green revolution. This revolutionary idea has turned us into Romantics, who love nature and wish for our return to nature. Consequently, "the countryside has been partially pulled in to the cityscape…The distinctions between city and country are now, perhaps more than ever, dissolved" (Donnelly 43-44).

But have we really become natural men again? Our Postmodern return to nature is in fact often a vicarious return. We "plant" plastic flowers instead of real flowers. We "raise" electronic chicks instead of real chicks. Our many farms are for sports rather than for farming. We shoot and hunt on screens or in imitation forests. We fish in man-made ponds rather than in natural rivers or lakes. As technology promises to make everything possible, our Romantic primitivism is aided by all kinds of substitutes. The Romantic ideal of having communion between man and nature is "fulfilled" in this Postmodern Age by the blending of natural and artificial ingredients. At the end of this century, we are told, "we are all cyborgs now."[8] The cyborg, as we know, is a hybrid blend of organism and machine.

The hybrid blend of organism and machine certainly needs high technology. But in this hi-tec world, hybrid blending is a very common phenomenon. As we see, male and female can blend in appearances, manners, ways of dressing or thinking, walks of life, etc. Class distinctions are disappearing, and so are racial discriminations. People of different classes and races have mixed together at work or at play. Marriage is possible between any two. All styles of arts, all habits of living, all customs of life, all features of culture, as well as all disciplines of study are trying every minute to blend and merge. The Classical ideal of purity has waned. The Romantic ideal of promiscuity has waxed, in this Postmodern world.

Blending is more often a way to produce a new species, than a way to enlarge an old body. When new species of all things keep coming into this world, can the old body hold its ground? Impossible. Jean-François Lyotard has told us that in the Postmodern condition, all past "metanarratives" (*grands recits*) have lost their credibility. Indeed, Postmodern Romantics can find no authority (or "legitimation") in any old body, be it a body of things or a body of ideas.

Where do Postmodern Romantics attach their values, then? In the unreal. Jean Baudrillard has told us that we are living in an epoch of "simulation," where reality is gone for good. As communication technologies improve, our world is proliferated with media images. We recognize not a man, but the image of that man; not a company, a product, etc., but the image of that company, that product, etc. Romantics like to imagine. Postmodern Romantics are provided with imaginings and led to believe such as true. What a world is ours!

B. The Medium

In his *The Death of Literature,* Alvin Kernan tells us convincingly that we are now "in the midst of a transition from a print to an electronic culture" (127). Furthermore, he agrees with McLuhan that the medium is the message, that each of the major historical information technologies--oral, written, printed, and electronic--has modified perception and posited a different kind of "truth."

> *Oral societies seek wisdom, manuscript and print societies knowledge and information, and, now, electronics manipulate bytes to produce data. The Greek world was transformed--philosophy for poetry, Plato for Homer--in the fifth century B. C. by the appearance of writing in an oral society, and the Western world was transformed again by the appearance of print in the mid-fifteenth century. And in the late twentieth century print culture is giving way to an electronic culture that stores and transmits information by means of such electric devices as the telegraph, telephone, radio, television, and computer.* (128)

In a book culture, Kernan explains, print "helped to shape the dominant modern character type, inward, alienated, puzzled, Hamlet or Ivan Karamozov" (132). Print also made philosophy concern itself "almost exclusively with the epistemological issues that became of first importance when the reading situation became the standard setting of understanding" (132). It was in such a culture that literature throve lavishly. All canonical works, some originally oral or manuscript, were printed, and readers were made to experience reality on the printed pages. But now "economics as well as chemistry seems to be favoring the electronic future over the printed past" (136). Perhaps Huxley is not correct in predicting the absence of books for our future in *Brave New World*. But truly the older books are disintegrating on the library shelves. What come in alarming quantity are actually new forms of computer printouts and desktop publishing, microfilm and microfiche, laser disks storing millions of words, computer databases containing masses of information in readable form (138).

What happens, then, in such an electronic age? There is, first, the so-called "literacy crisis." More and more people are found lacking the skills of reading and writing, and the amount of reading, particularly of books, is steadily diminishing while the amount of watching TV or the computer screen is steadily increasing.

In the former book culture, people read words on the page; in the present television culture, people watch images on the screen. What visual images give us are "simple open meanings not complex and hidden, transience not permanence, episodes not structures, theater not truth" (Kernan 151). TV programs, as we know, are often entertainment consumables, quickly used and soon discarded, unlike printed literary classics which are often serious texts, to be perused for their intricacy of structure, complexity of meaning, etc.

What is worse, Jean Baudrillard warns, owing to the flooding of media-created images, we have lost the real; we have let the depthless "simulacra" determine the real; and we replace our "real" external world with a world of "hyper-reality," in which no truth-claims are possible.

C. The Language

It is well known that Dante wrote a document in Latin prose (*De Vulgari Eloquentia*) to defend the use of the vernacular Italian instead of the official Latin for literary works. And his use of the vernacular for his masterpiece, the *Divine Comedy*, is indeed a success. In fact, as more and more modern nations with their native tongues came into existence, the problem of whether it is proper or not to use the vernacular for literary works has ceased to exist.

Dante's position against the official language can be thought of as a Romantic pose of revolting against authority or aristocracy. Another similar position is found in the later Romantics' distrust of poetic diction and in their belief that poetry can be written in "a selection of language really used by men" and that there can be no "essential difference between the language of prose and metrical composition."[9] Today, for all the influence of the Russian Formalists' concept that literature is a special use of language which achieves its distinctness by deviating from and distorting "practical language," we know writers are increasingly disregarding the levels or class distinctions of language. They use any kind of language that can serve their purposes. And certainly we have many many new languages ready for use, from technical terms to campus slang, from the jargon of the stock market to the cant of gangsters, plus all sorts of pidgins. Sometimes, writers themselves are creators of specialized literary creoles. Think of Joyce's *Finnegans Wake*. Think, too, of Lewis Carroll's nonsense language, E. E. Cumming's verbal reprocessing, Wallace Steven's hermetic style, and Nabokov's Orphic writing, not to mention the language of dada poems or Surrealist poetry.

Facing the new Babel, it is observed, some writers have responded by saying less and less. "Increasing amounts of silence and a minimization of words were for Hemingway, Beckett, Kafka, William Carlos Williams, Pinter, Larkin, and many others the only honest speech still available, and they deliberately reduced the language of literature to the barest and plainest terms, distrusting larger and grander statements as empty and likely to break down in the face of actuality" (Kernan 162). Meanwhile, most educated people begin to protest against the jargon of blight and bloat that floods the media and accuse fools of coining words without any concern for truth or logic or decency. Although this new Babel "purposely tries to sound like the down-to-earth words of the folks," the language is freely made by "modern language engineers, the public relations flacks, entertainers, media specialists, television personalities, advertising hypesters, bureaucrats, celebrity manufacturers and marketers, politicians and their image makers, technocrats, and singers of popular songs" (Kernan 170). Such a language is intended to be seen and heard rather than read through such modern inventions as TV and VCRs, video disks and cassettes, and its purpose is "political in the sense of providing people with what they want, technological in the utilization of new methods of communication and information storage, economic in the sense of big payoffs for the ability to shape attitudes with words" (Kernan 172).

The serious use of language for political or economic purposes is much influenced in our age by Foucault's idea that power is gained through discourse: there are no absolutely "true" discourses, only more or less powerful ones. Today's writers, creative or critical, familiar or unfamiliar with Foucault, are using their languages like politicians or merchants to gain power, to gain profits. For them literary language is no different from business language.

On the other hand, however, there are writers who are influenced by the poststructuralist thought (especially the Derridean thought) that language is but a process of "différance," of using one sign for another, achieving at best a sort of supplementarity (addition-substitution), never a guarantee of "presence." For such writers (e.g., Borges) writing is a game: it plays with linguistic signs much like a musician playing with musical notes or a chess-player playing with chessmen. For them language is nonreferential. Therefore, they can employ language for language sake.

D. The Author

The author's fate has not often been a happy one in the West. Since Plato there have been detractors of the author, who is variously called "the artist," "the writer," "the poet," "the playwright," "the novelist," "the essayist," or any other name pertaining to a specific genre of literature. However, the author has sometimes enjoyed a high status. In the Romantic Period, for instance, the poet is considered to be "the author to others of the highest wisdom, pleasure, virtue and glory, so he ought personally to be the happiest, the best, the wisest, and the most illustrious of men."[10]

The author's status or function has indeed changed with times. In his *The Wake of Imagination* Richard Kearney argues very plausibly that the premodern cultures of Jerusalem and Athens tended to construe the author primarily as a *craftsman* who, at best, models his activity on the "original" activity of a Divine Creator. The modern movements of Renaissance, Romantic and Existentialist humanism, then, substituted the original *inventor* for the mimetic craftsman. But this figure is himself replaced in the Postmodern time by a *bricoleur*, a "player" in a game of signs or an "operator" in an electronic media network. In an essay I have also contended that the author has never "died." He or she only undergoes "transformation" all the time. In our age, when computers have become our daily necessity, the author may no longer be a "writer" writing on book pages, but a "programmer" handling some kind of "software."[11]

The fact that the author's status shifts constantly does not annul our impression that as our media of communication keep improving, the author seems to grow in number and variety. Today, amateur as well as professional writers of all kinds are found everywhere. Famous authors are no longer restricted to the male sex, nor to the powerful nations, nor to the major languages, nor to the higher social class, nor to the governing race, nor to any particular region, age, genre, style, etc. Authorship in this Postmodern time is certainly as diversified as personality.

E. The Reader

Undoubtedly, the reading public has also grown in number and variety as history develops. In the ancient days when literature existed only in oral form, in the mouth of the scop for instance, there were of course practically no readers. In those days there were only hearers or listeners of literature, and the audience were in fact limited to a lucky few who belonged to the nobility.

Later, when literature appeared in manuscript form, the world began to have readers. But the readership was likewise limited to a few privileged noblemen who were able to read and had access to the few current manuscripts. It was only after the invention of the printing machine that the reading public could grow to an enormous size. Think of Blake and his engraved writings. How many people could have the opportunity to read his prophetic books? Then think of Dickens and his novels. How many more people could have the opportunity to read them? As more and more books were printed and became available to ordinary people, more and more men, and women too, were educated and became readers of literature. Today, as cheap printed materials are flooding, the readership has naturally reached its biggest size.

A greater number of readers allows a greater variety. Who are readers nowadays? They are surely not confined to a certain class, nor to a certain gender, nor to a certain race. In this highly industrialized world people of all walks of life, of all ages, and of all regions can be readers. In fact, the readers have become so diversified that their different tastes have to be considered. "Just as a cohesive, homogeneous reading public fragments into a series of reading publics, 'artistic expression' fragments into a network of competing discourses" (Collins 4). In this consumers' society, a literary masterpiece cannot hope to appeal to everybody; it can only hope to cater to a majority of readers.

Readers are indeed of various types. One particular type, however, deserves our special attention. That is the critic. It is said that with a few earlier exceptions, criticism became a standard literary genre only in the eighteenth century, when print made letters into a business (Kernan 64). After its formalization as a standard literary mode, "the critical impulse was used for a host of mundane tasks, such as advertising and reviewing the new books pouring from the press, improving the taste of the now common readers, and providing expert judgments about literary questions" (Kernan 65). Thus, the status of the critic has not been high in literary history. Compared with the author, especially the creative genius called the poet, the critic seems to be merely a menial servant of literature.

This situation has somewhat changed, however. Since literature entered the university curriculum and criticism became a big industry in the late nineteenth century, the literary scholar and the critic have merged into one person. The scholar/critic conducts research to publish original contributions to literary knowledge, standing to literature much as a physicist does to nature. In this highly-technologized world, the social position of critics and criticism has indeed improved enormously by achieving professional status. There are even literary professors (Geoffrey Hartman, for one) who begin to believe that criticism today is no less creative than contemporary literature. In truth, a large quantity of creative writing today is presumably brought forth under the influence of critical theories. Therefore, such writing would be difficult for readers ignorant of the involved theories. Take Samuel Beckett's *Endgame* for example. If a reader does not know that it is a very "open text" based on the methods of the theater of the absurd to expose existentialist ideas, the reader would find it very difficult to approach.

Critics may really be literary specialists. Nevertheless, not all readers today are critics. In fact, the vast majority of readers are still common readers. Such readers demand but common literature, that is, texts easily available and readable. So it is not surprising that such difficult authors as

Joyce, Faulkner, Beckett, and Robbe-Grillet cannot be popular with the populace while cheap books of science fiction, detective stories, romances, mysteries, as well as pornography can always attract so many readers.

Serious critics may worry about the reader's superficial tendency today. But what can they do about it? In this world of "hyper-reality," of images mirroring images rather than truths, how can they expect readers to have "depth"? In effect, authors have begun to invite readers to join their depthless enterprise on the computer screen. As authors become programmers designing "hypertexts" on the computer, readers cannot but become watchers and players of the texts. As they watch and play on, they are creators of games. In this sense, the reader is "writing" his own text. With the advent of modern technology, reader and writer are one, after all.

F. The Work

Different times have different genres of works. In the West, three basic literary types have come down from classical antiquity: drama, epic, and lyric. But many more than the three have since become current and popular. In the Middle Ages, for instance, the chivalric romance was created. And the novel then came as the later modern version of the long narrative. Meanwhile, almost all basic genres keep developing into big genres with many sub-genres. The broad category of the lyric, for instance, has now contained such subgroups as elegy, epithalamion, threnody, dirge, ode, sonnet, ballad, and the short song-like poem also called the lyric. The kinds of drama, too, have proliferated vastly in the course of time. Today drama includes not only the ancient types: tragedy and comedy. It also includes such types as miracle play, mystery play, morality play, chronicle or history play, tragicomedy, masque, problem play, and all sorts of modern or postmodern theaters. The long narrative poem called the epic has indeed lost its popularity. But its modern related prose version, namely the novel, has developed to the full. It now covers a wide variety of types: picaresque novel, epistolary novel, Bildungsroman, Kunstlerroman, psychological novel, sociological novel, proletarian novel, novel of the soil, Gothic novel, philosophical tale or conte, etc. In fact, we have nowadays used the name "fiction" to cover all the varieties of novels plus such things as fabliau, fable, novelette or novella, detective story, and short story. Likewise, the name "poetry" is used to refer to the aforementioned lyric types together with epic and such things as epigram, philosophical poem, descriptive nature poem, dramatic monologue, pastoral poem, satiric verse, etc. Therefore, the three basic modern genres come to be drama, fiction, and poetry instead of drama, epic, and lyric. But this is not the whole story. In the course of genre classification, we find we have such special genres as allegory, pastoral, and satire, which can enter almost all other genres to form allegorical romance, pastoral elegy, mock-epic, etc., etc. And finally, we begin to find it necessary to distinguish fiction from "non-fiction," the latter comprising also a large group of writings: biography, autobiography, memoir, diary or journal, letters, essay, dialogues, maxims, etc.

Here we have as yet not mentioned all existing genres, of course. We have left out some popular genres such as science fiction, mystery, love romance, and pornography, for instance. But it is enough to show that our world is certainly full of all kinds of literary works. Literary genres are now as diversified as individual authors or readers.

Regarding this genre ramification or complication, however, several things are particularly noteworthy. One is the rise of the formal, critical essay as an important genre for reading. Today, we must admit, many people have no time to read literary works. They read, instead, reviews or critical essays. Common readers, for lack of time or skill in reading, prefer story summaries to stories themselves. Serious readers—students or scholars of literature--may be obliged to read the text, but they often seek the aid of criticism in their efforts to write reviews, papers, dissertations, or books about literature. Thus, they seem to be more interested in works about works than in works themselves.

Another thing worthy of our notice is the rise of hypertext. This new genre is of course the offspring of our new media—the "hepermedia" which range from "electronic books" and CD-ROM or CDI devices to "personal assistants," wireless pocket computers connected with telephone and data networks (Joyce 21). It includes a far higher percentage of nonverbal information than does print. Besides providing such visual elements as illustrations, maps, diagrams, flow charts, or graphs, it supplies "the cursor, the blinking arrow, line or other graphic element that represents the reader-author's presence in the text" (Landow 45-46). It can utilize color and sound effects, too. This new genre, to be sure, "represents a shift in human consciousness comparable to the shift from orality to print" (Joyce 20). I dare presume that in the near future, literature is to be divided first into two big genres, i.e., text and hypertext. Then, we will find that hypertext can take in all the traditional textual genres mentioned above. That is, we will have hypertextual poetry, drama, fiction, and prose with all their subgroups.

A third thing we should note here is the rise of cyberpunk. Cyberpunk is no doubt a barefaced marketing device of science fiction publishers (McHale, *Constructing Postmodernism*, 243). But it is "the latest in the succession of phases or 'waves' constituting the modern history of the SF genre" (244). Most cyberpunk motifs have precedents in earlier SF, indeed. Yet, it is innovative in that it selects certain motifs, foregrounds them, and arranges them so that it "translates or transcodes postmodernist motifs from the level of form (the verbal continuum, narrative strategies) to the level of content or 'world'" (246). As Brian McHale has observed, there are three bundles or complexes of motifs which cyberpunk SF shares with mainstream postmodernist fiction: motifs of what might be called "worldness"; motifs of the centrifugal self; and motifs of death, both individual and collective (246-7).

These motifs, as will be touched on below, are designed to raise and explore ontological issues—a thematic tendency of our epoch.

A fourth thing pertaining to our present generic problem is the idea of generic purity. We know Classicism values purity of genre (wants a tragedy to contain purely tragic elements, for example), while Romanticism often breaks the rule. Now, in our Postmodern time when literary genres have grown to a countless number, we find literary works often do not belong purely to certain genres. A work is more often than not a hybrid. Thus, we often find it hard to assign a work to a single genre. For example, Robert Ray finds that Julian Barnes's *Flaubert's Parrot* (1985) is nominally a novel. Yet, it achieves the effect of both biography and criticism as woven into the narrative are "brief, playful compelling forays into biography and criticism, conducted in a variety of forms" (140). Other unclassifiable texts Ray has mentioned include Borges's *Labyrinths*, Calvino's *If on a Winter's Night a Traveller*, Derrida's *Glas*, Barthes's *Roland Barthes* and *A Lover's Discourse*, Levi-Strauss's *Tristes Tropiques*, Godard's films, Cage's writings, Syberberg's *Our Hitler*, and Lacan's seminars (142). For Ray these works "stage at the level of representation the collapse of modernism's privileged oppositions: avant-garde and mass culture, private and public spheres, theoretical and practical activity" (142). Indeed, today we can find countless examples to show that works are trying, purposely perhaps, to blur any generic distinction just as we are trying in many ways to eliminate class distinction among people. And just as people can be mongrels, so can works be hybrids.

Talking about genres of works, we must finally come to the recognition that in our present age the idea of "work" is giving way to the idea of "text" and that of "discourse." In an article I have already pointed out that the ideas of work, text, and discourse respectively stress literature as an illocutionary, locutionary, and perlocutionary act, to use J. L. Austin's terms. The three ideas echo three types of criticism: the Romantic-Humanist, the Formalistic-Structuralist, and the Marxist, which are respectively oriented towards the author, the code, and the context. And the three ideas also correspond to three traditional classes of literary theories: expressive, mimetic, and affective, which are respectively concerned with the origin, reference, and function of literature.[12] So, when people prefer to use "text" or "discourse" to talk about literary "work," we know they are emphasizing textuality (plus intertextuality) and contextuality rather than the creator who finishes the work and gives originality to it. Under such circumstances, we should not be surprised to find so many "open texts" and "powerful discourses" poured out to explore ontological problems of literature and to exercise political influences on our world.

But how can ontological texts or political discourses be concretized into literature in our present world? Our Romantics seem to have despaired of ever becoming originals. Some people seem to agree with Harold Bloom that since Milton poets have suffered an awareness of their "belatedness"; their poetic fathers have used up all the available inspiration; hence all they can do now is just to misread their masters intentionally and use such "poetic misprision" to bring out revisionary texts.[13] But some others would agree with Fredric Jameson that in our late capitalist society where no unique self and no private identity is possible as the old individual or individualist subject is "dead," pastiche--that is, blank parody, or mimicry of past styles without purpose or irony--is the characteristic mode of writing ("Postmodernism and Consumer Society," 15-17). And still many would agree with Linda Hutcheon that parody--be it variously called ironic quotation or pastiche or appropriation or intertextuality--is the postmodern way of representation. By parody the postmodern artists rummage through the image reserves of the past and utilize the past, not nostalgically but critically, through a double process of installing and ironizing, to signal how present representations come from past ones and what ideological consequences derive from both continuity and difference (*Politics,* 93). This is the way Umberto Eco writes his best-seller, *The Name of the Rose.*[14] This is also the way so many other Postmodernists write their intertextual works, including such Russian dramatists as Vampilov, Amalrik, and Aksënov.[15]

To parody is to imitate in a way. And to imitate is to focus on sameness rather than difference. The Postmodernists, however, are extreme Romantics. They cannot let go the Romantic temper of posing differently even though they know they cannot be unprecedentedly original in anything. Therefore, to accord with their principles of diversity, multiplicity, polyphony, pluralism, heterogeneity, etc. (all of which focus on difference rather than sameness), the Postmodernists have sought to vary their works in all methods possible so that some kind of originality can still be felt. There is William Faulkner, for instance, who lets his *The Sound and the Fury* be told in four sections, each with a different narrator, each supplying a different piece of the plot. There is also John Fowles, who leaves the readers of his *The French Lieutenant's Woman* with four endings of the story to choose from. And there is Italo Calvino, whose *If on a Winter's Night a Traveler* is composed of many different novel beginnings but without middles or ends. If we want to think of more, we then have Thomas Pynchon, whose *V* is a quest story, but the target of the quest is an unidentifiable "who" and an indescribable "what," as the "V" can stand for anybody and anything (Tanner 45). We also have Thomas Disch, whose *The Businessman* is fraught with "playfully random minglings of the banal with the horrific and sublime," and Denis Johnson, whose *Fiskadoro* is full of "sudden, inexplicable point-of-view shifts from character to character" so that "any sense of narrative development is undercut" (Pfeil 61,67,68). And finally we have Alain Robbe-Grillet, whose collage-like technique has produced such "objective literature" as *The Voyeur* and "The Secret Room," in which description replaces narration, and the story, if any, is open for the reader to conjecture.

G. The Theme

As tens of millions of literary works (call them texts or discourses if you like) classifiable into hundreds of genres are available in our world today, one would certainly be crazy to attempt to exhaust all they have to say, that is, all their themes or messages. However, one will surely be right if one says that there seem to be certain themes particularly dominant and noteworthy in our Postmodern literature.

We know every piece of literature has something to say. This "something" is often what we call "truth." And we know Romantics are especially fond of telling us "truths" since they often pose as seers or prophets. Think, for instance, Blake's "Without contraries is no progression" (*The Marriage of Heaven and Hell*, plate 3), Wordsworth's "Nature never did betray/The heart that loved her" ("Tintern Abbey," 122-3), Shelley's "If Winter comes, can Spring be far behind?" ("Ode to the West Wind," 70), or Keats's "Beauty is truth, truth beauty" ("Ode on a Grecian Urn," 49). Aren't they all statements of truth, and themes or messages of their works?

But the time has come when we are fed up with truths, when we begin to doubt all truths, when we feel all truths are relative truths, not absolute. Thus, Luigi Pirandello's works win our acclaim, as they directly expose the theme. In our Postmodern age, in fact, the same theme is suggested time and again if only indirectly. It seems that Derrida's attack on "logocentrism" has really helped writers to beware of proclaiming truths.

One type of works that make no pretensions of truth is pop literature. Writers of this type seem to believe in Baudrillard. For them, since nothing really has any depth, literature cannot hope to provide any serious truth. Therefore, their stories, characters, settings, techniques, etc., are all commonplace and superficial. And their common theme is: "For all our efforts, we seek but temporary joy, not permanent truth."

Another type of works that dare not claim truth is ontological literature. Writers of this type seem to believe in Lyotard. For them, since no "metanarrative" is legitimate, literature cannot but be skeptical about itself. Therefore, they pose questions bearing "either on the ontology of the literary text itself or on the ontology of the world which it projects" (McHale, *Postmodernist Fiction,* 10). According to Brian McHale, such writers include Faulkner, Beckett, Robbe-Grillet, Fuentes, Nabokov, Coover, and Pynchon. And the cyberpunk writers (Bruce Sterling, Walter Williams, Michael Swanwick, John Shirley, Marc Laidlaw, Greg Bear, Lucius Shepard, etc.) also belong to this group, as they all try to deal with the "worldness" of microworlds created in their "cyberspace," or with the centrifugal self which, like the world, is plural, unstable, and problematic, or with the boundary between life and death, which is also problematic in its machine-operated or its "bio-punk" forms (MacHale, *Constructing Postmodernism*, chapter 11).

A third type of works that seemingly try to bypass truth is linguistic literature. This type is nonreferential in that it treats literature as a game, a linguistic game which is self-contained, with its own elements and rules of structure sufficient for the game without having to refer to the outside world, the world beyond the linguistic universe. The lack of reference naturally renders no sense, no meaning, no truth except the understanding that no sense is a sense, no truth is a truth. Works of this category comprise the L-A-N-G-U-A-G-E poetry of Tina Darragh, the riddle-like fiction of Pynchon, the game-like fiction of Borges, the French writers' *nouveau roman* and the *Tel Quel* novels. They are often self-reflexive or metafictional.

Besides suggesting the prevailing theme that there is no absolute truth, or no deep truth, or no transcendent truth, our contemporary works also suggest the concomitant theme that all truths are created equal. Since God is already dead and Godot will never come, each human has a right to make his or her little narrative and regard it as a provisional truth. Feminist writers, postcolonial writers, and writers of new historicism are all supporting this theme.   In defending the weak, the oppressed, the underprivileged, the marginal, the neglected, etc., they are using their discursive power to persuade us that others' truths or values can always be deconstructed, thus leaving their own to be believed for the time being.

But what will happen if everybody really has his own say and presents or represents his own truth for our recognition?   We will exhaust truths, then. We will then have all truths, and to have all is as meaningless and harmful as to have none.   We will find "the main preoccupation of intellectuals is no longer wisdom, nor prudence, nor reason, but second-order descriptions"; they will just "describe how others describe what others describe" (Luhmann 182). Surfeit is a great risk, indeed.   Today, we know we are at the risk of having too much or going too far.   Therefore, much of our contemporary literature is also preoccupied or obsessed with the theme of death or the theme of end. Consciously or unconsciously, we speak or act as if we were really playing "the Endgame," in "Finnegans Wake," seeing "Things Fall Apart," and crying "Death Constant Beyond Love!"[16]

VI. The End

This paper is drawing to an end.   Many people feel our century is also drawing to an end.   What is an end, then?   Is Postmodernism an end of Modernism?   The controversy has not yet ended.

My end here is not to end the debate.   But I must agree that the end cannot be located in a non-linear, non-Euclidean space of history; it is conceivable only in a logical order of causality and continuity (Baudrillard, *Illusion*, 110).   When we talk of the end of the subject, of history, of philosophy, of anything, we are but using a metaphor to stress the fact that something is caused to change to such an extent that it *seemingly* no longer continues to be the same thing while it may *de facto* be still there, only in another form. Thus, Frank Kermode is right in referring to *fin-de-siècle* crises as "myths" that are shaped by a common pathology, stories that "grow together" and demonstrate a "pattern."[17] And thus, Rita Felski is also right in asserting that the epigram "Fin de siècle, fin de sexe" coined by the French artist Jean Lorrain to describe the symbolic affinity of gender confusion and historical exhaustion in the late nineteenth century seems even more apt for our own moment (226), since for her as well as for many of us, gender confusion and historical exhaustion seem to be even more conspicuous right now when feminism has leveled both sexes in many respects and Postmodernism has used up all possible themes and methods of literature.

But my main concern here is not with the end of sex but with the end of literature. This paper has drawn largely on Alvin Kernan's *The Death of Literature* (1990), a book whose title suggests that literature has come to an end. Yet, what has Kernan actually said in the book? Among other things he says, "If *literature* has died, *literary activity* continues with unabated, if not increased, vigor, though it is increasingly confined to universities and colleges" (5). "What has passed, or is passing, is the romantic and modernist literature of Wordsworth and Goethe, Valéry and Joyce, that flourished in capitalistic society in the high age of print, between the mid-eighteenth century and the mid-twentieth" (5-6). "...the disintegration of romantic-modernist literature in the late twentieth century has been a part not only of a general cultural revolution but more specifically of a technological revolution that is rapidly transforming a print to an electronic culture" (9), "where creativity and plagiarism are increasingly hard to define, where advertising and image making have captured the language" (10). So, in Kernan's mind literature refers only to "printed matter," excluding oral text and hypertext. And for him the end or death of literature means only the change of literary genres or forms, not the cease of literary activity.

Kernan's idea strengthens my belief. I believe man always has a strong will to live. In the age when man sees death everywhere, one way to guarantee survival is by producing literary offspring. Although our Postmodernists have come to realize that in this culture only language has remained--"Being that can be understood is language" (Gadamer xxii) or "Being that can be imagined is language" (Madison 183)--they know they can still "play freely" with linguistic signs, and do it so freely indeed that they may claim that they can feel some erotic pleasure (*jouissance*) in their text production, no matter whether it is on desk or on keyboard or anywhere else, and no matter whether their offspring are printed texts or hypertexts. After all, the scene of textualization is like the scene of sexualization, isn't it?

With this understanding, then, we will bring our end back to our beginning. In the beginning of this paper, I point out that the history of Western literature is a dualistic history because it is assumed to begin with two traditions: Hellenism and Hebraism. But, as we see, the spirits or values these two traditions represent seldom blend equally at any supposed period of the history. The Classic/Romantic contrast and the Modernist/Postmodernist dichotomy are in fact the result of having some Hellenistic or Hebraic qualities serving as the dominant. It is only that the Postmodern style seems to be the consequence of pushing the Romantic movement, with its Hebraic/Dionysian tendencies, to an extreme. Thus, we find waywardness, randomness, absurdity, indeterminacy, immanence, popularity, nonreferentiality, anti-form, intertextuality, heterogeneity, nihilism, etc.—those Postmodern attributes—have all stemmed logically from Romantic characteristics.

Logical inference needs to be strengthened by factual evidence. In considering the world situation today together with its changes concerning the medium, the language, the author, the reader, the work, and the theme of literature, we cannot but admit that the Romantic spirit of loving freedom, change and difference has really brought about an unthinkable revolution in our art of literature. For our literature today, the Postmodern kind, is often so different that it becomes simply anti-art, anti-literature--a trend worshiping Chaos, a voice full of sound and fury, signifying nothing.

In the Romantic period, Thomas Peacock postulated a theory called the Four Ages of Poetry. In his view, poetry has been rising and then declining all the time cyclically from the age of iron through the golden age, the silver age, and the brass age, back to the age of iron again. For him the iron age of classical poetry is the bardic; the golden, the Homeric; the silver, the Virgilian; and the brass, the Nonnic. For him modern poetry also has its four ages: the Dark Ages can be considered the iron age again; the Renaissance, the golden; the Neoclassical Period, the silver; the Romantic Period, the brass. As Peacock placed himself in the brass age, he did not live to see the next iron age. But the satire he directed against his contemporary poets was enough to impel Shelley to write his *Defense of Poetry*.

Peacock's theory might be a joke. Yet, it is not without sense. The criterion he has used to differentiate the four ages of poetry is the relative dominance of Hellenistic/Classic/Apollonian virtues or Hebraic/Romantic/Dionysian virtues. The iron age comes when the latter virtues overwhelm the former completely whereas the golden age arrives when the former suppress the latter thoroughly. The silver and the brass ages are respectively somewhat dominated by the former and the latter. In this light, then, our present age could be the iron age again, as our Postmodernists do not want reason, sense, order, and culture; they want irrationality, nonsense, disorder, and anarchy instead. "When the lamp is shattered," certainly "the light in the dust lies dead."[18] The Romantic lamp has now shattered itself, and so darkness is everywhere. Although the Postmodernists are striving with all sorts of lens to inspect, reflect, or refract each other, what avails in sheer darkness?

Happily, however, change is the permanent rule. We can predict that after some decades of darkness literature is sure to see light again. Another lamp may bring with it another form of art. As this Postmodern phase wanes, another full moon is expectedly in sight. If the *fin-de-siècle* goes, can the millennium be far ahead?

Notes

1. Jokingly, F. L. Lucas counts 11,396 definitions of the term in his *The Decline and Fall of the Romantic Ideal* (1948). Jacques Barzun has surprisingly listed some attributes (e.g., "conservative," "materialistic," "ornamental," and "realistic") in his *Classic, Romantic and Modern* (1961).
2. In J. A. Cuddon's *A Dictionary of Literary Terms* (1979), Modernism is said to be associated with Anti-novel, Anti-play, Beat Poets, Dadaism, Decadence, Existentialism, Expressionism, free verse, Happening, Imagists, New Humanism, nouveau roman, Nouvelle Vague, stream of consciousness, Theater of the Absurd, Theater of Cruelty, Ultraism, Vorticism, etc.
3. The table first appeared in *The Dismemberment of Orpheus* (1982) as part of a "Postface" article titled "Toward a Concept of Postmodernism," which was later reprinted in his *The Postmodern Turn* (1987).
4. See Keats's letter to John Taylor (February 27, 1818).
5. See Shelley, "Mutability," l. 14.
6. Cf. Hassan's statement: "the capacity of mind to generalize itself in symbols, intervene more and more into nature, act upon itself through its own abstractions and so become, increasingly, im-mediately, its own environment" (*The Postmodern Turn*, 93).
7. I have replaced Jakobson's context, contact, code, addresser, addressee, and message with world, medium, language, author, reader, and theme so that the factors have names closer to literary studies. For Jakobson's factors, see his *Language in Literature*, p.66.
8. This is Donna Haraway's statement quoted in Rita Feslski's "Fin de Siècle, Fin de Sexe," p. 229.
9. See Wordsworth's Preface to *Lyrical Ballads*.
10. See Shelley's *A Defense of Poetry.*
11. See my paper "Is the Author 'Dead' Already?" *Journal of the College of Liberal Arts*, Chung Hsing University, 26 (1996), 1-15.
12. For detailed discussion, see my paper "Work, Text, Discourse: Literary Problems, Old and New," *Journal of the College of Liberal Arts*, Chung Hsing University, 25 (1995), 31-44.

13. See his *The Anxiety of Influence* (1973) and *A Map of Misreading* (1975).
14. This work, as we know, is a detective thriller combining gothic suspense with chronicle and scholarship and boxing narrative within narrative, to prove Eco's belief that "plot could be found also in the form of quotation of other plots" and that "the past, since it cannot really be destroyed, because its destruction leads to silence, must be revisited: but with irony, not innocently" (Eco 226-7).
15. The three Russian dramatists all use the code of the absurd theater and intertextuality to achieve their artistic purposes. See Herta Schmid's analysis in "Postmodernism in Russian Drama."
16. Here I refer to the works of Beckett, later Joyce, Chinua Achebe, and Gabriel Marquez.
17. See his *The Sense of an Ending* (1966), quoted in Donoghue, pp. 4-5.
18. Shelley, "When the Lamp Is Shattered," ll. 1-2.

Works Consulted

Arnold, Matthew. *Culture and Anarchy.* Ed. Samuel Lipman. New Haven & London: Yale UP, 1994.

Baudrillard, Jean. *Simulations.* Trans. P. Foss et al. New York: Semiotext(e), 1983.

-----. *The Illusion of the End.* Trans. Chris Turner. Cambridge: Polity Press, 1994.

Bercovitch, Sacvan. "Game of Chess: A Model of Literary and Cultural Studies." *Centuries' Ends, Narrative Means.* Ed. Robert Newman. Stanford, CA: Stanford UP, 1966. 15-36.

Bertens, Hans. "The Postmodern Weltanschauung and Its Relation with Modernism: An Introductory Survey." *Approaching Postmodernism.* Ed. Douwe Fokkema & Hans Bertens. Amsterdam & Philadelphia: John Benjamins, 1986. 12-51.

Best, Steven & Douglas Keller. *Postmodern Theory: Critical Interrogations.* New York: The Guilford Press, 1991.

Brooker, Peter, ed. *Modernism/Postmodernism.* London & New York: Longman, 1992.

Cazzato, Luigi. "Hard Metafiction and the Return of the Author-Subject: The Decline of Postmodernism?" *Postmodern Subjects/Postmodern Texts.* Ed. Jane Dowson & Steven Earnshaw. Amsterdam & Atlanta: Rodopi, 1995. 25-41.

Collins, Jim. *Uncommon Cultures: Popular Culture and Postmodernism.* New York & London: Routledge, 1989.

Docherty, Thomas, ed. *Postmodernism: A Reader*. New York & London: Harvester Wheatsheaf, 1993.

Donnelly, K. J. "A Ramble Through the Margins of the Cityscape: The Postmodern as the Return of Nature." *Postmodern Subjects/Postmodern Texts*. Ed. Jane Dowson & Steven Earnshaw. Amsterdam & Atlanta: Rodopi, 1995. 43-56.

Donoghue, William. "Ends and the Means to Avoid Them: Skepticism and the *fin de siècle*." *Substance*, xxvii, 1 (1998), 3-18.

Eco, Umberto. "Postmodernism, Irony, the Enjoyable." *Modernism/Postmodernism*. Ed. Peter Brooker. New York & London: Longman, 1992. 225-242.

Felski, Rita. "Fin de Siècle, Fin de Sexe: Transsexuality, Postmodernism, and the Death of History." *Centuries' Ends, Narrative Means*. Ed. Robert Newman. Stanford, CA: Stanford UP, 1996. 225-237.

Gadamer, Hans-Georg. *Truth and Method*. New York: Seabury Press, 1975.

Hassan, Ihab. *The Dismemberment of Orpheus*. 2nd ed. Madison: U of Wisconsin P, 1982.

-----. *The Postmodern Turn*. Columbus: Ohio State UP, 1987.

Horton, Rod W. & Vincent F. Hopper. *Backgrounds of European Literature*. New York: Appleton-Century-Crofts, 1954.

Hutcheon, Linda. *A Poetics of Postmodernism: History, Theory, Fiction*. New York & London: Routledge, 1988.

-----. *The Politics of Postmodernism*. London & New York: Routledge, 1989.

Jameson, Fredric. "Postmodernism and Consumer Society." *Postmodernism and Its Discontents*. Ed. E. Ann Kaplan. London: Verso, 1988. 13-29.

-----. *Postmodernism, or the Cultural Logic of Late Capitalism*. London: Verso, 1991.

Jokobson, Roman. *Language in Literature*. Ed. Krystyna Pomorska & Steven Rudy. Cambridge, MS & London: The Belknap Press of Harvard UP, 1987.

Joyce, Michael. *Of Two Minds: Hypertext Pedagogy and Poetics*. Ann Arbor: U of Michigan P, 1995.

Kearney, Richard. *The Wake of Imagination*. London: Hutchinson Education, 1988.

Kernan, Alvin. *The Death of Literature*. New Haven & London: Yale UP, 1990.

Landow, George P. *Hypertext: The Convergence of Contemporary Critical Theory and Technology*. Baltimore & London: The Johns Hopkins UP, 1992.

Luhmann, Niklas. "Why Does Society Describe Itself as Postmodernism?" *Cultural Critique*, 30 (Spring 1995), 171-186.

Lyotard, Jean-François. *The Postmodern Condition*. Manchester: Manchester UP, 1984.

McHale, Brian. *Postmodernist Fiction.* London & New York: Routledge, 1987.

-----. *Constructing Postmodernism.* London & New York: Routledge, 1992.

Mack, Maynard, et al., eds. *The Norton Anthology of World Masterpieces.* 6th ed., vol. 2. New York & London: Norton, 1992.

Madison, G. B. *The Hermeneutics of Postmodernity.* Bloomington: Indiana UP, 1988.

Musarra, Ulla. "Duplication and Multiplication: Postmodernist Devices in the Novels of Italo Calvina." *Approaching Postmodernism.* Ed. Douwe Fokkema & Hans Bertens. Amsterdam & Philadelphia: John Benjamins, 1986. 135-55.

Norris, Christopher. *What's Wrong with Postmodernism: Critical Theory and the End of Philosophy.* Baltimore: The Johns Hopkins UP, 1990.

Peacock, Thomas Love. "The Four Ages of Poetry." *Critical Theory Since Plato.* Ed. Hazard Adams. New York: Harcourt Brace Jovanovich, 1971. 490-7.

Pfeil, Fred. "Potholders and Subincisions: On *The Businessman, Fiskadoro,* and Postmodern Paradise." *Postmodernism and Its Discontents.* Ed. E. Ann Kaplan. London & New York: Verso, 1988. 58-78.

Ray, Robert B. "Postmodernism." *Encyclopedia of Literature and Criticism.* Ed. Martin Coyle, et al. London: Routledge, 1991.

Schmid, Herta. "Postmodernism in Russian Drama: Vampilov, Amalrik, Aksënov." *Approaching Postmodernism.* Ed. Douwe Fokkema & Hans Bertens. Amsterdam & Philalephia: John Benjamins, 1986. 157-82.

Smith, Guy E. *American Literature: A Complete Survey.* New York: Littlefield, Adams & Co., 1957.

Tanner, Tony. *Thomas Pynchon.* London & New York: Methuen, 1982.

* This paper first appeared in1999 in *JLA*, pp. 117-53.

The Augustan "Wit" Re-examined

The word "wit"—along with such words as "sense," "reason," and "taste"—was a key critical term in the Augustan Age of English literature. It carried the Age's value, and it indicated the ideology in which the Age was immersed. Regrettably, however, the key word, just like any other critical term after frequent usage, has been so abused that it often cannot render any clearly-defined sense even in a simple context. Scholars have noticed this difficulty and have tried to clarify the word's meanings. But previous efforts still leave us enough room to re-examine this problematic word.

The word "wit" can be a noun, a pronoun, or a verb. Our discussion here is concerned with it as a noun only. But, even if it is restricted in its nominal usage, the word has shown a very wide variety or unstable range of meanings. The *O.E.D.* (1989), for example, has provided no less than 14 ways of explaining the word, grouped into four categories:

I.   Denoting a faculty (or the person possessing it)
II. Denoting a quality (or the possessor of it)
III. Senses, chiefly obsolete, corresponding to those of L. *scientia* and *sentential*
IV. [Occurring in] Combinations

Yet, even this *O.E.D.* scheme is not very helpful in inspecting the real usage of the word in some 18th century English literature. In Pope's *Essay on Criticism*, for instance, the word "wit" (together with its cognates) occurs 48 times.   Many of the occurrences are troublesome, since the meaning of the word is irritatingly vague.   For example, what is meant by the word "wit" in such a passage:

> *Such once were Critics; such the Happy Few, Athens and Rome in better Ages knew. The mighty Stagirite first left the Shore, Spread all his Sails, and durst the Deeps explore; He steered securely, and discovered far, Led by the Light of the Maeonian Star. Poets, a Race long unconfin'd, and free, Still fond and proud of Savage Liberty, Received his Laws; and stood convinced 'twas fit, Who conquered Nature, should preside o'er Wit.*   (643-52)[1]

Here Pope was talking about the great critics of the past.   First, he mentioned Aristotle, the "mighty Stagirite."   He said that Aristotle was led by Homer, the "Maeonian star."   When he stated that poets received his laws, we know he was referring to Aristotle's laws as brought forth in *Poetics*.   Yet, when he said that poets "stood convinced 'twas fit,/Who conquered Nature, should preside o'er Wit," was he referring to Aristotle as a conqueror of nature?   Did he think Aristotle, rather than Homer, "should preside o'er Wit"?   Obviously, "Wit" here is a collective noun.   It denotes all people who possess the faculty or quality of "wit."   But, who did Pope think were the possessors of "wit"? Critics like Aristotle or writers like Homer?

Before we answer this question, let us probe into the nature of wit as a faculty or quality first.   To do so, let us first read these lines:

> *My love in her attire doth show her wit,*
> *It doth so well become her;*
> *For every season she hath dressings fit,*
> *For winter, spring, and summer.*

> *No beauty she doth miss*
> *When all her robes are on;*
> *But beauty's self she is*
> *When all her robes are gone.*

These lines constitute an anonymous "Madrigal" appearing in an anthology entitled *A Poetical Rhapsody* published in 1602.[2] They clearly claim that the speaker's mistress is a possessor of wit. Besides that, they also suggest, at least, these two points: First, wit is a faculty of knowing what becomes or fits whom. Second, wit is an adorning quality, just like fit dressings. The first point brings us naturally to Dryden's comment that "[Wit] is a propriety of thoughts and words,"[3] for "propriety" is what is fitting or becoming. The second point, then, leads us to Pope's famous saying: "True Wit is Nature to Advantage drest" (*Essay on Criticism,* 297-8). Nature, like beauty, needs wit to dress it to advantage.

In fact, the idea of propriety and the idea of adornment are closely tied together: propriety lies in the fitting or becoming aspect between the adornment and the adorned, and no adornment is considered good without this fitting aspect. Therefore, it can be presumed that the idea of "proper adornment" is an essential idea of the Augustan Age for "wit" as a faculty or quality. In effect, many problems, as we shall see, are mere ramifications from this basic idea.

Take the problem of "true wit vs. false wit" for example. It depends actually on the criteria of propriety and the status of adornment assigned for wit. On one hand, for instance, we have Cowley, who says, "In a true piece of Wit all things must be,/Yet all things there agree" ("Ode: Of Wit," 57-8). For Cowley, then, propriety is equal to agreeability among all things in the whole. This is no other than the criterion of *discordia concors* proposed by Johnson in his criticism of Cowley in *Lives of the Poets* (Johnson 15). On the other hand, we have Addison, who, echoing Locke, at first says that "true wit generally consists in this resemblance and congruity of ideas, false wit chiefly consists in the resemblance and congruity sometimes of single letters …," but later elliptically says that "true wit consists in the resemblance of ideas, and false wit in the resemblance of words."[4] "Congruity" means actually the same as "agreeability" or *discordia concors*. Nevertheless, it is shown here that in Addison's mind propriety of wit is judged primarily on the basis of resemblance rather than congruity. And at the same time we see that by disparaging the resemblance of words as false wit, Addison is echoing Cowley's idea that wit is "not to adorn and gild each part … not when two like words make up one noise …" ("Of Wit," 33-54), since words are considered as adornment for ideas.

As we know, Addison's discriminating true wit from false wit originates in Locke's differentiating wit from judgment:

> … *wit lying most in the assemblage of ideas, and putting those together with quickness and variety, wherein can be found any resemblance or congruity, thereby to make up pleasant pictures and agreeable visions in the fancy; judgment, on the contrary, lies quite on the other side, in separating carefully, one from another, ideas wherein can be found the least difference, thereby to avoid being misled by similitude, and by affinity to take one thing for another.* (II, xi, 2)

For Locke, then, wit is an assembling faculty, not a separating faculty (which is attributed to judgment). And wit functions with ideas, not with words. But wit is not mere "assemblage of ideas." To qualify for wit, the ideas should be put together "with quickness and variety."[5] They should have "resemblance or congruity" in themselves. And they should "make up pleasant pictures and agreeable visions in the fancy." Postulating such qualifying conditions, Locke says as much as: A wit is able to, quickly and with variety, assemble ideas with resemblance or congruity in themselves, so as to make up pleasant pictures and agreeable visions in the fancy.   Hence, the attributes of wit as a faculty or quality include quickness, variety, synthesis, and pleasure, besides resemblance and congruity.

Addison accepted Locke's explanation of wit, but he added: "every resemblance of ideas is not that which we call wit, unless it be such an one that gives delight and surprise to the reader.   These two properties seem essential to wit, more particularly the last of them" (*The Spectator*, No. 62, in Bond 264).   So, for Addison wit includes, furthermore, the property of surprise.   This particular property, he suggested, stems from finding likeness in apparently dissimilar ideas: "In order therefore that the resemblance in the ideas be wit, it is necessary that the ideas should not lie too near one another in the nature of things; for where the likeness is obvious, it gives no surprise." (*The Spectator*, No. 62, in Bond 264)

Actually, Addison did not rest with accepting and modifying Locke's account of wit.   He finally came up with a casual remark which virtually collapses Locke's dichotomy between wit and judgment.   He said that "not only the resemblance but the opposition of ideas does very often produce wit," as he "could show in several little points, turns, and antitheses," that he might "possibly enlarge upon in some future speculation" (*The Spectator*, No. 62, in Bond 270).   Yet, he never returned to the topic.   Earlier, in fact, he had objected to Dryden's definition of wit as "a propriety of words and thoughts adapted to the subject," and had lauded Bouhours for showing that "the basis of all wit is truth" (*The Spectator*, No. 62, in Bond 268).   It seems that for Addison truth, found in resemblance or opposition of ideas, is more essential to wit than propriety of words and thoughts.

To emphasize the truth-finding ability, rather than the adorning art, is to return to what C. S. Lewis calls "the old sense of wit."   According to Lewis,

"Anglo-Saxon *wit* or *gewit* is mind, reason, intelligence" (86). The word is originally very close to *ingenium* in Latin:

> *What is being talked about is the thing which, in its highest exaltation may border on madness; the productive, seminal (modern cant would say "creative") thing, as distinct from the critical faculty of* judicium; *the thing which he who has it may love too well and follow intemperately. It is what distinguishes the great writer and especially the great poet. It is therefore very close to "imagination."* (92)

But in practical usage the old sense gradually gave way to "the dangerous sense of wit," namely, "that sort of mental agility or gymnastic which uses language as the principal equipment of its gymnasium" such as found in "pun, half pun, assonance, epigram (in the modern sense) and distorted proverb or quotation" (97). It is this dangerous wit that makes the constant skirmish between Benedick and Beatrice in Shakespeare's *Much Ado about Nothing*, creates Falstaff's humor, and, to be sure, builds up Lyly's Euphuism. As we know, Lyly's *Euphues* is subtitled "The Anatomy of Wit." But it is in effect not an analysis of the truth-finding intelligence, but a display of "witty," stylistic features: an elaborate sentence structure with a wealth of ornamental skills, showing the Elizabethans' fascination with language.

It is in the second half of the 17th century, Lewis tells us further, that "we find the most abundant and amusing evidence of the word's drift towards its *dangerous sense*" (100). Lewis gives examples from Davenant, Flecknoe, Shadwell, and Dryden, and lists such things as conceits, clenches, quibbles, jingles, poor antitheses, poor paranomasia, repartees, and other trifles. In the Age, indeed, important men of letters had already felt the danger and had tried to provide a correct definition of wit. Cowley in his "Ode of Wit," for instance, had warned the world by his negative definitions of it. And in the Preface to his *Annus Mirabilis* (1667) Dryden had divided it into "wit writing" and "wit written" and positively defined thus:

> *... wit in the poet, or wit writing ... is no other than the faculty of imagination in the writer which, like a nimble spaniel, beats over and ranges through the field of memory, till it springs the quarry it hunted after; or, without metaphor, which searches over all the memory for the species or ideas of those things which it designs to represent. Wit written is that which is well defined, the happy result of thought, or product of imagination.* (i, 97-98)

Dryden's equating "wit writing" with "the faculty of imagination in the writer," and "wit written" with "the happy result of thought, or product of imagination," is a clear proof that wit is for him a creative power. And his explanation shows that for him the aim (the "quarry") of creative wit (the "nimble spaniel") is to catch what "it designs to represent," that is, good "species or ideas of things" lurking in the memory, not the ways of expressing the ideas. Therefore, Dryden is here emphasizing the truth-finding faculty, not the adorning art of language. This emphasis surely goes against his later conception of wit as "a propriety of thoughts and words" or "thought and words elegantly adapted to the subject."

Dryden's lack of consistency was felt by Pope, perhaps. For, after Dryden's death, Pope wrote to William Wycherley and said: "Our wit ... is but reflection or imitation, therefore scarce to be called ours. True wit ... may be defined a justness of thought and a facility of expression, or (in the midwives' phrase) a perfect conception with an easy delivery" (Goldgar 29). Pope conceded that "this is far from a complete definition," but we know it is much more complete than Dryden's "spaniel definition" or "propriety definition." It actually takes into account both Dryden's "wit writing" (the nimble spaniel for "justness of thought" or "perfect conception") and his "wit written" (the proper adaptation of words and thoughts to the subject, the "facility of expression" or "easy delivery").

Although Pope has a much more complete definition of wit, his use of the term, as we have said above, is most confusing. And now we can say: that is due to three reasons. First, as many scholars have pointed out, Pope refuses to separate wit from judgment cleanly. For him wit "becomes not only a faculty which provides quickness of insight and liveliness of expression, but also a controlling and ordering faculty," and thus, wit and judgment "seem to be … differing aspects of the same faculty" (Audra & Williams 218). That is why in the *Essay on Criticism* he tells us that "Some to whom Heaven in Wit has been profuse,/Want as much more, to turn it to its use" (80-81).

Second, Pope makes no true distinction between the writer's wit and the reader's. And this is nowhere more manifest than in his *Essay on Criticism*. As we all can see, the Essay starts with "describing the highest form of artistic talent in the poet as true genius, and the highest gift of the critic as true taste"; it yet (in lines 15-16) "proceeds to the principle that the best critics are those who excel as authors" (Hooker 226). Therefore, the Essay is actually not just on criticism; it is clearly also on creative writing as well. One can justifiably say: it is even more on creative writing than on critical reading. That is why more authors than critics are referred to, and seemingly more art of poetry than art of criticism is taught, therein. And that is why, as mentioned above, there are cases where his "wit" can ambiguously refer to a poet like Homer and a critic like Aristotle at the same time.

The third reason for Pope's confusing use of the term "wit" is his tendency to fuse criticism, poetry, and morality altogether. Patricia Spacks has pointed out that for Pope, "the identity between the good critic and the good man is not just possible but almost necessary" (27). That is why in the *Essay on Criticism* wit is often associated with good breeding, and we are reminded that "As Men of Breeding, sometimes Men of Wit,/T'avoid great Errors, must the less commit" (259-60), and that "Good Nature and Good Sense must ever join;/To Err is Human; to Forgive, Divine" (524-5). Pope, of course, was not the first to consider wit in the light of a whole person's whole character. In Shakespeare's time, for instance, when people talked about the "university wits," they also had in mind such people's conduct, besides their ability to criticize and write. Nevertheless, Pope was certainly the greatest to attack those who lacked wit in criticism, creativity, and social conduct. In truth, he called those who lack wit dunces, and the *Dunciad* is his mock-epic for those "lack-wits," false wits or witlings.

William Empson has truthfully pointed out that a wit in the Augustan Age may be a bright social talker, a critic of the arts or of society, or a poet or artist, who applies his wit in mocking, acting as judge, or giving aesthetic pleasure or expressing new truths (86). But it is to be doubted that "in the smart milieu which Pope was addressing," the most prominent meaning of "wit" is something like "power to make ingenious (and critical) jokes" (Empson 85). We can agree that there must have been people then who would be pleased with Mercutio's joking wit. But it was unlikely that the Augustans could forget such "patriarch-wits" as Homer and Aristotle in their praise of a mere jester like D'Urfey. As far as we can see in Pope's *Essay on Criticism*, true wit is indeed "the sum of the characteristics in the human mind that make intellectual, cultural, and (to a great extent) moral life possible"; it is "a fusion of all the best elements of the human mind in the right proportions" (Isles 262-3).

To take "wit" for its most general sense is to comply to the neo-classical propensity for generality. Ironically, however, even great wits have been unable to do so since classical times. So far in this paper we have pointed out, directly and indirectly, many important attributes of "wit" as a faculty or quality: propriety, adornment, quickness, variety, synthesis, pleasure, resemblance, congruity, surprise, truth, creativity, etc. But these are still far from a complete list. By the time of Pope, it is said, the word "wit" had accumulated "a score or more of synonyms, including ingenuity, invention, imagination, fancy, extravagancy, epigrammatic conceit, humor, raillery, satire, irony, criticism, and ridicule" (Milburn 29). Furthermore, it was found in a wide variety of manifestations:

> *Sometimes it lieth in pat allusion to a known story, or in seasonable application of a trivial saying, or in forging an apposite tale; sometimes it playeth in words and phrases, taking advantage from the ambiguity of their sense, or the affinity of their sound; sometimes it is wrapped in a dress of humorous expression; sometimes it lurketh under an odd similitude; sometimes it is logged in a sly question, in a smart answer, in a quirkish reason, in a shrewd intimation, in cunning diverting, or cleverly retorting an objection; sometimes it is couched in a bold scheme of speech, in a tart irony, in a lusty hyperbole, in a startling metaphor, in a plausible reconciling of contradictions, or an acute nonsense; sometimes a scenical representation of persons or things, a counterfeit speech, a mimical look or gesture passeth for it; sometimes an affected simplicity, sometimes a presumptuous bluntness giveth it being; sometimes it riseth from a lucky hitting upon what is strange, sometimes from a crafty wrestling obvious matter to the purpose.[6]*

Besides, by the time of neoclassicism the word had become a "signal word" for "extending those arguments that had beset the Renaissance rhetoricians and critics: simplicity versus ornamentation, word versus thought, reason versus imagination, delight versus instruction, and, finally, imaginative perception versus the literal statement of truth" (Milburn 75). And, in the light of psychology, it had indeed been variously identified with intellect, understanding, the antithesis of dullness, judgment, imagination, *and* both judgment and imagination.[7] Facing such a complicated situation, what can we say of this wit-racking "wit"?

First, no matter how many attributes it may have, no matter what word may be its synonym, no matter on what occasion or in what case it may be used, and no matter with what argument it may be connected, the Augustan "wit" is either a human faculty or a quality of an object. In terms of writing, the faculty-quality dichotomy is no other than the distinction between what Dryden calls "wit writing" and "wit written," respectively. In terms of conversation, however, it should be "wit speaking" and "wit spoken" instead. In actuality, if we want to extend it to the most general usage, we may well call this bifurcation "inward wit" and "outward wit," meaning that it is either a faculty inherent in a person or a quality expressed in a perceivable object.

Second, we know Coleridge divides imagination into the primary and the secondary.[8] And, as most critics agree, what Coleridge calls the primary imagination is the power of human perception, the secondary the power of artistic creation. Under this broad understanding, however, different interpretations have been made about Coleridge's description of the dichotomy.[9] My view is: the primary imagination is indeed a perceptive power, a power leading to the poet's insight or vision, that is, a pre-composition power employed to "see into the life of things," or, to use a common phrase, to "get ideas for writing," whereas the secondary imagination is indeed a power of artistic creation, a composition power employed in the writing stage to "re-create" the poet's insight or vision, to express in a suitable form the idea the primary imagination has obtained for him (Tung 119-20). Now, if we consider the Augustan "wit" in the light of this differentiation, we find the Augustans certainly lacked this critical acumen. They should have understood that as a synonym for imagination, "wit" could likewise be both a truth-finding "pre-composition power" and an expression-finding "composition power." Besides, they should have agreed that "the expression ... is not the result of a separate act but exists in the most intimate and necessary relationship with the ideas, emotions, and attitudes of the artist, being engendered along with them" (Hooker 245).

We have mentioned above that critics like Addison followed Locke to discriminate wit as an assembling faculty from judgment as a separating faculty. Furthermore, true wit as resemblance of ideas is discriminated from false wit as resemblance of words. But this further discrimination is somewhat invalidated by the observation that wit is very often produced not only by the resemblance, but also by the opposition as well, of ideas. In truth, no faculty can assemble without separation, nor can any faculty separate without assemblage: a true wit must be able to analyze and synthesize at the same time. In real life, it is true that one may tend to judge better than write; therefore, one can be more a critic than a poet. Yet, a truly great wit, like Homer or Aristotle, ought to have enough sense or intellect to see both similarities and differences, that is, he must have the ability both to fuse, blend, or combine and to break, sever, or disunite. What makes Homer differ from Aristotle is not that one lacks judging wit while the other lacks writing wit, but that one's work is called poetry while the other's is called criticism. In actuality, they both must have exercised their analytical and synthetic power at once in getting their ideas and in writing their works. In other words, true wit is both critical and creative all the time.

It follows, then, that to treat resemblance of ideas as true wit and resemblance of words as false wit is itself a false discrimination. Certainly it takes great wit to see meaningful resemblances in chaotically different ideas. Nevertheless, it takes great wit, too, to see useful resemblances in multitudinous words (with regard to their sound, shape, and sense). In fact, it takes nothing but great wit as well to find contrasts, oppositions, inconsistencies, etc., in similar ideas or words. In a time when method is judged as no less important than matter, and when expression is found hardly distinguishable from content, we really have no position to hold that wit can be called true or false merely due to its being exercised on ideas (content) or on words (expression).

Third, the Augustan wits, as neo-classicists, derived their ideas and problems from the classical times.   Since antiquity there had been a struggle "between the custodians of pure idea and pure fact, dialecticians and scientists, on the one hand, and on the other, the custodians of the riches of the 'word,' grammarians, rhetoricians, critics, exegetes" (Wimsatt & Brooks 222).   This struggle came to a critical point during the 17th century.   Many followed the French logician Peter Ramus to separate rhetoric cleanly from dialectic. Originally, the art of rhetoric was alleged to have five parts: Invention, Disposition, Elocution, Memory, and Delivery.   Now the Ramists "took invention, disposition, and memory away from rhetoric and gave them securely and univocally to dialectic, leaving to rhetoric proper only elocution (that is, style) and delivery" (Wimsatt & Brooks 223).   This separatist move, I believe, was no less consequential than the "dissociation of sensibility." With a view to its bad effect up to the Augustan Age, I believe it had, at least, given rise to whole generations of dunces, of false wits, who sought only rhetorical ornaments in writing.

It should be noticed that the Augustan Age was an era in which art rather than nature was highly promoted.   Hence Pope's statement: "True Ease in Writing comes from Art, not Chance/As those move easiest who have learned to dance" (*Essay on Criticism*, 362-3).   In writing, therefore, the art of using language (i.e., rhetoric) became a crucial discipline and the finding of insightful truth for the content became seemingly less important.   Under the circumstances, interestingly, linguistic expression was often compared to dress.   Besides Pope's "True Wit is Nature to Advantage drest," we have, for instance, Johnson's direct statement:

> *Language is the dress of thought: and, as the noblest mien, or*
> *most graceful action, would be degraded and obscured by a garb*
> *appropriated to the gross employments of rusticks or mechanicks;*
> *so the most heroick sentiments will lose their efficacy, and the*
> *most splendid ideas drop their magnificence, if they are conveyed*
> *by words used commonly upon low and trivial occasions, debased*
> *by vulgar mouths, and contaminated by inelegant applications.*
> (51)

This remark surely emphasizes the idea of proper adornment. In addition, the dress-metaphor implies that thought or idea is the body. It follows, then, that we can argue: "Which is more important, the body or the dress?" In the "Madrigal" quoted earlier above, we hear the speaker praise his love first for her having the wit to wear fit dressings and miss no beauty on all her robes, but his ending comment is: "But beauty's self she is/When all her robes are gone." This comment, for all its sexually playful tone, suggests seriously that the body itself rather than the attire can be, and should be, the real object of beauty sought after. The great Augustans, to be sure, were not unaware of the value of the body. Swift, for instance, said satirically in his *A Tale of a Tub* that there were currently 9743 wits in England, belonging to many different schools including the school of critics and the school of poetry (25), but "Wit, without knowledge, being a Sort of Cream, which gathers in a Night to the Top, and by a skilful Hand, may be soon whipt into Froth; but once scumm'd away, what appears underneath will be fit for nothing, but to be thrown to the Hogs" (138). Nevertheless, the Augustan society, as Dryden and Pope had suggested, was full of dunces. For most ordinary Augustans, what easily counted as wit was certainly not the finding of the knowledge (truth, body, content) underneath, but the making of the cream (froth, dress, expression) on the surface.

The Augustans are certainly better considered in terms of contrast with the Romantics who followed after. Indeed, we must admit that both Augustans and Romantics want beauty and want truth. However, they are obviously different in their emphasis, and their difference is best seen in the fashionable use of critical terms. By nature and by definition, "wit" is more easily linked to proper adornment, and "imagination" to visionary truth. So it is only natural that the rhetorically-inclined Augustans talked more of "wit" while the dialectically-inclined Romantics talked more of "imagination." And no wonder, too, that while the Augustans strove most painstakingly with their *wit* to polish their dress and language, the Romantics expected most faithfully with their *imagination* or vision "to pierce into and illuminate the most profound truths of human experience" (Audra & Aubrey 214), or to reveal essential truth or "thought lying too deep for tears" as Wordsworth put it. Furthermore, the course of wit's losing ground to the rise of imagination was but a natural outcome of its going too far. To tell it clearly, the shift from the Augustan to the Romantic was a shift from rhetoric back again to dialectic. To replace "wit" with "imagination" in the vogue of phrases was but another sign of historical swing between two extremes or phases, with one (rhetoric) serving as the thesis and the other (dialectic) as its antithesis.

Notes

1. Hereinafter the parenthesized line numbers of Pope's *Essay on Criticism* refer to the reprinted version of the work in John Butt, ed., *The Poems of Alexander Pope* (1989).
2. Reprinted in M. H. Abrams, ed., *The Norton Anthology of English Literature*, 5th edition (1986), vol. I, p. 999.
3. See Dryden's "The Author's Apology for Heroic Poetry and Heroic License," an essay prefixed to *State of Innocence*, the libretto for an opera based on *Paradise Lost*. The key phrases are reprinted in Abrams, p. 1848. Pope also defined wit as propriety in a letter dated November 29, 1707.
4. See *The Spectator*, No. 62 (Friday, March 11, 1711).

5. John Sitter in his *Arguments of Augustan Wit* says: "... with and judgment are not distinct actions but different manners: one 'quick,' the other 'careful.' To Matthew Prior, at least, Locke's judgment would seem a name for slow wit." See Sitter, 67.

6. This list was prepared by Dr. Isaac Barrow, a 17th –century divine, as part of a sermon preached about 1677 on the subject of foolish talking and jesting. Reprinted in Milburn, pp. 30-31, from *Theological Works* (Oxford, 1830), I, 386.

7. See Milburn, pp. 77-118 ("The Psychology of Wit").

8. See his *Biographia Literaria,* Chapter XIII.

9. See Tung, *Imagination and the Process of Literary Creation,* Chapter 3.

Works Consulted

Abrams, M. H. ed. *Norton Anthology of English Literature*, vol. 1. New York: Norton, 1986.

Audra E. & Aubrey Williams, eds. *Pastoral Poetry and An Essay on Criticism.* London: Methuen, 1961.

Bond, Donald F., ed. *The Spectator*, vol. 1. Oxford: At the Clarendon Press, 1987.

Coleridge, S. T. *Biographia Literaria.* Revised & ed., J. Shawcross. Oxford: Clarendon P, 1954,

Cowley, Abraham. "Ode: of Wit," rpt. In Abrams, 1664-5.

Dryden, John. "The Author's Apology for Heroic Poetry and Heroic License," rpt. In Abrams, 1847-8.

--------. Preface to *Annus Mirabilis.* In *Of Dramatic Poesy and Other Critical Essays*, 2vols. Ed. George Watson. New York: Dutton, 1962.

Empson, William. *The Structure of Complex Words.* Cambridge MS: Harvard UP, 1989.

Goldgar, Bertrand A. *Literary Criticism of Alexander Pope.* Lincoln: U of Nebraska P, 1965.

Hooker, Edward Niles. "Pope on Wit: The Essay on Criticism." *The Seventeenth Century: Studies in the History of English Thought and Literature from Bacon to Pope.* Ed. Richard Foster Jones, et al. Stanford, CA: Stanford UP, 1951.

Isles, Duncan. "Pope and Criticism." *Writers and Their Background: Alexander Pope.* Ed. Peter Dixon. Athens: Ohio UP, 1975.

Johnson, Samuel. *Lives of the Poets.* In *The Works of Samuel Johnson*, vol. 7. Oxford English Classics. New York: AMS Press, 1970.

Lewis, C. S. *Studies in Words*, 2nd Edition. Cambridge: Cambridge UP, 1967.

Locke, John. *An Essay Concerning Human Understanding*. Booko @ Adelaide 2004, II, xi, 2.

Milburn, D. Judson. *The Age of Wit: 1650-1750.* New York: Macmillan, 1966.

Pope, Alexander. *Essay on Criticism*, rpt. in *The Poems of Alexander Pope.* Ed. John Butt. London: Routledge, 1989. 143-68.

Sitter, John. *Argument of Augustan Wit.* Cambridge: Cambridge UP, 1991.

Spacks, Patricia Meyer. *An Argument of Images: The Poetry of Alexander Pope.* Cambridge MS: Harvard UP, 1971.

Swift, Jonathan. *A Tale of a Tub.* 5th Edition, rpt. in *A Tale of a Tub with Other Early Works.* Ed. Herbert Davis. Oxford: Basil Blackwell, 1957.

Tung, C. H. *Imagination and the Process of Literary Creation.* Taipei: Bookman Books, 1991.

Wimsatt, William K. Jr., & Cleanth Brooks. *Literary Criticism: A Short History.* New York: Vintage Books, 1957.

*This paper first appeared in 2005 in *JH,* pp. 333-52.

Biotechnology and Creative Writing

Life Science

Is there any relationship between biotechnology and creative writing? Many people, including biotechnologists and creative writers, may doubt if there is any, even though we are manifestly living in a time when interdisciplinary considerations are highly promoted. With "Biotechnology and Creative Writing" as its topic, this essay aims, of course, to show that there are indeed some noteworthy relations between these two disciplines. But before we probe into details, let me remind everyone, at the outset, that biology deals with life in the concrete; it studies such perceivable things as cells, tissues, organs, systems, and other forms of living beings whereas literature deals with life presumably in the abstract and yet it comprises no less perceivable things than organisms, as it refers to interactions among living (especially human) beings in connection with their environments, and to the linguistic signs which express the interactive relations. Thus, biotechnology as the skills of handling life forms is certainly not unlinkably far from creative writing as the skills of expressing life manners. Both are "life science" despite their different concerns.

Organic Form

Science as systematized knowledge has various branches. Different branches of science never cease to influence one another. Natural sciences, for instance, have been providing ideas, sometimes terms along with ideas, for the stamina of developing social sciences. In the field of literature, for example, we see the 17th-century metaphysical poetry was obviously "contaminated" by the ideas of such natural sciences as physics, astronomy, and geography.

Biology is an old science as Aristotle is considered to be an ancient biologist. But the great strength of biology had never been felt so deeply until the 19th century when Darwin produced his theory of evolution by natural selection. Before Darwin, however, biological ideas had entered literati's thinking. The early 19th-century poet-critic S. T. Coleridge, for instance, had the idea of "organic form vs. mechanic form":

> *The form is mechanic when on any given material we impress a predetermined form, not necessarily arising out of the properties of the material, as when to a mass of clay we give whatever shape we wish it to retain when hardened. The organic form, on the other hand, is innate; it shapes as it develops itself from within, and the fullness of its development is one and the same with the perfection of its outward form. Such is the life, such the form.* (462)

The same emphasis on the "organic" aspect of vitalism is also seen in the pre-romantics (e.g., Edward Young) as well as the later romantics (e.g., John Keats). Yet, this organic thinking extends even to some realistic fiction writers. The late 19th-century novelist-critic Henry James, for example, says:

> *A novel is a living thing, all one and continuous, like any other organism, and in proportion as it lives will it be found, I think, that in each of the parts there is something of each of the other parts.* (*The Art of Fiction,* 666)

And for him a statement of merely ten words overheard on a Christmas Eve was a sufficient "germ" to develop into a novel.[1]

If the process of literary creation is a growing and ripening process like that of a living organism, the technique involved in the process is naturally not just a throwing in or piling up of all available elements, much less of irrelevant odds and ends. To be sure, it needs the culling of proper elements and the proper arrangement of the culled parts to make a nice, harmonious whole. Thus, this process is very similar to that of modern biotechnology in producing things by recombinant DNA methods.

The Text

Even though a piece of literary creation is often conceived as a living organism, it is often referred to as a text as well. And the word "text," as we know and as Roland Barthes has repeatedly mentioned, in its etymology simply means a tissue, a web, a fabric or something woven. This meaning has played down the implication of "life or living" for sure. But it has increased the sense of structure. Now, what has a text or structure? Everything, of course. In a biologist's eyes a tissue is an aggregate of cells usually of a particular kind together with their intercellular substance that form one of the structural materials of a plant or an animal. And every living thing is a composite of tissues which are often organized into organs. In fact, in a naturalist's eye even a rock has its texture, that is, its structural pattern. Indeed, modern scientists have told us that things are all made up of atoms in accordance with certain structures, and even atoms are structures of even smaller things called protons, electrons, neutrons, etc. If we turn from the microcosmic worlds to the macrocosmic worlds, we find, for instance, the solar system, too, is a text or structure with its constituents displaying a sort of pattern. As to the galaxies, we know they are each a unit of billions of systems each including stars, nebulae, star clusters, globular clusters, and inter-stellar matter that make up the universe. So, we can proclaim that all things, great and small, are texts indeed.

Creative writing is to produce literary texts. What is a literary text, then? In most people's minds, the literary text usually refers to the written text. That is why Paul Ricoeur can say, " a text is any discourse fixed by writing" (331). And that is why G. Thomas Tanselle can state that "As artifacts, literary texts are analogous to musical scores in providing the basis for the reconstitution of works" (24). When the text is restricted to the notion of the written text, it is often accompanied with a sense of permanence, which led Shakespeare to claim, in his sonnet 55, that "Not marble, nor the gilded monuments/Of princes, shall outlive this powerful rhyme," and led Roland Barthes to say "the text is a weapon against time, oblivion and the trickery of speech, which is so easily taken back, altered, denied" (32).

But in point of fact, our notion of the literary text should not be restricted to the written text. In the final analysis, every literary work is a composite of words, and words have sound, shape, and sense. Therefore, a literary text is a structure of sounds, shapes, and senses. What are the ingredients in such essential elements of poetry as meter, rhyme, imagery, symbol, denotation and connotation? And what are in such structural elements of fiction and drama as plot, character, setting, and theme? Aren't they all words with sound, shape, and sense? Indeed, when a writer wields the pen to demonstrate his talent by bringing forth ambiguity, metaphor, metonymy, paradox, irony, allusion, etc., or double plot, surprise ending, split personality, flat character, innocent narrator, humor, fantasy, local color, stream of consciousness, etc., can any of the techniques dispense with words which have sound, shape, and sense?

It follows, then, that as literature is a verbal art, its text is but a verbal structure. According to Roman Jokobson, there are two basic modes of arrangement used in verbal behavior, namely, selection and combination (71). These two modes (called paradigmatic and syntagmatic relations in semiotics) are indeed the basic ways of constructing a textual pattern of any kind. All texts are certainly representable as networks of their horizontal syntagms plus their vertical paradigms, thus suggesting the idea of woven fabrics. It is only that for many the literary text does not appear to be so well-knit or so neatly woven with homogeneous materials. For Jeremy Hawthorn, for instance, the literary text resembles "a fortified medieval town" in which "foreigners and outsiders are repelled, or allowed in only after rigorous checks, but within all is bustling life; exchange, mutual interdependence and influence are the rule" (41). And for the New Critics who persist in seeing "tension" or "irony" or "paradox" in a text, "conflict elements" are to be selected and "conflict structures" are to be combined in the literary text.

Now, does biotechnology use the same basic modes of arrangement in producing (or reproducing) a form of organism (a biological text)? And is it concerned with the problem of "homogeneous or heterogeneous" constituents?

According to the definition of the Office of Technology Assessment of the United States Congress dismantled in 1995, biotechnology is "any technique that uses living organisms or substances from those organisms, to make or modify a product, to improve plants or animals, or to develop microorganisms for specific uses" (quoted in Barnum 2). Thus, biotechnology uses no single tool or technique to bring out its product. Yet, if we choose to narrow down its reference and refer it only to recombinant DNA technology (and this narrow sense is for many the sense most commonly understood), we will find the basic principles of biotechnology are similar to those of creative writing.

Gene cloning, as we understand, is the work of recombinant DNA technology. Its process begins with the isolation of a gene which is well characterized. If this isolated and well-characterized gene is really good for use, it will then be inserted into a DNA molecule that serves as a vehicle or vector, thus combining two DNAs of different origin and making a recombinant DNA molecule. The molecule can then be moved into a host where it can be reproduced.[2]

Now, the isolation and characterization of a gene is equivalent to the stage of selection in creative writing (selecting a linguistic unit with its particular sound, shape, and sense), and the insertion and combination of genes or DNAs is equivalent to the stage of combination in creative writing where the selected linguistic unit is inserted into a syntactic sequence. The resultant, i.e., the recombinant DNA molecule, is similar to a phrase which can be put in use in a larger unit of syntax ("moved into a host") and used repeatedly ("reproduced").

It is said that "two major categories of enzymes are important tools in the isolation of DNA and the preparation of recombinant DNA": "restriction endonucleases that act as scissors to cut DNA at specific sites and DNA ligase that is the glue that joins two DNA molecules in the test tube" (Barnum 58). It is not necessary here to explain how these two categories of enzymes are obtained and made to work. Suffice it that the restriction enzyme is like the power of judgment while the enzyme DNA ligase is like the power of imagination in creative writing. For, as we know, judgment is an analytical power, a power employed to cut apart, to recognize differences in similitude, whereas imagination is a synthetic power, a power employed to glue together, to make a whole of parts.[3]

In fact, it is not only a creative writer but also a biotechnologist that needs both judgment and imagination. It takes a biotechnologist's judgment, for instance, to decide which particular gene (as different from others) ought to be separated from the rest of the chromosomal DNA and transferred to a foreign host cell. And it takes a biotechnologist's imagination to envisage the result of introducing some genetic material into foreign cells to be replicated there and passed on to progeny cells. In this process of judgment and imagination, whether a genetic property is homogeneous or heterogeneous to other properties in the cell is naturally a problem to be taken into consideration, just as the homogeneity or heterogeneity of a certain textual property in a certain context has to be considered by a creative writer when constructing a certain text.

The Code

We have said that literature is a verbal art and hence a literary text cannot but be a verbal structure, a text woven with words, a tissue concocted with sounds, shapes, and senses of words. This description, in effect, implies a semiotic dimension. Words, as we know, are signs, and signs are not the things but stand for the things. In Ferdinand de Saussure's view, a linguistic text is a linear sequence of words, and words as symbols or signs are made up of two parts: the signifier (the mark, either written or spoken, that represents) and the signified (the concept, thought, or meaning that is represented by the mark).[4] In truth, before the writing system was invented, mankind only used oral words, hence only had sounds for the signifiers to signify the senses to be communicated in ordinary speech or poetic (literary) discourse. Later, after the invention of the writing system, mankind began then to use visual words to communicate, and hence word shapes began to signify word sounds which in turn signify word senses.

It is interesting to note here that a genetic text is also a linear sequence with genetic substance signifying genetic content, and, moreover, that (according to the central dogma of molecular biology) "the flow of genetic information is from DNA to RNA to protein" (Barnum 42). And this process includes a stage of transcription and one of translation. In the stage of transcription, "RNA is synthesized, or transcribed, from a DNA template by the main replication enzyme RNA polymerase," and through this transcription "the genetic information stored in the DNA (gene) is used to make an RNA that is complementary" (Barnum 44). In the stage of translation, the information encoded in the RNA is converted into a sequence of amino acids forming a polypeptide chain by transporting the newly synthesized RNA into the cytoplasm, the site of translation. This final stage is a stage of protein synthesis carried out by mRNA, tRNA, rRNA, etc.[5]

Now, if we equate genetic message to verbal message, the genetic transcription of RNA for DNA is much like the transcription of speech for thoughts (of sounds for senses), and the genetic translation of RNA into protein (sequence of amino acids) is much like the translation of speech into writing (of sounds into shapes). This comparison seems to be all the more pertinent if we recognize the fact that for all its importance in the entire coding process, RNA appears to function but as an intermediate or transitory factor just as in a literary or linguistic text the phonological system appears to be complementary to the graphic system and serve merely as an intermediate or transitory factor between senses and shapes. This understanding, to be sure, may add piquancy to Jacques Derrida's attack on "phonocentrism," the privileging of speech over writing for its being closer to an originating thought from a living body.

In biotechnology, the genetic code refers to "the relationship of nucleotides to amino acids," and "the genetic language of the gene is the nucleotide" while "the language of proteins is the amino acid" (Barnum 42). Therefore, a biotechnologist engaged in cutting and joining DNA is one involved in manipulating the genetic language or the genetic code so as to change the natural result of genetic transcription and/or genetic translation.

This is analogous to a creative writer's manipulation of the verbal language to reshape his image of the experienced life by imaginative transcription of ideas into sounds and translation of sounds into shapes. In other words, a biotechnologist tries to "write" or "rewrite" a sequence of amino acids in order to express his intended genetic information while a creative writer "writes" or "rewrites" a sequence of words in order to express his image of the experienced life.

The System

Creative writing produces literary texts by using the linguistic (or literary) code; biotechnology creates genetic products by using the genetic code. A code is a system made up of a finite number of symbols although the ways of combining the symbols for various meanings can be infinite. The English language, for instance, has less than 40 vowels and consonants to make up its sound system, and only 26 letters to make up its shape (writing, graphic) system. Yet, the words, phrases, sentences, texts, etc., engendered from the sounds or letters are really infinite. Likewise, life forms or living organisms are infinite in number. But the proteins which constitute the unlimited number of things are all made up of 20 amino acids that vary their ways of combination in accordance with the various genomes the organisms possess.

The idea of "system" has entered many branches of social science. When structural linguists talk of such terms as "phonemes," "morphemes," and "graphemes," they are considering speech sounds, word forms, and writing shapes as systems. Similarly, when Claude Lèvi-Strauss talks of "mythemes," when Umberto Eco talks of "sememes " and "stylemes," and when Frederic Jameson talks of "ideologemes," they certainly have in mind the mythical, semiotic, stylistic, and ideological systems.[6] All these "-emes" are the basic units of the social sciences concerned, just as genes are the basic units of genetic information.

A system may contain systems. The cosmos contains galaxies, which contain stars. The earth contains things, which contain chemical compounds, which contain elements with atoms. In biology, bodies contain systems, which contain organs, which contain tissues, which contain cells. Biotechnologists even find that amino acids contain codons, which contain nucleotides; or that nucleic acids contain polymers, which contain nucleotides, the basic units of DNA or RNA. And in creative writing, texts contain sentences, which contain phrases, which contain words. In words, again, we find morphemes and in morphemes we find phonemes, while in ideologies we find ideologemes, and in styles stylemes. Thus, a literary work (e.g., a novel or a poem) is a large composition of words in different levels of syntax which ultimately are made up of phonemes, graphemes, sememes, etc., whereas a plant or an animal is a big composite of cells in different formations which ultimately are composed of cellular ingredients including amino acids with their nucleotides. So, both biotechnologists and creative writers are engaged in very complicated systems of systems which ultimately give each of us ever-changing impressions of what we call "life."

The End

There is no end to any type of creation. Since the Original Creator (call Him God or the First Cause if you please) started creating the universe with all things in it, the process of natural creation has never ceased: every minute, every second, certain life forms (flora or fauna, bacteria or viruses) are popping up. The same with the process of human creation. On one hand, mankind is forever producing or reproducing copies of their own kind (propagating with their offspring). On the other hand, human beings are constantly creating what they want: the constructions, the products, the articles, devices, tools, all the items that make the so-called culture or civilization. It seems that man is other than other animals just because he has a strong determination, and strong power too, to continue his creative activities. Therefore, creative writers will continue to create literary texts for all the rumor that "the author is dead."[7]   And presumably, biotechnologists will continue to create genetic products.

The romantics used to call the poet "the Second Deity," deeming his creative power only next to that of God. Some radicals even agree with Sir Philip Sidney that "lifted up with the vigor of his own invention," the poet "doth grow in effect another nature, in making things either better than nature bringeth forth, or, quite anew, forms such as never were in nature," and that "nature never set forth the earth in so rich tapestry as divers poets have done... Her world is brazen, the poets only deliver a golden" (157). In this age of ours when the Divine Author and the human author are both proclaimed dead, no scientists, I believe, will be so radical as to believe in the poets' emulation over nature. Nevertheless, man's overweening pride seems to have been transferred from the poets to the scientists themselves. Aren't there, for instance, enough biotechnologists who proceed with confidence to "improve plants or animals" with their techniques?

If there is no end to literary creation, and to genetic creation as well, what then is the common end of biotechnology and creative writing? Literature has been assigned the function of delight and instruction. To delight and instruct (mankind) is very good, but somehow it rings with human selfishness. Biotechnology professes to "improve plants or animals," thus apparently sounding not so man-centered. But do we improve plants or animals really for their sake, not for our own sake?

Today's biotechnology has been applied in immunology, in commercial production of microorganisms, in plant genetic engineering, in animal transgenic engineering, in aquaculture, in gene therapy, and in many other fields of study or industry. But are we sure that all these applications are really beneficial to mankind and to non-human beings? There have been opponents of recombinant DNA technology. Many concerns have been voiced:

> *They fear that we will not know where to draw the line. For example, we now have sophisticated cloning technologies. Will we one day be free to clone humans? Will we be able to use them as organ donors? Are we able to select characteristics in our engineered children? At what point will these technologies become acceptable? Other fears include the effect of genetically engineered foods on our health, hidden dangers in transgenic organisms, pollution of the environment by genetically engineered organisms (for example, displacing other organisms), and manipulating (and as some say, tampering with) the natural world.* (Barnum 58)

Since a long time ago, there have been detractors of literature, too. Plato, as is known, had his good reasons for banishing poets from his ideal republic. Today when we face so much pornography and "bad literature," don't we think censorship is often necessary? Indeed, both biotechnology and creative writing are liable for good and bad influences on not only mankind but also the entire universe. Hence, no matter whether the title of "Second Deity" is placed on a biotechnologist or a creative writer, the creator certainly ought to keep a good end forever in his creative consciousness.

But what is a good end? Remember: both biotechnology and creative writing deal with life, and all living organisms have a strong "will to live." Consequently, what is good is that which can best ensure one another's survival, be it a literary text out of creative writing or a genetic text out of biotechnology. It is not enough to use "organic forms." The best message for any text, code, or system is the language that signifies the harmonious end (outcome), not the ruinous end (death), of life.

Notes:

1. See his Preface to "The Spoils of Poynton" in Ghiselin, 151 ff.
2. This description of the process is based on the description in Barnum, p. 58.
3. John Locke in his *An Essay Concerning Human Understanding* first discriminates wit from judgment: "wit lying most in the assemblage of ideas ... wherein can be found any resemblance or congruity, thereby to make up pleasant pictures and agreeable visions in the fancy; judgment, on the contrary, lies quite on the other side, in separating carefully, one from another, ideas wherein can be found the least difference, thereby to avoid being misled by similitude, and by affinity to take one thing for another." Henceforth, the contrast between imagination as a synthetic power and judgment as an analytical power is established since imagination is no other than fancy and fancy is equated to wit.
4. See his *Course in General Linguistics*, p. 65 ff.
5. For the details of genetic transcription and translation, see Barnum, 42-55.
6. See Lèvi-Strauss' *Structural Anthropology*, Eco's *The Role of the Reader*, and Jameson's *The Political Unconscious*.
7. It was Roland Barthes that popularized the theme of "the death of the author." For a discussion on this theme, see my article "Is the Author 'Dead' Already?"

Works Consulted

Adams, Hazard, ed. *Critical Theory Since Plato*. New York: Harcourt Brace Jovanovich, 1971.

Barnum, Susan R. *Biotechnology: An Introduction*. 2nd ed. Belmont, CA: Thomson, 2005.

Barthes, Roland. "Theory of the Text." *Untying the Text*. Ed. Robert Young. London & New York: Routledge & Kegan Paul, 1987.

Coleridge, S. T. "Shakespeare's Judgment Equal to His Genius" in Adams, 460-63.

de Saussure. *Course in General Linguistics*. Trans. W. Baskin. London: Fontana/Collins, 1974.

Eco, Umberto. *The Role of the Reader: Explorations in the Semiotics of Texts.* London: Hutchinson, 1981.

Ghiselin, Brewster, ed. *The Creative Process.* Berkerley & Los Angels: U of California P, 1952.

Hawthorn, Jeremy. *Unlocking the Text.* London: Edward Arnold, 1987.

Jakobson, Roman. *Language in Literature.* Cambridge, MS: Belknap P of Harvard UP, 1987.

James, Henry. "The Art of Fiction" in Adams, 661-70.

--------. Preface to "The Spoils of Poynton" in Ghiselin, 151 ff.

Jameson, Frederic. *The Political Unconscious: Narrative as a Socially Symbolic Act.* London: Methuan, 1981.

Lèvi-Strauss, Claude. *Structural Anthropology.* Trans. C. Jacobson & B. G. Schoepf. London: Allen Lane, 1968.

Locke, John. *An Essay Concerning Human Understanding.* Booko @ Adelaide 2004, II, xi, 2.

Ricoeur, Paul. "What Is a Text? Explanation and Understanding." *Twentieth-Century Literary Theory.* Eds. Vassilis Lambropoulous & David Neal Miller. Albany: State U of New York P, 1987.

Sidney, Philip. "An Apology for Poetry" in Adams, 155-77.

Tanselle, G. Thomas. *A Rationale of Textual Criticism.* U of Pennsylvania P, 1989.

Tung, C. H. "Is the Author 'Dead' Already?" *Journal of Liberal Arts.* Taichung: National Chung Hsing U, 1996. 1-15.

This paper first appeared in 2006 in *JH*, pp. 327-44.

語言文學類　　AG0075

Literary Theory: Some Traces in the Wake

作　　者 / 董崇選
發 行 人 / 宋政坤
執行編輯 / 林世玲
圖文排版 / 張慧雯
封面設計 / 莊芯媚
數位轉譯 / 徐真玉　沈裕閔
圖書銷售 / 林怡君
法律顧問 / 毛國樑　律師
出版印製 / 秀威資訊科技股份有限公司
　　　　　台北市內湖區瑞光路 583 巷 25 號 1 樓
　　　　　電話：02-2657-9211　　傳真：02-2657-9106
　　　　　E-mail：service@showwe.com.tw
經 銷 商 / 紅螞蟻圖書有限公司
　　　　　台北市內湖區舊宗路二段 121 巷 28、32 號 4 樓
　　　　　電話：02-2795-3656　　傳真：02-2795-4100
　　　　　http://www.e-redant.com

2007 年 11 月 BOD 一版
2007 年 12 月 BOD 二版
定價：320 元

讀 者 回 函 卡

感謝您購買本書，為提升服務品質，煩請填寫以下問卷，收到您的寶貴意見後，我們會仔細收藏記錄並回贈紀念品，謝謝！

1.您購買的書名：＿＿＿＿＿＿＿＿＿＿＿＿＿＿＿＿＿

2.您從何得知本書的消息？

□網路書店　□部落格　□資料庫搜尋　□書訊　□電子報　□書店

□平面媒體　□ 朋友推薦　□網站推薦　□其他＿＿＿＿＿

3.您對本書的評價：(請填代號　1.非常滿意 2.滿意 3.尚可 4.再改進)

封面設計＿＿　版面編排＿＿　內容＿＿　文/譯筆＿＿　價格＿＿

4.讀完書後您覺得：

□很有收獲　□有收獲　□收獲不多　□沒收獲

5.您會推薦本書給朋友嗎？

□會　□不會，為什麼？＿＿＿＿＿＿＿＿＿＿＿＿＿＿＿

6.其他寶貴的意見：＿＿＿＿＿＿＿＿＿＿＿＿＿＿＿＿＿

＿＿＿＿＿＿＿＿＿＿＿＿＿＿＿＿＿＿＿＿＿＿＿＿＿＿＿

＿＿＿＿＿＿＿＿＿＿＿＿＿＿＿＿＿＿＿＿＿＿＿＿＿＿＿

＿＿＿＿＿＿＿＿＿＿＿＿＿＿＿＿＿＿＿＿＿＿＿＿＿＿＿

讀者基本資料

姓名：＿＿＿＿＿＿＿＿＿　年齡：＿＿＿　性別：□女 □男

聯絡電話：＿＿＿＿＿＿＿　E-mail：＿＿＿＿＿＿＿＿＿

地址：＿＿＿＿＿＿＿＿＿＿＿＿＿＿＿＿＿＿＿＿＿＿＿

學歷：□高中(含)以下　□高中　□專科學校　□大學

□研究所(含)以上 □其他＿＿＿＿＿＿＿

職業：□製造業 □金融業 □資訊業 □軍警 □傳播業 □自由業

□服務業 □公務員 □教職　□學生 □其他＿＿＿＿＿

To：114

台北市內湖區瑞光路 583 巷 25 號 1 樓

秀威資訊科技股份有限公司　　　收

寄件人姓名：

寄件人地址：□□□

(請沿線對摺寄回,謝謝!)

秀威與 BOD

BOD（Books On Demand）是數位出版的大趨勢，秀威資訊率先運用 POD 數位印刷設備來生產書籍，並提供作者全程數位出版服務，致使書籍產銷零庫存，知識傳承不絕版，目前已開闢以下書系：

一、BOD 學術著作—專業論述的閱讀延伸
二、BOD 個人著作—分享生命的心路歷程
三、BOD 旅遊著作—個人深度旅遊文學創作
四、BOD 大陸學者—大陸專業學者學術出版
五、POD 獨家經銷—數位產製的代發行書籍

BOD 秀威網路書店：www.showwe.com.tw
政府出版品網路書店：www.govbooks.com.tw

　　永不絕版的故事・自己寫・永不休止的音符・自己唱